Secrets of the Royal Maid

Annie Seymour is a historical-fiction writer who lives in Cambridgeshire and is at her happiest when she is researching and writing true untold stories about women's lives, combined with anecdotes about our royal family, whose lives continue to fascinate. Annie is a former journalist and started writing women's features for her local newspaper at the age of sixteen. She believes the skills she learned then equipped her with an endless curiosity and fascination for people's lives that will remain with her for ever. Her new Royal Maid series is inspired by Rosa Edwards, a poor pit-miner's daughter from Merthyr Tydfil in the Welsh Valleys, who in real life became a royal maid during World War II, and lived a life beyond her wildest dreams.

Secrets of the Royal Maid

ANNIE SEYMOUR

PENGUIN BOOKS

PENGUIN BOOKS

UK | USA | Canada | Ireland | Australia
India | New Zealand | South Africa

Penguin Books is part of the Penguin Random House group of companies
whose addresses can be found at global.penguinrandomhouse.com

Penguin Random House UK,
One Embassy Gardens, 8 Viaduct Gardens, London SW11 7BW

penguin.co.uk

First published 2026

001

Copyright © Annie Seymour, 2026

Set in 12.5/14.75pt Garamond MT Std
Typeset by Six Red Marbles UK, Thetford, Norfolk
Printed and bound in Great Britain by Clays Ltd, Elcograf S.p.A.

The authorized representative in the EEA is Penguin Random House Ireland,
Morrison Chambers, 32 Nassau Street, Dublin D02 YH68

A CIP catalogue record for this book is available from the British Library

ISBN: 978-1-405-97910-8

To Rosa, who touched the lives of royalty with her sweet nature, hard work and humbleness, and to her loving daughter Jan, who proudly shared her story with me.

Prologue

Christmas Eve 1926,
Merthyr Tydfil, South Wales

'Please, Thomas. Leave now, and return with God's speed,' pleaded Eira, doubling over her swollen belly.

The expectant woman's eyes widened as she reached forward and gripped her husband's arm, digging her nails through his shirtsleeve and feeling his bones beneath it. She pressed her body weight against him for support.

'I don't like to leave you alone in this state,' he replied, his voice strained.

She winced, her words sticking in her throat. 'I'm scared, Thomas. You must go and find Mrs Craddock. I need her.'

'Alright, I will, but—'

'Go. Please, go now,' she wailed, her face contorted.

'Very well, my love. I'll be back as quickly as I can.' He gently released her grip, rubbing his arm where her nails had dug in. 'But first, let me help you to bed.'

Thomas pulled back the covers and gently assisted Eira over. She rested her arms on his shoulders and lowered herself onto the mattress, swinging her legs onto the bed and laying back on top of the sheet.

He lowered his face, brushed his lips against her moist brow and stroked her face as she panted and groaned, twisting her head from one side to the other.

He straightened. 'I'll go now. I'll go with lightning speed.'

Eira placed her hands on her swollen stomach and managed a weak smile. 'Hurry. It won't be long now until our babe enters the world.'

Thomas went to the door and turned his head for a final glance at his young wife before dashing down the stairs. He pulled on a sweater he had earlier discarded on a chair and grabbed his black overcoat and cap from the peg on the back of the door. The door opened into Nantygwenith Street, Georgetown, an area of cramped back-to-back homes inhabited by miners. A gust of freezing air smacked his face as feathery flakes of snow fluttered softly from the sky, making a crisp white carpet on the ground, softening the sound of his hobnail boots. His steps became brisker and more urgent as they gathered pace.

The faint sound of carollers could be heard a street away, ringing out the haunting melody of 'Silent Night'. Merthyr, like the rest of Wales, was renowned for its harmonious, angelic voices. Singing was a way of life here, and Merthyr could boast its fair share of strong male choirs. Thomas had been known to raise the roof with his melodic tone, which Eira had complimented him on. Tonight the festive season was the last thing on his mind and he didn't notice the voices fading in the distance as he moved quickly in a different direction.

The only voice he could hear was Eira's anguished cry, over and over again, as he quickened his step in search of the midwife. After a few minutes he reached the top of a narrow road and turned left, panting for breath and pressing his body against the elements as he strode up a steep incline, a row of terraced houses on each side.

What kind of existence was this for a baby to be brought into, he pondered.

His troubles had begun six months ago when he and his fellow miners dropped tools and stormed out of the pits, never expecting their strike would drag on so long. He cursed the life of a miner, working in a dark underground world for little pay, for bosses who cared more about profits than improving poor working conditions.

Thomas stomped along Penry Street, his heart pounding as he contemplated his dire straits. His eyes flickered as he spotted Mrs Craddock's home a short distance away.

A woman's voice called out from across the street, stopping him in his tracks. 'Hello there, Thomas. Would you be heading for Mrs Craddock?'

Thomas glanced at her, narrowing his focus on the woman. 'Why yes, I am. It's Bronwen Morgan, isn't it?'

'Aye, it is. How is Eira faring? It must be her time any day now.'

'That's why I'm here. The baby's on its way as we speak and I'm heading to the midwife's house to take her to Eira. So if you excuse me, I can't hang about.'

He turned to walk away, but the woman raised her hand. 'I thought as much. Hold your fire, Thomas Edwards. I've something to tell you.'

Bronwen hurried across the road, limping slightly, her eyes showing concern. She was dressed warmly against the elements, a knitted hat resting on her grey curled hair.

'I'm sorry to tell you, but she's not in. I saw her leave an hour ago for a delivery across the valley. She went off with Alwyn Jones on his horse and cart. His Frida must have started labour too. Oh my, it is a night for it, and Christmas Eve too.'

Thomas's lips trembled. 'But she promised Eira she would be there for her. What am I to tell her? She was in agony when I left and pleaded with me to bring Mrs Craddock to her quickly.'

'Well, she wasn't to know Frida's baby would come early,' Bronwen quipped. The woman's eyebrows furrowed as she thought for a moment. She was in her fifties and had known Eira and Thomas since they were both born twenty-two years ago. Everybody in Georgetown knew each other, living shoulder to shoulder in the two-up, two-down miners' houses.

'What am I to do, Bronwen? Eira is in a desperate state.'

Bronwen bit her lip. Her eyes fixed on his face. 'I have an idea. You will have to trust me on this.'

'Tell me, what is it?' he pressed.

'Well, you could ask Angharad to do the delivery.'

Thomas's dark eyes widened. 'Angharad? You mean, Angharad Craddock? Her daughter?'

'I do. She's assisted her mother many a time. I do believe she's in. I saw her carrying an armful of holly up the street just five minutes ago.'

Thomas scoffed. 'But she can't speak. She's dumb. She's slow-witted—'

'Now halt your tongue this instant, Thomas Edwards. It's true the girl can't speak, but she's as sharp as a needle You don't think I would suggest her if she couldn't help Eira, do you?'

'Surely there must be someone else?'

'There might well be, but none that we can reach quickly

or who I would recommend as highly as Angharad. That girl has a special way about her that is calming, while setting about what needs to be done in a no-nonsense way. Your Eira couldn't be in better hands. Come now, let's go and ask her, and stop your babbling.'

Feeling helpless, Thomas shrugged his shoulders and followed Bronwen. Within a couple of minutes he was outside the house shaking the snow off his cap and coat. Bronwen opened the front door without knocking; most folk in these parts didn't lock their door as they had nothing of value to steal – and besides, Thomas realised there would be no point in knocking as Angharad wouldn't hear.

He wiped his feet on the mat and followed Bronwen's instructions to remain in the hallway so as not to alarm the girl by his sudden appearance.

Bronwen entered the living room, leaving the door ajar, and he watched as she approached a girl of around eighteen who was arranging holly on the mantelpiece, her back to them, with sheets of dark hair hanging down like a black velvet cape.

Bronwen positioned herself in front of her and explained the urgent purpose of their visit by making sweeping gestures with her hands over her belly and moving her lips to emphasise words for Angharad to lip-read. She finished by pointing towards Thomas.

As she did so, Angharad turned and Thomas drew a breath, taking a few steps into the room. She had delicate features with a milky complexion and wide-set hazel eyes which stared intently at him. She held her head in a confident pose that he had not been expecting.

He cleared his throat and pleaded, holding her gaze. 'Please, can you help?'

Angharad turned to Bronwen, who took her hands in hers. 'There's no one else. I know you can do it.'

She turned to Thomas, who pressed his ham-like hands against his chest. 'Please. Please help. I beg you.'

Angharad nodded and pointed upstairs, indicating that he should remain where he was as she left the room.

'Where has she gone?' he asked Bronwen, a catch in his throat. 'She is coming, isn't she?'

'You're in luck, Thomas, and you should thank God, on this holy night. She is upstairs getting her things.'

He surveyed the room while he waited. It was spotless and similar to neighbouring houses in the slanting street; a sturdy table in the centre of the room and four plain chairs placed around it. A photograph displayed on a mahogany sideboard showed a smiling Mr and Mrs Craddock with a young Angharad, aged around ten years old, sitting formally. Mr Craddock had died long ago in a pit explosion and didn't live to see his daughter grow up.

An alabaster clock was positioned in the centre of the black cast-iron mantelpiece which had a drying rail across it. Some linen hung from it, and the embers glowed in the grate below. Thomas positioned his feet as close as possible to warm his freezing toes.

Within a couple of minutes the midwife's daughter returned carrying a small brown leather case. She had tied her hair back and tucked it under a felt hat and was wearing a thick coat.

Bronwen eyed the bag. 'It's just as well Mrs Craddock has spare equipment for emergencies.'

Thomas was suddenly swarmed with feelings of guilt for having listened to idle gossip about the girl, and realised how much he depended on her now for the safe arrival of his firstborn.

'Thank you,' he said to Angharad, mouthing the words slowly.

She nodded, her face expressionless, and brushed past him. She opened the front door, and Bronwen and Thomas followed into the street. The church clock struck six times as the door closed behind them. Thomas realised it was around forty minutes since he left his house. There wasn't a moment to lose.

The snow was falling even thicker now, the chill in the air pinching his cheeks. He pulled his collar up to his ears and dug his hands deep into his pockets. They trudged along the street, the snow slowing their pace. After a few minutes Thomas spotted a couple of men in jovial spirits on the opposite side of the road. They hailed Thomas and wished him the season's greetings. He hollered back, 'I can't stop. The baby, it's on its way.'

They bellowed, 'Haven't you heard, boyo? The strike could be over tomorrow. All being well, we'll be back down the pits within a day or so.'

'Is this true? Are they paying us more?'

'Nah, what do you think? We had to give in. We've been out for months and the men, they've had enough of empty pockets.'

Thomas froze. 'The bastards! I can't believe we've got nothing. Is everyone going back?'

One of the men, Dolby Hobson, shrugged his shoulders. A thin roll-up dangled from his bottom lip. 'We can't say for sure. They're drawing up a list of who they'll have back, but the word is that they won't take any trouble-makers.'

Thomas shook as he said, 'Trouble-makers? Decent men who stand up for a fair wage and working conditions?' He was suddenly panicked. What if his name wasn't on the list? He had been seen by one of the pit managers distributing leaflets for a protest meeting and was warned then that his name would go on a blacklist.

Thomas had joined the men making a stand after their unprincipled bosses had refused to honour an agreement on minimum pay, and the strike had followed. *What choice did we have? Who could have known it would last so long?* Thomas reflected, rubbing the back of his neck. The embittered men could never accept the unfair changes demanded of them – working longer hours for less pay. Thomas winced, felt a knot tightening inside his gut as he recalled his bravado, which could now cost him dearly, just as he was about to have his first child.

How times had changed. Merthyr had once been an innovative industrial town and made its name when the world's first steam-powered railway journey set off from there in 1804. In its glorious heyday, Merthyr boasted the largest ironworks in the world and, with its high wages, drew in people from all around the country, and even parts of Europe. Later, as the coal industry developed, unscrupulous owners ran the mines and put profits first.

'Merry Christmas to you, Thomas, and congratulations on your new baby,' the men chortled, walking off. 'And good luck to you and your missus.'

Thomas hadn't noticed Angharad walking on ahead, oblivious to the discourse he had stopped for. Bronwen pursed her lips and dragged Thomas by the arm. 'Come along, man. What will be will be. This is no time to hang about and dwell on the past.'

Half an hour later he flung open the door of his home and flew up the stairs, pushing aside his worries about work. Eira sat on the side of the bed, stroking her swollen belly. She caught her breath, her face contorting as she exhaled slowly.

He ran to her. 'I came back as quickly as I could, Eira.'

Eira's pale face stared over her husband's shoulder, her expression confused as her eyes rested on Angharad, who was unpacking the contents of her bag on a chair behind him.

'Why is that girl here? Where's Mrs Craddock?' she croaked, wincing and biting her lip as another contraction intensified.

Thomas took her hand. 'Mrs Craddock's out on another delivery and we don't know when she'll be back. I bumped into Bronwen and she says Angharad has assisted her mam at many births and we can place our trust in her.'

Bronwen stepped forward. 'You've nothing to worry about, Eira. Angharad and I will look after you. It's been a while since I delivered Jenny Jones's little un, but we're all you've got for now, and I promise we will deliver you a bonny baby. Try not to fret, my lovely, everything will be alright.'

Eira arched her back and screeched, a long high-pitched cry, her face covered with sweat.

Thomas's hand flew to his throat, feeling utterly help-less. 'She's not going to die, is she?' he warbled, shooting Bronwen an anxious glance.

'Enough of that talk,' chided Bronwen in a firm tone.

Angharad came over and Thomas moved aside. She positioned herself next to Eira, rubbing her back to ease her discomfort.

Thomas paced the room, pausing to rub the back of his neck, his face etched with anxiety. Bronwen said, 'If you want to help, boyo, can you bring us up a bowl of hot water and some towels. Then it's perhaps best if you stay downstairs until you hear a baby's cry. You'll only get in our way here.'

Thomas did as he was asked. Downstairs he saw that Eira had set everything out that she might need for the birth. The bowl and towels were on the table, with a baby's vest and terry nappy next to them, along with a small, soft blanket. The water was bubbling in a kettle on the range and he filled up the bowl and returned upstairs with it and the towels. When he entered the bedroom he was relieved to see Eira responding to Angharad, who was rubbing Eira's back in a soothing way, while Bronwen held his wife's hands and made encouraging sounds.

'How long will it be?' he spluttered.

'As long as it takes. Nature will decide,' Bronwen pronounced without glancing up, an edge to her voice.

Eira attempted to wriggle and move positions, her weight supported by Angharad. The midwife's daughter pressed her lips together and breathed slowly and purposely through them, as if blowing smoke rings. Bronwen urged Eira to focus on her breath and copy the way Angharad was breathing.

'That will be all, thank you, Thomas,' Bronwen said curtly as he hovered by the bed. 'Go and make a brew and calm yourself.'

Thomas returned downstairs feeling utterly useless. His hands shook as he lit the stove and poured a scoop of tea leaves into the brown teapot. He considered himself a strong man, yet he felt weak and powerless watching the woman he loved crying in pain.

He paced backwards and forwards in the room, stopping every few minutes and catching his breath, tilting the side of his head upwards and hearing more cries.

A couple of hours had passed when Bronwen called from upstairs. He rushed to the steps.

'You'll have to be patient a bit longer. We're parched up here and could do with some tea.'

Thomas's face fell. 'Right you are.' Ten minutes later he entered the room carrying the tray with their drinks. Bronwen and Angharad were showing signs of tiredness, while Eira looked exhausted. Angharad mopped her sweaty brow, her eyes shut.

'What's happened?' he asked anxiously.

'The labour wasn't as advanced as we thought. Poor girl, she's exhausted,' said Bronwen, who flopped on her knees by Eira.

'Promise me she's alright, Bronwen. And the baby too. Eira and I have been together since infant school.'

'Of course she's alright, stop your fretting. As I said, these things take time, and Angharad has been just wonderful. Your wife is in good hands, Thomas. I couldn't manage without her. If I were you, I would try and have a nap while you can.'

'A nap? At a time like this?' he retorted, his nostrils flared.

Once again he retreated downstairs and slumped in an armchair. His heart raced and he had no desire to rest at a time like this. After a few minutes he leaped out of the chair and paced the room, stepping backwards and forwards over the threadbare rug. His eyes flickered towards the hands of the clock ticking on the mantelpiece, watching as each second and minute passed.

It was now approaching half an hour to midnight and Thomas felt increasingly anxious.

He shuffled from foot to foot, paced the room and stepped to the window where he pushed apart the curtains and stared outside at the wintry scene. The snow was still falling fast in large flakes, and the white sugary coating on the street made Merthyr look as pretty as a Christmas card. But the picturesque scene belied the poverty and suffering of families caused by unemployment.

He cocked his ears on hearing a sound that broke his despondent train of thought. Bronwen's voice was louder, and even though he couldn't make out her words, he could sense the urgency in her tone. He went to the bottom of the stairs and his heart lurched as Bronwen yelled, 'Push harder, Eira, it's coming now.'

He belted up the stairs two at a time, and paused at the top, unsure whether to enter the bedroom. The sounds from inside the room were drowned out by the ringing of the church bells two streets away.

'Push, push, Eira. One more push,' boomed Bronwen.

The high-pitched cries of a newborn entering the world followed. Thomas could hold back no longer. He flung open the door, a lump forming in his throat, as the infant was passed to Eira by Angharad, who had just snipped the cord tying the newborn to its mother.

'Congratulations, Eira. You have a beautiful daughter,' Bronwen cooed.

Eira kissed her daughter's cheek. 'She is a little beauty, isn't she? She is just perfect.' She smiled at Thomas. 'Come and meet your daughter.'

Thomas wiped his eyes and sat on the edge of the bed, staring in awe at his wife and baby. He trembled, overcome with emotion. 'She is a beauty, just like her mam.'

Joy spread across Eira's face. 'Look at her eyes, staring up into my face. I love her more than I can say. Tell me, what day is it?'

Thomas gently kissed his wife. 'It's Christmas Day, my love. I'm afraid I don't have a present for you, Eira, seeing how things are. But I promise you this. I promise you our daughter will want for nothing, whatever happens at the mines.'

'Let's forget the mines for today, Thomas. Our baby is my present to us. What shall we call her?'

Thomas raised Eira's chin and lowered his lips on her mouth. 'You are both the dearest things in the world to me. I want nothing else now we have our daughter. Why don't you pick a name for her?'

Eira gazed adoringly into her baby's face. 'Well, just look at those rosy cheeks, just like two red apples. We'll call her Rosa. Welcome to the world, Rosa Edwards.'

'Rosa Edwards it is, my darling wife.'

Thomas turned to Angharad. 'Thank you for what you've done. We couldn't have managed without you. What do I owe you?'

Angharad shook her head and collected her instruments, cleaning them in the water and packing them away.

Bronwen placed a hand on his shoulder. 'You've been blessed, Thomas Edwards. Be sure to find peace with your work at the pits or find another job. You're a family man now, and Eira and Rosa are counting on you.'

Seventeen years later: Christmas Eve 1943

'I think that's it for today. I doubt we'll have any more customers,' Rosa announced, turning the sign on the door of the printing company where she worked to *Closed*.

She addressed her comment to Dylan Williams, whose parents owned the business.

'I think you're right, seeing as it's four o'clock on Christmas Eve. Before you go, Rosa, I have something for you.'

'For me? But I don't have anything for you.' She frowned, and stared at Dylan's pale, freckled face, crowned with chestnut hair parted at the side, a caterpillar sliver of moustache spread across his upper lip.

'I'm not expecting anything from you. It's back here,' he replied, lifting the flap on the wooden counter to let Rosa through.

She followed him into the back room, where he opened a drawer then turned to face her.

'I hope you like it. It's for your birthday.' Dylan pressed a small package into Rosa's hand, his face reddening.

Rosa's eyes widened as she stared at the gift. 'I don't know what to say. I don't usually get birthday presents. Can I take it home and open it tomorrow?'

'If it's alright with you, I'd like it if you opened it now so I can see your face. I thought you might miss out on your birthday, seeing as it falls on Christmas Day.'

Rosa's hand flew to her throat and a warm glowing sensation rippled through her as her sapphire-blue eyes fixed on Dylan, who stared at her expectantly, his lips curling up at the corners.

'Very well then, I will,' Rosa said, carefully unwrapping the pink tissue paper to see lying in the folds a gilt brooch in the shape of three pink rosebuds. 'Why, it's beautiful,' she beamed. 'I love roses. It's the prettiest brooch I've ever seen.' A smile stretched across her face as she held up the gift to admire it closely. The roses were tied with a pale pink enamel ribbon. 'It's really lovely. Thank you, Dylan. It must have cost a fortune,' she gushed.

'I thought you would like it. I wanted you to have it as soon as I saw it,' he replied. 'My parents have a present for you too.'

At that moment Rosa and Dylan were joined by Huw and Jane Williams. Huw was a cheery, round-figured man dressed in the same brown overalls as Dylan, a badge engraved with his name pinned to his chest pocket. His eyes twinkled as he spoke, his good nature shining through.

'We didn't want you to miss out on your birthday, Rosa, and there's an extra week's pay by way of a Christmas bonus. Most people could do with a bit of extra money at this time, and it's a tradition we follow every year.'

Rosa's eyes widened as she took a small package from him. 'I wasn't expecting anything. That's very generous.'

Jane piped up, 'It's almost a year since you came to us, Rosa, and we have become very fond of you. Even if money is tight, you've made a favourable impression on our customers.'

Jane also had a rounded figure and was as cheerful as

her husband, with dimpled cheeks and twinkling eyes. Mr and Mrs Williams were the most jovial couple Rosa had met, always looking on the bright side. 'What will be will be,' they had agreed when paper restrictions were introduced by the government at the beginning of the war, severely impacting their business.

'Go on, you can open it now,' Mrs Williams beamed, resting her hand on her husband's arm and exchanging a warm glance.

'Very well,' smiled Rosa, unable to contain her excitement. She unwrapped the pretty floral paper and gasped when she saw the exquisite gift inside. 'This is just perfect, I can't believe you knew I wanted it.' She stared in wonderment at the prettily decorated pink and gold bottle of Floris Rose Eau de Cologne and opened the bottle, dabbing some of the perfume on her fingers and rubbing it next to her ears.

Mr Williams placed an arm around his wife's shoulder and they exchanged a warm smile. 'We're so pleased you like it, Rosa,' said Jane. 'I recall you mentioning you had set your heart on it.'

'I'm lost for words. Thank you both. I don't know how I can ever repay your kindness and generosity. I don't feel I deserve it.'

'You let us be the judge of that,' beamed Jane amiably.

Rosa glanced at Dylan, who had inherited his parents' goodness, and felt truly blessed to have been taken on to work for them. She had quickly grasped the tasks expected of her after joining Williams & Son, following a recommendation from a mutual acquaintance at the chapel she attended.

The small family printing business had been started by Dylan's grandfather and passed on to Huw and his wife, living above the shop, after he died. They built on its reputation by introducing new machinery to print faster, clearer and cheaper orders, ranging from business cards, public notices and posters, to leaflets, brochures and calendars. They also stocked office stationery and calendars featuring local scenes.

The war had had a drastic impact on their business as paper had become a valuable commodity. At the beginning of the war a national campaign had encouraged the recycling of paper and cardboard into things like bullet cartridges, while cigarette cartons were recycled into mortar bomb carriers. The message on the posters was clear: *FROM WASTE PAPER TO MUNITIONS OF WAR*. Salvage officers were appointed to gather what paper they could, and Huw and Jane were actively involved. Paper was imported from Canada, and the government was keen to stress that *'a ship carrying paper to replace paper you destroy is a ship wasted'*. Books were gathered from library shelves, and Huw and Jane would never risk the fine of up to £2,500, or even a two-year prison sentence, for contravening the campaign. Mrs Williams was a keen member of the Women's Voluntary Service and knocked on doors in the neighbourhood for paper donations, with every tiny scrap counting.

During these challenging times for the business, they continued to trade by winning contracts from the local authority to print public notices, posters and leaflets, and designed artwork for newspaper advertisements, which Rosa had a natural talent for.

The Williamses admired Rosa for her keenness to learn, her diligence and neatness, and particularly her easy way with customers, who frequently praised her excellent service.

Rosa had not courted Dylan's attention, having seen how Hettie Pritchard, the daughter of the ironmonger across the road, was smitten with him and would call in at the smallest pretence. She was simply grateful for the opportunity to learn about the family trade from him.

Rosa's cheeks flushed when she recalled how earlier in the week she was in the back room when her ears pricked up at hearing her name. Mrs Williams was telling Hettie's mother, Agnes Pritchard, who had called in to discuss the next WVS meeting, how well Rosa was doing. Smarting, Mrs Pritchard had spat out, 'I really don't know where she gets it from, with a no-good father and a divorced mother who cleans day and night. In fact, Mrs Thomas used to clean for us, and we had to let her go. Her standards fell far short of what we accept.'

'I'm afraid I don't know what you are talking about,' Mrs Williams replied defensively.

Mrs Pritchard turned up her nose. 'The whole family is no good, if you ask me. The boy, Billy, is always up to no good, running away from home and getting into all sorts of scrapes. Now, take my Hettie. Not only is she very bright and amongst the top of her class, she is a hard-working and gifted daughter any son would be proud to introduce to his family.'

Fire had seared through Rosa's veins and she stormed into the front of the shop. A thin woman with wiry ginger hair and thick-rimmed spectacles spun around, her thin lips disappearing as she pursed them tightly. She glanced down her nose at Rosa, whose nostrils flared.

'Cleaning is an honest job,' Rosa said, 'and, from what I heard, Mr Pritchard tried to take advantage of Mam and she walked away from you, there and then. I have my mam to thank for being the person I am today. I'm not ashamed of who I am and Mr and Mrs Williams will vouch for me if you have any concerns about my working standards,' she blurted.

'As for my father, if your man worked in the pits like he had for a pittance, you would know what it was like. Look around you and you will see many more like him. It breaks my heart to see the broken man he has become. But he is still my da, and I shall always stand by him. It's true Billy runs off sometimes, it's because he wants to be with his da, any boy does, it's called love, what's wrong with that?'

Mrs Pritchard stared wide-eyed in astonishment. She fumed, 'Well, I've never in my life been spoken to in such a disgraceful manner by a—'

Before she finished her sentence Rosa turned on her heels and flew into the back room, her cheeks burning. Tears streamed down her cheeks and her heart pounded. She almost knocked Dylan off his feet in her distressed state, blinded by tears.

'Hey, what is it?' he asked, his eyes filled with concern. He closed the door and blocked out the furious strains of Mrs Pritchard's voice. 'Is it anything to do with our customer in the shop?' he asked gently, fishing a handkerchief from his pocket and handing it to her.

She sniffled. 'I'm afraid I let my tongue get the better of me and was rude to Mrs Pritchard. I shall be sacked for it. Mam will be furious. I may as well get my bag now and leave.'

'Steady on, I'm sure it won't come to that,' he consoled. 'We all know how sour she can be.'

Rosa shook her head. 'No, you don't understand. I was rude to her. Someone in my position should know better.'

'Come, come,' he comforted. 'Let's wait and see what Mam says. I'm sure it will all blow over.'

Jane entered the room, a serious expression on her face. 'Well, Rosa Edwards, I'm lost for words. What in heaven's name got into you to speak in that way?'

Rosa whimpered, 'I'm sorry, Mrs Williams. It was hearing the horrid things she said about my family. I couldn't stand by without putting her right. I know I did wrong. I'll get my coat and leave.'

Mrs Williams shook her head. 'You'll do no such thing. That woman needed to be put in her place, coming in here with her snooty ways and trying to force her daughter on Dylan. Ah, yes, I know what she is up to.'

'What are you talking about?' Dylan interrupted. 'I've never for a moment encouraged that girl. She's a bit of a pest, if truth be told, hanging around the shop and getting on my nerves.'

Dylan's mother fixed her eyes on Rosa's face. 'I think Hettie is put out that you and Dylan are close and . . .'

Rosa screwed up her face. As far as she was concerned, Dylan was just a friend. 'Surely Mrs Pritchard doesn't think that Dylan and I . . . ?' She let her words trail, unable to finish the sentence, feeling it would sound ludicrous to presume that Dylan would court her with her humble beginnings.

Jane shrugged her shoulders. 'Now I think of it, she could be seeing you as a rival, treading on Hettie's toes, but in truth I admire a girl who stands up for her family. Your mam should be proud of you, and your da, too.'

Having calmed down, Rosa said, 'I wish I hadn't let my hot head get the better of me, but I couldn't stop myself. I love my mam and da. It's not their fault the way their lives turned out. And I do worry about Billy, if I'm honest.'

Rosa felt protective towards her brother, who was two years younger than her. She could see he sorely missed their father since their mother threw him out thirteen years ago.

Mrs Williams rested her hand on Rosa's shoulder. 'Try and forget it, my dear. Come on, hang up your coat and finish off what you were doing.'

Rosa spluttered, 'You honestly mean I can stay?'

'Of course you can. We don't want to lose a good worker like you.'

'Thank you, Mrs Williams. I promise I'll hold my tongue in future, I won't let it get the better of me again. I hope you haven't lost a good customer because of me.'

Dylan winked. 'You don't think we're going to let you go that easily, do you?'

Later that evening Rosa brimmed with delight as she showed her birthday presents to her best friend, Alice Evans, whose birthday treat to her was a night at the town's Castle Cinema.

They giggled their way through *Du Barry Was a Lady*, a musical comedy featuring the biggest American stars of the day, Lucille Ball, Gene Kelly and Red Skelton, with music by the popular Tommy Dorsey and his orchestra.

As they left, Rosa said, 'Thank you, Alice, for an unforgettable night. Seeing the show in colour and singing along to it was a real treat.'

They linked arms, humming along to the tunes as they headed to Rosa's home first.

Alice chided, 'You do know Dylan is potty about you? I've seen the way his eyes follow you when I've waited for you at the shop at the end of the day. I think you may feel the same way, seeing how dewy-eyed you were when you showed me the brooch.'

Rosa's cheeks flushed. 'I do like him, but we're just chums. Besides, I don't have time for boys, what with helping Mam with her cleaning jobs and doing my weekend waitressing shifts at the Valleys Hotel.'

Alice was a year older than Rosa and seemed very worldly and much more confident than her, particularly when it came to boys. She had been the most popular girl in her class, a year ahead of Rosa and Hettie. Alice had always stood up for Rosa, and when she saw a classmate take Rosa's lunch from her hand and scoff it in front of her, she dragged her up by the collar and made her apologise.

A few months before that, Rosa had returned home from school one day and found her mother in a furious state. 'How dare that man think he can put his grubby hands up my skirt when he likes? Mind you, I shouldn't be surprised, seeing that dried up old prune he is married to.'

'Mam, what are you talking about?' Rosa asked.

Eira spat out the words. 'That slimy Mr Pritchard and his stuck-up wife! I quit cleaning for them this morning after he pushed his hand right up the top of my thigh and tried to unclip my suspenders. I whacked him between his legs with the broom.'

Since that day, Hettie had made her dislike of Rosa clear, bringing Rosa and Alice closer together. After leaving school, they had gone their separate ways, but fate had brought them together at the Valleys Hotel two years later.

Rosa grinned. 'Talking about boys, you are always surrounded by admirers – are you dating anyone?'

After a pause Alice replied cagily, 'Well, there is someone I've been seeing, he's with the American Air Force. You might have seen him at the hotel on a couple of occasions.'

'Yes, I know who you mean, seeing as he can't keep his eyes off you. He's very good-looking and laughs a lot. He's the luckiest fella to have you as his girlfriend.'

Alice's face creased. 'I am keen on him, Rosa, but you know what these Yankies are like, and he's leaving in a couple of days. Unfortunately, I attract attention from men who want more from me than just an eyeful – more than I'm willing to give. Even Sid thinks he can take liberties.'

Rosa's eyes widened. 'Never! You mean Sid, the head waiter?'

'Exactly. But don't worry, I can handle him.'

Rosa was astonished at Alice's revelation. Sid was a married man in his mid-fifties with slicked strands of thinning black hair plastered over the top of his balding head and eyes like slits that lit up when an attractive lady entered the restaurant.

The Valleys Hotel was positioned on the outskirts of Merthyr and frequented by the town's affluent residents. It had seen better days in the 1930s and was in need of a lick of paint, but it was regarded as *the* place to be seen. Rosa had started there six months ago. Her mother asked her for a share of her earnings on top of what she was already giving her from Williams & Son, saying she was struggling to make ends meet. 'It's not been easy for me to find more cleaning work. I'm sure the Pritchards have been saying things about me.'

Rosa's cheerful manner and impeccable table etiquette were quickly noticed and complimented by customers. As well as silver service she was shown the correct way to serve coffee, and soon she was being requested to attend to their most influential customers and her tips were mounting up.

Alice was a flirtatious head-turner with bouncing curls. She had a perfect pout, porcelain skin and a curvaceous figure that Rosa envied. She also stood three inches taller than Rosa, who measured only 4 foot 11½ inches in her stockinged feet. Rosa felt dowdy in comparison when she ran a comb through her brown wavy hair that never went the way she wanted.

Alice assured Rosa she was a beauty, possessing a heart of gold, a good brain, a very pleasing, happy face and a kind heart that people warmed to, and would get her far.

'I wish I could do something with my cheeks. They're always so pink,' Rosa complained one day.

She had been born with the colour in her cheeks, and

had believed her mother when she told her as a child that they had been kissed by an angel. However much powder Rosa plastered over them, she couldn't disguise the redness. Alice assured her it was endearing, like a sweet blush, but it irritated Rosa, particularly if her face became warm, which was quite often when she passed through the kitchens while waitressing.

They were now within spitting distance of the steps leading up to Rosa's home, lodgings she shared with her mam and brother, and Rosa stared up at the night sky, lit only by the stars and moonlight. The windows were blacked out and street lights switched off, the same as in all towns during the war.

'Thank you again for my birthday treat. You are a very special friend,' Rosa told Alice when they arrived.

'I enjoyed it too, Rosa. I . . .' Alice's voice trailed off and she paused for a moment. 'There is something I must tell you.'

Rosa could tell from Alice's tone, and the way she was shifting uncomfortably from one foot to the other, that something important was on her mind.

'You've got me worried now. What is it you want to say?'

Alice blurted, 'I'm leaving Merthyr. I've been offered a job in one of them big houses in London. I'm going to be a maid and start straight after Christmas.'

Rosa was stunned. 'A maid? In London? But why would you want to be a maid? And what about your new American fella?'

'Oh, it's still early days, and he'll be leaving soon on another posting. It was fun while it lasted. I just want to get out of this place. It's the chance of a fresh start for me.'

Rosa's voice wobbled. 'But a maid? Isn't that beneath you?'

Alice shrugged her shoulders. 'I don't expect to be doing it for long. It's my getaway ticket from this dump.'

'It's not that bad here, surely?' squeaked Rosa.

'It is as far as I'm concerned. I'm only going because I was told I won't be a maid for long.'

'What do you mean?'

'I saw an advertisement for the post in the paper and had an interview at an agency in Cardiff last week with the master of the house where I'll be working. He was there on business and seems very nice. Their last maid left them in the lurch without giving notice, apparently, and he seemed to be impressed by me.'

'Well, I'm happy for you, if it means so much to you,' Rosa stuttered. 'Who will you be working for?'

'I'll be working for a real lord and lady – Lord Jeremy Hesketh-Robbins and his wife, Iris. He said if I do well he will send me to secretarial school and train me up to help in his office. He told me he could see potential in me. I'm not intending to be a maid for ever, Rosa. It's a way of getting my foot in the door.'

Rosa frowned, concerned that it all sounded too good to be true, but she didn't want to put a dampener on Alice's enthusiasm. With so many girls taking up new wartime occupations, domestic household positions such as this had become harder to fill, and a part of Rosa wondered if the promise of being trained as a secretary was the cherry on the cake that Alice couldn't resist.

'Well that all sounds wonderful, Alice, if you're sure. It's come as a shock, so sudden, like. I shall miss you.'

'They have to check out my references first and be sure I'm not a spy. Seriously, I shall miss you too, Rosa. You've been the best of friends.'

'When do you start?'

'Very soon – in the new year. I'm getting sentimental about leaving you, Rosa, the soft sod I am. But truthfully, I want you to be happy for me. I want some excitement in my life. I want to see the bright city lights, that's the way I am. I've seen pictures of London and can't wait to be there and see it for real.'

As if reading the doubtful look on Rosa's face, Alice added, 'I do have an aunt in London, my father's sister, who I'll look up. She lives in Stepney. I've told Mam I shall visit her for tea on Sundays, but I don't intend to do that for long. You know me, Rosa. I make friends easily, war or no war.'

'Of course I'm happy for you, Alice, only it's such a big step to take. And you know what they say, the grass is always greener . . .'

'Oh yes, "The grass is always greener on the other side of the valley," recited Alice. 'Even if it isn't, I feel I have to leave. Don't worry about me, I can look after myself. Everything is arranged and I had excellent references from the hotel.'

'I shall worry about you, nevertheless,' Rosa retorted, unable to shift the deep sense of unease she felt about Alice's plans.

'There's nothing for you to fret about. Once I'm settled in, you can come to London and visit me, spend some of your tips on yourself. In fact, once I've settled in, I could ask around for a position that would suit you. How about it? We'd have a whale of a time.'

Rosa's hand flung to her face. 'Oh no, I couldn't leave Mam, Da and Billy. I couldn't leave Merthyr. It's my home-town, it's all I've known. And Mr and Mrs Williams rely on me now as well.'

'Oh yes, and Dylan too, no doubt,' Alice teased. 'At least promise me you'll think about it. Here's my address, I've written it out for you.' She handed Rosa a scrap of paper with an address in Piccadilly and pressed it in the palm of her hand. 'Promise you'll write, Rosa. You're my best friend and I don't want to lose touch. I want to hear about Dylan, and even slimy Sid. I shall want you to keep in touch, if only to remind me what I'm not missing in Merthyr.'

'I promise, Alice. I wish you well, I really do. I shall miss you terribly.'

Rosa and Alice embraced, clutching each other tightly. She didn't at first notice the man's shadowy figure as she glanced over her friend's shoulder. As he got closer she stepped back and scrunched her eyes to improve her focus; there was something familiar in the man's gait. Alice followed Rosa's gaze.

'Do you know him?'

The man stopped alongside them before Rosa could answer. He was shabbily dressed and wearing an old worn jacket with frayed edges. A hand-knitted scarf was wrapped around his neck and his shoulders were hunched and shook slightly, shivering in the cold. He was small in stature, his swarthy face covered in rough stubble.

He cleared his throat of phlegm, spitting a blackened gooey substance on the path, and wiped his mouth with his sleeve. He spoke coarsely. 'Happy birthday, Rosa.'

'Da! What are you doing here? What if Mam sees you?'

Alice's jaw dropped. She edged closer to him and stared intently, turning up her nose. 'Rosa, is this man really your father?'

Rosa ignored the question and addressed her father with an anxious voice. 'Da, you shouldn't be here.'

'Your mam has no right to stop me seeing my own daughter. Just like she can't stop Billy running away to see his da.'

Alice extended her manicured hand. 'I don't believe we've had the pleasure, Mr Edwards. My name is Alice Evans and I'm very pleased to meet you. Rosa and I have had a wonderful evening at the cinema to celebrate her birthday. Have you come to bring her a present?'

Thomas Edwards shuffled uncomfortably, digging his hands deep into his pockets, his eyes staring down at his feet. Rosa noticed the soles were becoming unstitched from the leather uppers of his boots and she worried that his feet were cold and wet. What had made him risk her mother's wrath? She couldn't recall the last birthday present he gave her and for a moment she was hopeful.

'Do you have a present for me, Da?' Her eyes brightened for a moment.

He coughed, bending over and bringing up more phlegm. His voice cracked as he cleared his throat. 'You know I would if I could, Rosa. Truth is, my pockets are empty. Seeing as it's Christmas, I've come to ask if you'd give your da a few pounds to pay off my tab at the Miner's Arms. I promise, if you help me out now, I'll get myself sorted and buy you the best birthday present as soon as I can. I heard there's some work going—'

Rosa didn't wait for him to finish his sentence. 'How could you, Da? How could you come here begging me again for money for that horrible stinking place, and on my birthday? I'm going in, before Mam comes out and makes a scene when she sees you.'

A solitary tear fell down her father's cheek. Alice quickly opened her handbag, fished out a white handkerchief and offered it to him.

'You're right. I shouldn't have come asking you for money,' he croaked, dabbing his eyes. 'I'll be off, then. Happy birthday, Rosa. You've made your da proud. You've turned into a fine young woman and you're the light of my life.'

Rosa gulped as her father turned and shuffled off into the darkness. She cried out, 'Where are you going now, Da? It's Christmas Eve.'

Her words fell on deaf ears and she felt wretched watching him shuffle off in the darkness, his hacking cough becoming softer until he faded from sight altogether. Her cheeks burned scarlet from the guilt that engulfed her after refusing to pay off his debts at the boozer.

Alice placed a comforting arm around her friend's shoulder. 'Let him be, Rosa. It's not your place to clean his slate. You have your life to live,' she whispered.

Rosa whimpered, 'It breaks my heart to see him so down. Mam tells me they were happy at first, but the mines and their wicked owners broke him, both mentally and physically. He's not a well man, you can tell by his chesty cough.

Da doted on me and Billy, but the illness on his lungs dragged him down. And us with him.'

Alice spoke gently. 'I know how tough your early years were, Rosa. I hope you will think about what I said and leave these troubles behind you. There will be plenty of opportunities in London for a bright girl like you.'

2

January 1944

Rosa flicked idly through the discarded *Merthyr Express* lying on the kitchen table. She paused on the *Situations Vacant* page, but saw nothing of interest.

Paper restrictions meant the *Express* contained only half the number of pages from before the war, and print numbers were reduced. Eira managed to bring one home with her from the house where she worked, and Rosa would then pass it on to Mrs Williams to add to her salvage collection.

Her mind turned to Alice and she wondered how she was doing. She had written to her twice since the new year; the first time to wish her well in her new position, followed by another letter just a few days ago to inform her that the Valleys Hotel had changed hands, but had had no response. The hotel was now owned by a retired army officer who was running the business like a battalion – barking orders, belittling his workers and making cuts to increase his profits – and she included this information in her latest letter to Alice, commenting on how customers complained that standards had dropped, and that she was missed by many of the regulars.

She found herself reflecting on Alice's parting words and her friend's comment about Dylan having feelings for her. Initially she had dismissed such an idea. But she felt now, one month later, that there was some truth in it.

She was conscious of his presence at work, feeling a shyness around him, and found she enjoyed his company, their easy conversation and the interest he showed in her. If she worked at the counter and he leaned over her to point out something, his arm brushing against hers, she felt a flutter rising inside her which was a new and pleasurable sensation she had never experienced before.

He had a mixture of maturity belying his seventeen years, and a boyishness that Rosa found attractive. He was being groomed by his parents to take over the family business and, when the time came, she was sure he would excel at it.

One afternoon at the end of January, Rosa noticed Dylan hovering closer than usual, their faces close as they conversed. Out of the blue he blurted, 'I can't imagine a lovely girl like you doesn't have a fella.'

'Oh yes, I have them lining the street,' she replied cheekily.

'Oh, I see,' he replied despondently.

'Of course I don't, you silly thing. I'm teasing you.'

Rosa wished at that moment that he would take her in his arms, but he maintained his distance, giving her sideway glances and grinning.

The weather was atrocious and rain lashed down all day. At five o'clock, Dylan flicked over the *CLOSED* sign and approached Rosa.

'Seeing as I have to leave for RAF training very soon and will be going your way, maybe we could walk together?'

Before Rosa could answer his mother smiled and said,

'I think that's an excellent idea. I've heard there's a rowdy group of American Air Force men out on the town. We don't want Rosa bumping into any high-spirited young men while she is out on her own, do we?'

Rosa opened her mouth to reply, but Mrs Williams glanced at her son and declared, 'Don't forget to take an umbrella.'

Dylan grinned at Rosa as they wrapped themselves up in their overcoats and stepped outside. Rosa's little legs moved at a faster pace to stay in step beside Dylan, sploshing in the puddles while he held the umbrella above their heads. They bent forward as they climbed up some of the steeper streets leading to the rows of terraced houses and her lodgings. The air force men loitered with giggling girls on their arms. Rosa nodded at a couple of the girls she recognised and they tittered as she passed them with Dylan alongside her.

'Everything alright?' Dylan asked, observing the girls gossiping together.

For a moment Rosa swivelled round and stared at the group. She thought she recognised one of the Yanks as Alice's admirer from the hotel, yet here he was with another girl. He stared intently at her, his eyebrows meeting, and flicked out his cigarette, stubbing it with his shoe into the pavement. Rosa coyly placed her arm in the crook of Dylan's elbow, pulling him towards her, and gave him a shy sideways glance. A tingling sensation ran along her spine at their closeness.

'That feels nice,' Dylan beamed, drawing Rosa closer towards him.

Rosa gulped. 'I didn't mean to be forward, but I thought I recognised one of those Yanks as someone my friend

Alice was seeing and I think he recognised me too. I don't think he's a good sort. I'm worried about her, I haven't heard from her since she left Merthyr for a new job in London after Christmas. I hope you didn't mind?'

'Mind? I've wished for this moment for so long, Rosa. I hope you didn't do it just for pretence though?'

Her cheeks flushed. 'Well, I wasn't sure . . .'

He stopped abruptly, the umbrella falling by his side and the rain trickling down their cheeks. His words spilled from his lips, his Adam's apple juddering. 'Rosa Edwards, we've known each other for a very long time now and I think about you all the time. I've been holding back, but you must see that I am fond of you.' He tenderly flicked wet strands of hair from her face.

Rosa's voice was soft. 'I never dreamt for a moment that you and me . . .'

'I find myself looking forward to you stepping through the door and coming to work every morning.'

Rosa's expression was incredulous. 'You do? That's exactly how I feel, though I didn't realise until recently. I'm just a pit-miner's daughter and used to char with Mam before I was taken on by your family nine months ago. I'm nobody special.'

'You're special to me, Rosa. I admire you all the more for your humble beginnings, how you haven't let it hold you back. We know about your da, and none of that is your fault.'

'You and your family are so kind to me. If only there wasn't a war.' Rosa's heart pounded as she stared up at his kind face, his eyes brimming with love.

'It won't be for ever,' he said, smiling. 'Come, we'd better move on, else we'll get soaked.'

A silence followed as they picked up their walking pace again, their arms firmly interlocked. Rosa felt like she was walking on air. When they reached her front gate Dylan took her hands in his. 'Rosa, can I ask you something?'

'Of course, Dylan.'

'Will you be my girl, Rosa? What do you say?'

Her heart was fit to burst. She could barely believe what she was hearing and gasped, 'Yes, I will, Dylan.'

He leaned forward and pressed his lips gently on hers. Their mouths softly locked in passion, arousing her womanly desires. Her heartbeat soared and she felt butterflies fluttering inside her, making her feel giddy, until Dylan finally pulled away.

'That felt so good, Rosa. You've just made me the happiest lad in the country.'

She smiled coyly. 'I've never been kissed by a boy before.'

'And I've never kissed a girl before, not like that,' he blushed. 'I hope you liked it.'

'I think I did,' she teased. 'Shall we do it one more time, just to be sure.'

Rosa closed her eyes and lifted her chin towards his face. As he pressed his lips down more firmly this time, the warm glowing feeling inside her intensified as the kiss lingered. When their lips parted, Rosa's heart pounded faster than ever before.

'Oh Dylan, I feel all giddy.'

She softened her body as his arms enveloped her in an embrace, resting her head against his chest. Dylan stroked her hair. 'I'm sorry. Your hair is dripping. Your mam will think I don't take proper care of you.'

Rosa laughed, feeling a shiver of excitement run down her spine. 'I'll see you tomorrow then.'

'Until tomorrow, my sweet Rosa,' he said. 'I can't wait until then.'

She watched him walk away, her heart beating fast. She pinched herself. *Did he really kiss her? Was she really his girl now?* Her head was in the clouds as she ran up the steps, unlocked the front door and climbed the stairs to their rooms.

Eira was seated at the kitchen table, resting her seamed stockinged feet on a chair and inhaling on a cigarette.

'My God, look at the state of you,' she commented, glancing at Rosa's drenched appearance.

Rosa couldn't contain her excitement. She clasped her hands in front of her chest and blurted, 'Oh, Mam. I have some news for you. It's about Dylan.'

'What about Dylan? Spit it out, girl.'

'He's asked me to be his girl.'

Eira's eyebrows arched. 'He has? Well, you're a dark horse. You could do a lot worse than settle for a lad like him, with the family business and all.'

Rosa flung her arms in the air. 'It's nothing to do with the business, Mam. How could you think such a thing? Dylan and I enjoy each other's company.'

'I'm sure you do, love. Now don't go getting up to hanky-panky and finding yourself in the family way. I remember the advice my mother gave me: "Don't do any-thing with a fella that you wouldn't do in front of your mam," then you'll have nought to worry about.'

Rosa blushed. 'Mam! How could you even think such a thing.'

Eira stubbed out her cigarette and reached for her black stilettos, sliding her feet into them and rising, picking up her coat which was draped over a chair. Although she cleaned people's houses in the day, at night she could transform herself into a glamorous woman-about-town, wearing the latest fashions, slicking bright red lipstick on and rouging her cheeks.

'I'm pleased to hear it, Rosa, honest I am. I'm happy for you. Don't wait up for me. I'm seeing Charlie tonight. He'll be picking me up in a minute. And do get out of those wet clothes before you catch your death.'

Charlie was Eira's latest gentleman friend who lived a couple of streets away. A widower, he was balding, in his late fifties, with a chipped front tooth, a big smile and a big heart, and was smitten with Eira, who he'd begun courting six months ago. He seemed to have plenty of cash to splash and was generous with her mother, who was intent on keeping him at arm's length until he popped the question. 'It's security I want at my time of life, someone I can rely on, not like your da,' she told Rosa. 'And if I am patient, Charlie will give it to me.'

Two weeks later, just days after Dylan's eighteenth birthday, he asked Rosa to meet him on the Sunday morning before her lunchtime shift at the hotel. For his birthday she had given him a book on aircraft, knowing he was an avid air cadet, and the family had celebrated quietly with a meal at their home, which Rosa was invited to.

Since they had declared feelings for each other, they had enjoyed a couple more walks, and her desires for him had intensified when he took her in his arms and she melted, but there was little free time to see each other as Dylan was required to attend training with the Air Cadets most evenings and weekends.

He had dropped a note off at her lodgings the previous evening asking her to meet him at Cyfarthfa Castle the following morning. The castle was the town's distinguished landmark high on a hill, surrounded by lush parkland, looking down across the town and the valley.

Rosa arrived on her bicycle and dismounted, a knot forming inside her as she fretted over the reason for needing to meet up so urgently. Dylan walked over to her and took her hand. 'Thank you for coming, Rosa. You must be wondering what this is about.'

A tingling sensation swelled through Rosa's body as her hand touched his. 'Well, yes, you said it was urgent. I must confess I am curious. Is everything alright?'

He pointed to a wooden bench in a secluded spot a few feet away. 'Shall we sit over there?'

She followed him to the seat, taking in the view. 'What is it, Dylan? What is so urgent it can't wait?'

Dylan cleared his throat. He bit his lip and his eyes creased. 'There is something important I need to tell you.'

Rosa's eyes filled with concern. 'Have you found another girl? Do you want us to break up?'

'Oh no, it's nothing like that, you silly thing. I only have eyes for you, you should know that by now.'

Dylan rose from the bench and paced a few steps. She watched him, unsure whether to stand too. He then stopped in front of her and blurted, 'I had a letter yesterday, and . . .'

Rosa's stomach tightened as she guessed what he was about to say.

'My call-up has come to join the air force.'

Rosa's voice wobbled. 'Oh no! I was dreading this. When do you go?'

'I leave next week. There's a special mission coming up and I will be trained in some kind of support role. I can't tell you any more.'

'But so soon?' Rosa quaked, her stomach flipping, overcome with sudden feelings of tenderness towards him, fearing he could die in action.

'Pilots are desperately needed. I know I'm young to enlist, but they say my navigational skills are exceptional and badly needed. I must serve my king and country, Rosa. I'm proud to do so. I feel honoured that my training will stand me in good stead.'

Feeling numb, Rosa replied softly, 'I see. I knew it was coming, but it's still a shock. How have your parents taken the news? With you being an only child, they must be very anxious.'

'Of course they are, but they know how much it means to me. I have no choice. I have to go. I want to go.'

Rosa said tenderly, 'You know I'll keep an eye on them and will do my best for the business.'

'I know you will, Rosa. My parents think the world of you, you must see that.'

Rosa nodded. 'I think the world of them too. Will you promise me one thing?'

She patted the seat and he sat next to her, taking his hand in hers. 'Anything, if I can.'

Rosa stared at him earnestly, their eyes locking. 'I want

you to promise you will take care of yourself and return to Merthyr in one piece, that you won't do anything stupid and try to be a hero.'

'Of course, that's what I want too. Part of me is scared, but I'm also excited, Rosa. I'm no coward and I'm going to do my best to help win the war.'

'I know you will,' Rosa whispered, feeling a warm rush of emotions course through her body.

'I wish I'd had the courage to ask you out before, Rosa. I've been so happy with you this last month.'

Rosa placed her hand on his arm and her eyes brimmed with tenderness. 'We must make the most of the time we have left.'

Dylan smiled. 'Yes, we must. I'm crazy about you, Rosa Edwards. Not knowing when I will see you again after I leave is too awful to think about.'

Rosa choked. 'I feel the same, but we have a week to make more special memories.'

She rested her head against his chest and felt his pounding heartbeat. He caressed her face and wrapped his arms around her in a tight embrace. 'Careful,' she teased. 'You'll mess my hair up and I have to be at work soon.'

He pulled away, patting her loose strands of hair in place. They stared across the valley, clasping hands tightly, sitting in silence. After a few minutes Dylan inhaled deeply and said, 'Wherever I am, I shall think back to this moment, of us together in my favourite part of Merthyr.'

'I shall come here and think of you when you are away, Dylan.'

'I appreciate that, my sweet Rosa. I've always been fond of this place. You know we have William Crawshay to thank for Cyfarthfa Castle. He owned the Cyfarthfa Iron-works down there, the other side of the town. It was once even visited by Admiral Lord Nelson, as his cannons were made there.'

Rosa paused to take in the imposing building before her. 'I always enjoyed history lessons, but I never knew that. I wonder what Mr Crawshay would think if he knew it was being used as a school today and filled with evac-uee children from Folkestone? Can you answer me this, Dylan, if you know so much? I've always wondered what *Cyfarthfa* meant.'

'As strange as it sounds, it means "barking place", after the barking hunts that were held around here. The dogs would be sent to chase their prey, which would climb trees or hide in underground burrows, and the dogs would signal their position by barking.'

'Well, that makes sense, I suppose.'

'Enough of history,' Dylan grinned, scooping Rosa up in his arms and swinging her around, then placing her gently on the ground. He took her hand in his. 'There's something I would like to ask you. I would like a photograph of you to take with me. I shall carry it with me at all times and when-ever I'm afraid, I shall look at your sweet face and remind myself that you are here waiting for me in Merthyr.'

Rosa's eyes moistened. She stared up at his chocolate-brown eyes. 'I'll bring you a photograph that I really like tomorrow, that was taken by Alice before she left.'

Dylan began to speak again, turning his head away as if struggling to find the right words.

'Is there something else, Dylan?' Rosa coaxed, taking hold of his arm.

'Yes there is. I've been putting off telling you.'

'What do you mean?'

'Mam and Da need more help with the business when I'm gone. They've asked Hettie Pritchard to come in. She helped out last year when Mam was taken poorly and was surprisingly good. I know you two don't see eye to eye, but the truth is she's first rate at design layout and has always shown an interest in the business.'

'Oh, I see,' muttered Rosa, her throat tightening. 'When does she start?'

'Tomorrow, so I can show her the ropes before I leave.'

A long silence followed and then Rosa gave Dylan a light peck on the cheek. 'You have nothing to worry about on my account. Your parents must do what's right for the business. I'm sure Hettie and I will get on just fine.'

3

March 1944

Eira slapped a letter on the kitchen table. 'It's for you, Rosa. Now who would be writing to you from London?'

Rosa's eyes lit up as she grabbed it and read her name on the front. 'I recognise that writing – it's from Alice. I hope she's getting on alright.'

Each morning Rosa skipped down the stairs to see if there was a letter for her. Two weeks had passed since Dylan left Merthyr and she had had one brief letter from him saying he was enjoying his training, but that it was tough, and he would write again when he could.

This was her first letter from Alice since her departure ten weeks ago. Her fingers burned to rip open the envelope and devour every word, but a glance at her mother's face showing a slight scowl made her feel this was not the time to do so.

Eira pulled out a chair and sat, resting her elbows on the table. She rolled a cigarette, flicked a match and lit it. She inhaled deeply, blowing out puffs of smoke. 'I saw the London postmark and guessed who it was from. She used to fancy herself, that one. I heard she was free with her favours too and hanging around with a Yank. I never liked you associating with her and was glad when she left Merthyr. Good riddance to bad rubbish, that's what I say.'

45

Rosa blurted, 'That's not true, Mam. People were jealous of Alice because she was popular. She had a friendly way about her that some people took the wrong way.'

'Huh, you live in cloud-cuckoo-land, girl. Before you open that letter and let that girl fill your head with rubbish, there are jobs to be done here before you go to work.'

'Yes, Mam, I know,' replied Rosa dutifully, slipping the letter into her skirt pocket and picking up a vegetable knife. She was itching to read Alice's news, but wanted to savour every word her friend had to say in peace and privacy, without interruption.

Eira barked, 'The potatoes need peeling and our bedding needs changing. And if Billy runs off again, I swear I shall lose my rag. That boy gives me a bad head and doesn't know when he's lucky.'

'Don't be so hard on Billy, Mam. He misses his da. He's fifteen soon, he's almost a man, and it won't be long before he leaves school.'

Eira stubbed out her cigarette and scowled. Her hair was piled on top of her head and crowned with a headscarf, and she wore a pinafore over her woollen jumper and skirt in readiness for her charring. She scoffed, 'I have no idea why he wants to hang around with his father. Thomas Edwards is no role model for the boy. Billy doesn't appreciate what a good home he has here, skulking off when he fancies and skipping school.'

Rosa reflected on her mother's harsh words, knowing they were true, but feeling sympathy for her father, whose bad health and misfortunes had led him to seek solace from the bottle, taking his moods out on Eira, his young wife, his childhood sweetheart, his one and only love.

In their early married days there was no bitterness between them. But like countless other miners, her father's health had deteriorated due to his working conditions. His lungs were riddled with coal dust and he suffered from silicosis, leaving him short of breath and with coughing fits, sometimes bringing up black phlegm. He was a shell of a man, losing his melodic voice too.

His inability to work had forced Eira to swallow her pride and take on three cleaning jobs in order to put food on the table. Occasionally Thomas picked up casual work, once as a chimney sweep, then as a porter at the railway station. He helped on a farm during lambing season too, but opportunities were sporadic. On a good day you couldn't find a better worker, but after a night at the boozer Thomas couldn't be counted on to turn up for work and was given his cards. Then his temper would get the better of him when he stomped off home in the foulest of moods, lashing out at his wife.

The final straw for Eira came after her mother, Grandma Meryl, was summoned to their house early one evening. A neighbour had rushed to her saying they had never seen Thomas in such a filthy mood. He was in an uncontrollable rage, shouting and thrashing his arms around. Eira had shielded herself by holding Rosa up in front of her chest, while Billy, who was only a toddler at time, hid his face in the folds of her skirt. Meryl had thundered, 'Get out of this house this minute, Thomas Edwards. If you so much as lay a finger on my daughter or the children, I swear you will be floating face down in the river this time tomorrow.'

Thomas had raised his fist, but Eira squared up to him,

burning with rage, and he turned and skulked off. The following day, when he'd sobered up, he regretted his anger and promised to change, pleading with Eira to give him another chance.

'I've heard it all before. You've had your last chance.' She spat the words at him on her doorstep and slammed the door behind her, turning him away whenever he turned up on her doorstep to see Rosa and Billy in the years that followed. She took on work wherever she could, usually cleaning, to put food in their bellies and a roof over their head.

In the end, Thomas's visits became infrequent, timed around their birthdays and Christmas. Nowadays Thomas had mellowed as his health deteriorated and he cut a lonely figure in the local pubs he still frequented, which troubled Rosa.

The lodgings Eira, Rosa and Billy shared were in a three-storey house on Plymouth Street owned by sisters Vera and Betty Hughes. Vera was the elder by two years, at forty-five, and they lived on the ground floor. Rosa and her family had two rooms on the first floor – a small kitchen-cum-sitting room and a bathroom – and two bedrooms on the floor above in the attic space. Eira and Rosa shared one partitioned room, while Billy slept in a much smaller space with room only for a single bed. The furnishings were dated, but the rooms were clean and it suited them.

The sisters had inherited the property from their father, a pastor who had died ten years ago. At the time Eira cleaned his chapel and the sisters offered her the chance to move in with her family, paying a reduced rent in return for cleaning their private rooms on the ground floor. Eira was struggling to pay her bills, getting no money from Thomas, and grabbed the offer with open arms.

The sisters kept themselves to themselves. Rosa knew from what she had been told by her mother that they had both been engaged to marry, but their sweethearts were killed in the Great War. Since then, they had pledged to remain true to their lost loves, with the belief that true love only came once in a lifetime.

The sisters could not have looked more different. While Vera was tall, fair and slender with slate-grey eyes and a sculptured bone structure, Betty was dark and swarthy and had a less refined air than her sister. Rosa would ask Eira about them, but she told her sharply that their affairs were none of her business.

One day when Eira was cleaning their rooms, Rosa was walking down the stairs on her way out. Knowing the sisters were out, she pressed their living-room door and opened it slightly.

She pushed it further open and stood rooted to the spot, her hand flying to her face. She took a few steps inside and looked around in astonishment. Photographs of two young men in army uniforms, surrounded by crucifixes and small mementoes, covered the top of the sideboard, and the wall was plastered with photographs too. It was a shrine to the men these sisters had planned to spend the rest of their lives with, whose own lives were tragically cut short. There were pictures too of their father with the sisters, and framed Bible quotes declaring God's love for his flock.

Her mother appeared and scolded her: 'What are you doing here?'

'I had no idea this is how they lived. It seems so sad,' said Rosa.

'It's none of our business. I think you should leave now, before they return.'

Rosa retreated, wondering if the sisters were right, that you can only love one man in a lifetime.

Clutching Alice's letter, Rosa retreated to her room before leaving for work, having completed her chores in record time.

She carefully slid her index finger inside the back of the envelope and brought out two small sheets of white paper. It was addressed from 139 Piccadilly, London.

Dear Rosa,

You must think I am a poor friend to have taken so long to write to you, but I've been run off my feet. Working at the Valleys Hotel was child's play compared to what's expected of me now!

Not that I'm complaining, seeing as I work alongside some friendly people and have settled in well. I've become friendly with another maid called Susan, who helps Cook in the kitchen, while I assist Lord and Lady Hesketh-Robbins. I couldn't believe my eyes when I met her. She is only in her twenties, while he must be old enough to be her father! You certainly wouldn't match them up as a couple.

His lordship is out most of the time, he is something to do with the theatre, though I'm not exactly sure what. He goes out at night smartly dressed, saying he is off to see his protegees at the Queen Mary Theatre. She is the prettiest lady, with milky white skin, violet eyes and perfect rosebud lips. She flings her arms about a lot in a very dramatic way, and Susan mentioned she had been on stage once, and that's where she met her husband.

I'll try and find out more from Susan, but she says it's none of our business as upper-class people get up to all sorts of rum things that you could never imagine.

I did spend one morning with his lordship in his office helping him sort out his paperwork. It was such a mess, with papers up to his elbows. He was busy writing letters and he told me not to disturb him. I know I shouldn't have peeked, but when he slipped out of the office for a minute I picked up one of his letters. It was from a bank saying he owed them £10,000. That's a fortune! I'm wondering now how secure my position here is.

I asked him yesterday about the secretarial classes, and he said all in good time. Lady Iris rolled her eyes when I asked her and she wouldn't talk about it, saying it was for her husband to arrange.

Anyway, Susan has invited me to join her in a cellar bar where jazz musicians play. I've not heard from the Yank in Merthyr, so sod him and his stockings. Susan is cheering me up. She's made friends with some of the musicians and told me not to act surprised when I introduce her to Bernie and Jimmie, who are American GIs and have dark skins. She says they are good fun and very generous and we won't have to put our hands in our purse all night. It sounds lots of fun, a world apart from Merthyr.

Oh, I forgot to say, I wasn't surprised when you told me about you and Dylan. You make a lovely couple and I hope you will be happy. I hope you don't forget me, my offer stands if you want to come to London, it would do you the world of good. If things don't work out, Susan has good connections with other households and I can ask her to keep her eyes peeled for you if you fancy moving here, though I guess that's not on the cards now you and Dylan are together.

Rosa placed the letter back in the envelope and contemplated its contents with a sense of unease. The lord and lady of the house seemed to live unconventional lives – and she wondered how long Alice would remain there if the family were in such huge debt. Her hunch about the offer of secretarial training being too good to be true was proving correct.

She frowned, feeling the sense of unease increase. While Alice might feel able to handle unwanted male attention in Merthyr, would this be the same in London, where men were bound to be slicker and more sophisticated?

Hettie had already arrived at work when Rosa stepped through the door. She was perched on a stool behind the counter alongside Mrs Williams, their heads locked together, poring over the contents of a letter, in animated conversation.

Hettie had recently turned eighteen and was a miniature of her mother, having inherited her thick black hair, sallow skin, thick lips and haughty manner.

Hettie purred, 'It's so nice that Dylan asks after me, Mrs Williams. Please tell him how much I appreciate his kind words. Or maybe I should write to him myself, seeing our families are so closely connected.'

Before Mrs Williams could reply, Rosa came over to

them, forcing a smile. 'Good morning, Mrs Williams. Is that a letter from Dylan you have there?'

Mrs Williams gushed, 'Why yes, it is, Rosa. You may read it too. He says he is rushed off his feet, with barely a minute to himself, and promises to write to you the following day. He mentions you by name several times.'

Turning to Hettie, she continued, 'Dylan was only asking how you have settled in here. As you know, he is very fond of Rosa.'

Hettie gritted her teeth and scowled, her face reddening. 'I was only trying to be friendly.'

Rosa's eyes shone. 'I'm so pleased you've heard from Dylan, Mrs Williams. Does he say what he's doing?'

'He's not allowed to say much, but at least we know he's alive.'

Hettie glared at Rosa. Trying to make peace, Rosa added, 'Feel free to write to Dylan if you wish. I'm sure he would enjoy hearing your news too. Any letters from home are bound to help keep his spirits up.'

Hettie's throat juddered. 'Well yes, if I have time, I shall write to him later today.'

Mrs Williams demurred. 'That's very sweet of you, Rosa. By the way, is there any news of your friend, Alice?'

'There is actually – just arrived. I was able to read it quickly before I left this morning . . .' Rosa's voice trailed, and Mrs Williams picked up on her anxious tone.

'How is everything with Alice?'

'I'm not sure, if I'm honest.'

Mrs Williams said soothingly, 'It was a big step moving to London. I'm sure she's fine. I hear she's working in a distinguished household.'

'That's what she said. And she's made a good friend in the house there, a maid called Susan.'

'I'm pleased to hear it. Try not to worry about her. We must press on now. Mr Fry will be in to collect his posters this afternoon to promote his new art exhibition in Merthyr. It's very exciting by all accounts, with paintings by soldiers from the frontline, the likes of which have never been seen before in Wales. You did an excellent job there, Rosa. And I want to spend time with Hettie this morning, showing her where everything is. I'm afraid Mr Williams is away on business for most of the day and due to attend a Home Guard meeting late afternoon, so it's just us.'

Rosa barely had time to catch her breath that morning. Mr Jiggings from the general stores called in to order new promotional leaflets, which Rosa took charge of. He also brought in some cardboard for Mrs Williams's WVS salvage collection. After this, the pastor's wife, Mrs Bonnett, collected service sheets for a funeral parlour. 'It's the choirmaster's funeral, Mr Alwyn, and everyone is expecting the choir to be heard across the valley,' she said, putting the carefully wrapped package in her basket. She placed two more orders for services in the next week before she left, promising to return the previous service sheets so they could be recycled.

Rosa then recalled Mrs Williams asking her to double-check Mr Fry's order for thirty copies of the poster for the forthcoming *Soldiers at War* exhibition. She was confident there were no problems, though, having carefully proof-read the draft and written clear instructions for thirty to be printed. The poster featured a painting depicting the horrors of war, an injured soldier kneeling on a battlefield, his eyes filled with terror, surrounded by corpses, flames and gunfire in the background. It was a haunting image showing the brutality of war, and Mr Fry had expressed his delight.

Hettie was out seeing a potential client, promising to return with any used paper from her call for Mrs Williams, when Rosa heard her name being called.

'Rosa!' cried Mrs Williams. There was a hint of urgency in her tone.

Rosa rushed to the front of the shop. An irate gentleman demanded, 'Tell me, how could such a mistake have been made?'

Mrs Williams looked close to tears. She appeared visibly shocked as she replied, 'I have no idea, Mr Fry, but I intend to find out.'

Mr Fry was tall and distinguished-looking, with grey hair and a thin moustache on his upper lip. He shook his head and pointed to a pile of posters on the counter. 'I don't need three hundred copies, a scandalous amount in these times. I only ordered thirty. Look, here is a carbon copy receipt of my order showing thirty copies. I certainly have no intention of paying for three hundred.'

Mrs Williams's face was creased. 'Please forgive me, Mr Fry. I don't understand how such a mistake could have happened. Ah, here is Rosa now. Perhaps she can explain.'

Rosa's eyebrows furrowed. 'This isn't right. I am certain I wrote down thirty copies, as you requested, Mr Fry. How could it have been mistaken for three hundred? I would never have done that. If you ask Bryn, Mrs Williams, he'll tell you that's what I wrote. He saw it with his own eyes.'

Bryn Price was the Williamses' print manager of forty years, who collected orders from the shop at the end of each day with Rosa's instructions, and produced them at their small printing press on another site in town. Mrs Williams scrutinised the order sheet. Rosa had never seen her so cross. She fumed, 'I shall do that, but from what I see on the copy I have, it shows an order for three hundred copies of the *Soldiers at War* exhibition, while Mr Fry's order shows thirty, with the promise they would be returned and recycled afterwards. It would be quite preposterous to believe we would print as many as three hundred when there is a shortage of paper. How could this have happened?'

Rosa took the order sheet and read it. 'But I don't understand. I swear I didn't write three hundred.'

Mrs Williams pressed. 'I asked you to check Mr Fry's order. Did you do so?'

'Well, no,' mumbled Rosa, the words sticking in her throat. 'I didn't expect anything to have changed since I wrote the order. I was busy seeing to another customer and assumed everything was still in order.'

Hettie returned as Mrs Williams berated Rosa. 'How many times have we said all orders must be checked again and again to avoid mistakes happening?'

'Is anything wrong?' asked Hettie with a smirk.

After being put in the picture, Hettie denied knowledge of any wrongdoing.

'I will just take the thirty copies, and we will leave it at that. It is an excellent design and I must be on my way now to an appointment,' said Mr Fry, exasperated.

Mrs Williams rubbed the back of her neck. 'Well, we could recycle the excess numbers. But I have another idea.

Rather than disposing of them, perhaps you could make use of them. This was a genuine error and you will not, of course, be charged for them.'

Mr Fry considered the suggestion. 'Well, if you are sure, Mrs Williams. It would be a pity to waste them. I'm sure we could place them around the town, and once the exhibition is over, they can be returned for the salvage collection. After all, waste not want not.'

'Exactly,' she retorted, sighing with relief.

Hettie sidled up to Mr Fry. 'If you like, I will help you put them up. I can do it when I finish work. Your exhibition will raise money for an excellent cause and the more people hear about it, the better. You'll be able to have posters on every street corner in the town.'

Mr Fry beamed. 'How very kind, young lady. I gladly accept your offer.'

'My name's Hettie Pritchard, sir. And it's my pleasure. Shall I come to your studio after work today?'

Rosa squeaked, 'Can I help too?'

Mr Fry replied crisply, 'It's all in hand, no thanks to you. I think I can rely on Miss Pritchard's assistance.'

'You certainly can,' Hettie gloated.

After he left Mrs Williams turned to Rosa. 'In future, if I ask you to check an order before it leaves the premises, will you please do as I ask. That was most embarrassing.'

A lump formed in Rosa's throat. 'Of course, Mrs Williams. I'm very sorry. I really don't know how this could have happened.'

The rest of the day dragged on and Hettie was given permission to leave an hour early to assist Mr Fry with putting up the posters. Just before closing time, Bryn strolled into the shop. Barrel-chested with short legs, he was always cheerful, however busy they were. 'What's got into you today, Rosa? I've never seen you looking so down. Have you had bad news?'

She shook her head. Mrs Williams beckoned him into the back room. 'There's something I need to ask you, Bryn, and I would like you to answer truthfully.'

Bryn followed her through and the door was left ajar so Rosa could hear every word. Mrs Williams explained the mess up.

He replied, 'It's funny you say that. I could see Rosa was busy with a customer and the new girl gave me Mr Fry's order sheet. I had called in earlier, that's when Rosa gave it to me, but the new girl told me to forget it, and gave me a different one.'

'I see,' muttered Mrs Williams. 'Or rather, I don't see. Why would she do that? How did the mix-up happen with the figures?'

Bryn continued, 'I thought it strange that three hundred copies were written down. I told the new girl it must be costing the organiser of the art exhibition a small fortune and that it was a huge number, with the paper shortage. She said "So what of it?" or words to that effect. Cocky little thing, I thought.'

Rosa burst into the room. She could hold back no longer and confronted her employer, her face burning. 'I heard that. It's as I said. I swear I only wrote thirty copies. Bryn saw that's what I'd written down.'

Bryn rubbed his chin. 'So that means . . .'

'It means what, Bryn? What are you saying?' pressed Mrs Williams, putting her hand against her forehead.

'Someone changed it deliberately,' he stated. 'Rosa is right. She wrote thirty.'

'But I don't understand?' queried Mrs Williams, as the full realisation of Bryn's words slowly sank in.

He declared, 'I'm sure it wasn't Rosa. She is meticulous and I've never had problems with her orders before.'

Mrs Williams's eyebrows arched. 'Exactly. Those are my thoughts too. It could only mean— You don't think Hettie was responsible, do you?'

Bryn shrugged his shoulders. 'If it wasn't Rosa, who else would it be? She gave me the second order sheet. I can't say I've really taken to the girl – she seems sly to me.'

Mrs Williams murmured, 'I am so sorry, Rosa. It seems I owe you an apology for doubting you. I have never in all our days had such a calamity, and one that has cost us dear, both reputationally and financially. I hope you can put it out of your mind.'

'I'll try,' mumbled Rosa, a sense of rage building up inside her.

Bryn chided, 'Chin up, Rosa. Mr and Mrs Williams will get to the bottom of this. That girl really seems to have it in for you.'

Rosa couldn't face returning home straight after work, wanting time to herself after the unpleasant event that left her shaken. She walked to Cyfarthfa Castle and sat on the bench where she had met Dylan, reliving the time they had spent there together, feeling a sense of comfort. How she yearned to be in his arms again, his hungry lips pressing on hers and arousing in her a burning desire and longing she didn't know she possessed.

Their embraces had always been chaste, and once when his hand strayed onto her breast she was so shocked that she pulled away and almost fell over. It wasn't that she didn't want to further explore their passions, but she was terrified of giving in to them and ending up in the family way, without a ring on her finger.

Before she realised, two hours had passed and she rushed home. She flew up the stairs and threw open the door.

Her mother was still up, and stared at her with a dark expression. 'What time do you call this?' Eira demanded.

Rosa caught Billy's expression in the corner of the room. He tilted his head, raising his eyes towards the ceiling. 'I told Mam not to worry, that you would have an explanation.'

Rosa blurted, 'I'm sorry, Mam, I didn't mean to worry you. I wanted some time alone to think. I've not had a good day, if you must know. Why all the fuss?'

'It just so happens we had a couple of visitors earlier on – your Mr and Mrs Williams. They were hoping to see you and gave up waiting,' her mother informed her, her arms folded across her chest.

'Mr and Mrs Williams? Why would they come here in the evening? They know I'll be in tomorrow.' Rosa's hands flew to her mouth. 'Unless . . . they haven't given me my cards, have they?'

'It seems the Pritchards phoned the Williamses to say they were furious to learn of the accusations made against Hettie. From what I could gather, Mr Pritchard has threatened to use his influence on the local authority to suggest they take their trade to Boswell's Printers instead, unless they take back what they said about Hettie. Mr Williams got so worked up he thought his heart would pack up.'

'None of this is my fault,' Rosa cried. 'Does it mean Dylan's parents are taking Hettie's side and want me to leave?'

'I'm sorry, Rosa. I think the Pritchards are taking out their dislike of me against you. It's disgusting,' her mother spat.

Billy butted in. 'If I were you, Rosa, I'd tell them where to stick their job.'

'But I can't. Why should I? I haven't done anything wrong.'

Eira rested her hand on her daughter's arm. 'I had to bite my tongue and stay shtum about why I left my work with the Pritchards. I don't want to stir things up and make matters worse for you. Try not to worry – I'm sure it will all blow over in a week or so. Mrs Williams was saying how highly they think of you, but the Pritchards have put them in a difficult position. After all, money talks.'

'I don't want their business to suffer because of me, Mam. Maybe it would be for the best if I left. Hettie will never like me, especially now.'

Her eyes fell on a small white envelope on the mantelpiece. She saw her name written on the front and her heart skipped a beat when she recognised the handwriting. Rosa's face brightened. 'It's from Dylan. Why didn't you say?'

Her mother waved a hand. 'I'd forgotten about that with all this fuss. It came with the last post.'

Rosa eagerly ripped open the envelope and her eyes devoured the words on the page.

Rosa clutched the letter to her chest, her eyebrows knitted together. *A mission* — what could Dylan mean? It sounded dangerous, and she was being asked to keep it to herself. What would she tell his parents? How she wished Alice was here to confide in at moments like this.

'Well? Is everything alright?' her mother asked.

'I don't know, truth be told. I don't think Dylan would tell me if things were not OK — or his parents,' she replied cagily, turning away from her mother's enquiring gaze. 'How I miss him. I wish he was here right now. He'd make everything right again.'

'Well, what does he say? Can you tell your mam?'

Rosa's hands trembled as she read an extract from his letter, omitting mention of the mission, and trying her best to mask her anxiety.

'I know you, Rosa Edwards. I get the feeling there's something you're trying to hide. Am I right?'

'I'm sorry, Mam. I can't say. Dylan asked me not to, and I have to keep my word to him.'

Eira tilted Rosa's chin up to face her. 'I know Dylan meant well, but if he's asked you to keep some information about what he's doing a secret, then that's a huge burden for your shoulders. His parents should be told – at least his father.'

Rosa gulped. 'I'll sleep on it, Mam. I think you're right.'

'And don't go fretting about that Pritchard girl. You're worth ten of her, and she knows it, that's why she's so spiteful,' her mother consoled her.

'Thank you, Mam. I know how important the Pritchards are for their business. I promise I won't let Hettie get the better of me.'

'That's the spirit, my girl,' beamed her mother, as Billy punched his fist in the air.

4

That night Rosa tossed and turned, her head filled with conflicting thoughts on whether she should break Dylan's trust. In the end, she agreed with her mother that it was too big a secret to keep to herself. If everything went well, he would have no excuse to be cross with her, and if it didn't, well, that option didn't bear thinking about, and she dismissed the thought from her mind.

She also needed to summon up all her courage the following morning and have a word with Mr and Mrs Williams and Hettie to clear the air before customers came in.

The door was still closed for business when she arrived ten minutes before opening time, the *Closed* sign still up. She pressed her face against the window and could see Mr Williams behind the counter. She knocked on the door and he let her in.

'Good morning, Rosa. I'm afraid Mrs Williams is resting upstairs today. She has a bad head after that unpleasant business yesterday.'

'I'm sorry to hear that. I wanted to come early and let you know there's no ill feeling on my part and I'll go along with anything you say.'

'You're a good girl, Rosa. You mother's told you about our predicament, has she?'

Just as she was going to mention Dylan's letter while

they were alone, the bell above the door jangled as Hettie breezed in.

'Ah, here's Hettie now.'

Hettie stared at them both, her body rigid. 'Why do I get the feeling you are talking about me?'

'Rosa's just arrived, Hettie,' Mr Williams blurted. 'We want to let bygones be bygones. Let's start today afresh, shall we?'

Rosa extended her hand to Hettie. 'I agree. I hope we can be friends and put this misunderstanding behind us.'

Hettie glared at Rosa.

'Hettie,' urged Mr Williams. 'Come on now. We're a small business and everyone needs to get on.'

'Perhaps we could go out together at the weekend and get to know each other properly,' suggested Rosa magnanimously.

The muscles on Hettie's face tightened. After a moment she gulped, 'I will accept your apology for trying to blacken my name. But as far as the weekend goes, I have responsibilities supporting the poor people in Merthyr. You might know some of them?'

Rosa's jaw dropped and Mr Williams raised his arms in exasperation.

'I give up,' he said. 'All I ask is that you are civil towards each other at work. What you do in your spare time is your own business. Now, where is the ledger for today's orders?'

Hettie followed Mr Williams into the back room. 'Is this what you are looking for?' she replied, smiling sweetly and holding out the book.

'Thank you, Hettie. Now then, I believe Mr Bellamy is calling in later for his new business cards. Are they in?'

'Yes, they are. I checked the order before I left yesterday.'

Rosa joined them, but felt excluded, seeing them nattering together, reviewing orders in the ledger, and barely glancing in her direction. Fighting back tears, she picked up a broom and began sweeping the front of the shop, desperate for something to do.

'I see you've done an excellent job sweeping here too, Rosa. I do like it when staff show initiative,' Mr Williams praised her a few minutes later.

Rosa was relieved when Hettie left an hour early, having been given permission to slip away to continue distributing the surplus posters promoting the art exhibition. She rushed to her bag and picked up Dylan's letter, pressing it close to her chest. She felt conflicted by his request not to divulge news about his mission to his parents to protect them from worrying about him, but decided that surely they had a right to know too.

Rosa tentatively approached Mr Williams.

'What is it, Rosa? Is everything alright?'

She opened her mouth to speak, then shut it, avoiding his gaze.

His eyes fell on the letter. Rosa said, 'It's from Dylan, Mr Williams. It came yesterday afternoon, only—'

'Oh my dear child, why didn't you say earlier? Jane is worried sick about him. We both are.'

'I'm sorry. I meant too, but—'

'May I see it?'

'I don't wish to betray Dylan's trust by showing it to

you, but I think you should know what's happening. I hope he doesn't feel I'm being disloyal to him.'

She handed him the letter to read. His face became anxious. 'A mission?'

'I thought you should know, even though Dylan didn't want you to. It's really worrying, isn't it? I barely slept last night. Do you think it's already happened?'

'You did the right thing showing it to me, Rosa. I can't let Jane know of this, though I shall tell her he has written to you, which will give her some peace of mind.'

'You're sure I did right to tell you?'

His eyebrows furrowed and he rubbed the back of his neck. 'You did, but let's keep this to ourselves for now. Will you give me your word?'

'Of course. I won't even tell Mam and Billy.'

'There's one other thing, Rosa.'

'Yes, Mr Williams?'

'I wanted to thank you for your hard work and for not letting Hettie get under your skin today.'

Rosa beamed. 'Thank you, Mr Williams. I'm only doing my job and it pleases me to know you're happy with what I do.'

He hesitated. 'There's another thing. With Dylan being away, and with Mrs Williams planning to step back from her duties here . . .' He paused.

'Yes? Is there more I can do to help? You only have to ask.' She sensed a discomfort in his manner as his eyes shifted to the floor. He cleared his throat and rubbed the back of his neck again.

'We've been put in a very difficult and delicate position, I'm afraid, Rosa.'

'What do you mean? Are you saying you want me to leave?'

'Oh no, nothing of the sort. The thing is, the Pritchards have made it clear that they want us to promote Hettie. She enjoys working here and, despite her difficult ways, her artwork is excellent, as is yours. Her parents say a promotion for her would be regarded favourably by many businesses in the town they have ties with.'

Rosa's jaw dropped. 'You mean, Hettie would be my boss? I would have to take orders from her?'

Mr Williams nodded, avoiding her stricken face. 'I'll speak to her about her manner towards you.'

Rosa flew out the door, her eyes brimming. She thought for a moment that some kind of promotion was coming her way, but it was being offered to her nemesis instead. It felt like a punch in the stomach.

Fighting back the tears, she stumbled down the path into the town centre. She ran until she became breathless, pausing outside a department store to catch her breath.

Through a mist of tears she staggered into a doorway of Goodwin & Co, where the best-heeled folk in Merthyr shopped. She barely noticed the mannequins adorned in the latest spring fashions, but her attention was caught by a large number of young women whose eyes were fixed on the front window. A young shop assistant was carefully stepping around the mannequins, holding a card in her hand. She taped it to the window and the women surged forward. Curious, Rosa also pressed forward and read:

Her face brightened as an idea came into her head. She caught the eye of the assistant, who smiled at her. *She seems friendly*, Rosa thought. *Maybe I should think about it. I'll never be happy working under Hettie.*

The more she thought about it, the more she liked the idea. She was used to working with the town's most respected citizens at the hotel, and maybe this was the break she needed as she dreaded having to take orders from Hettie, knowing she was intent on making her life a misery. She hoped Dylan's parents would understand it would be best for their business if she found herself another position, and this way they could all remain on good terms.

She memorised the contact details, her spirits lifted. As she turned to walk away, from the corner of her eye she spotted the same assistant stick another notice on the window. She tried to push her way forward, but the small group of young women were crowding round and blocked her view. She craned her neck, but the girls in front were much taller. She heard one of them yelp: "'Maids wanted to work in large respected household in London for distinguished family. Impeccable references required.'"

Rosa's ears pricked up on hearing London mentioned,

curious to know more. Her thoughts turned to Alice's letter, and a seed planted in her mind that maybe this would be a way for her to be close to Alice.

Rosa cursed her short legs as she leaped up to try and read the notice. 'I can't see a thing. Will someone let me through?' she hollered.

A girl in front turned and stepped back, inviting Rosa to take her place. She told her, 'It says maids are wanted to work at a big house in London. It's not for me, I don't want to be a maid, on my hands and knees making up fires. Nah. I might go for the sales jobs at Goodwin's though. That's more my cup of tea.'

A couple of older girls craned their necks, read the notice, and turned away. 'I'd have given it a shot, but I'm being called up for National Service soon, seeing as I turn twenty next week,' one of them said.

'Me too,' her friend said. 'My call-up is due any day.'

Women could opt to work in munitions factories, aircraft and tank factories, or in shipbuilding, or become a Land Army girl. They could also choose to join one of the uniformed services, either the Auxiliary Territorial Service, the Women's Auxiliary Air Force, or the Women's Royal Navy Service, leaving huge staff shortages in shop work and domestic service.

Rosa read and reread the notice.

Housemaids and coffee maid needed as soon as possible.
Silver service experience required. Must be of excellent character.
Apply in writing with impeccable references to:
Miss Penelope Rogers, care of Mrs Pettigrew's
Domestic Agency, Cardiff.

The group was dispersing, their initial excitement dimming. Rosa was surprised they didn't all leap at the chance. 'Who wants to work in London and get bombed?' commented one girl. 'I'd be homesick. I couldn't bear to be so far apart from my family,' another girl retorted, shaking her head. 'My hand would shake if I had to serve soup to any of those posh folk. It would end up in their lap,' giggled another.

Rosa was oblivious to their chatter as they walked off and she was left alone, her eyes reading the words over and over again. She wondered if the agency was the same recruitment company that placed Alice in her position. Alice's advice about her leaving Merthyr rang clear in her ears. This could be the chance she needed. After all, she could do silver service, and she was of excellent character.

As quickly as she talked herself into it, a voice in her head talked her out of it, then changed her mind back. After churning it over and over in her head, Rosa made her decision: she would give it a go, even though a part of her was convinced there would be far better applicants than her.

5

Rosa's heart thumped as she sat at the kitchen table later that evening and stared at the plain white sheet of paper in front of her. She'd never applied for a job before, not in the formal sense.

Now her position at the print business was untenable, she decided to apply for both positions in the hope she would be offered an interview for at least one of them.

Billy hovered over her shoulder. 'What's this then?'

'If you must know, I'm applying for a position at Goodwin's as a sales assistant.'

'Why would you do that? I thought you were happy with the Williamses. What would Dylan think of it?'

Rosa shrugged. 'Look, don't keep pressing me. I was happy there, but now Hettie will be my manager, of a kind, I would rather leave. I saw the advertisement in the window quite by chance and thought I would give it a go.'

Billy's face reddened. 'Hettie Pritchard, your manager! Why, you're ten times better than her.'

'Well, that's the way it is. Please don't say anything to Mam, until I know for sure. You know how she relies on my wage packet each week, and I don't want her to think I'll be leaving her short.'

Billy gave his word and left Rosa to write her application, telling her he was popping out for a while.

'Where are you going, Billy? Are you off to see Da again?'

'It so happens, I am. Where's the harm in that?'

Rosa gulped. 'How is he doing? I haven't seen him since Christmas, and he was trying to cadge money off me then. I don't like it when he's like that.'

'Neither do I, Rosa, but he's my da, and he lets me be myself, not like Mam, always nagging about something.'

'Mam's had it tough, Billy. She worries about you and doesn't want you ending up like Da.'

'Well I won't, because there's no way I'm going down those pits. I'll see you later.'

'Tell Da to take care,' Rosa said as Billy left.

Eira was out for the evening so she didn't have to rush her applications. She read her first attempt for Goodwin's and screwed it up and threw it in the bin, having smudged the ink. She took more care with her second attempt and completed it neatly, to her satisfaction. Her heart skipped a beat as she read it, feeling scared yet excited at the same time. She named Mr and Mrs Williams for her reference – asking to be informed in advance of them being approached if she should be successful – as well as her last teacher, who she was still in touch with.

I don't sound too bad at all, she thought. Top of the class for writing and arithmetic is something to be proud of, though I'm not sure if I will need them if I'm selling hats.

She repeated the same attributes in her application for the position in the London household, adding a paragraph stating she was accomplished and experienced at silver service and serving coffee, and had waited on the town's leading figures without mishap.

When she was satisfied with her letters, she sealed

them in their respective envelopes and addressed them accordingly.

It was now nine o'clock and she would normally be getting ready for bed. But there was one more letter she needed to write, although she decided to keep her work news to herself for now, until she knew for certain what would happen. A warm sensation coursed through her as she pictured Dylan in her mind's eye, seeing his kind face and smile, recalling the womanly desires he awoke within her, as she put pen to paper, yearning for the day they could kiss again.

My darling Dylan,

I pinch myself when I write those words, for I can still scarcely believe that you have fallen for me and we are sweethearts. I tingle all over when I think of the short time we had together before you left Merthyr. I'm so thankful for it, and I replay those memories in my head all day. The other day your mam caught me smiling and mumbling to myself — she must have thought I was half mad. I think she guessed I was daydreaming about you because she laughed and said 'Tell my boy his mam tells him not to get up to any nonsense.'

I was over the moon to receive your letter and I am anxious to hear from you again very soon, to know that you are safe and well after your mission. It fills my heart with dread to think what danger you might put yourself in. I know you are the kind of person not to hold back and this fills me both with pride at your bravery and a fear of what might happen.

I wear your brooch on my coat lapel and feel your love as I run my fingers over it, and I kiss your photograph by my bed before closing my eyes and giving in to sleep, which will be very soon now.

She licked the envelope with a smile and stuck on the stamp just as her mother returned home and kicked off her shoes in the corner of the room, followed by Billy, whose eyes shot in her direction. She swiftly concealed all three letters under a magazine and rose to greet her mother.

Eira scowled. 'Look who I found hanging outside the Miner's Arms hoping to catch a word with that no-good father of his. God knows how long he would have been there if I hadn't passed by.'

'It's not a crime to want to see your da. What were you doing there anyway?' he replied with a defiant tone.

Eira confronted him. 'You're not planning anything stupid, are you, Billy, like running off again? There'll be work for you down the mines if you want it. The government is bringing Bevin boys here and training them to do the job. If it's good enough for them, why can't you do it?'

The 'Bevin Boys' scheme had been introduced in 1942 by Ernest Bevin, Minister for Labour and National Service, to make up the shortage of men working in the pits at a time when labour was short and coal was needed more than ever to make materiel for the war. Mines were taking in lads from fourteen and fifteen, but there were still too few men available to do the job, and soldiers' names were picked at random for it.

'You must be joking!' Billy shot back. 'I'm not going down there. You saw how it ruined Da's life.'

Eira pointed upstairs. 'Enough of your back-chat. It's time for your bed. Now!'

Rosa's mouth opened wide into a yawn. 'I'm tired too, Mam. I'm off to bed as well.'

Rosa and Billy retreated to their respective bedrooms. The attic room Rosa shared with her mother had two iron-framed single beds under the eaves. The small window was framed with pink floral curtains. Their eiderdowns, made from matching fabric, had spines of feathers poking through the covers and wouldn't fluff up no matter how hard Rosa shook them.

A bedside cabinet was placed on each side of their beds. Rosa was afraid the loose drawer handle would come off in her hand and she'd be blamed for damaging it, so she left hers half open. She gently opened it another inch and placed her letters inside, covering them with a magazine, then left it slightly open. A photograph of Dylan dressed in his uniform sat on top of her cabinet. In the dim light she could see his face bursting with pride, and his smile tugged at her heartstrings.

The room was brightened thanks to its white-painted walls. Paraffin for their lamps was in short supply but candles were always at hand, and it was surprising how easily her eyes adjusted to the smallest light in the darkness. An oak chest of drawers was covered with her mother's cosmetics.

There was also a small wardrobe for them to share and a pink straw linen bin almost full of dirty washing.

Billy's room was sparse and airless, a quarter of the size of theirs. There was room only for a small bed, chest of drawers and a chair in the corner piled high with clothes that Billy didn't have room for in his drawers. A cable hanging from the ceiling provided a dim yellowy light. It was claustrophobic, and little wonder that Billy wanted to leave as soon as he could.

Rosa slipped her shoes off and felt the rough grain of the wooden floorboards through the worn patterned carpet. 'Blast!' she yelped, catching her foot on a tiny splinter and swearing under her breath as a ladder spread quickly up her stocking from the heel.

Under her pillow lay her cream floral winceyette nightgown. She removed her clothes and laid them neatly on a chair, then slipped her nightgown over her head as a wave of overwhelming tiredness flooded her body.

Pulling back the bed clothes, she turned on one side and returned Dylan's smile. '*Goodnight, my love. Wherever you are, I hope you are safe and will return home soon,*' she murmured. She yanked the covers up to her chin as her heavy eyelids clasped shut, and drifted into a deep sleep.

She was still in another world when her alarm clock went off at six-thirty. She switched it off in a flash, and leaped out of bed, remembering the letters she had to post on her way in to work.

She glanced at her mother, thankful she hadn't disturbed her, and tiptoed out of the room. She looked in on Billy and he too was still sleeping.

Rosa hastily washed and returned to her room, dressing

as quietly as she could. With the lightest touch she opened the drawer beside her bed and removed the letters.

After wolfing down a slice of toast and marmalade, she looked at her reflection in the mirror, turning her head one side and then the next.

'You'll do, Rosa Edwards. Today could be the first day towards your new life.'

She crept down two flights of stairs, past the rooms occupied by the sisters, and slipped out of the front door.

She patted her bag where she'd placed the letters and set off for Goodwin & Co. She reached the store within ten minutes. The notices were still in the window and Rosa stared at them, wondering how many would apply.

'Good morning,' said a well-spoken woman's voice. Rosa spun around. She had been so engrossed in her thoughts that she hadn't noticed the woman stop alongside her.

She was confronted by a beautifully dressed lady wearing an elegant pale grey suit and white silk blouse, but couldn't instantly place her. Her make-up and light brown hair were coiffured perfectly, and in Rosa's eyes she could have stepped from the pages of a fashion magazine. She estimated she was around her mother's age, but her gloved hands and smart black leather heeled shoes were evidence of their vastly different backgrounds.

Rosa blurted, 'I'm sorry, I didn't mean to stare. Only—'

The woman smiled. When her pale pink lips opened, Rosa saw a beautiful row of teeth, as perfectly maintained as every inch of her body. 'You must excuse me as I was staring too. I believe we have met before, though I cannot recall your name. It's always difficult to put a name to a face when you see a person you recognise in a different setting. But I certainly recall your face for your rosy cheeks and lovely smile.'

'You do?' Rosa gulped, feeling embarrassed at the compliment.

The lady smiled. 'It's come to me now and I'll put you out of your misery. You have waited on me at the Valleys Hotel. I remember you because I complimented your excellent service to the manager.'

The penny dropped and Rosa's eyes flickered. 'Of course I recognise you now. I apologise for not knowing straight away, Mrs—'

'I'm Lady Gwendoline Goodwin. This is my husband's family business and I advise their fashion buyer, as I have excellent contacts with the fashion houses in London.'

Rosa's cheeks flushed and she fumbled her words. 'It's an honour to meet you, milady. I mean, I'm pleased to make your acquaintance.'

Lady Gwendoline threw back her head and laughed. 'Enough of those formalities. Will you tell me your name?'

'It's Rosa. Rosa Edwards, ma'am.'

'Tell me, Rosa, I see you are staring at the notices in the window. Are you considering applying for either of the positions?'

'As a matter of fact, I am. I'm interested in the sales position here. I'm just dropping my application off now, but I'm on the early side.'

Lady Gwendoline's arched eyebrows furrowed. 'Are you applying for the position at the London household too, my dear?'

Rosa's eyes stared downwards. 'I am, as a matter of

fact, but I don't know for sure if I want to be a maid. My friend Alice is one in a big London house and I thought I should try it too so I could see her. I don't know if I'd be considered good enough, though.'

'That's a ridiculous thing to say,' chided Lady Gwendoline. 'I've seen how well you work and your meticulous approach to detail. You would be very well qualified. In fact, I would be happy to vouch for you as I have personally experienced your work. You are most accomplished and shouldn't put yourself down.'

'That's what my Dylan says,' blurted Rosa.

'And who is Dylan, though I think I can guess?' she asked, her voice warm.

Rosa found herself confiding in Lady Gwendoline about her woes at work and her reason for wanting to leave and spread her wings.

When she had finished speaking, Lady Gwendoline extended her gloved hand. 'If you give me your two applications I will make sure they both reach the right people. I am personally involved with the interviews here. And, as I said, I think you would also be very well suited working for this particular family in London, whom I know personally. I can pass your letter on to the agency in Cardiff. The owner, Mrs Pettigrew, is a regular customer here and I have her ear. It was my suggestion to place the advertisement in our window.'

Rosa gulped. 'You really think I should try for it?'

'I really do. The London household has a high regard for girls from the Valleys, as they are known to be honest, truthful, diligent and reliable – good Chapel girls they can count on during these particularly challenging times, not flighty or likely to be involved in espionage. I have no doubt that you meet all those criteria.'

Rosa became flustered, biting her lip. 'I wouldn't know a spy if I saw one. And I've never been the flighty type. I'm a homely girl.'

'Of course you are. Believe me, I wouldn't suggest you would be suitable if I didn't think so.'

Rosa's face brightened. 'That's most kind of you to say, milady. If you think I should apply for the London job, then I will.' She fished in her bag and brought out both applications. 'I was on my way to post the letter for the London job after dropping the other letter here first, but I'll leave it with you then.'

'I'll take care of it for you. Mrs Pettigrew will be in later this week. I can give it to her then and she will contact you personally.'

Rosa handed both envelopes to her. 'That's very kind of you. Thank you, Lady Gwendoline. Thank you so much. May I ask a question?'

'Of course, what is it?'

'I can't understand why you should be so kind to me, seeing as we barely know each other.'

'I like to help people improve their position in life, if I'm able to, seeing as my grandfather owned the mines that have since closed and caused so many problems for families – including yours, I suspect. If I am able to help in any way, I see it as my duty to do so. Good luck, Rosa, though I don't think you'll need it. Just be yourself, and you'll be fine and sail through life.'

Rosa's head was spinning as her benefactress tilted her head and walked around the side of the store, leaving her gobsmacked. If ever there was a fairy godmother, she had just met her, and been sprinkled with a dusting of kindness and goodwill.

She skipped off down the road feeling on top of the world and full of confidence. She could scarcely believe that a titled lady had remembered her, a lowly pit-miner's daughter. She vowed that nothing was going to spoil her good mood that day – not even Hettie Pritchard.

Still beaming, Rosa arrived at work early and was pleased to see Mrs Williams behind the counter. 'How are you today, Mrs Williams? I hope you are feeling much better,' Rosa asked cheerily, removing her coat and hanging it in the back room.

'I'm very well, thank you,' her employer replied, eyeing her closely. 'And it's a relief to see you so cheered. We were worried how you might feel about Hettie's step up here.'

'I understand that it's good for your business. I intend to keep my head straight and do my best for you.'

Jane's eyes levelled on Rosa's. 'That's very good of you to say, my dear. I assure you we will reward you for your understanding one way or another. And when this war is over and Dylan is back, who knows how different things will be here for you.'

A moment later Hettie swept in with an air of grandeur. Rosa smiled. 'Congratulations, Hettie, on your new position here. I should have said before, but it was a bit of a shock.'

Hettie frowned. 'You mean you don't mind? Well, it's just as well you know what your position is here.'

Mrs Williams raised her arm. 'Now, Hettie, there's no need to speak to Rosa like that.'

Rosa spoke lightly. 'It's of no matter. What would you like me to do today?'

Mrs Williams stared at both girls. 'Today is a busy day, so all the more reason for you to put any differences aside. Hettie, I believe your father has recommended us to a new trader in town and he would personally like you to see him and discuss his requirements.'

'Of course, Mrs Williams. You can rely on me,' Hettie declared, her nose in the air.

She headed out, leaving Rosa to work on the latest posters promoting recycling.

An hour later, Hettie returned beaming with an order that brightened Mr Williams's face. 'You will have done exceptionally well if you can get this extra business, Hettie,' he gushed. 'I must thank your father for his kind introduction.'

The day convinced Rosa that she was doing the right thing. Hettie was superb at her job and Rosa began thinking she wouldn't be missed after all, which softened the guilt she felt for planning to leave. Her fate now lay in the hands of her new acquaintance who had become like a fairy godmother and could help change her life for ever. She couldn't wait to write to Alice and tell her she might join her in London, but decided to wait and see if she was invited for an interview first.

6

Later that evening Eira slapped on her ruby-red lipstick and slid her feet into a pair of stilettoes. 'You look nice, Mam,' Rosa said. 'Are you going anywhere special?'

'Seeing as it's Friday night, I thought I would go to the dance at the Palais with Charlie. A new band's playing there and I'm in the mood for some fun.'

'Have a good time,' she called as her mother opened the door to leave.

As soon as they heard the front door slam, Billy turned to his his sister. 'I'm not hanging around just to end up in the mines to please Mam. I have another idea. I'm going to enlist.'

'But you can't. You're too young. You'll only be sixteen on your next birthday and you have to be eighteen.'

'I look older than my age and from what I hear they're desperate for men and will look the other way. That's what happened to one of my mates, and I'm going to sign up with him,' he retorted, a determined flash in his eyes.

'Oh Billy, think again. It will kill Mam when she finds out.'

He walked to the door. 'She'll survive. I'm going to see Da now, he understands. I'll be back later.'

'What if Mam sees you with him?'

'I'll tell her he's finding somewhere for us to live together. She knows I want to be with him, she'll be glad to see the back of me. One way or another, I want to move out.'

'Oh Billy, don't say that. Mam loves you, you know it.'

But Rosa could see from his set expression that his mind was made up, as was hers, and she was not going to let this change her mind.

After a week of not hearing from either job, Rosa began to feel anxious, and even questioned in her mind if Lady Gwendoline had delivered her letters as she had promised. Neither had there been news from Dylan, and she was desperate for reassurance that he had survived his first mission.

That morning, as she skipped down the stairs on her way to work, her face brightened as she spotted three letters on the doormat and eagerly picked them up.

Her heart sank as she placed two envelopes on the hallstand, both addressed to the Hughes sisters.

The third, a crisp cream envelope, was addressed to her. At the top right corner it was stamped with the words *Mrs Pettigrew's Domestic Agency*.

'This must be it,' she cried, as her shaking hands prised open the envelope. Her eyes shone as she read the letter and her hand flew to her face. 'Oh my God, I can't believe it.'

She was asked to go for an interview the following Monday. And in Merthyr too, as Mrs Pettigrew would be in town that day, at Goodwin's. It was only five days away.

She reread its contents. The letter informed her that this would be a first interview to consider her suitability, and if she was to be recommended for the position in London, she would be invited for a second interview at the family home. She was asked to telephone Mrs Pettigrew at her earliest convenience to confirm she would attend her interview at six o'clock, after the store had closed.

Rosa placed the letter back in the envelope and rushed to the nearest telephone box on the street corner. It was early, around eight-thirty, and she hoped the agency was taking calls. A woman was already inside the booth making a call and she shuffled impatiently from foot to foot. It seemed an eternity before the door swung open and she leaped inside and telephoned the number.

A well-spoken lady answered straight away and gave her name as Mrs Pettigrew. Rosa put on her best voice. 'Good morning, Mrs Pettigrew. My name is Rosa Edwards and I am calling in reply to your letter which I received today, to confirm I can make my interview next Monday. The letter said I had to call you as soon as possible.'

'You're the girl who knows Lady Gwendoline, aren't you. Thank you for your speedy response, Miss Edwards. Lady Gwendoline has kindly made a room available for us. The front of the store will be closed, so go to the back door and ring the bell, and someone will meet you and bring you to me.'

'Thank you, Mrs Pettigrew. I appreciate this opportunity.'

Her clipped voice replied, 'I wouldn't go counting your chickens, Miss Edwards. We have had many applications. Goodbye for now.'

'Good day to you, Mrs Pettigrew.'

When Rosa stepped outside the booth she stood rooted to the spot. Her legs wobbled. *What have I done? What will Dylan say about it?*

For the rest of that week, Rosa kept her head down at work. When the day of the interview arrived, she paid extra attention to her appearance, ensuring her skirt and blouse were freshly laundered and well pressed. Her black shoes shone until she could see her reflection. She also washed her hair and clipped her fingernails so her hands looked presentable. Her final attention to detail was to fasten the rosebud brooch Dylan had given her to her jacket lapel.

When it was time to leave work, Mrs Williams wished Rosa a good evening. 'There's still no further news from Dylan, Rosa. I'm very anxious about him.'

'I am too,' Rosa responded. 'We must keep hoping that no news is good news – isn't that what they say?'

'I suppose so,' Dylan's mother replied, her shoulders slumped.

Rosa walked briskly to Goodwin's and down a side passage, where she found the back door with the company's name on a plaque. She patted her hair in place, smoothed her skirt, pulled her shoulders back and took a deep breath as she rang the bell. Within seconds it was answered by a porter wearing grey trousers and matching waistcoat.

'Miss Edwards, is it?' he asked cheerily. 'Follow me, they're waiting for you upstairs.'

His pace was slow and he limped slightly, pausing at the top of the first flight to catch his breath. He tilted his head upstairs. 'We've one more flight to go.'

They stopped outside a door that was slightly ajar where voices could be heard inside. He knocked, and Rosa recognised Lady Gwendoline's voice calling out, 'Come in.'

The porter entered and announced Rosa's name. She heard Lady Gwendoline say, 'Thank you, Mr Bennett. Could you now see to the blackout curtains, and then that will be all for the day.'

'Very good, ma'am,' he replied, winking to Rosa as he stepped aside and opened the door for her.

Lady Gwendoline was seated behind a desk, accompanied by an older lady. She rose to welcome Rosa. 'I would like to introduce you to Mrs Felicity Pettigrew, of Mrs Pettigrew's Domestic Agency. We have known each other for many years.'

'How do you do, ma'am,' Rosa said in her best voice.

Mrs Pettigrew bowed her head slightly at Rosa, then rose from her seat. She was a small wiry woman and wore a cloche hat. Her clothes looked of good quality, Rosa noted, eyeing the shiny brass buttons down the front of her dark blue jacket, which had a velvet collar and cuffs, and a matching skirt that fell below the knee.

Mrs Pettigrew circled Rosa, who stiffened under her intense gaze. Lady Gwendoline gave her an encouraging nod and Rosa instinctively raised her chin, holding her head high.

'That's what I like to see,' Mrs Pettigrew said approvingly. 'A girl who knows how to hold herself upright and wears sensible shoes. The family in question rely on my recommendation that the candidate I put forward has the highest morals, sense of duty, is trustworthy and does not gossip. They require staff who maintain discretion, and do not have wagging tongues.'

'Yes, ma'am, I understand.' Rosa's voice quivered.

Lady Gwendoline invited Rosa to take a seat.

Mrs Pettigrew probed, 'Tell me, Miss Edwards, why are you seeking this position?'

Rosa stumbled over her words at first. She had prepared an answer, but the bluntness of the question threw her off track. She mentioned her friend Alice who had found a position in a London house, and her wish to spread her wings, and how they had both worked together at the Valleys Hotel.

'I recall the young lady you refer to, a pretty thing. She has settled in well, from what I've heard. What of your present employers?'

Rosa twisted her fingers in front of her and her stomach clenched. 'I'm sure Mr and Mrs Williams will provide a reference to vouch for my honesty, if I am offered the position. They have been very kind to me and it will be a wrench to leave, but I feel this is the right time for me to move on.'

'That's all very well said, Rosa,' Lady Gwendoline encouraged. 'I can also vouch for her waitressing and coffee-making skills.'

'May I ask a question?' Rosa asked.

'You can, but the nature of it will depend very much on whether I can answer it,' Mrs Pettigrew replied crisply.

'I wanted to ask about the family in question, what they are like.'

'I thought so, and that is a reasonable question, but I am not at liberty to divulge that information at the moment. Thank you for coming, Miss Edwards. I will be in touch soon and inform you of the next step, if you are successful for a second interview.'

Mrs Pettigrew rose and Rosa took her cue and followed suit.

Lady Gwendoline took a torch from the desk and led Rosa to the door. 'I'll show you out.'

Rosa went cautiously downstairs, following the dim

torchlight in the blacked-out stairwell. When they reached the bottom, Lady Gwendoline said, 'You did very well, Rosa. Now hurry home. I'm sure you will hear very soon.'

When Rosa reached home, the smell of stew made her stomach rumble. 'Your dinner's in the pan. Good day at work?' her mother asked.

'Well, yes . . .' Rosa stumbled, her heart sinking at not seeing a letter for her on top of the sideboard from Dylan or Alice. *Maybe I'll hear from them tomorrow*, she thought wistfully.

While there was still no news from her sweetheart or best friend by the end of that week, a letter arrived inviting Rosa for an interview in London the following week. She was told she would be sent a return rail warrant and a driver would meet her at Paddington Station and take her to the household.

Rosa needed to confirm she could attend, and realised this was a chance for her to see Alice at the same time. She was owed two days' leave from work and decided to request this time off from the Williamses, using Alice as her excuse.

Her face reddened when Mrs Williams willingly gave her consent. 'Of course you may have time off to see Alice. Just promise me you will take good care of yourself there, after all the bombing it has had.'

It occurred to Rosa that the worst could have happened to Alice, with all the air attacks London was suffering, but surely she would have heard about this. Now she planned to see for herself and discover the truth.

Next Rosa telephoned Mrs Pettigrew to confirm her

attendance. 'I will post you a rail warrant for your journey,' Mrs Pettigrew told her. 'If you present this at the station, you will be given a ticket and the household will settle the account. The housekeeper, Miss Rogers, will be expecting you.'

'What time is my appointment, please?'

'Your interview is at two o'clock. You may want to arrive half an hour earlier to catch your breath and have some refreshment before your appointment. I appreciate you are making a long journey, but the trains run regularly, I believe.'

'Yes, Mrs Pettigrew. Thank you very much.'

Rosa scribbled a quick note to Alice telling her of her imminent arrival. In the days leading up to it, her nerves jangled at the prospect of making her first visit to London on her own, overcome with fears that she might miss her train or connection, that she would get lost and make a fool of herself.

The evening before her journey she packed a snack of bread and cheese and pressed her best blue skirt and dark grey jacket, then laid out a crisp white blouse and sensible flat black shoes that shone. As her head fell on her pillow that night, with Dylan's kind face watching over her, she prayed that she would have a reply from him soon. Mrs Williams was also waiting to hear, but as Mr Williams frequently pointed out, his war duties came first, and they must be patient.

Eventually her tired body succumbed to sleep, and she managed just over five hours before the shrill ringing of her alarm made her leap up. She glanced over to her mother, who moaned and told her to switch the racket off, before turning over and dozing off.

Within half an hour she was washed and dressed, with Dylan's rosebud brooch pinned on her jacket for luck. She left the house clutching her rail warrant, the letter inviting her for the interview, a small overnight case with a change of clothes and her gas mask. She also had Alice's letter in the hope of seeing her too.

The nerves she felt about the long journey ahead were pushed to the back of her mind as she imagined the golden opportunities that beckoned.

The town was waking up and a dim sun began to brighten as she walked briskly. Few people were out and about at six o'clock, but there were a couple of delivery boys and milkmen, and the smell of fresh bread wafted under her nose as she passed the bakery.

The station was a ten-minute walk from Plymouth Street, and Rosa pushed her little legs as fast as she could, arriving on the platform just as the Cardiff train arrived. She stepped into the carriage and walked along the corridor, opening a door to a compartment and choosing a window seat. She was joined by an elderly lady who produced a pair of knitting needles and wool and promptly began knitting. Whenever Rosa had tried knitting, she was all fingers and thumbs, and she watched in admiration as the bundle of dark grey wool being worked on clearly began to take the shape of a sock.

'It's for our soldiers,' the lady said, smiling, noticing Rosa staring at her nimble fingers. 'My neighbour had some wool left over when she died, and her husband gave me her craft box. It's all I can lay my hands on at the moment, and I'm thankful for that.'

A couple of well-dressed gentlemen came into the

compartment and enquired if the seats were occupied. 'Oh no, you're welcome to come in,' invited Rosa. The knitting lady seemed oblivious. They glanced at Rosa and took their seats. From the snippets of conversation she overheard, they were a father and son involved in insurance. The knitting lady kept herself to herself for the duration of the journey. As they approached Cardiff, the older man looked down his nose at Rosa and said, 'And what brings you to Cardiff so early in the day?'

'I have an appointment in London today.'

Both father and son looked surprised. The son's eyebrows rose. 'Really? Fancy you making a big journey like that.'

'And why shouldn't I?' Rosa replied indignantly.

The two men smirked and buried their faces in a newspaper, and Rosa spent the remainder of the journey staring out of the window.

She felt relieved when a few minutes later the train's brakes screeched to a halt and she saw the Cardiff sign on the platform. The men disembarked with more smirks and cursory nods. The woman packed her knitting away and commented, 'What very disagreeable men. It's very courageous of you to go all that way on your own, quite an adventure, I would say. You need platform six, and from memory it will leave in fifteen minutes.'

'Thank you, ma'am. Those gentlemen were stuck-up, but I wasn't going to let them spoil my day.'

The train was waiting where the lady had said, and Rosa found a seat. The remaining journey seemed tortuous and slow, stopping at every station along the way. As Rosa munched her snack she reflected on how the kindness of strangers could lift your spirits. She recalled Lady Gwendoline's words of encouragement too. *Just be yourself*, she had advised, and that's what Rosa would do, she vowed. Finally, three and a half hours after setting off from Cardiff, the train screeched to a halt at Paddington.

She clasped her bag and gulped. Everyone around her appeared to be in a rush as they alighted from the carriage. As she stepped onto the platform, she held her head high and inhaled deeply.

A voice inside her head told her, 'You can do this, Rosa Edwards.'

Smiling, she nodded and affirmed *Yes, I can.*

7

Paddington Station was vast compared to Merthyr, with numerous railway tracks and trains steaming in and out. It was packed with servicemen and their loved ones, as well as brisk workers who marched along the platforms with purpose. Porters, many of them women, scurried along pushing trolleys piled high with luggage, while guards raised their flags and blew their whistles, shouting out imminent departures.

Rosa found a porter, a cheery woman around the same age as her mother, who directed her to the exit at the far end of the platform. It was easy to spot those on the platform who had lost loved ones by the black armbands they wore, their faces etched with sorrow.

She walked out of the station and her eyes swivelled in all directions, feeling at a loss, like a tiny ant in a jungle. Then she spotted a stocky man with greying hair a few yards away. He wore a navy-blue battledress with the initials G.R.V. embroidered on the breast pocket, and a row of ribbons from his service in the Great War. She sighed with relief when she spotted the large card he carried with her name written on it. She walked towards the driver, feeling nervous. 'That's me. I'm Rosa Edwards.'

He held out a hand. 'Mr Brownlow.' He took her bag and smiled. 'Is it your first visit to London?' he asked with a warm tone.

She nodded, biting her lip.

'I thought so. I imagine it's a lot to take in, at first glance.'

Mr Brownlow's friendly manner instantly made Rosa relax a little. She stared at the shiny car parked at the kerbside. 'It's so big and busy, much more than I'm used to at home. And I've never been in a posh car like this before.'

'Step inside and enjoy the ride,' he grinned.

'That sounds very nice, but I've no idea where I'm going or who I'll be working for.' They must be very important people, Rosa mulled, if they had their own driver and their names couldn't be divulged in advance.

Mr Brownlow held open the rear nearside door, she slipped onto the soft leather upholstery, and he took his place behind the wheel. 'You'll find out soon enough,' he smiled. 'We should be there in half an hour. My name's Andrew, by the way. You can call me Andy, unless we're with senior staff, in which case it should be Mr Brownlow. How was your trip here? I can tell from your accent you've had a long journey.'

She babbled a reply and sank deep into the comfy seat, pressing her back into the soft cushioning, her lips curling in the corners. *If only Hettie Pritchard could see her now!*

'A penny for your thoughts?' he teased.

'I can hardly believe I'm in London. I'm thinking what people back home would say if they could see me now,' she replied with a smile.

'It's quite a sight, though not so pretty in some parts where it's taken a hit. I'll take the scenic route past Marble Arch, Hyde Park and Piccadilly.'

Rosa's eyes widened and she stared in awe at the city as the chatty driver swept along the roads lined with eye-boggling buildings. After pointing out the large town-houses in Piccadilly her eyes soaked up the elegance of Belgravia, then they swept into Victoria, along Buckingham Palace Road and up to a huge memorial statue of Queen Victoria which faced a vast building.

The car slowed, and they halted at some elaborate iron gates with a coat of arms fixed on them. The building in front of her was breathtaking, with more windows than she could count and huge pillars stretching up to the sky. Armed guards were positioned at various locations around the building.

'That's just for the view,' the driver grinned. 'Our entrance is at the side.'

Rosa gawped in disbelief. Her head swivelled in all directions to take in the sprawling facade. 'Is this—?'

'That's right,' grinned Mr Brownlow. 'It's Buckingham Palace.'

'But that's where the King and Queen and princesses live. What am I doing here?'

'You've come about a maid's job, I believe.'

'But nobody said—'

'Of course they wouldn't, for security. Anyone could apply otherwise, spies and all. No doubt you were well vetted first.'

'You mean to say I've come for an interview with the King and Queen?' she asked, incredulous.

'No, you daft thing. You'll be interviewed by Miss Rogers, the housekeeper, but yes, you will be serving the King and Queen if you are successful today.'

'Well I'll be damned, I had no idea. I'm terrified now.'

'There's no need to be. You look like a sensible girl. Just be yourself, and you'll be fine.'

They approached a less elaborate set of iron gates at the side of the palace. Two armed guards in khaki uniforms peered into the window, and Rosa was asked to hand over her letter inviting her for the interview. They checked her name on a list, then handed it back to her and nodded.

Mr Brownlow proceeded straight into a quadrangle, where he parked. She stepped out of the car before he had a chance to assist her, and glanced all around. The building seemed to stretch in height and breadth for many yards around her. She had never seen such an enormous place, and pinched herself at the thought of standing in front of the home of the King and Queen of the United Kingdom. Like ordinary homes all over the country, the windows had been blacked out. She marvelled at the bravery of the King and Queen to work there every day after it had been struck by German bombers.

Andrew nudged her. 'Are you ready? Follow me then. I'll show you to the kitchen for refreshments before you see Miss Rogers.'

Rosa's knees began to knock. 'What is she like, this Miss Rogers?'

'She's a hard taskmaster who takes no nonsense from anyone. But while it might seem that she's as hard as nails, she's soft as putty on the inside. If you do what is expected of you and don't poke your nose where you shouldn't, you'll do just fine.'

She followed Andrew to a doorway, where two guards acknowledged him and moved apart to let them through. They continued down narrow winding steps, turned along a corridor, and down more steps. They came to a dimly lit corridor with doors on either side, names on each. At the end of the corridor, Andrew opened a door and invited her into a large kitchen. A cook was rolling out pastry, and small dainty sponge cakes were cooling on a tray nearby. The sweet aroma made Rosa's mouth water.

Cook looked up. 'Are you the girl Miss Rogers is expecting?'

Rosa nodded. Andrew turned to leave. 'Good luck, Miss Edwards.'

'Thank you, Andrew. I mean Mr Brownlow.'

Cook pointed to a seat at the end of the table. She wiped her hands clean, fetched a cup and saucer, and poured tea for Rosa.

'I expect you're in need of that after your long journey.'

Cook was in her mid-forties, short and round, with short curly auburn hair and twinkling eyes that wrinkled at the corners.

'I recognise your accent,' Rosa said. 'Are you from Wales, by any chance?'

'I hail from Aberdare, near Merthyr. Which part are you from?'

'You never are! That's just a stone's throw from my home. I'm from Merthyr. Fancy coming all this way and meeting someone close to home. Er . . . may I ask you a question, Miss——?'

'It's Mrs Jones, though Mr Jones is no longer with me. What is it you want to ask?'

Rosa fumbled with her fingers. 'How easy was it for you to settle here after leaving Wales? I worry I shall miss it dreadfully if I'm offered the position.'

'Oh, you'll be so busy and in awe of your surroundings and the goings on here that you won't have a spare moment to think about it. Everyone here is friendly and you'll soon get used to seeing the royal family walking around. There's no need to be scared of them, they're human beings just like us, though they are hard taskmasters and expect their staff to be dedicated and loyal.'

'I see – and yes, I am reliable and honest.'

'I can see in your face that what you say is true,' said Cook as she pushed one of the freshly baked cakes in front of Rosa, who devoured it, washed down with a second cup of tea.

'I remember someone else saying the royal family are normal human beings, but royal ones. In fact, Princess Elizabeth is the same age as me. I would love to see her, though I'm sure I wouldn't know what to say.'

Cook stared at Rosa. 'The princesses spend most of their time in the country. They are lovely young ladies with no airs and graces. We see them here from time to time, so you will be sure to meet them. Now, it's time for you to see Miss Rogers. You have a lucky face, Rosa, with those rosy cheeks of yours. Good luck.'

Rosa straightened her skirt and tidied her hair in a mirror on the kitchen wall by the door.

'Miss Rogers is an excellent judge of character,' Cook continued. 'If you pass her sharp-eyed scrutiny you'll have done very well for yourself. Sir Piers will be there too, I expect. He has the final word on all new staff, to make sure no spies are taken on.'

'Sir Piers?' asked Rosa, thinking how posh the name was and wondering if he'd look down on her.

'He is Master of the Household. It's his job to make sure you are up to the task. Don't let it worry you. You wouldn't have been invited here today if you weren't up to it. Hold your head up and speak truthfully, and you'll be just fine.

Cook's kind words helped quell Rosa's nerves as they walked along the flagstone corridor, past a number of doorways before stopping outside one with Miss Rogers's name on. It was slightly ajar, and inside they could see a woman talking to a distinguished-looking gentleman.

Cook knocked on the door and nudged Rosa to enter after hearing a woman's voice invite her in. The woman rose and came to the door, thanking Cook and dismissing her.

'You must be Miss Edwards. Please take a seat.'

Miss Rogers appeared to be a few years younger than Cook. She was taller, slimmer and well-spoken. Her thick, wavy hair was tied back into a neat bun sitting at the nape of her neck. Below this she wore a neat black skirt and a pair of sensible black shoes.

Rosa sat where indicated, in front of a large desk. A window behind the housekeeper was blackened, and a light suspended on a cord from the ceiling shone on the paperwork in front of her. A telephone rested on the corner of the desk. She picked up Rosa's application letter, and another sheet of paper with writing alongside it and read them both. The gentleman sat next to her and leaned forward slightly, staring at Rosa with interest. He was dressed in a smart suit and had thinning hair and thick, bushy eyebrows.

'This is Sir Piers Legh. As Master of the Household he must be fully confident that the calibre of staff employed here is of the highest and most trustworthy standard.'

'Of course. I'm very pleased to meet you, Sir Piers,' Rosa

said coyly, returning his gaze with as much confidence as she could muster.

The housekeeper cleared her throat. 'Sir Piers and I have been reviewing your job application and it would seem you have had plenty of experience.'

'Thank you, Miss Rogers.'

'Very good, yes, very good,' she muttered under her breath, picking up Rosa's letter and scanning the lines.

When she had finished reading she looked up. 'I see you have been approved by Mrs Pettigrew and have a reference from Lady Gwendoline, who speaks very highly of you. She may not have mentioned this, but she is acquainted with one of the queen's ladies-in-waiting and is held in the highest regard. She states she has had personal experience of you as a waitress.'

'Yes, Miss Rogers, that is correct,' replied Rosa, overcome with shyness. 'I waited on her at the Valleys Hotel, but I had no idea she had connections with the royal family.'

'I see your main employment is at Williams & Son, a family printing business. You are clearly an industrious young lady.'

'I don't mind hard work. At home, I have to give Mam most of my money as we get nothing from Da and she worries about making ends meet.' Rosa's cheeks flushed, wondering if she had said too much. She bit her lip.

Miss Rogers leaned forward. 'That is most commendable. We approve of hard work. Can you tell me more about yourself, Miss Edwards? I'd like to know everything if you are to be considered for a position in the royal household.'

Rosa blurted out everything, about Dylan and how she helped with her mother's cleaning jobs too. She told her about Billy running away, about wanting to move to London to stand on her own feet after Hettie had been promoted, and how she was spurred by the words of encouragement from Lady Gwendoline.

She finished breathlessly, 'I'm a hard and reliable worker who never takes a day off sick. I'm honest and loyal too. Mr and Mrs Williams will vouch for me, I'm sure.'

Sir Piers listened attentively, then said, 'I can believe it, Miss Edwards. The King and Queen live simply and have ration books like anyone else. From time to time they will entertain on a much smaller scale, and like things to still be done properly. When you are waiting at tables with silver service and making tea and coffee, are you able to do so without spilling it?'

'Oh yes, Sir Piers. Honest, I never have spillages when I'm serving refreshments.'

'May I ask, would you feel unnerved serving noble people, those with titles, our royal family? Would you become flustered pouring for the King?'

Rosa quipped, 'Well, I've never waited on a king before. But I shall try and look on him as any man and give my best service. I never had any complaints from Lady Gwendoline, and she's . . . well, as posh as they come in Merthyr.'

Miss Rogers covered her mouth with her hand to conceal her smile and stared sideways at Sir Piers, whose eyes crinkled. They exchanged a glance and he nodded at her, resting back in his chair.

Miss Rogers said, 'I think that's everything. Thank you for coming today and for your frankness. I have to say

I am impressed by what I have seen and heard. I will need to check your references if we decide to offer you the post. We do have other applicants to interview this week and will let you know very soon.'

'Thank you for seeing me, Miss Rogers, Sir Piers.'

Miss Rogers rose. 'What are your plans now, Miss Edwards? Are you returning to Wales this evening?'

'No, I'm going to Piccadilly. My friend Alice works there as a maid, though she's being trained as a secretary. I want to see how she's getting on. I'm hoping she knows of a cheap room I can stay in for the night before travelling back tomorrow.'

'Well, goodbye then, Miss Edwards. I hope you have an enjoyable evening with your friend and I wish you a safe journey back.'

Sir Piers rose. 'Thank you for coming today, Miss Edwards. We will be in touch.'

Miss Rogers walked Rosa to the door and called out to a maid of about Rosa's age who was walking along the corridor. 'Miss Deakin? Could you please show Miss Edwards the way to the visitors' entrance.'

'Thank you again, Miss Rogers,' Rosa said, accepting her outstretched hand.

Miss Deakin approached and was introduced to Rosa as Molly. Rosa found herself retracing the steps she had taken earlier with the driver, noticing passages along the way that had escaped her attention earlier. She thought it resembled a rabbit's warren as she stepped gingerly along the dingy passageway, lit by a single bulb, and feeling overwhelmed by the corridors that snaked in different directions.

When they reached the top of the stairs and the door that led to the courtyard and daylight, Rosa squinted her eyes.

'You get used to it,' Molly commented, as if reading her mind. 'It feels like yer cut off from the outside world down 'ere. In the winter I came out one day and saw it'd been snowing. What job are you after, then?'

'A maid, serving at the table, I believe. How long have you been here?'

'Almost a year now. My ma worked here and put a word in for me, but she gave it up to look after us. The royal family are very kind. They don't look down on you when they speak to you. I wouldn't want to work anywhere else now.'

Rosa confessed, 'I have to admit I am scared of the palace being bombed. It's taken a few hits and could be a target again, with us as sitting ducks.'

Molly's green eyes focused on Rosa's face, her eyebrows furrowed. 'I thought the same too. If the King and Queen stay in London, it must be safe enough. They look after us, I've no complaints. We used to sleep in the servants' quarters upstairs, but our beds 'ave been moved to the basement alongside the air-raid shelters.'

'That's a relief. I hope I'm offered the position. I like all the people I've met here so far. Cook is from Wales, like me, and it will be a comfort for me to hear the same accent.'

Molly pointed out the door. 'You say you're heading for Piccadilly? You should take that gate and walk through Green Park, across the road — that's the quickest way. Good luck, Rosa, I 'ope to see you again.'

'I hope so too, Molly, and thank you. I've enjoyed our chat.'

She left the gate as directed, suddenly becoming conscious of the time. It was almost half-past three and an ache in her stomach reminded her she had barely eaten all day. The sense of excitement and nerves remained with her as she soaked up her surroundings, crossing the road into Green Park. Oh, this is just so lovely, she said to herself, taking in the sprawling parkland that strollers were enjoying with their children. A savoury smell wafted under her nose and she followed it until she reached a stall selling potato and vegetable pie, bought one and found a bench to devour it. Within seconds she was surrounded by pigeons swooping for crumbs. She shooed them away, finishing the meal with the disposable cutlery she had been given.

Once her stomach was full she took in her surroundings. Spring was arriving, with buds bursting into bloom, and the blossom of the cherry trees making a pretty picture. she reflected on the contrast to Merthyr's rows of terraced houses, the smoke from the ironworks' giant chimneys across the valley, the blackness of the coal mines that broke the men who worked there.

While a part of her bristled with excitement at the thought of sharing her news with Alice, she felt a sense of trepidation following Alice's lack of response, and hoped the reason was simply that she had been busy living life to the full, and not because she was giving her the brush-off.

She arrived at Alice's address, 139 Piccadilly, within twenty minutes and stared up in awe at the impressive property. It was a double-fronted white house and had six floors that she could see. Blimey, thought Rosa, Alice has done well for herself landing a job here.

She walked nervously up seven white steps to the front door. There were two bells on the panelled door, one for Lord and Lady Hesketh-Robbins, Alice's employers, and the other with the word *Housekeeper*. Rosa rang the second bell and waited, shuffling from foot to foot. There was no reply and she rang it again, pressing it twice.

Eventually a young maid, her cheeks flushed, answered the door. She was breathless and her hair and clothing appeared dishevelled. She opened the door slightly and peered through the gap, eyeing Rosa curiously. 'Yes, can I 'elp yer?'

'I'm sorry to turn up out of the blue like this, only I'm a friend of Alice's. She gave me this address as being where she lives and works. Could I see her please?'

The maid's face clouded. 'Alice?'

'Yes, Alice Evans. Is she in please? I do have the right address, don't I?' Rosa pressed. She opened her bag and pulled out the scrap of paper where she had written it down. 'Here it is, 139 Piccadilly.'

The maid stepped outside and whispered, 'She ain't 'ere any more. She's left.'

'What do you mean *she's left*? There must be some mistake.'

'I can't say any more. It was very sudden, like.'

'When is she coming back?'

'She ain't. I 'ave to go now, before Lady Iris wonders where I am.'

'Do you think she's returned to Merthyr?' Rosa asked, totally flummoxed.

But the maid shut the door hastily, leaving Rosa open-mouthed.

As she walked down the steps, she turned to look at the house and paused, feeling a deep sense of unease. A shadowy woman's figure was peering at her from the side of a curtain and quickly disappeared behind it. What was she to do now? Where was Alice? She could think of no alternative other than to return to Merthyr that night.

She found her way to Paddington Station, and, to her relief, secured a seat on a train for Cardiff Central, where she would be able to change for Merthyr. On the journey home she decided she would contact Alice's parents, in case her friend had suddenly returned to Merthyr and not had time to let her know. There must be a simple explanation, she surmised.

It was almost midnight when she finally reached Merthyr and began to navigate her way home in the blacked-out streets, spotting familiar landmarks. Her legs were about to give way and she could barely keep her eyes open when she reached home. She sneaked in as quietly as she could, her mind whirring from the events of the day. She fell asleep instantly, a long, deep sleep, and only woke at eleven o'clock the following morning.

Her mother was out when she emerged downstairs bleary-eyed after her late night. Her thoughts drifted back to the palace, to her interview, and the fondness she instantly felt for Molly. But it was her concern over Alice's whereabouts that filled most of her thoughts. She decided to call her family straight after breakfast.

After devouring a quick slice of toast and marmalade,

she made her way to the nearest telephone box. A woman's voice answered that she recognised immediately.

'Good afternoon, Mrs Evans. I'm Alice's friend, Rosa. I'm sorry to trouble you, but I was hoping to speak to Alice. Is she at home, by any chance?'

A long silence followed, then a sniffling sound.

Rosa pressed: 'Only, I was in London yesterday and called in to see her at the address she gave me, and a maid there told me she had left. I was hoping to see her.'

Following another pause, Mrs Evans spoke shakily. 'I'm afraid Alice was taken ill and is staying with her aunt in London. I'll be sure to let her know you called.'

'Can you give me her address, please? I'm hoping to have a position in London myself and thought we could meet up.'

'I'm afraid I can't help you. I have to go now,' she replied, hanging up abruptly.

'What——?' gasped Rosa, stunned by the sudden end to their conversation. 'Alice taken ill? What could have happened to her? Something is wrong,' she gulped, a sinking feeling in her gut as she replaced the telephone handset.

A few days later, Mr Williams took Rosa to one side. 'A most extraordinary thing, Rosa – we've been asked for a reference for you from *Buckingham Palace*. What's this all about? We thought you were happy here.'

'I'm sorry, I should have said something, but I wasn't sure it would come to anything.'

'Is it to do with Hettie? I thought you were getting on better now.'

Rosa squirmed. 'In a way. I can see she is really good at

her job and now she's working here, you should be able to get on without me. I'm not going for ever. I shall return when Dylan is back, if you will have me. But it would be an honour to work in the royal household.'

'I've no doubt it would, but Mrs Williams is very upset at the thought of losing you – we both are. And off to London too! We can't help but worry about you there with all them bombings.'

'I didn't mean to upset you.' Rosa's voice wobbled, overcome with guilt, wondering for a split second if she should stay.

Mr Williams rubbed the back of his neck. 'Are you sure this is what you want to do?'

Rosa took his hands into hers and stared directly at his anxious face. 'Yes, I'm sure. As I said, it's not for ever, just till Dylan is home again, I promise.'

'Well, if that's what you want, so be it, and I will write your reference today. We will miss you dreadfully.'

The words stuck in Rosa's throat. 'Thank you, I shall miss you both very much too. I feel I need to do more with my life, and serving the King and Queen as a maid is my contribution to the war while Dylan is making such a sacrifice.'

Her employer rested his hand on her shoulder. 'That's a very fine thing to say. We're all proud of you, Rosa. There's no need to wait for the end of the war, you can come back and see us any time if it doesn't work out. You won't forget us, will you?'

The job had not yet been officially offered to Rosa, but hearing that the palace was following up references was a sign for her to be optimistic. Brimming with excitement,

Rosa threw her arms around Dylan's father. 'I'll never forget you and Mrs Williams and your kindness towards me.'

The following week a letter with a Buckingham Palace franking stamp on the envelope was delivered to Rosa's lodgings. She held the royal cipher-headed notepaper as if it were the most delicate, precious porcelain.

We would like to offer you the position of Royal Maid with a salary of £60 per year, as well as a daily allowance of 3s. 6d. for your board and a £7 washing allowance. Please confirm you accept the offer and will be able to start on 5 April, 1944.

Rosa whooped with joy.

'You look happy about something.' Billy said. 'Good news, is it?'

Rosa leaped up and spun around on the spot, waving the letter in the air. 'It is – I have a new job!'

'Job? What job?' queried her mother.

'I'm going to work at Buckingham Palace, Mam. I've been offered the position of royal maid. See, look here how much money I'll be paid.'

Eira fumed, 'When did all this happen, then? Never mind about telling your mam. You must be crazy to want to work in London at a time like this.'

'I wanted to be sure before saying anything. I'll be alright. Don't worry, Mam, I promise I'll send you what I can each week.'

'Well, make sure you do,' she replied.

'And I'll come home and see you when I can, Billy.'

Later that evening, Rosa wrote to accept the offer, and then to Dylan telling him her news and asking him to write to her care of the Servants Quarters, Buckingham Palace, London.

On Rosa's final day at work Mrs Williams was teary-eyed and made a fuss of her, giving her a fruitcake, some toiletries and a writing pad and envelopes to stay in touch. 'It's not goodbye,' she said, 'just a short separation, that's what I tell myself, Rosa. I'm hoping Huw will take me to London one weekend to see a show and we can see each other then. We'll take you out to the theatre.'

'I'd like that very much,' beamed Rosa.

She ignored Hettie's disdainful expression, her narrow eyes observing as Mrs Williams affectionately embraced her. Mr Williams appeared from the back room and held out a small blue box.

'It's a gift from us both, Rosa. You don't want to keep our King and Queen waiting now, do you?'

Rosa took the package and exclaimed, 'But you've already given me so much. What is it?'

'Open it and see,' Mr Williams said, smiling.

Rosa undid the box and lifted out a gold watch with a thin brown leather strap. She stared at it in disbelief, tears springing to her eyes. 'Why, it's so beautiful.'

Hettie scowled. 'I don't know what the fuss is about. She's only going to be a maid, after all. I wouldn't want to be in London with all those bombings going on, no matter what job I was offered.'

Mr Williams bristled. 'I'm sure you would like to wish Rosa well, Hettie. And don't forget, while Merthyr is fortunate not to have been the target of air raids, we have had our share of tragedies too, if you recall – those two

Canadian planes that collided and crashed over Merthyr, killing five people.'

The shop door suddenly flung open and Mr Williams went to answer it. 'Is Rosa here?' a woman's voice enquired.

'Rosa,' he called, 'you have a visitor.'

'Me? Whoever could it be?' she mused, stepping into the front of the shop.

'Hello, Rosa. I'm so pleased to have caught you before you left. I hear you are going to be a royal maid and I would like to congratulate you. Only girls of a high calibre, who meet the highest standards expected in the royal household are offered these positions. I have every confidence you will do yourself and Merthyr proud.'

Rosa gawped. 'That's very kind of you, Lady Gwendoline. I promise I'll do my best.'

'You deserve it.'

'Thank you for delivering my application. The funny thing is, I met Cook there and she is from Aberdare. I couldn't believe what a small world it is.'

Lady Gwendoline chuckled. 'Ah, yes, that would be our Mary Jones. She used to be my personal cook and when the palace suddenly found themselves short of one, I lent them Mary, and she's stayed there ever since. That was ten years ago after her husband ran off with their neighbour's daughter.'

Rosa tilted her head to one side. 'Oh, I didn't know that. May I ask you a question, Lady Gwendoline. I'm curious about the other application, for the sales assistant's post. I never heard back from the store.'

Lady Gwendoline raised her gloved hand to her mouth.

'Ah, please forgive me for that. I have no doubt you would have been most suitable for that post too, but I held on to it to see the outcome of the Buckingham Palace application. This is your chance to make something of your life, Rosa. If you find once you are there that it isn't for you, if you are unhappy, you only have to say the word and you can return to Merthyr any time and I will put a word in for you at the store.'

'Oh no she won't. She'll be welcomed back here any time. The palace is lucky to have her,' said Mr Williams, brimming with pride.

'Indeed they are,' concurred Lady Gwendoline.

Rosa's eyes moistened, her heart touched by everyone's kindness. When she finally closed the shop door behind her, she took a deep breath, her chest swelling. She imagined the thrill of her new life unfolding in two weeks' time, a life beyond the Valleys and its collieries and its gigantic ironworks.

I can't believe that little ol' me, a pit-miner's daughter, is going to work in a palace with the King and Queen of England.

8

5 April 1944

Rosa shook her umbrella and folded it up, placing it in the crook of her arm. The rain that, despite the umbrella, had soaked her through had stopped, and the sun was breaking through.

She fished out a handkerchief from her coat pocket and patted her face dry. She unclasped her black handbag and fumbled inside until she found her comb and ran it through her damp hair, ruffling it with her fingers. *I must look like a drowned rat. Some first impression I'll make*, Rosa thought as she stood in Buckingham Palace Road.

Clutching her brown leather suitcase, she straightened her back and, plucking up courage, approached a gate where two guards stood erect. Instead of the scarlet jackets with shiny gold buttons and black bearskin hats worn by the Grenadier Guards in peacetime at the palace gates, they were dressed in khaki gear and steel helmets.

She caught the eye of one of the armed guards and gave him her name. His colleague handed him a clipboard which he glanced along. Looking up, he smiled and said, 'Good morning, Miss Edwards. Miss Rogers is expecting you. First day, is it?'

Rosa bit her lip. 'It is. Is it that obvious? Look at me, I'm wet through.'

'You'll have a chance to dry off once your inside.'

'That's a relief.'

He leaned forward. 'Am I right in thinking I recognise that soft accent of yours?'

'Depends on where you think it's from,' she replied, brightening a little.

'We have another Welsh lady here, so you'll be at home here, Miss Edwards.'

'I've already met Mrs Jones. I hope hearing the Welsh accent will make me feel less homesick.'

'My name's Gerald Snaith. Have a good day now. You need the entrance over there. Someone will be on hand to direct you inside the door.'

'Thank you,' replied Rosa, suddenly noticing his bright blue eyes. He was tall, much taller than the men she knew in Merthyr, around six foot, and it was impossible not to notice how very handsome he was in his uniform.

Rosa's hand flew to her cheek, suddenly feeling it become flushed. She turned and walked quickly towards the entrance, where an attendant took her details. He wore a policeman's uniform and had an officious manner. He ushered her into a small office, and she stood rigid as he picked up the phone and made a call, telling someone she had arrived.

'I'm glad to see you're punctual,' he commented, checking the clock on a shelf which showed eight o'clock. 'Someone will be with you in a moment, Miss Edwards. Please take a seat. I'm Bernie Parkins, by the way, Sergeant Bernie Parkins. You'll see me here, keeping an eye on people coming in and out.'

'I didn't know there were coppers here,' Rosa commented as she sat where indicated, her feet just reaching the floor.

'That's right, Miss Edwards. The palace has its own police. There's a few of us here.'

'I'm very pleased to hear it.'

A moment later there was a knock on the door. 'Come in,' Sergeant Parkins bellowed.

Rosa's face lit up as she saw Molly step into the office. Their eyes met and they exchanged a smile, with Molly winking.

'Ah, I see you know each other. Can you show Miss Edwards to her room. I believe she is sharing with you, Miss Deakin.'

'I'm really pleased to hear it. We met when I came here for my interview,' said Rosa, smiling.

Molly picked up Rosa's suitcase and grinned. 'I'm pleased too, as long as you don't snore. Follow me. I'll take you to 'ousekeeping and get you kitted out in your uniform.'

They descended one set of stairs and walked along a carpeted corridor with elegant wallpaper. At the end, a door led to more stairs. Rosa halted, staring at the dinginess of the lower floor. They twisted and turned on the flagstones along dingy, dimly lit corridors for what seemed an eternity. 'I'll get lost, I know I will,' blurted Rosa.

'Don't worry, everyone does at first, but you'll soon be able to memorise the route by looking out for names on the doors.'

'I hope so,' replied Rosa softly, feeling nervous. 'The doors all look the same to me though.'

'This is our room,' pointed Molly, throwing open a brown-painted door, flicking on a light switch and stepping back. 'We share a bathroom down the corridor. You'd best get out of your wet coat and tidy yourself up before seeing Miss Rogers. This 'ousehold runs on perfect timing.'

Rosa entered the room, her eyes scanning its sparseness: a couple of iron beds, a wardrobe, two chests of drawers and a bedside table by each bed. The flagstone flooring was covered with a rug in the centre of the room, and a small rug was placed beside each bed. There was an armchair in one corner near a blacked-out window. A mirror in a bamboo frame was the only wall fixture.

Rosa stared in silence. As if reading her mind, Molly said, 'I know what you're thinking, it's not very 'omely. But I promise you'll soon settle in.'

'Who did you share with before me?'

'Another maid by the name of Jennifer Stanley. When the palace found out she was up the duff she 'ad to leave. There was a bit of a scandal about it 'cause she wasn't married, and the fella she was with 'ad three nippers too.'

Rosa's hand flew to her mouth. 'I would rather die than get in the family way like that. What happened to her?'

Molly shrugged her shoulders. 'Nobody's 'eard of her since, poor sod. With the war going on, more people are living for today, and don't think of the consequences. It's the poor girl who lives with the shame of it.'

Rosa picked up a photograph on the nearest chest of drawers. It showed a careworn woman surrounded by children. Molly pointed them out. 'That's me ma, Annie, and me brothers and sisters. They live in Stepney.'

'Stepney? That's a coincidence. My friend Alice has an aunt who lives there. I wonder if it's close to you. Do you go home at night?'

'No, they like yer to sleep in, and it's easier all round,

with working late sometimes. I get fed here too, so that's one less mouth for Ma to worry about, and the company can be good – well, in most cases.'

'What do you mean?' asked Rosa, picking up on Molly's change of tone.

'You'll find out in good time. Why don't you put your things away and get yerself sorted, and then we'll get you kitted out and see what Miss Rogers has lined up for you today.'

Rosa put her clothes and few possessions away and rubbed her hair dry using a towel Molly handed her, listening as her new friend rattled on about her family. Molly was the eldest of six children, and Rosa listened agog as she told her how, five years ago, their father ran off with the wife of the landlord of the pub next door – and they had heard nothing of him since.

'That must be awful for you,' said Rosa wistfully. 'At least after my parents split up, there was just Billy and me for Mam to look after, and I know where my da is and see him from time to time. He's having it tough right now. Working in the mines must be the worst job there is, it broke my da. How does your mam manage?'

'She just does, she finds a way. Ma goes without to make sure the little'uns get fed.'

'They look a playful bunch. What are their names?'

'That's Phyllis next to me, with the fair hair, she's two years younger than me and works as a maid for a family in Park Lane, and Thomas is on the other side of me, he's fifteen, and the spitting image of Dad. In front is Benjamin, Rosemary and Helena, aged thirteen, ten and nine. Quite a brood, but I love them to death.'

'I can see that,' murmured Rosa.

'You'd get on like an 'ouse on fire with them, and Ma too. If you're ever in trouble, Rosa, just remember that our 'ouse is your 'ouse. You'll find us next to the Three Blind Beggars boozer in Stepney, just remember that.'

'I will. I would very much like to meet your family. I suppose all families have their problems.'

'Of course they do, even the royal family,' chortled Molly.

Rosa stroked Dylan's face with her fingers as she placed his photograph next to her bedside.

'And who is this?' Molly probed with a glint in her eye, 'or can I guess, judging by your expression?'

'Oh yes. That's my Dylan. He's the most thoughtful and kind boy I've ever met.'

'I can see he has a kind face.'

Rosa's eyes clouded. 'I'm worried – it's been six weeks since I heard from him. He was going to make his first active flight, and I gathered it could be dangerous. What if he's been killed?'

'Oh, Rosa, try not to dwell on that. Dylan could well be alive, but unable to write, in a hospital somewhere or missing. The palace has its own post office, so you can post a letter from 'ere. But now we 'ave to report to staff housekeeping. Are you ready?'

'Thank you, Molly. I'm ready. How do I look?'

Molly faced Rosa, flicked a few stray hairs into place and eyed her up and down approvingly. 'You look just grand.'

'I must admit I'm nervous. I won't know what to say when I see the royal family. What are they like? Do you see them very much?'

'Well, yes, seeing as the King works from here and has meetings with all sorts of dignitaries. They're very kind people. You see a different side of them from this side of the fence, so to speak. Just keep your eyes down and don't speak to them until you're spoken to, and then you'll be fine.'

Rosa and Molly walked quickly along the labyrinth of seemingly endless passages until they reached a door that read *Deputy Housekeeper, Miss Bruce*. A lady with greying hair, a sturdy build and no-nonsense manner greeted them brusquely in a Scottish accent. 'Come on in, girls. I haven't got all day. I was expecting you half an hour ago.'

'I do apologise,' Rosa stuttered.

Miss Bruce sized her up with a penetrative, expert eye. She stepped into a side room and returned with two garments. 'Here are two outfits for you to wear whilst in the employment of the royal household. It is your duty to ensure they are clean at all times. Is that clear?'

Rosa's bottom lip trembled as she took hold of her uniform. 'Yes, Miss Bruce. I promise.'

'Please change your stockings before you report to Miss Rogers. There is a ladder behind your right ankle.'

With a wave of her hand, Rosa and Molly were dismissed.

'I don't think she liked me,' Rosa mumbled when they were out in the corridor.

'You haven't seen Miss Bruce on a bad day. Don't let her worry you. Sorry I didn't spot the ladder. That woman has razor-sharp eyes – it's so tiny it's hardly noticeable.'

They returned to their room and Rosa excitedly slipped into her new garments and a fresh pair of stockings. She raised her chin, stared at her reflection in the mirror and smiled as she patted her hair.

'I'm ready, Molly. I'm ready to serve the King and Queen. It may not be war work in the true sense, but I am serving King and country in my own way and hope this makes Dylan and my family proud.'

It seemed to Rosa that she had to take two steps to every one of Molly's for her short legs to keep up as they strode along another passageway on their way to Miss Rogers's office.

Her eyes caught some of the names on the doors they passed: food stores, wine cellars and linen, and vital trade areas were marked, including a seamstress, plumber's shop, carpenter's and cabinetmakers; everything but a candlestick-maker, Rosa mused.

'It's like a village down here. We even have our own public bar in the servants' staffroom on the ground floor,' explained Molly when she paused for a moment.

Everyone they passed politely wished Molly good morning. Female staff wore the same black dress, white apron and white cap as Molly and Rosa, while male household staff wore the navy-blue battledress with royal cipher that the driver Andrew had worn.

'I thought the attendants here wore scarlet coats with gold braiding and fancy stuff like that,' Rosa said.

'Not any more – at least not while the war continues. All the men at the palace and at Windsor have to wear the same outfit, none of the fancy stuff they used to wear, the tailcoats and scarlet jackets with embroidered waistcoats and gilt buttons bearing the royal cipher. They all wear plain military-style battledress now.'

'Oh, I didn't know that, but I suppose it makes sense,' Rosa commented.

'I can tell you it didn't go down well with some of the old-timers here. A couple said it was tantamount to treason for them to abandon their royal attire. The King's mother, Queen Mary, sorted them out. She accused them of rebellion, and forced them to follow suit.'

'Never!' gasped Rosa.

As they turned the next corner they spotted Miss Rogers speaking to the gentleman who had been at Rosa's interview.

'That's Sir Piers Legh, Master of the Household. I hope everything's alright,' Molly whispered behind her hand.

Rosa held her breath as Miss Rogers called her over and Sir Piers glanced briefly at them, before walking off in the opposite direction.

Rosa stepped into the housekeeper's office, with Molly behind her. Her cheeks flushed as Miss Rogers walked around her, conscious she was eyeing her up and down.

'Yes, very good. And we hope to see you as immaculately dressed each day.'

'Yes, of course, Miss Rogers.'

She handed Rosa a staff card before taking a seat behind her desk, indicating to the two girls to take a seat too. 'Sir Piers kindly brought this down for you. You must show it to the duty officer when you leave and return to the palace. For obvious reasons, security here is very tight. We need to know who is on the premises at all times.'

'Oh, thank you. And yes, Miss Rogers, I will take good care of it,' Rosa spluttered.

'Do you have your ration card with you?'

'Yes, it's in my room.'

'You will need to show it to Mr Corbitt as you are having meals here. He is in charge of ordering supplies and it will have to be added to his list. We follow rationing to the letter. Even the King and Queen, the princesses and their royal refugee relatives comply with the country's ration regulations, though they are allowed extra rations to entertain guests on state occasions.'

'Yes, Miss Rogers. I can pick it up and give it to him.'

'Molly will take you to him later. Now, I need to tell you that there are rules you must follow while working for the royal household.'

Rosa's eyes widened and she shot Molly a sideways glance. Molly responded with a reassuring wink.

'Maybe Miss Deakin can tell us. Let's see if she can recount them.'

Molly rubbed her hands together, inhaled and began reciting. 'The first is that everything must be done properly and promptly, there must be no mistakes or tardiness. There is no room for error.'

'Correct. Please continue,' instructed Miss Rogers.

'The second is that we must not approach the royal family or speak to them unless they speak to us first. Saying that, they are friendly and will stop and ask 'ow I'm doing. I've even been in the air-raid shelter with them once, and we 'ad a good chat then.'

A slight curl formed on Miss Rogers's lip. 'That may be so, and we are fortunate that they do care for the safety and well-being of their staff. Nevertheless, the strictest decorum must be adhered to. Now tell me, what is the third important rule?'

Molly blurted, 'Nobody must mention the names of

the Duke and Duchess of Windsor. And who would want to anyway?'

'Indeed, and don't forget it, Miss Edwards. It pays to remember that if you do so, you will be overheard, however softly you whisper it. It will not be tolerated, and if you should do so, it will be reported to Sir Piers, who will view it very dimly.'

Rosa, along with the rest of the country, knew the reason for this. In 1936 the King's brother, Edward VIII, had abdicated the throne in order to marry Wallis Simpson, a twice-divorced American woman. This led to George VI becoming King, and his eldest daughter, Princess Elizabeth, aged seventeen now, becoming heir to the throne. What a huge weight of responsibility on her young shoulders it must be, thought Rosa.

Another rule was to follow. Miss Rogers's voice deepened. 'The fourth rule states that what you see and hear is not repeated. You must abide by the strictest code of secrecy and discretion. Remember, "Careless Talk Costs Lives", and we must never put the lives of our royal family at risk.'

Miss Rogers asked Rosa to repeat the four rules and promise to abide by them.

'That's very good. Before you leave, I would like to mention that what you do in your own time is your own business. We know our Welsh girls have a proper Chapel background and good morals, and I'm sure we can count on you to keep your nose clean and stay on the straight and narrow.'

'Oh yes, Miss Rogers. You can count on that.'

Miss Rogers rose, the corner of her lips again curling

up, indicating that it was the end of their meeting. Rosa took the hint and stood up.

'Welcome to the royal household, Rosa. I've every confidence you will settle in very well. Now, I believe it's coffee time in half an hour. You'd better get a move on. The King and Queen don't like being kept waiting.'

9

Cook's sleeves were rolled up as she beat her ingredients in a bowl. 'Well bless my soul, if it isn't my little friend from Merthyr. It's good to have a friendly face from the Valleys working alongside us, isn't it? Agnes, I'm talking to you.'

Her question was directed to a maid whose back was turned. She appeared to be occupied weighing flour on a set of scales, and spun around, staring daggers at Rosa. Rosa was taken aback by the hostility of her scowl and a shiver ran along her spine. 'If you say so,' Agnes replied sullenly.

She turned and wiped flour from her hands on her long white apron. She appeared older than Rosa, in her early twenties perhaps. She was tall and slender, with round currant eyes, a pointed nose, and dark brown hair tucked behind her ears. Rosa thought how pretty she would look if she didn't scowl.

Cook admonished her, 'Try and put a smile on your face. You sealed your own fate by kicking the Queen's corgi. You know how dear it is to her.' Agnes was tight-lipped as Mrs Jones turned to Rosa. 'How are you with dogs, my dear?'

'I don't mind them at all. I think they're really sweet.'

Agnes's tone became friendlier. 'I apologise, Rosa. I shouldn't take it out on you. The blasted hound asked for it, and I'm not the only one who thinks so. It will have a nip at anyone, given the chance.'

Rosa gasped. 'Oh no. Surely they can control it.'

Cook threw back her head and roared. 'You'll see. Dookie is a bit of a handful. He has a sweet tooth, and the Queen is most particular about what he eats, but is known to pander to it. Agnes dropped a biscuit and he immediately swooped across the room to grab it, and had a nibble of her ankle at the same time. She dropped her tray of drinks kicking the dog away, smashed the china and made a terrible mess, and was lucky not to be given her cards there and then. As a result she's now working on pastry instead of upstairs.'

'It wasn't my fault. If that hound hadn't been there, it would never have happened. What about the fright I had?' Agnes huffed.

'I think it's because they realise what Dookie's like that you're still here, so be warned, Rosa.'

'It must have been a horrible experience for you, Agnes,' Rosa acknowledged. 'I hope we can be friends.'

Agnes accepted Rosa's outstretched hand. 'Welcome to the palace.'

Cook turned to Molly and said, 'Can you prepare the tray for the King's coffee. He has a meeting in his study, so you'll need another couple of cups. Rosa can help you.'

Molly led Rosa to a worktop in the corner away from Agnes. Reaching up to a cupboard, she opened the door and brought out a canister with 'Fortnum & Mason' written on it, and a storage jar with sugar. She opened another cupboard and produced fine white porcelain cups, saucers, two small plates and a matching milk jug, all edged in gold gilt with the royal crest. Rosa picked up one of the cups and ran her fingers softly around it. 'It feels so soft and smooth, like a newborn's skin, silky and satiny,' Rosa murmured.

'It's only a cup,' quipped Molly. 'We need to get a move on. If you open that cupboard you'll find the coffee jug, and if you open the drawer above it you'll see the linen tray cover and napkins.'

Rosa did as instructed. 'What else can I do?' she asked, her eyes narrowing.

'What's on yer mind, Rosa?'

'What if they don't like me, the King and Queen, or I mess things up?'

'That will only be the case if we're late – they can't abide being kept waiting. Pass me the kettle of water that's just boiled, and then watch me closely, and you can do this tomorrow.'

Rosa's eyes were fixed on Molly as she placed two scoops of fresh coffee in the silver pot. She knew it would need to infuse for a few minutes before plunging the coffee. 'Shall I bring the trolley over,' offered Rosa, spotting it out of the corner of her eye. 'I can place everything on the tray while the coffee is brewing.'

'Very well, I can see how keen you are. While you do that, I'll put the fresh shortbread biscuits on a plate. They're the Queen's favourite and made to a very precise recipe from her childhood in Scotland.'

When the coffee was brewed, Molly placed a small vase with colourful spring flowers on the trolley and pushed it out of the kitchen, Rosa on her heels.

'How do we get this up upstairs?' Rosa asked with an air of innocence.

'We take the lift, silly.'

'Of course, silly me. I never thought about there being a lift here. I'm thinking of Dookie and worried I might kick out at him too,' Rosa replied, feeling foolish.

'Dogs can sense when you're nervous. I've not had a problem with him, but he can probably sense that Agnes doesn't like him.'

The lift had an iron cage that they had to secure firmly, then Molly pressed the button to take them up a flight. When they reached the first floor, Rosa spotted the room by the policeman standing on duty outside. They knocked, and the door was opened by a butler in the now-familiar battledress.

Rosa couldn't stop staring at the King. He looked exactly as she had seen him in the newspapers, with his thin face and small frame, dressed in his naval uniform. He was seated at his desk opposite a severe-looking man with a thick moustache dressed in a dark suit.

The butler instructed, 'Leave it over there.'

The King looked up and Rosa asked, 'Will you be needing another cup and more coffee, Your Majesty?'

'The Queen is . . . out . . . on shooting practice . . . killing the palace rats . . . and will join us . . . shortly. That will be all . . . thank . . . you.'

Rosa curtseyed and walked backwards towards the door. 'Thank you, sir,' she mumbled, relieved not to have encountered the corgi with the ferocious reputation.

The King looked up, his piercing eyes penetrating Rosa's. He stuttered, 'I don't recognise that Welsh voice. Are you . . . you . . . new?'

Rosa's cheeks turned scarlet. Her eyes were fixed on the carpet as she curtseyed again. 'Yes, Your Majesty – I mean sir. I started today.'

'I see. Thank you . . . for the . . . coffee.'

The butler pointed to the door and Rosa and Molly continued to walk backwards slowly, their heads down, turning just before they reached the door and closing it behind them.

He followed them out and hissed, '*You* never speak to the King unless spoken to first. Wasn't that explained to you?'

'I'm sorry. I was only asking if he needed anything else. It won't happen again.'

'The correct way for staff to address the King or Queen after saying "Your Majesty" is *sir* or *ma'am*. Is that clear?'

'I was nervous, it won't happen again,' Rosa replied, biting her bottom lip.

The butler continued in a stern tone. 'However, when speaking to the princesses or anyone who is HRH – His or Her Royal Highness – you first address them as *Your Highness*, and afterwards as *sir* or *ma'am*. Is that understood?'

Rosa nodded, her face anxious at having so much to remember.

'Don't worry about it. The King didn't seem to mind,' Molly consoled her.

Rosa pressed her back against the wall and gasped, 'I hope I haven't messed up. I came over all strange. I never imagined I would be seeing the King on my first day here. Wait till I tell Dylan! And Mam won't believe it. Who was that man with the King, Molly? He seemed awfully stern. I wouldn't want to get on the wrong side of him.'

'That's Sir Alan Lascelles, the King's Private Secretary. And no, you don't want to get on the wrong side of him. The King and Queen, well, they're more friendly, but he's very stuffy, though you couldn't meet anyone more loyal and devoted.'

'I couldn't help notice the King's slowness of speech.'

'You'll get used to it,' said Molly as they made their way along the corridor. 'Never try and finish his sentence, that's the worst thing you could do.'

After a few more steps Rosa stopped in her tracks. 'I can hear shooting. It sounds very close. Is that what the King meant?'

'It is. You'll get used to it. The Queen needs to know how to protect herself if the worst should happen. She's an excellent shot, by all accounts, and there are fewer rats in the palace as a result, the little blighters. They're everywhere, so watch out.'

'Rats! I'm petrified of rats. Oh no, they're not running around in our rooms, are they?'

'Well if they are, we know who to ask to shoot them, don't we?' Molly replied with a grin.

'No! Not really. You mean the Queen?'

'Oh Rosa, you are green, aren't you.'

The rest of the morning flew by, with Cook taking Rosa under her wing, giving her simple tasks to do in the pastry kitchen, and instructing her where different items were kept.

After clearing away in the kitchen, Molly grabbed Rosa's arm and she found herself in the staff canteen, where trestle tables were set up. Rosa suddenly realised she was famished and stepped in line behind Molly in front of a counter.

'What do you fancy, love? I can recommend the shepherd's pie and veg,' suggested the friendly serving lady.

'That will do nicely, thank you,' Rosa responded nervously.

'There's jam roly-poly and custard too, if that takes your fancy.'

Rosa's eyes popped out at the scrumptious dessert, and she nodded. She followed Molly to a space on a bench and was about to tuck in when a man's voice asked, 'How's your first day been so far?'

Rosa looked up quizzically at the man opposite.

'Have you forgotten me already? Gerald Snaith,' he teased gently.

The penny dropped and her face broke into a smile. 'No, not at all, only I wasn't expecting to see you down here,' she replied coyly.

'Well, us guards have to eat too, you know. So tell me, how has your morning been?'

'I met the King and he spoke to me, and I spoke to him when I shouldn't have done, but he didn't tell me off,' she gushed. 'He seems very nice.'

'Well, that's something to write home about,' he said, grinning.

'I intend to, this evening. I shall write to Mam and Dylan, my boy back home.'

Molly interjected, 'And she's a one-boy type of girl, if you get me drift.'

'Hold your horses. I was only being friendly,' he retorted. 'Dylan is a very lucky young man.'

Rosa shot Molly a glance, feeling her comment was unnecessary. It had never occurred to her that Gerald's questions were anything but kindness.

'I wonder when I'll get to meet the princesses. Elizabeth is the same age as me,' Rosa commented, turning her back on Molly.

'They come here from time to time,' Gerald replied. 'But mostly they're at a secret location in the country, for security reasons. The Nazis would kidnap them if they thought they could, so their whereabouts are not known, not even to me, until I need to know – I'm one of their security guards.'

Rosa absorbed this information with interest.

Gerald whispered to her, 'I do apologise if I made you feel uncomfortable a moment ago. It can be daunting on your first day. I promise you I'm a perfect gentleman and merely wish you well.'

'I didn't think anything else, and am glad you asked – it was kind of you,' she replied.

'You can call me Jerry, by the way. That's Jerry with a J, just like the Yanks spell it. I must dash. I'm sure I'll see you around again.'

After he'd left, Molly turned to Rosa. 'I'm sorry if I spoke out of turn. I was only looking out for you in case he had thoughts of trying it on and you didn't know what to say, on account of Dylan.'

'I know, and I appreciate it. Let's forget it. I wonder what I'll be doing this afternoon?'

'Cook has said that we'll be taking the afternoon tea up. I believe the Queen has a committee meeting in her sitting room. Afterwards we can see Mr Corbitt and give him your ration card.'

'I'm pinching myself. I can't believe I'll be seeing the Queen today as well. I shall be very nervous.'

'Well, you'd better get used to it and remember what Cook said about making sure everything is perfectly prepared on time – and do not speak to the royal family unless they speak to you first. If the Queen is occupied when we arrive, a lady-in-waiting will ask us to lay the tea and cakes out on a table. We may be asked to stay and wait on them, but if it's highly confidential stuff they're discussing, we will have to leave.'

A tingle ran up Rosa's spine. It sounded so exciting and she was desperate not to put a foot wrong.

A few hours after lunch they carefully prepared two trolleys laden with Earl Grey tea, milk and sugar, dainty egg-and-cress and ham sandwiches with the crusts cut off, as well as shortbread, scones, home-made jam, cream and lemon drizzle cake. It looked so inviting.

Rosa operated the lift and followed Molly's directions to the Queen's sitting room. She knocked lightly on the door as instructed, waited to be told to enter, then the two girls pushed the trolleys inside.

'If you set everything out on the table, that is all that's required and you can then leave us,' a woman with a posh voice instructed.

Rosa dared not glance over in the direction of the four women grouped together at the end of the room. She could see from the corner of her eye that two of them were seated on a deep sofa, while two were in armchairs. The ceilings were high and ornate, while the walls were pastel and white with elaborate gilt finishings.

Her pulse soared when she glanced up and saw the Queen, then heard a short bark.

A corgi bounced towards Rosa and Molly, running circles around them.

'Dookie! Behave,' snapped the Queen as her corgi yapped.

'Shush, you silly thing,' Rosa said, instinctively bending down to stroke the dog. Dookie wagged his tail and she reached for one of the biscuits Cook had made and fed it to Dookie, who gulped down every crumb and licked Rosa's hand. He returned to his mistress, where he was patted and made a fuss of.

Was it her imagination, or did the Queen really glance over in her direction and tilt her head sideways, smiling and nodding at her as she stroked Dookie?

Once they had been dismissed, Molly blurted, 'You managed that really well, Rosa. Did you see the Queen give you a nod of approval?'

'Do you think so? I wasn't sure he was allowed a biscuit. I hardly dared look at her,' she replied, her head still in a daze.

'You can be sure it was noted by her, just as Agnes kicking out at Dookie was. Cook will be pleased, but I expect Agnes's nose will be put out of joint.'

'Oh no. The last thing I want is to upset anyone.'

'Come on, let's drop off your ration book now, before we forget.'

After stopping off in their room to collect Rosa's ration book, they set off for Mr Corbitt's office. It was close to the kitchen, and as they made their way there Molly gabbled on, telling her he was nicknamed the Magician because he could obtain anything the King and Queen desired, however unobtainable it seemed.

'I don't know how he does it, but he has contacts all

over London,' Molly prattled as they approached a door with *Frederick Corbitt, Comptroller of Supply* on it.

The door was slightly ajar and, peering through the gap, Rosa saw a balding man speaking on the phone. 'Don't let me down, Stan. This is requested personally by the Queen and I gave her my word.'

After he thumped the phone down on the corner of his desk next to a huge ledger, he leaned back in his chair, produced a white handkerchief from his pocket and proceeded to mop his damp brow.

'We'd better knock first,' Molly whispered, and proceeded to do so.

Mr Corbitt bolted upright. 'Come in.'

Molly stepped inside first, followed by Rosa clutching her ration book.

Mr Corbitt was a stout, besuited man in a crisp white shirt and dark tie. 'Ah, this is the new girl,' he said. 'I'm sure I would have remembered those rosy cheeks if I'd seen them before.'

'Yes, sir. My name is Rosa Edwards. I started today. Here, this is my ration book.'

'Very good. I'll take that and keep it with the others. It's not just staff whose ration books I mind. I also have those for the royal family I cater for, as well as their royal relatives who are displaced by the war, otherwise the kitchen cupboards would not be stocked. The King and Queen are keen to set a good example.'

'What are you after now, Mr Corbitt?' Molly asked.

Mr Corbitt pondered, rubbing his ear. 'It's a tough one. I might even have to admit I'm beaten, which would be a first, but I haven't given up yet.'

'What would that be for? Rosa enquired.

'Tabasco sauce, so not an item that is used in everyone's home.'

'Tabasco sauce? I've not heard of that before. What is it?' asked Molly.

'It's a hot sauce made from tabasco peppers, vinegar and salt. That will put some fire in your belly,' he grinned.

'Yuck. It sounds horrid.' Molly said, pulling a face.

'I've heard of it, Mr Corbitt, from my time working at the Valleys Hotel in Merthyr. I believe it's used for cocktails, though I don't know what it tastes like.'

Mr Corbitt smiled. 'I see we have a very knowledgeable young lady here, Miss Deakin. Miss Edwards, I very much doubt your establishment in Merthyr has been able to lay its hands on Tabasco sauce in the last few months. There doesn't appear to be a bottle of it anywhere in the country. It can also spice up a meat dish like shepherd's pie if your palette so desires, or be enjoyed with a plate of fresh oysters.'

'I never knew that,' marvelled Molly, her mouth open.

'Her Majesty is partial to a drop or two of Tabasco in her lobster cocktail as well. We have scoured London in search of it. I've just tried my last contact in the East End. He's also trying to source the French Negri toothpicks the King likes to use after every meal. He's never let me down so far, but it comes at a cost and I will have to make sure the books balance at the end of the day. I'm never one to admit I can't get an item our King and Queen desire. It's the least I can do, after all they are doing right now.'

'Oh, it does sound a difficult challenge,' Rosa sympathised.

'Her Majesty has said she will understand if I cannot

get hold of the sauce, but I'll lay my hand on it somehow or other.'

Rosa listened in awe. Tabasco sauce for lobster cocktail and French toothpicks – what a different life the royal family had. Her eyes strayed to the ledger.

'Ah, that is my bible. Everything I order gets logged there and all the food that comes in is accounted for. If so much as a packet of salt or sugar needs ordering, I'll be able to check if they really need replenishing now, or if – how should I put it – if they were slipped into someone's bag, which has happened.'

Molly caught Rosa's eye and tilted her head towards the door. 'Thank you, Mr Corbitt,' she said. 'We must be on our way. We have to collect the trays from the Queen's sitting room now. They won't want dirty crockery hanging around.'

'It was a pleasure to meet you, Mr Corbitt,' Rosa added.

'Good day, Miss Deakin, Miss Edwards,' Mr Corbitt responded, just as the telephone rang.

As Rosa closed the door behind her, she heard Mr Corbitt say, 'Splendid work, Stan. How much do we owe you? . . . What? That's outrageous! . . . Very well. I don't want it said that Freddie Corbitt couldn't supply our King and Queen with whatever their hearts desire.'

10

At the end of her first day, Rosa penned letters to her Mam and Dylan, followed by a reassuring note to Dylan's parents too. She posted them in the palace post office the following morning and was told they would leave with the first post of the day. Her thoughts then turned to Alice, anxious about what might have happened to her and how she could reach her.

She had to put it to the back of her mind as she fell into a routine over the next few days, quickly picking up the duties that were required and marvelling every time she saw the King or Queen in the distance. She'd seen Jerry in passing, and he nodded at her when he caught her eye. She was relieved to see that he wasn't ignoring her after Molly's comment.

When their duties finished on Friday evening, Molly changed out of her uniform and slipped into a green dress, pulling a cardigan over the top. 'I'm going home for the weekend to help Ma with the little'uns. Do you want to come too? As long as you don't mind sleeping on the couch.'

'It's very kind of you to ask, but I couldn't possibly impose on your mam, and besides, she won't want a stranger tagging along with you. It must be lovely to be part of a close family.'

'Ma wouldn't mind a jot. She'd say what's another

mouth to feed, as long as it's an 'appy house, that's all that matters.'

'I'm going to find Alice, the friend from home I told you about. I shall revisit the house she used to work in and see if I can find out anything more about why she moved out so suddenly. I have a feeling she must be in some sort of trouble.'

'Well, promise me you'll be careful.'

'I promise. Have a lovely time with your family.'

Molly hugged Rosa. 'I'll see you on Sunday evening then and want to hear all about it.'

After she'd gone, Rosa took a deep breath. She felt her eyes fill up and a queasiness stir inside. She picked up Dylan's photograph and pressed it to her chest. 'Where are you, Dylan Williams? I didn't realise how much I missed you until now. I miss Merthyr too, but it's not the same without you. I even miss Hettie Pritchard. Please come home safely. You promised, remember?'

Rosa felt alone without Molly's companionship. After eating in the canteen, she returned to her room and lay on her bed, staring up at the ceiling. She realised she was homesick, and a lump formed in her throat.

Lady Gwendoline had assured her she could return any time she wished, and maybe she should. Maybe being a royal maid wasn't for her. But first, she vowed she would find out what happened to Alice.

Rosa shielded her eyes from the sun as she emerged from the palace the next morning, checking she had Alice's address and her staff pass for when she returned.

She spotted Jerry on duty, standing stiff, a rifle held

tightly inside his left arm, and went up to him. He chortled. 'It's alright for some having the day off. Enjoy your day.'

'I'm actually on a mission,' she explained.

'That sounds mysterious.'

'I'm trying to find my friend Alice, who is also from Merthyr. She left her position suddenly without telling me and moved in with an aunt in Stepney, but I don't have an address. Her mam told me she's ill, but none of this makes any sense and she hasn't replied to my letters, so I'm going back to the house where she worked to see what I can find out.'

'Turning detective, are we? Take care, and good luck. I hope you find your friend, Rosa.'

As Rosa set off across Green Park, she spotted Agnes across the road talking to an older man in a pin-striped suit and trilby hat pulled down over his face, the kind of man her mother would call a spiv. They appeared to be having an animated discussion, and Agnes opened her handbag, fished out an envelope that she handed to him, then spun around and stomped off.

Rosa shrugged her shoulders, telling herself it was none of her business, and hastened her steps towards Piccadilly, barely noticing her surroundings: children running along the path and servicemen walking arm-in-arm with their sweethearts.

She soon found herself back at 139 Piccadilly and climbed the first step before noticing that on the right there were steps leading to a basement.

That must be the trade entrance, she surmised, turning and walking down them. At the bottom was a window and she pressed her face against the glass and stared inside.

She saw an ironing board and piles of linen, a washing machine, a wooden table and four chairs, but there didn't appear to be anybody in the room.

She straightened her back and was about to press the bell when a well-spoken man's voice from above asked, 'Can I help you?'

She spun around and glanced to the top of the steps. A smartly dressed man in a well-cut suit looked down on her. He wore a trilby hat and carried a cane with a silver top.

Rosa's heart pounded. 'I'm looking for my friend, Alice Evans. She used to work here and I know she's left, but I don't have a forwarding address. Is there any chance you might have one?'

'I can tell you are from the same part of the world as Alice. I might be able to help you.'

Rosa's face brightened as she ascended the steps. 'Thank you, sir. I can't tell you how worried I've been. Are you—?'

'Lord Hesketh-Robbins. I must say I was very surprised when Alice upped and left suddenly a month ago. I could see she was a bright girl and had plans for her, but there you go – as my dear wife says, you can't rely on staff these days. We had hoped she'd be different, more reliable, coming from Wales.'

'You say you might be able to help, sir?' Rosa pressed, ignoring his reference to her Welsh roots.

'I don't have an address myself. But I believe the girl left some belongings behind and our maid may be able to help. If you wait at the bottom of the stairs, I'll send her down. Good day, Miss . . . ?'

'Miss Edwards, sir . . . your lordship. Thank you for your help.'

Rosa could hardly believe her luck. She went back to the bottom of the basement steps, and after a few minutes the maid she had seen before opened the door. She clutched a small brown suitcase and three letters and handed them to Rosa.

'I was hoping to see you again, and that you could help me,' Rosa gushed.

'I can't say for sure, but here's her case and these letters. She left quickly, but I thought I should 'ang on to them, just in case,' the maid replied. 'If you find her, tell her Susan sends her best wishes, and 'opes we can go to the club again.'

Rosa scanned the letters, recognising her own handwriting on two of the envelopes. She opened the third that had a London postmark. It was signed by Alice's Aunt Ruby in Stepney. Rosa felt guilty reading it, but she felt it might give her a clue as to her friend's whereabouts. The letter had a warm tone and Ruby was inviting her niece to tea on her day off. Rosa recalled Alice speaking with fondness of her mother's sister, who was widowed and worked in a bakery in the East End. With huge relief, Rosa noted that she had included her address, 26 South Grove, at the top of the page and placed the letter back in the envelope.

'Thank you for these, Susan, Alice mentioned you to me in her letter. I have her aunt's address now and will return the case to her. It seems strange she left it behind.'

'I thought the same, but their ain't much in it. I 'ope she's alright.'

'I'll go now. Do you know how I get to Stepney? I'm not used to the Underground and buses here.'

Susan gave Rosa careful instructions, asking her to repeat them. 'When you get off the Tube, or if you get lost, just ask. They're a friendly lot in the East End when you get to know them, but some of them are a bit rough around the edges, so watch yourself.'

'It can't be worse than the poorest parts of Merthyr where I hail from. There are some right sorts there.'

Susan tossed her head back and roared. 'So long. I 'ope to see you at the club with Alice one night, all being well.'

'That would be nice,' Rosa agreed as she mounted the steps. Clutching Alice's case, Rosa marched briskly to Hyde Park Corner Tube station, with instructions to change at South Kensington and take the District line to Stepney Green. She double-checked the route at the ticket office with a kindly member of staff, who warmed to her and wanted to hear what she was doing in these parts.

Rosa knew the Underground had been used as a shelter by thousands during the Blitz and felt apprehensive descending further and further down. The depth was only a fraction of what her father would have been used to in the pits, but it was deep and dark enough for her as she continued to make her way down into the bowels of the station. She stood on the platform and leaped in surprise when the train thundered in and halted alongside her.

She almost fell off her seat when the train moved off, and again when it jolted to a halt at South Kensington station, where she changed lines. As she waited for her connection, she imagined what it must have felt like to sleep on the platforms; perhaps not that different to being underground in a coal mine. As her train pulled in and Rosa clambered on board, she was relieved to see Stepney Green on the map inside. An elderly lady wearing a tweed skirt and jacket produced her knitting out of a bag and a roll of pale blue wool and clucked as the needles wound the wool around them, line after line.

'Do you mind if I ask, what are you knitting?' asked Rosa.

She turned to Rosa and beamed. 'Why, a baby's bonnet, my dear, for my new grandson. What a time my daughter had, going into labour at home as bombs fell on the street behind them.'

'That must have been so frightening. Are they alright?'

'She has a bonny boy now. Fortunately for her, an ambulance was there in a flash and attended to her. Tell me, what's a nice girl like you from the Valleys doing here then?'

Rosa told her about her search for Alice. The woman placed her knitting on her lap and listened attentively, and before she knew it Rosa heard Stepney Green being announced.

'That's my stop, I mustn't miss it,' said Rosa.

'It so happens that this is my stop too. If you tell me your address, I might be able to show you the way, seeing as you're a stranger to these parts.'

Rosa gratefully accepted the lady's offer and walked with her out of the Tube station. Rosa could immediately see she was in a less affluent area. The street was filled with traders and working-class people going about their business. Women with tired faces jostled along the path with their children in tow, and she blushed when a delivery boy wobbling on his bicycle whistled as he passed her, turning his head to wink at her. Some of the properties had shabby exteriors with flaking paintwork. Queues had formed outside a bakery for the loaves fresh out of the oven, and the best pickings had been snapped up from a fruit and veg store next door, with only a small amount of produce left. The fumes were more evident, with black, billowing smoke wafting up into the sky from numerous chimneys. The cars were smaller and less shiny. Despite all this, there was a cheerfulness and cheekiness in the demeanour of the East Enders. She passed on the offer of jellied eels from one trader on the street corner: 'Another time,' she promised, wondering what they tasted like but keen to hurry on and see Alice.

Within five minutes they turned off the main road and into South Grove. Rosa was surprised to see that although they were terraced houses, they were bigger and smarter than the back-to-back homes in Merthyr, with bay windows and front gardens, and a more prosperous feel to them, as if they were lived in by office workers rather than the lower ranks.

Rosa paused at the wooden gate of 26 South Grove, and the lady bid her farewell. She stared up at the house, neatly presented with a dark blue front door. She estimated it was built around thirty years ago, with a front bay window, a decorative brick porch. She lifted the latch of the gate and shot an upwards glance at a window. I swear someone there has seen me, she thought to herself.

Plucking up courage, she went to the door and knocked twice. Almost immediately the door was opened by a woman in her forties, her hair tied up in pin curls. She gripped a cigarette tightly between her lips, screwed her eyes and stared intently at Rosa. 'Can I help you, love?'

'I'm looking for my friend Alice Evans.'

The woman took the cigarette between her fingers and said, 'Who the blazes are you?'

'My name's Rosa Edwards. I'm Alice's friend from Merthyr. We used to work together there and now I have a job at Buckingham Palace. I was given your letter at the house in Piccadilly with your address. She left some of her belongings behind and I've brought them to her.'

Rosa produced Alice's bag and placed it on the door-step. 'Are you her Aunt Ruby?'

'Thank you for bringing her stuff over. I'll let her know you've called. It's very kind of you to go to this trouble, Rosa.'

'So you *are* Ruby, Alice's aunt? Is she in? Can I see her?'

'I am Ruby, but no, I'm sorry love, you can't see her. I can't say anything. Now, if you'll excuse me, I must go.'

Ruby took the bag. 'Please don't come again. Alice will be in touch with you if she wants to.'

'But—'

The door was slammed shut in her face. Stunned, Rosa took a few steps down the red-tiled path and paused, turning to look back at the house.

She glanced up at the first floor and saw the curtain flicker. She screwed her eyes, catching sight of a figure that quickly hid behind it.

Alice! So you are there. Why are you hiding from me?

<h1 style="text-align:center">11</h1>

No two days were the same at the palace and Rosa soon became accustomed to performing her tasks with ease.

She'd confided in Molly about her visit to Alice's aunt, and her friend advised, 'There's not a lot you can do. She must at least be safe if she's with her aunt, though it's strange you haven't been able to see her, and her ma is keeping you at arm's length too.'

'Alice wouldn't cut herself off from me. There must be a reason for it.'

'You can't put your nose in other people's business if it's not wanted. You've let her know where you are, so Alice can track you down if she wants.'

'But only if her aunt tells her,' Rosa wailed. 'It just didn't seem right that she lied about her not being in.'

'That does seem strange. Maybe you could write her a letter again, now you know the address. I could ask Ma to keep her ears peeled too in case she hears anything in the neighbourhood.'

Rosa's face brightened. 'That's a good idea, I'd appreciate that. Thank you for the suggestion about writing again – I shall do that.'

'And Dylan? Is there still no news from him?'

Rosa's face clouded. 'No, nothing. I'm beginning to think—'

'You must put such thoughts out of your mind. What's a few weeks in wartime?' Molly consoled.

Cook summoned Rosa and Molly over. 'There's no time for chit-chat today. The Queen is entertaining her royal relatives this afternoon and everything must be perfect, the way Her Majesty likes it. You will be expected to stay and wait on them too.'

'Yes, Mrs Jones,' Rosa replied. 'It will be an honour.'

'That's the spirit,' Molly said. 'Chin up. I wonder which foreign royals it will be, only some of them don't speak good English.'

'I don't know the answer to that. If anything isn't clear, ask the lady-in-waiting and she will be able to help.'

Agnes appeared carrying an armful of clean tea towels. 'I was passing and overheard you mention the Queen's relatives. If you need a spare pair of hands, I can help. I believe one of them spoke well of me when they were here before.'

Cook pressed her hands on her ample hips and considered the suggestion. 'It might be a good idea to have another pair of hands there, as long as you give me your word you will get along with the others and keep away from Dookie. I don't want Miss Rogers to give me a ticking off.'

'I promise,' replied Agnes in a silky voice. 'I'll just pack these tea towels away in the cupboard and be right back.'

Cook instructed the three maids on the final touches for the afternoon tea. Mr Corbitt had secured some fresh crab that the Queen was partial to, and salmon fillets straight from Balmoral had been cooked and mashed with home-made mayonnaise. Cook had surpassed herself with her iced buns, coffee and walnut sponge and short-bread, and Rosa's spirits lifted at Agnes's friendly offer to help fill the sugar bowls while Rosa folded the napkins. Now the laden trolleys rattled along the corridor to the lift. Rosa's trolley carried the tea and fine porcelain cups, plates and cutlery, and she strode along with a more confident air, having started at the palace just over two weeks ago. She was intrigued to see who the royal guests would be.

Once out of the lift, they reached the room with a police officer outside, and, after knocking on the door, were shown in by a valet.

A long table was placed against one side of the room, draped in a white tablecloth with the gold monogram that matched the china. Rosa heard the Queen's voice and glanced up briefly; she was surrounded by two other ladies and a gentleman.

Rosa couldn't contain her excitement whenever she saw the Queen, her cheeks burning. She watched in awe, admiring her gracious ways, how she waved a slim hand in the air as she spoke with a smile, laughing gaily to her companions. She was always beautifully dressed, and today she wore an elegant pale blue floral dress and rows of pearls at her throat, with matching earrings.

The Queen's lady-in-waiting, Lady Rosemary Carrington, a poised lady wearing a cream silk dress, came over and said, 'Ah, we are looking forward to this. Can you please place the tea on the left side of the table and the food next to it with the plates. I must say, it looks very appetising.'

After Rosa had done this the Queen beckoned her over. Rosa could barely believe it was her the Queen was summoning, but Molly nudged her forward.

'Your Majesty,' said Rosa, bobbing her knee in a nervous curtsey.

'You're our new Welsh maid, aren't you? How are you finding it here?'

'Very well, thank you, *ma'am*.' Rosa emphasised the word, pleased she had remembered the correct form of royal address.

'We are very fond of Wales. The people of Wales were most generous to my dear girls when they were young, presenting them with their own little house, a dear little cottage complete in every detail that has given them endless pleasure.'

'I am delighted to hear it, ma'am,' replied Rosa looking puzzled.

'It was gifted to them ten years ago, and is in situ at Windsor. It really was the most thoughtful and delightful gift. You know, the princesses still dust it themselves, no servant is allowed in there, the house is their responsibility alone.'

'I am so pleased to hear it,' replied Rosa, delighted at the Queen's attention and her compliment to her fellow countrymen.

Rosa returned to her position and admired the spread in front of her. Molly grinned from ear to ear. Rosa glanced at the guests and asked Agnes, 'Do you know who they are?'

'Of course. The slim young man is King Peter of Yugoslavia, the older lady is the Dutch queen, Queen

Wilhelmina, with King Haakon and his son, Crown Prince Olav of Norway. Quite a mix, hey?'

'Goodness, so many royals. I can hardly believe I'm in the same room as them,' Rosa gulped.

Agnes raised her head and smiled as the Queen's guests rose and came towards them. She pushed herself in front of Rosa and beamed at Prince Olav. 'Can I be of assistance, Your Highness?'

'Just tea for now, thank you.'

Rosa swiftly moved over and picked up the silver teapot and poured the liquid into a cup. 'How do you like your tea, Your Highness?'

'With just, how do you say, a dash of milk and one teaspoon of sugar.'

Rosa duly complied and handed the prince his tea. Queen Wilhelmina, small in stature and stout, made a beeline for the sandwiches and cake. Rosa offered to pour her some tea when Prince Olav pulled a face. 'This tea tastes very strange.'

His voice resonated throughout the room and Rosa felt everyone's eyes burning through her body. He placed it on the table. 'I can't drink this. It is bitter, it is not tea as I know it.'

The lady-in-waiting rushed to his assistance. 'May I?' she asked.

He pointed to the cup. 'I have never tasted tea like this before. It is undrinkable.'

Lady Rosemary picked it up and sniffed it and then took a sip. She screwed her face and reached for a glass of water.

'Miss Edwards, why have you put salt in the sugar bowls? This tastes disgusting.'

'But it can't be. That's impossible.'

Rosa turned to look at Agnes as the penny dropped. Agnes had offered to fill the sugar bowls, but instead of being a gesture of kindness it was a ploy to set her up. But who would believe her?

Agnes feigned ignorance, shrugging her shoulders, a shocked expression on her face.

Rosa's legs wobbled as she recalled Miss Rogers's words on her first day, how the first rule of working in the royal household was that everything had to be done perfectly.

Prince Olav gallantly intervened. 'Please do not make a fuss on my account. No harm has been done. It's not as if she was trying to poison me. You're not a spy, are you?'

'No . . . no . . . sir,' Rosa wailed. 'I swear on my life.'

'I believe you,' he replied, staring at her stricken face. 'There are far more serious matters we need to concern ourselves with if we are to beat Hitler.'

Molly stepped forward. 'I have some sugar here, Your Highness. I can promise you it is sugar as I have tasted it.'

The prince roared with laughter. 'Ah, so I have my own food-taster now, dear Elizabeth. I applaud your thoughtfulness.'

He smiled in Rosa's direction and she felt her cheeks turn crimson as she bobbed a curtsey. The Queen smiled in her direction too. What could have been a disaster had been averted and she heaved a huge sigh of relief.

On their way back down to the kitchen, Rosa thanked Molly for coming to her rescue. 'If it wasn't for you, I don't know what would have happened, Molly. I wonder what Cook will have to say about it when I tell her.'

Molly stopped her and said, 'It wasn't your fault, but I

couldn't say that there and then. I saw Agnes filling the bowls, but couldn't see what she was filling them with. I felt suspicious, so I took a spare sugar bowl on my trolley.'

Rosa's jaw dropped. 'I don't understand why she would do such a wicked thing and lay the blame on me.'

'It's pure jealousy, because she's having to roll her sleeves up in the pastry kitchen while you get to serve the King and Queen. Let's keep this between ourselves for now, nobody here is interested in staff tittle-tattle. I must say, Prince Olav took it very well.'

It was impossible to hide the salt incident from Cook – news of it spread like wildfire. Molly spoke up and recounted what Agnes had done. When Cook questioned Agnes about it, she insisted it had been a mistake. Cook discussed the situation with Miss Rogers and it was decided that Agnes should be sent to work in the laundry after a girl there had been taken sick.

Cook assured Rosa, 'I don't believe you were responsible. Agnes has a sly way about her. I've seen the way she looks at you out of the corner of her eye and I don't like it. But she shouldn't bother you any more now.'

Deep down, Rosa wasn't so sure, feeling her nemesis might want to avenge her.

Miss Rogers asked Cook to send both Rosa and Molly to see her the following day when she could spare them.

'I hope it's nothing to do with the salt,' Rosa quaked.

'You've done nothing wrong,' said Molly. 'I don't think they'd want to lose you, especially now Agnes is no longer in the kitchen.'

'No one is indispensable, that's what we were always told at the Valleys.'

'Well, let's get this over with now,' said Molly, knocking on Miss Rogers's door.

Holding her breath, Rosa followed Molly in the room. Miss Rogers was with a slim lady in her mid-fifties wearing a dark suit and white blouse. 'This is Mrs Hargreaves. She is Deputy Housekeeper at Windsor Castle. She has asked for extra staff to assist there for a short duration and I put your names forward.'

Rosa shuffled from one foot to the other. 'Windsor Castle? Where is that?'

'It's easily reached by train, just thirty-five minutes, I believe, from Paddington, and then a six-minute walk to the castle,' Miss Rogers replied, glancing at her companion.

Mrs Hargreaves nodded. 'That's exactly right. You would be doing the same kind of work as here and will sleep there. Would you agree to that?'

'Well, yes, of course,' replied Molly, nudging Rosa.

'May I ask a question please?' Rosa said nervously.

'Of course,' Miss Rogers nodded.

'Can I tell Mam and Dylan of my whereabouts, in case they want to write or contact me? Only, I'm waiting for news from Dylan. I haven't heard from him for a month now.'

Mrs Hargreaves answered: 'I understand your concern, and delays in communication are quite common during these turbulent times, but you cannot – and must not – tell them anything about your whereabouts. I must insist on that for security reasons. They can still write to you here and any mail that arrives for the two of you will be taken to Windsor Castle. Is that understood?'

Both girls nodded in unison, staring at each other.

'I'm pleased to hear that. You will be provided with a rail warrant and the royal household will settle the cost. You will start next Monday and will only need to bring a small bag of possessions with you, as the placement is just for a short while.' She leaned forward, her voice deepening, and continued, 'I repeat, you must swear with your life not to tell a soul about who or what you see there.'

'I swear with my life,' Rosa uttered in a serious tone. The same words were repeated by Molly with equal gravity.

Each week Rosa sent a postal order to her mother covering half her wages, and that Sunday when she dropped it off at the palace post office, there were two letters for her.

The first was a note from Eira thanking her for what she'd sent, while asking if she could spare more money as she was struggling to make ends meet. Rosa noted this didn't seem to stop her mother from splashing out on make-up and new clothes, insisting it was one of life's pleasures. She whinged too about Billy, saying he still caused her headaches by running away to his father. The second letter was from Mrs Williams asking Rosa how she was settling in. She and Huw were increasingly concerned there was still no news from Dylan, but were determined to remain hopeful.

Tears came to Rosa's eyes, knowing Mrs Williams's words were written from the heart. She wrote: *I feel numb, but we carry on each day because we have to. We are thankful that Hettie is with us and business is ticking over. We would love to see*

A lump formed in Rosa's throat. She felt wretched that she couldn't say when she would have time off to return home. Her initial feelings of homesickness had passed and going to Windsor meant she had a new chance to serve the royal family, which she had begun to look forward to.

She swiftly wrote back to both her mother and Mrs Williams, telling the former she couldn't spare any more money for now, while promising Mrs Williams she would visit her the first chance she had.

She finished by writing: '*I pray for my dear Dylan every night and for his safe return. I have his photograph by my bed and it reminds me what a truly good person he is, selfless and brave through to his core, always putting the needs of others before his own. If there is a God, he will surely spare him as the world needs men like our Dylan.*'

She made no mention to either about going to Windsor.

Her mind turned to Alice, but she was unsure of the best way to approach the matter after being sent packing from her aunt's house in Stepney. For now, that would have to wait while she mulled it over.

After dropping off the letters in the post office, Rosa returned to her room and packed for Windsor. Molly was there too, packing her bag. She declared, 'It may not be war work in the sense of working in a munitions factory or serving in one of the forces, but it is war work nonetheless. We are serving the King and Queen who are leading this country to bring this war to an end. We should be honoured, Rosa. I wonder why we were suggested by Miss Rogers?'

'I expect Miss Rogers sees we work well together. And just as I was getting used to finding my way around these passages.'

'At least we'll be together. It will be new for me too,' Molly said.

'I wonder what Windsor will be like?' Rosa asked. 'I mean, it is a castle, so there's no way the Nazis could get in, is there?'

'Huh! Let them try. Seeing as it is a well-guarded fortress that's been standing for hundreds of years, I doubt it very much.'

Windsor railway station was a stone's throw from the castle. The two maids didn't need to ask for directions; the castle's Round Tower was easily spotted from a distance, up Castle Hill. It loomed high above, with vast numbers of turrets, towers and battlements.

Miss Rogers had told them how it was the oldest inhabited castle in the world, founded by William the Conqueror in the eleventh century, and had been home to almost forty British monarchs.

Rosa pinched herself as she stood at the guardhouse on the perimeter of the castle grounds, awed by the imposing surroundings and imagining the fierce battles that had taken place there. Compared to Buckingham Palace, it was gigantic. This castle had been the scene of many bloody conflicts and was now having to defend itself against its biggest threat in living memory.

Rosa and Molly walked tentatively up to the archway and introduced themselves to a policeman, showing their letter of introduction. He checked their names and directed them past the massive Round Tower to the trade entrance, where they reported to another police officer who instructed them to wait while he made a call.

As she waited, Rosa felt reassured at seeing guards in khaki dotted around the castle walls. Within a couple of minutes, Mrs Hargreaves arrived. Rosa hadn't taken much notice of her before, but now her eyes rested on her slender stature and her dignified air. Her greying hair was swept back in a neat bun behind her long, swan-like neck, and her violet eyes washed over Rosa and Molly.

'I hope you had a pleasant journey. Please follow me.'

They clutched their cases and fell into step behind Mrs Hargreaves, down one flight of steps and along a dark, dingy stone-flagged corridor, passing occasional trophies of ancient armour that underlined the history of this oldest of British royal homes, finally stopping at a door with her name on.

Once inside, she offered them a seat in front of her desk. It was an airless room with files piled on a shelf behind her. A dim lightbulb dangled from the ceiling and the small window offered only a glimpse of light. A table lamp and telephone were positioned neatly on her desk, alongside her stationery and ink blotter. She sat behind the desk and leaned forward, resting her elbows on the top.

'Unfortunately, two maids, Jessica and Emma Simms, who usually attend to the princesses, have mumps. They are sisters and contracted it from their younger brother. They are recuperating at home and you will be filling in for them until they can return.'

Rosa exchanged an astonished glance with Molly, whose eyes widened. 'Did you say the *princesses*? They're here? But they can't be. I thought they were in the country somewhere.'

'As you can imagine this is strictly confidential,' Mrs Hargreaves continued. 'You will be their temporary maids, taking instructions from their governess and other senior staff.'

'I can't wait to see them,' gushed Rosa. 'You can count on me to do my best. And what an honour it is too.'

'I couldn't tell you this before, for security reasons. To start with, it is Princess Elizabeth's eighteenth birthday on the twenty-first, and the King and Queen plan to hold a luncheon here for family and close friends.'

'It's my eighteenth birthday too this year. I was born on Christmas Day,' Rosa piped up.

'I'll be sure to buy you a special present,' whispered Molly behind her hand.

'The best present we could all wish for is peace, an end to this war,' Mrs Hargreaves commented, rising from her seat. 'Do you have any questions?'

Rosa piped up. 'I have one. I was wondering who the Head Housekeeper is here, and when we get to meet her?'

'That's a very good question. Dear Miss Brown is on compassionate leave at the moment. Her mother and brother were killed recently when their house was struck by the Nazis. You'll answer to me until further notice.'

'Oh that's terrible, poor lady,' Rosa replied.

Mrs Hargreaves opened the door, went into the corridor and called out to somebody nearby, 'Mr Proctor, can you spare a moment please?'

A stockily built man with greying hair entered the room. 'Of course, Mrs Hargreaves. How can I help?'

'Could you show our new maids to their room. They are taking the place of the Simms sisters until they are able to return and can use their room. They need to change into their work clothes. Afterwards, can you show them to the kitchen.' Turning to Rosa and Molly, she added, 'I will be there in half an hour to collect you and take you to the princesses' rooms.'

Rosa could scarcely believe what she was hearing and followed the cheerful porter out of the room. 'My name is Cyril Proctor, I've been a porter here more years than I can remember.'

Molly paused and extended her right arm. 'I'm Molly Deakin, and this is Rosa Edwards. We've come over from Buckingham Palace, just until the sisters are better.'

The porter moved forward to take their bags. Noticing he had a slight stoop, Molly took hold of it. 'I don't mind carrying it, Mr Proctor.'

The porter squared up to her. 'Are you trying to do me out of a job? You'll do no such thing. I'm quite capable.'

She handed over her case and he took Rosa's too and they followed him outside and along the corridor. 'Come on then, follow me down to the dungeons.'

Rosa stopped in her tracks and glanced, horrified, at Molly. 'I'm not sleeping in a dungeon. I thought we had the sisters' room.'

Molly looked apprehensive too and glanced sideways at Cyril. He winked and she sighed with relief. 'Come on, he's only joking.'

'I wouldn't be too sure. You wouldn't say no if your life depended on it. The dungeons are the safest place in the castle and even the princesses spent a night or two there at the beginning of the war,' he asserted.

Rosa shivered. 'It still sounds horrible. I would think of the men who died down there, in case it's haunted, but you're right.'

The maids followed the porter, passing numerous doors, until they reached the staff quarters, and Rosa was relieved to hear that the dungeons were in a separate part of the castle.

Like at the palace, the room they were to sleep in was sparsely furnished with only essential items. There were few personal effects showing the room had been occupied by anyone else and the iron-framed beds were freshly made. Rosa plonked herself down on one of them and pulled a face. 'I can feel the springs under my mattress. What does yours feel like?'

Molly sat on the edge of the other bed and bounced up and down. 'I don't think I have any springs at all!'

'Oh well, we'll get used to it, I suppose. At least we have a bed, and we're safe and well protected with all those police and guards around the castle. It's not just the royal family being protected – we are too.'

Mr Proctor coughed. 'I have a quick job to attend to, and then I'll be back to take you to the kitchen.'

Rosa's bag contained only a few items for a short stay. Dylan's photograph was soon placed by her bed. 'I wonder where you are now, my love,' she whispered. She turned to Molly and asked, 'Have you ever been in love?'

'Nah. I don't have time for that, not with Ma and the family. I'm not saying I don't want to, just that this isn't the right time.'

Rosa glanced around the room. 'I don't like it here, knowing that down in them spooky dungeons, men would have been chained in the cells and starved or tortured to death.'

'I feel the same,' Molly shuddered, slipping into her maid's dress and securing her white apron over it.

A few minutes later Mr Proctor returned. 'Good, I see you are ready. The princesses have a dance class this afternoon and their friend Alathea Fitzalan-Howard is with them. They'll be ready for refreshments soon, so you need to look sharpish.'

Turning to Rosa, he added, 'Be sure to put sugar out and not salt.'

Rosa looked horrified and her cheeks burned. 'But how did you . . . ?'

He tapped his nose. 'You could say I have a mate who has a mate at the palace. We're always exchanging little snippets – you'd be surprised what I hear.'

'I can see we're going to have to watch ourselves,' Molly grinned.

'You have to laugh while you can. I'll take you to the kitchen to meet Cook.'

Rosa and Molly followed their guide along the stone passages, trying to take in their route, and followed him up a staircase into a large darkened room, the huge windows covered in blackout curtains.

At the end of the room they traipsed along another corridor and then down a winding staircase. The sounds of chattering and the sweet aroma of freshly baked cake was a sign they were close, and a few seconds later they entered the kitchen.

It was enormous, bigger than any kitchen Rosa had ever seen. A huge black range was positioned at one end and there was a spit for cooking large carcasses. Wooden dressers lined the walls with saucepans and copper kettles filling their shelves. There were numerous large wooden worktops and tables and alcoves leading off from the kitchen to various stores.

Rosa and Molly spotted Mrs Hargreaves talking to a gentleman wearing a white chef's outfit and toque on his head, and sporting a distinctive handlebar moustache with curls at the end. Mrs Hargreaves beckoned them over and introduced them to head chef, Monsieur Phillipe Gaston.

'I am glad you are here,' he said in a thick French accent. 'We have a busy few days ahead of us and I insist on perfection.'

A tray of fresh lemonade was laid out on a trolley, along with some cheese straws. 'If you push this, Molly, we will take it to the princesses,' Mrs Hargreaves instructed. 'And please do try to memorise the route so you can do it alone.'

Rosa made a mental note of the corridor, a suit of armour standing at the corner. Her ears pricked up when she heard a piano being played and a woman's voice chanting, 'One, two, three, one, two, three.' The music stopped and the voice said, 'That is superb, you are all natural dancers.'

Mrs Hargreaves knocked on the door and entered the room, indicating for Molly to enter, followed by Rosa.

Rosa felt her insides turn to jelly. She instinctively curt-seyed low, keeping her eyes down. She couldn't stop a gasp passing her lips, captivated and in awe of the two young royals, her eyes fixed on Princess Elizabeth's face and sparkling eyes. *She's so pretty, and her sister is too*, she thought, noticing the mischievous glint in Princess Margaret's eye. The two princesses both had shoulder-length wavy hair and Rosa recognised Elizabeth as being the taller of the two. She'd seen their photographs in magazines, but they looked much prettier in the flesh and had an exuberant air about them.

They both wore similar outfits, white Aertex blouses and checked skirts, which seemed to be the way they did things, as they were frequently pictured wearing identical clothing. Rosa thought this made good sense as it prevented them from squabbling over who wore the best clothing.

Their friend, Alathea, around the same age as Princess Elizabeth and also with shoulder-length brown hair, stood alongside them. They were all three applauded by their glamorous dance teacher, Betty Vacani, her hair swept up in victory rolls, the fashionable style of the day.

Elizabeth stared in their direction. 'Hello, you must be new. I don't think I've seen you before,' she said in a friendly tone, walking towards Rosa.

'Your Royal Highness,' Rosa said in a muffled voice, her eyes still facing the floor.

Mrs Hargreaves shot a glance at Rosa, tilting her head upwards to indicate she could now rise. But Rosa remained bent over.

Rosa extended her hand out to Mrs Hargreaves. 'I . . . can't . . . stand,' she whimpered. 'I have a sharp pain down one side of my leg.'

Miss Vacani came to her aid. 'It looks like your knees have locked. Are you not able to straighten them?'

Close to tears, Rosa winced as she bit her lip. 'I'm trying, but I can't. It hurts. What am I going to do?'

'I have seen this before, it might just be cramp. We will carry you to a chair and see if that helps. You may be able to strengthen them after resting them for a few minutes.'

Molly piped up, 'How about if we bring a chair over to Rosa and she can try to stretch her leg from there? That will be easier, won't it?'

Looking flustered, Mrs Hargreaves agreed and, aided

by Molly, eased Rosa into the seat. Her legs were still extended and she complained of feeling pins and needles. She burned with humiliation that this should happen on her first meeting with the princesses. She avoided looking in their direction, imagining them laughing at her predicament.

'Perhaps we should offer her a drink,' suggested Princess Elizabeth. 'What is your name?'

'It's Rosa Edwards, Your Highness.'

'That's a pretty name. I do like your Welsh accent.'

'Oh, thank you, Your Highness, I mean, ma'am,' replied Rosa, beaming from ear to ear.

Princess Margaret and Alathea gathered round, their eyes showing concern.

Molly poured some lemonade into a glass and passed it to her friend. After Rosa had finished the drink, Miss Vacani kneeled down and felt Rosa's leg. 'It is very tight. Try breathing deeply to relax your muscles. This is what I advise my dancers if they get a sharp pain in their legs. I think you had a spasm caused by bending in a certain way and pinched a nerve. It looks like a simple case of cramp. Then stretch your legs out as far as you can.'

'Cramp? What do you mean, try to breathe deeply? How's that going to help?' she bleated.

'Miss Vacani is trying to help. Please do as she says,' Mrs Hargreaves urged.

The dance teacher raised her head, and, puffing out her chest, inhaled deeply until her chest expanded fully with air, then, after a pause, released it slowly while pressing her hand against her chest.

Rosa followed her breathing example and stretched out

her legs. After repeating this four times, to her surprise, she was able to feel her toes and the tingling sensation in her leg dissipated. A minute later she was able to place her foot on the floor and bent down to rub her shins. After a few seconds it felt better and she rose, easing her full weight on it.

'I'm so sorry, I don't know what came over me,' stuttered Rosa, wishing the ground could open and swallow her.

'We're just so pleased you're feeling better,' chirped Princess Margaret sweetly, her eyes twinkling.

'Yes, indeed we are. Are you sure your leg is better? Maybe you should rest it a little longer,' suggested Princess Elizabeth.

Rosa shook her leg to test its range of motion. Miss Vacani stepped forward. 'It looks much better now. Let me see you walk across the room, just to be sure.'

Rosa did as instructed, taking each step inch by inch, mortified that she had been the cause of a pause in the princesses' dance lesson.

Princess Elizabeth's eyes followed her every movement and showed concern. 'Yes, that looks much better,' she said, smiling and clasping her hands together. 'It's not the first time I've seen this.'

Rosa straightened herself and arched her back. 'Thank you miss— ma'am,' she said, flustered.

Margaret cupped her hand and whispered in her sister's ear, looking in Rosa's direction. Elizabeth beamed. 'Why yes, that's an excellent idea. Margaret was wondering if sometime you would like to see our little house that was gifted to us by the people of Wales.'

Margaret grinned. 'We have been given many presents – jewels and things like that – but that little house remains our favourite.'

Rosa could scarcely believe her ears. 'It would be an honour. I would very much like to see it.'

Mrs Hargreaves tilted her head towards the door, indicating to Rosa and Molly it was time to leave.

Outside the room Rosa's eyes shone. 'I can't believe I've not only seen the princesses, but they have invited me to see their little Welsh house.'

Mrs Hargreaves blurted, 'They do seem to have taken to you, Miss Edwards, but I have never witnessed anything of the sort in my life before. What an unseemly scene! Are you sure you're well enough to work? Do you have an incapacity we should be informed of?'

'I swear I'm fit. I don't know what happened. I can't explain it, other than my nerves getting the better of me and having cramp, which I swear I've never had before.'

Rosa gripped Molly's arm as they made their way back to the kitchen. 'I always seem to mess things up. Maybe I'm not cut out for this, Molly. Maybe I should pack my bag and go back to Merthyr before I make a fool of myself or upset anyone else.'

Molly stopped in her tracks. 'Where would we be if our soldiers gave in as easily as you? The Nazis would be flying their flag over this castle right now. So stop that stupid talk. And let's help give Princess Elizabeth the best birthday she can have. That will be something to talk about one day, when this is all over.'

All day Rosa could think of nothing else. She had the biggest smile and her chest swelled, overcome with immense pride as she recalled how she had been in the same room as the two princesses, unbeknown to the nation, who were informed only that they were evacuated somewhere in the country.

That evening, back in their room, Rosa asked Molly, 'I wonder what one buys a princess for her eighteenth birthday. War or no war, she must have everything she wants.'

'Rations or not, I don't imagine there's anything she needs. What would you like for your eighteenth, Rosa?'

'That's easy. I want my Dylan back home, or news that he is safe. My birthday is still a long way off, so there's plenty of time to make my wish come true.'

Rosa twisted her fingers in her lap as she sat perched on the side of her bed. 'I feel guilty being here sometimes, and not with Dylan's parents. They are the dearest people and are going through agony right now. But how can I leave without knowing what has happened to Alice? I can't abandon her.'

Molly sat alongside her friend and held her small hand in hers. 'When we are back in London, I could come to see Alice with you if you like. Remember, Alice knows where to reach you if she needs you. I can't believe her aunt wouldn't have told her. As for Dylan – as they say, no news is good news, so that's what we have to believe.'

Rosa rested her head against her friend's shoulder. 'You're such a good friend, Molly. I shall never forget it.'

The next two days were spent cleaning the King's dining room, making sure the silvery cutlery and porcelain shone in readiness for the princess's eighteenth birthday luncheon. Rosa was also taken to Princess Elizabeth's rooms in the Lancaster Tower, which she was expected to keep clean under the instructions of the princesses' Scottish governess, Miss Crawford, and Bobo, their devoted nanny. Molly's duties were to attend to Princess Margaret's room next door, working under the instruction of Allah, who had been their nursery nurse. Their duties were carried out while the princesses had lessons, but there was little for them to do, as both maids had strict instructions not to move anything and to dust around items.

Princess Elizabeth had private lessons with a distinguished tutor from nearby Eton College, Henry Marten, with an emphasis on constitutional history. At the same time Margaret was taught by Miss Crawford.

Rosa had only seen Elizabeth once since her embarrassing curtsey. She had arrived early for her duties the next day, and the princess was talking outside her door with her sister.

'I hope your knee is better?' she asked Rosa, radiating a charming smile.

Rosa bent her knee to bob a curtsey, but the princess raised her hand. 'Please, there's no need. I wouldn't want you to get stuck again.'

Rosa chuckled. 'No, ma'am. Neither would I.'

'I haven't forgotten about showing you our Welsh house. You know we used to clean it ourselves, wash its little gingham curtains and shake the mats. The kitchen has everything you would expect to find in a real kitchen and Margaret and I have baked there. It is just divine.'

'It sounds the most perfect present. I'm pleased it has given you so much enjoyment.'

'As soon as my birthday is over, I will show it to you. I have classes to go to now.'

'Good day, ma'am.'

Rosa pinched herself; the friendliness of the princess made her all the more determined to work hard and not give cause for complaint.

Mrs Hargreaves checked their work was to the highest standards, holding up a crystal glass to the light to check for smears, and told Rosa her work had passed inspection.

Elizabeth's forthcoming birthday was announced in the newspapers, when it was reported she would spend her special day, Friday 21 April, quietly with her family in the country with a celebratory luncheon together.

Rosa simmered with eager anticipation, having been told she would serve coffee after the royal family had finished eating, and other staff would also serve them on that occasion.

When the special day arrived, there was much excitement in the castle. Two years before, on her sixteenth birthday, Princess Elizabeth had had a unique honour bestowed on her when she was made honorary colonel of the Grenadier Guards, the regiment in which Jerry and the other palace guards served at Buckingham Palace, fulfilling their duty to protect the monarchy. Now the princess was to inspect the Guards as part of her birthday celebrations.

'Ooh, I'd give anything to see that,' Rosa commented to Molly, elbow-deep in soap suds after the breakfasts were cleared away.

'Why don't we? We could make out we need to go to the bathroom and take a quick peek from one of the windows. We'll be back before anyone knows.'

'What if we get caught sloping off?' asked Rosa nervously.

'We'll be careful, trust me,' Molly assured.

The plan excited Rosa and the two friends seized their moment after wiping down the kitchen and excusing themselves to Cook, who nodded her consent, while carrying on a conversation with the housekeeper.

Molly grabbed Rosa's hands and they sprinted along a passageway and up some stairs, straining their ears for sounds of activity outside that became louder. They squeezed together on a narrow stone window ledge on the first floor, giving them a spectacular bird's-eye view across the Horseshoe Cloisters set within the castle walls, leading to St George's Chapel.

The guards marched briskly, their rifles pressed against their left shoulders, their hands firmly gripping the butts and their arms in a smart 'L' shape, then stomping their feet together and standing to attention. The next moment Princess Elizabeth walked past them with a slow and purposeful step, wearing a smart dark coat that skimmed her knees and a hat that pressed on her curled hair, while the eyes of the Grenadier Guards were fixed straight ahead. Her father walked alongside her wearing his military uniform and medals, and the Queen followed a few steps behind resplendent in an elegant pale grey suit, cream blouse and fur stole, a row of pearls around her neck. A small group of distinguished-looking guests followed and made approving sounds.

After the inspection had finished, one of the guards stepped forward and presented the princess with a flag representing the Colours of the King's Battalion.

Molly nudged Rosa. 'There's your answer. You wanted to know what you give a princess for her birthday? No one else in the land will receive such a precious gift for their eighteenth.'

They were jolted by a woman's sharp voice. 'What is the meaning of this? Why aren't you in the kitchen helping with the luncheon?'

Rosa leaped up. 'I'm sorry, Mrs Hargreaves. We only meant to be here for a second to see the princess.'

'It was my idea. I'll take all the blame,' Molly bleated.

The two girls exchanged anxious glances.

Mrs Hargreaves inhaled deeply. 'Well, on this occasion I shall let it pass. The kitchen is in desperate need of extra pairs of hands so please go there straight away.'

'Yes, Mrs Hargreaves,' they replied in unison.

They scooted to the kitchen sheepishly, keeping their heads down, where, despite Mrs Hargreaves's comment, everything was in order. Some of the staff gave them a sideways glance and muttered words they couldn't hear, but Rosa and Molly ignored them.

Rosa checked everything she needed for coffee was laid out on her trolley, having already laid out the china and the silver coffee pot on a table at the side of the dining room for the special occasion. Rosa and Molly's instructions were to wait in attendance until coffee was required, and to observe the way in which the senior waiting staff conducted themselves. They were informed the luncheon guests would include Elizabeth's grandmother, the Dowager Queen Mary, her two royal uncles, the Duke of Gloucester and the Duke of Kent, accompanied by their wives, and the Earl of Harewood, who was married to the princesses' aunt, Princess Mary.

Although the royal family used their wartime rations like everyone else, and restricted their water use to five inches in the bath, they insisted their food was of the finest quality. The King did not care for cold food at luncheon, and the birthday meal was to start with a fluffy cheese soufflé, followed by poached sole with vegetables, and steamed marmalade pudding and cream.

Rosa observed this intimate family celebration feeling greatly privileged. It was impossible not to overhear the exquisite gifts that Elizabeth had been given: a tiara from her parents, and more precious jewels and a fur coat from her relatives.

When the princess thought she had received all her presents, the Earl of Harewood excused himself and returned to the room carrying a small dog.

'We thought you would enjoy having your own,' he smiled.

Elizabeth leaped from her seat, her eyes bright and her smile stretching across her face. She took the corgi in her arms and hugged it. 'For me? Thank you so much. Look, Mama, isn't she sweet?'

'She is indeed,' the Earl confirmed, receiving an approving nod from the Queen.

'It's my best present ever. I can't wait to play with her.'

A moment later a trolley arrived carrying a white iced birthday cake topped with eighteen candles, along with champagne, which the royal household had managed to continue sourcing during wartime. A small cheer broke out and all eyes turned to Elizabeth as the cake was placed in front of her and the candles were lit.

A chorus of 'Happy Birthday' filled the room and Rosa couldn't help but join in under her breath and clap as Elizabeth rose and blew out all the candles. She glanced towards the head waiter for a sign for her to serve coffee, but the jollity and chatter continued as the champagne flowed.

A moment later Mrs Hargreaves stepped into the room. Rosa thought nothing of it, assuming she wanted to check all was in order. Rosa stood erect, her hands by her side, staring straight ahead. To her surprise, the deputy housekeeper approached her and whispered, 'Miss Edwards, will you please come with me. I need to speak to you on an urgent matter.'

Rosa screwed her eyes. What could be so urgent that she was being asked to leave now?

A thought occurred that panicked her – did this mean there was bad news about Dylan? Her face turned ashen and she shot an anxious glance in Molly's direction. Molly came over to her.

Mrs Hargreaves said, 'Molly, I'm afraid you will have to serve coffee by yourself. I need to speak to Miss Edwards on her own.'

Molly nodded. 'Of course, Mrs Hargreaves.'

Rosa followed the deputy housekeeper out of the room. 'Let's go into my office where we can have some privacy,' she said, leading the way.

Each step that Rosa took felt like her short legs were lifting a leaden weight and her mind ran riot. Her stomach twisted in knots and her mouth dried as she feared hearing the news she had dreaded.

Her heart was pumping fast and loud as they reached Mrs Hargreaves's office. Her head had been in such a spin that she didn't notice a woman standing inside.

Miss Rogers stepped forward, and the shock of seeing her made Rosa's knees give way.

'Miss Rogers? What are you doing here?'

'Take a seat, Rosa. I'm afraid what I have to say isn't very pleasant.'

Rosa gripped her hands in front of her chest. 'It isn't—?'

'No, it isn't anything of that nature, if you were anticipating bad news relating to your family or Dylan.'

Rosa shook her head, staring at Miss Rogers's face, and then Mrs Hargreaves. The tone of their voices made it clear that it was a serious matter.

'I don't understand. What is it then?'

Miss Rogers took a deep breath. 'There's no easy way to say this. After you left the palace some information came to light questioning your honesty.'

Rosa's body tensed, her eyes filled with confusion. *'Questioning my honesty?* What do you mean?'

'A witness claims to have seen you take silver cutlery from the kitchen after it had been cleaned and hide it in your room. It was discovered hidden in one of your drawers under some garments.'

'It's not true. It's a lie. Whoever this person is, they've made a terrible mistake. I've never taken a thing in my life, I swear to God, I swear on the name of the King and Queen.'

'Please don't bring our King and Queen's names into this. It's not respectful,' Mrs Hargreaves reprimanded her.

'But I'm innocent,' she cried, reeling from the shock of the accusation. Tears sprung to her eyes and her chest racked with sobs. 'Why do people take against me? Why is it happening again? Is it because I'm a poor pit-miner's daughter and people don't think I'm good enough?'

Her blood ran cold as she recalled when Hettie had tried to turn Dylan's family against her, then Agnes had given her the cold shoulder and tried to blame her for something she hadn't done.

'Who could have said such a thing against me?'

The palace housekeeper bit her lip. 'We can't state the source of our information, but the palace police are investigating. Other pieces have gone missing too, some small porcelain pieces and a silver milk jug and sugar bowl.'

Rosa cried, 'You surely don't think I have them. I swear I know nothing of it. How can I make you believe me?'

Miss Rogers spoke softly. 'You will have a chance to give your side. The police will be in touch.'

The maid rose, fell into the housekeeper's arms and sobbed, her body shaking. Tears cascaded down her cheeks until there were none left. Miss Rogers handed her a handkerchief and Rosa dabbed her face.

She sniffled, 'What happens now? Am I being given my cards, even though I'm innocent?'

'We think you should go home, back to Wales, while the investigation continues.

'I promise we will get to the truth. I have managed to secure a railway warrant for your return journey home and you will be given your wages up until the end of the week. If you gather your belongings, you should be able to catch the next train that will get you home by the end of the day. Your remaining belongings at the palace will be put aside for safekeeping.'

Rosa's mouth opened wide. 'So soon? I'm being treated like a criminal when I'm innocent. What will I tell Molly? How do I explain this to my family?'

'I'm sorry, Miss Edwards. For security reasons, there's no other way. You can't return to the palace until the investigation is completed. When you are exonerated, which I'm sure you will be, we will let you know and your job will be here for you.'

Mrs Hargreaves intervened. 'For what it's worth, Miss Edwards, I believe in your innocence. I can always sniff out a light-fingered member of staff, and we have had one or two in our time who were marched off the premises.'

'How long will the investigation take? I don't want this lie hanging over my head.'

Miss Rogers replied, 'We can't say. It's in the police's hands now at the palace.'

Rosa's shoulders shook. 'I see. I'd better get my stuff together then. I'd like to write a note for Molly with my address. I don't suppose I'll have a moment to speak to her before I leave.'

'I'm afraid not, she is on duty, as you are aware,' said Miss Rogers.

Rosa bit her lip and fought back her tears. She couldn't bear it if Molly thought the worse of her.

'I guess I have to go then. I can't believe it should happen today, of all days. I've never felt so happy as when

I was singing Happy Birthday to the princess. I should hate her to think I'm a thief.'

'I'll wait here for you while you get your bag and we can walk to the station together. I'm afraid I shall have to ask you for your staff pass too.'

Rosa obliged, feeling as if her life at the palace was at an end for good.

'Oh, there's one other thing before I forget. You have two letters.'

Miss Rogers produced them from her bag and handed them over. Rosa's face brightened for a moment. She recognised the writing on one of the envelopes as her mother's. Her heart skipped a beat when she instantly recognised Alice's handwriting on the second letter. Her relief was tinged with disappointment at seeing no letter from Dylan. Was no news still good news?

As she retreated to her room, she eagerly ripped open Alice's letter:

Dearest Rosa,

I hope this letter reaches you. I wanted to let you know I received yours and to thank you for being such a true friend. You must be thinking what a terrible friend I am, having not spent a minute with you since you arrived in London. Congratulations on landing yourself such a prestigious job with the royal family. You always did stand out with your cheery smile and rosy cheeks, your calm ways and natural ease with people. I often envied you, even though you lacked confidence in yourself. Well, I'm telling you now, Rosa, you are one in a million and I hope they can see that at the palace. Dylan has seen it and . . .

Tears trickled down Rosa's cheeks. Alice had never spoken of her this way before. A lump formed in her throat as she imagined what her friend would think of her now.

She gulped and read on.

. . . Dylan has seen it and he is a very lucky man. I feel your anguish in waiting for news from him. He has a sensible head on his shoulders, Rosa, and I will be keeping everything crossed for you that you hear from him very soon.

You must be wondering what's happened to me. I have got myself into a spot of trouble and Mam and my aunt Ruby are trying to sort it out. I would tell you about it if I could, but I promised I wouldn't tell a soul. I'm afraid there's nothing you can do for me right now, but when this trouble is sorted, well, let's wait and see what happens. I'm afraid I can't make any plans for the future right now, but I promise I will let you know when I can see you. It's not for not wanting, my dear Rosa. I miss you so very much. I never imagined I would say this, but I even miss Merthyr. I thank you for not forgetting me.

With love from your true friend,
Alice x

Rosa placed the letter in her lap and a shiver ran down her spine. It confirmed her friend was in terrible trouble and she was unsure what she could do, now she was returning to Merthyr.

She fingered her second letter. Her mother always wrote short letters, no longer than one sheet, and when she opened it, she noted it was dated one week ago:

The news came as a surprise, but not a shock. Rosa had guessed it would only be a matter time before Billy ran off for good.

She scribbled a quick note for Molly with her home address, saying she was in a spot of trouble and had to leave immediately until things were sorted. She promised to write again later.

Feeling humiliated and distraught, she dabbed her cheeks. Never in a million years did she imagine that she would be returning to Merthyr just a month after leaving – in disgrace and under police investigation.

Rosa was relieved to part company with Miss Rogers in London as they went their separate ways. She had been unable to speak as the seriousness of her position sank in. She bit on her nails as her train rumbled towards Wales, her face etched with anxiety.

It was ten o'clock when the train arrived in Merthyr. She stepped onto the platform with a heavy heart, looking around, relieved not to see anyone she recognised. She knew her way home in the pitch darkness like the back of her hand, and walked with her head down. As she placed her key in the latch, a cover-up plan came to mind for her sudden appearance: she would say she was homesick and that city life wasn't for her. The blackout curtains were drawn tight, so she had no idea if her mother was still up.

She took a deep breath and climbed the stairs, feeling anxious at what her mother's reaction would be when she saw her. She tapped lightly on the door and turned the handle slowly, hearing a male voice inside the room. Her mother flung open the door and swiftly stepped back, her jaw dropping in astonishment.

'Bloody hell. What have we got here?' she exclaimed.

'Hello, Mam. I've come back home.'

'I can see that. I'm not blind, but I thought you liked it there?'

'I do, but I was homesick and missed everyone.'

'Like hell you were. You'd better come inside then.'

Rosa stepped into the room, put down her bag and hugged Eira, her heart pounding. 'It was good to hear from you, Mam. I'm sorry to hear about Billy. I suppose it was going to happen one day, him running off like that. He wants to be a man so quickly.'

'From what I hear, he got himself into trouble when he was out with his da one night and that's the reason he joined up. He lied about his age and the navy took him on with his mate, no questions asked. God knows when we'll see him again.'

Rosa bit her lip to avoid her mother's inquisitive gaze. Eira asked, 'Is there any news of Dylan? I saw Huw the other day – he said they were on edge waiting for the post each day.'

Rosa shook her head. 'I've heard nothing for weeks, Mam. Huw and Jane must be worried sick. Everyone says it's to be expected in wartime, that it can be months, even.'

A coughing sound made her spin around. A nervous-looking boy, a year or so older than her, rose from his seat. Rosa stared at him and then turned to face her mother.

'I'm sorry, Mam. I didn't know you had company.'

She glanced again towards the stranger. He had a mop of blonde curls which he swept away from his face. He was casually dressed, but the dirty pile of clothing in the corner of the room were the kind worn by miners.

He noticed her staring at them. 'Please excuse the mess – they're mine. You're Rosa, then, Mrs Edwards's daughter? I've heard all about you. My name is George Potter. I'm what you call a Bevin boy.'

'I see,' replied Rosa, taken aback at an unexpected stranger in her home.

'I signed up to fight for my country, but my name was picked to work in the pits. I wanted to be a soldier, but here I am instead.'

'George is staying in Billy's room,' her mother added. 'I saw no sense in keeping it empty and George was desperate for somewhere to stay. The extra money will come in handy, which is more than I had from Billy.'

'I had no idea you'd taken a lodger, Mam. You didn't mention it in your letter.'

'What business is it of yours? Seeing as you're here, you can wash his dirties.'

'I don't mean to cause any trouble,' said George in a timid voice.

'You're not trouble, George. It's my own family that give me a headache. One of them runs off while the other, who had run off, comes back out of the blue without a word, which makes me suspicious.'

'Of course I'll wash them out, Mam,' Rosa said. 'First thing in the morning. It's no trouble at all.'

Turning to George, she asked, 'What's it like being a Bevin boy, then? It started the end of last year, didn't it?'

George nodded, his eyes clouding with sadness. 'If you want to know the truth, I hate it, working in pitch darkness from seven o'clock until four o'clock. I can't stand being in the darkness all day, it could be night-time for all I know. The worst part is the drop down from the surface to the coalface in the lift, eight hundred yards down. I'd swap places any day with a soldier on the front and do what I signed up for.'

'It must be a shock for those who aren't used to it. How long have you been here?'

'Three days, and it gets worse each day, not better.' George slumped in a chair and buried his head in his hands. 'I can't face going back tomorrow. I don't know how I'll be able to stick it. I tell you, the miners deserve every penny they earn – and more – if you ask me.'

Rosa shot an anxious glance at her mother. 'Da would agree with that, he used to be a miner. We need more coal than ever now for manufacturing. You are doing a really important job, George, it's still early days for you, it takes time to get used to it.'

George wiped his eyes with the back of his hand. 'You're right. I'm being stupid.'

Eira led her daughter out of George's earshot. 'He's been like it ever since he arrived. I don't know what to do with him.'

'I can't help but think if this was our Billy pouring his heart out somewhere, if he is scared, wouldn't we want someone to show him kindness and compassion?'

Eira stroked her daughter's cheek. 'You've a soft heart, Rosa Edwards. Maybe some of it will rub off on me.' In a rare moment of affection, Eira extended her arms and wrapped them around Rosa. 'You can stay as long as you like, but you have to work and give me half your wages. I'm sure Dylan's parents will have you back.'

'Thank you, Mam, I hope so.'

'And I shall want you to help around the house and see to George's laundry and meals, if I'm not around.'

'It's a deal, Mam. It's good to be back,' Rosa said, choked with relief.

'You'd better take your bag upstairs.'

That night, as Rosa placed Dylan's photograph on her bedside table and rested her head on her pillow, she stifled a sob, thinking of the black cloud hanging over her and how she could keep up the pretence.

The following morning Rosa kept her word and washed out the coal soot from George's work clothes and hung them out to dry. He had left the house by the time she awoke and made her way downstairs. Her mother offered her some toast on the table with a jar of marmalade and a fresh brew.

'So what are your plans for today, Rosa?'

'I'm going to see Mr and Mrs Williams to ask if I can have my old job back. They always said I could return any time, but I doubt they were expecting me so soon, and my sudden appearance will come as a shock to them too. I'm not sure how Hettie will take it either.'

'If that doesn't work out you can return to the Valleys Hotel, or try a munitions factory. With your experience at the palace and a reference from them, you shouldn't find it a problem to get another job waitressing.'

Rosa felt her cheeks burn when her mother mentioned a reference from the palace. She bluffed, 'Yes, I'm sure you're right.'

Keen to change the subject, she asked, 'How are things with Charlie, Mam?'

'Charlie had the pleasure of seeing your da the other night,' Eira drooled, lighting a cigarette.

'Oh no. Was Da—?'

'Drunk? He was,' Eira confirmed. 'Wanting to pick

a fight for no reason. Anyway, thankfully yer da's mate, Bert, pulled him away and no harm was done.'

As Rosa picked up her coat to leave, her mother asked casually, 'Is there any news of that girl Alice who went to London. Did you see her? Someone asked me about her the other day and mentioned her father is unwell.'

Rosa paused, then said, 'Oh? I didn't know that. We haven't had a chance to see each other in London yet, but I did get a letter from her the same time as yours. I shall try to arrange something.'

She left the house before her mother could ask more uncomfortable questions. As Rosa walked to the Williamses' shop, she paused in front of a harrowing poster displayed on a wall showing an injured soldier. She turned the corner and saw the same poster glued to a lamppost. Every turn she took she saw the same injured soldier's face staring straight back at her. She felt a wave of pride rising within her: this was the poster she had designed for Mr Fry's exhibition. She read it was due to finish in a few days and made a mental note to see it. Hettie did a great job putting up all these posters around town, she marvelled.

Further down the street a government poster warned *DON'T WASTE COAL. It takes 50,000 tons of coal to make the bombs alone! Coke – Gas – Electricity – Water. ALL MEAN COAL.*

She knew that these powerful words would make her father pleased – that at long last the value of coal was being recognised, and the urgent need for men like him, or the Bevin boys, to shovel tons of this black gold each day.

She continued, and stopped for a moment outside Goodwin & Co, wondering if the sales job was still available. But there were no signs in the window for job vacancies, and for a moment she regretted not pursuing that opportunity.

She planned to arrive at the print shop when it was due to open to have a quiet word with Dylan's parents. She saw the light was on and the door bell jangled as she let herself in. Mrs Williams came through from the back room. Her face was pale and her eyes wet.

'Rosa! We had no idea you were back,' she warbled.

'What is it?' Rosa exclaimed. 'Has something happened to Dylan?'

Jane's voice shook and she stumbled over her words. 'A telegram arrived yesterday. It says . . . Dylan is *missing in action.*'

'Missing?' cried Rosa, her hands flying to her face.

'We don't know any more. We were dreading something like this,' said Jane, the words sticking in her throat.

Rosa reeled as the news she had feared sunk in. 'I'm glad to be back here now,' she said in a quiet voice.

'It's a comfort to have you here, Rosa. How long are you staying for?'

'I can't say. As long as you want me, I guess, if you'll have me back here?'

'But won't you be needed back at the palace?'

Rosa turned her head away and bit her lip. 'The truth is, I can't say for sure. I was feeling homesick.' Rosa shuffled from one foot to the other and twisted her hands in front of her.

After a pause, Mrs Williams replied, 'Well, that's all the better for us.'

Rosa flung her arms around Dylan's mother and hugged her. When she pulled away she said, 'I have Dylan's photo by my bed and speak to him every night. I shall keep hoping and praying that he is alive somewhere. "Missing in action" doesn't mean he's dead. He could be a prisoner, or in hospital, he could still be alive, couldn't he, Mrs Williams?'

Mrs Williams rested her hand on Rosa's arm and spoke warmly. 'You can call me Jane when we are on our own, Rosa. There's no need for such formality between us. And the same goes for Huw – he is happy for you to use his first name.'

The welcome was more than she could have hoped for – or felt she deserved – and she felt grateful for Jane's lack of intrusiveness. She was determined to clear her name first before disclosing the true reason for her return.

As Rosa was hanging up her coat she heard the bell jangle on the front door. Hettie came in and stared at her in disbelief.

'Well, well, well. I didn't expect to see you back so quickly. City life wasn't for you, then?'

Jane stepped forward holding the telegram and dabbing her eyes. 'Hettie, we've had some bad news. It's Dylan . . .'

Hettie's cheeks turned scarlet, 'Oh no, he's not . . . ?'

'He's missing in action, Hettie. We don't know how or where.'

Hettie softened her tone. 'I'm so sorry, I had no idea.'

'Hello, Hettie,' Rosa said. 'I'm not looking for any trouble. I hope we can rub along and be friends.'

Before she could answer, the doorbell jangled again and a soldier entered the shop. He wore military uniform and stood next to Hettie. Her face lit up and she took hold of his hand.

'Hubert, darling. I'm pleased you could come. I'm afraid Mr and Mrs Williams have had bad news about Dylan. He's missing in action.'

Hubert frowned and bowed his head slightly. 'I'm so very sorry, Mrs Williams. It must be a very anxious time.'

Mrs Williams's eyebrows arched. 'Thank you for your kind words. Have we met?'

Hettie smiled. 'I would like to introduce Hubert, Captain Hubert Fry. He's the nephew of Mr Fry who organised the art exhibition. Hubert is one of the artists. Every one of his paintings has been sold and the money will go to support the war fund.'

The captain raised a hand. 'Thank you for the kind introduction, Hettie. I can't take all the praise as virtually all the paintings by other soldiers have sold well too. The exhibition has been an astounding success. People have queued round the corner to come and see it. I wanted to let you know in person.'

'I'm pleased to hear it is so well attended,' Jane said.

Hettie extended her arm. 'And this is Rosa Edwards, who worked here for a while before leaving for the bright lights of London.'

'I'm back now,' said Rosa, extending a hand. 'I should like to see the exhibition before it closes later this week. Will your paintings still be on show?'

The captain beamed. 'Yes, indeed they will, along with

the others. None of the paintings will be removed until the exhibition closes. I would be delighted if you could all come as my guests on Saturday evening when we'll be having drinks to mark the end of the exhibition.'

'Thank you for your invitation, Captain Fry,' Jane said. 'I'll mention it to Huw, but I'm not sure if we will feel like socialising.'

His eyes softened. 'If I may suggest, coming out for the evening may offer some solace for you, as people there will want to support you.'

'I hadn't thought of it that way,' Jane concurred.

'You're very welcome to bring a friend with you, Miss Edwards, if there is anyone else in your family who would like to see it,' the captain enthused. 'The artwork was very eye-catching and we have your posters to thank for drawing in such great crowds.'

Mrs Williams turned to Rosa. 'Yes, all credit for that must go to Rosa – and Hettie too, of course, for placing them in so many prominent positions in town.'

'I'm indebted to you both. I shall be making an announcement at the reception and will thank you publicly for your posters. I leave the following day for an overseas posting.'

Rosa hesitated. 'A reception? I'm not sure that's my kind of thing, though I'd love to see the paintings.'

'People will want to see who was behind the poster – it would be an honour if you could attend.'

Mrs Williams nodded her head.

'Well, if you put it that way,' stuttered Rosa, 'I should love to. I'll ask my mother if she can join me.'

'That's settled then. I'd better be off. I shall be thinking of you and hoping you hear good news about Dylan very soon,' said the captain, tilting his head slightly. Hettie followed him outside the door. She placed her hand on his arm as they chatted and shared a farewell embrace. She returned to the shop with a radiant glow.

'I didn't know you were so close to an Army captain?' quizzed Mrs Williams.

'It happened very suddenly after we met on the opening night of the exhibition,' Hettie replied, half in a daze. 'We have a lot in common with our shared love of the arts and have been seeing each other as often as we could while he was here training new recruits.'

'He seems very nice. I'm happy for you, Hettie,' Rosa commented.

'Thank you, Rosa. In fact, your return here is timely. There is something I need to tell you all.'

'What do you mean?' Mrs Williams probed.

'Hubert is going to announce it on Saturday, but I may as well tell you now, especially as Rosa is here.'

Rosa and Dylan's mother exchanged puzzled glances.

'It's to do with the success of the exhibition. There's demand for it to be shown in prestigious galleries around the country. Hubert says what they showed here is just a fraction of the artwork soldiers have done. Mr Fry plans to take it to Cardiff next, and then London, and then other cities around the country. Isn't it exciting!'

'It's very exciting. But what does it have to do with us? With Rosa?' asked Mrs Williams.

'Because they want me to curate it. I shall be setting it up with Hubert's uncle and travelling around the art galleries with them.'

'You mean to say you're leaving us?' exclaimed Mrs Williams.

'That's exactly what I mean. Now Rosa is back, I can leave with a clear conscience.'

Mrs Williams slumped into a chair. 'Well, I'm sure I'm pleased for you, but it's still very unsettling.'

Rosa stepped forward. 'I'm happy for you, Hettie. You'll do a fine job and Hubert seems very fond of you. I'm pleased to see you so happy together. I'll be here, so you need have no worries on that score.'

'I am very fortunate to have met Hubert. He comes from a very well-connected family and he's my ticket out of Merthyr. I suppose I have you to thank, Rosa, for opening my eyes to what I was missing. I told myself if you and Alice could leave Merthyr, then I could too. You made me question why I should want to stay here. Thanks to the success of the art exhibition, I have it all now at the tips of my fingers.'

'So are your feelings for Hubert real?' asked Rosa, her eyes widening. 'You're not just using him to leave Merthyr, are you?'

'You can see it that way if you like. His uncle needs to promote their exhibitions, he says I have flair and an eye for detail. Besides, even though Hubert is a good catch, there's no point getting too attached to a serviceman these days – anything could happen to him.'

Mrs Williams gasped. She rose and confronted the hard-hearted girl in front of her. 'How could you speak such cruel words when Dylan is missing and we agonise over him every day. I would like you to leave this minute!'

'With pleasure!' Hettie raised her chin, turned on her

heel and stomped out of the shop, sending Mr Williams, who was about to come in, hurtling to the ground.

'Hettie, what's going on?' he cried as he watched her march down the street. He got himself up as his wife rushed to his aid. 'Where's Hettie off to in such a state? She sent me flying.'

'Come inside, Huw, we don't want people seeing you like this. Forget Hettie, I have a surprise waiting for you.'

Rosa's voice choked and her eyes watered. 'Hello, Mr Williams. I'm back. I didn't realise how much I missed you all until now.'

A tear fell down Mr Williams's cheek. He dabbed it with a handkerchief from his pocket and said, 'My God, what a blessing this is. I only wish our Dylan was here too.'

Rosa saw his chest judder, fighting back tears. Jane's chin wobbled and she bit her lip, turning her head away to hide her tears.

Mr Williams composed himself. 'I'm going to do something I've never done before during opening hours. I'm going to put the *Closed* sign up on the door and then I want to hear all about your time in London. Jane, my dear, will you put the kettle on?'

After many tears and copious mugs of tea, a calm atmosphere was restored by the end of the day and Mr and Mrs Williams thanked Rosa for her surprise return and staying on.

'I believe fate has had a hand in this. It was meant to be, now Hettie has left,' Rosa commented.

'Maybe you're right. Her mind seemed set on going off with the art exhibition. She was good at her work, but I didn't always like her ways. She could be very bossy, couldn't she, Huw?' said Jane.

'That's true. Bryn nearly lost his rag with her a couple of times, thinking she knew better than him. Now she's left of her own accord, and there is no ill feeling on either side, I hope that's the end of her parents threatening to stir things up with the local authority,' Mr Williams said.

'Do you think Mr Fry will want us to make his new posters when the exhibition goes on tour?' his wife asked.

'Maybe you'll have a chance to ask him on Saturday, at the final viewing,' Rosa suggested.

As Rosa slipped into her coat ready to leave, she said, 'There is something I forgot to tell you. Mam has a lodger, in Billy's room. He's one of them Bevin boys and he's like a scared rabbit. I feel so sorry for him. It's not his way of life, he hasn't been brought up with it, but he has no choice.'

'Poor lad. We have a shortage of miners, but who would

have thought young men would be forced to do it when they signed up to fight in the army?' Mr Williams said.

'He's so young, and so homesick. I don't know how he'll manage.'

'Don't worry about him, Rosa. The war makes men of young boys. They have to grow up fast with the things they see and do.'

'It also breaks them, and breaks their mothers' hearts,' his wife said ruefully. 'Just look at the poster if you need reminding of that.'

She walked Rosa to the door and embraced her. 'You're like a daughter to us now, Rosa. We'll see you tomorrow then?'

'You will, and the day after,' Rosa replied, putting on a brave face for Dylan's parents.

When she reached home she was glad to see her mother was alone so she could break the news to her about Dylan.

'You poor girl, what dreadful news. I did wonder if something had happened to him, after not hearing for so long.'

'I'm trying to be strong for them, especially Dylan's mam. By the way, are you free on Saturday evening? I've been invited to join them at the final viewing of the *Soldiers at War* art exhibition at the Town Hall, and can take a guest for the reception afterwards.'

'Get you! Who's gone up in the world all of a sudden? After a few weeks working with the royal family you come home and get invited to socialise with Merthyr's high and mighty.'

'It's nothing like that, Mam. It's because I designed the poster to promote the exhibition, and they really liked it and are going to mention me at the reception.'

'Well done you – what a surprise you've turned out to be. I'm afraid I can't go, though. I'm out with Charlie and we'll be dancing the night away to the Chesney Five Fox-trot Band.'

'I have to admit that sounds more your cup of tea. Who else can I take, then?'

At that moment the living room door opened and George came in, a pained expression on his face and his back bent. He forced a smile when Rosa and her mother both stared at him and exchanged a glance.

Eira tilted her head towards him. 'Why not take the Bevin boy along?'

George narrowed his eyes. 'Take me where? What are you talking about?'

Rosa shot her mother a warning glance, but Eira persisted and told him about the exhibition and Dylan being missing.

He shook his head. 'I don't know. What will people say, seeing Dylan's girl out with another fella, just when he's been declared missing.'

'George is right. I don't think it would be a good idea. It might upset Dylan's parents.'

'Why don't you ask them?' Eira suggested.

'If it makes you happy, I'll think about it.'

'That's settled then. There's sausage casserole and dumplings left from last night on the stove. Help your-self. I'm going upstairs to dry my hair and will leave you to it.'

When Eira had left the room, George said, 'I'm sorry to hear about Dylan. It must be very worrying for you and his family.'

'It really is. I don't suppose he would have wanted to

swap places with you, though. How are you getting on down the pits?'

'I hate it. I can't say it gets better. I heard that one of the other Bevin lads appealed against being posted here, but it was rejected outright as he has no medical problems.'

'I'm sorry, George, I really am. Da found it tough after a while – with his health, I mean. He didn't mind the work, and neither did his father before him. Not only did his health suffer, but the pay and hours changed so much and he was quite vocal about it, which didn't go down well. He'll have some tales to tell you if you meet him.'

Rosa poured fresh water in the kettle and placed it on the stove, measuring out a scoop of tea leaves for the brew.

'I'd like to meet him. I'd like to know how he coped with the "big drop", when the cage gates shut and the lift shoots down to the bottom in total darkness. It feels like my stomach is coming out of my mouth and I'm shaking all over.'

'Da used to say that's how he felt at first, that you were down in a couple of seconds. He started down the pits at the age of twelve and had to crawl on his knees, as the tunnel was only two feet deep. His knees were often blistered and sore, but it was the cold coal dust on his lungs that got him in the end.'

'Well, thanks very much for cheering me up, Rosa.' George said, rubbing the back of his neck.

'I'm sorry, I didn't mean to panic you.'

Later, after they had eaten and were washing up, Rosa told her mother, 'It seems strange seeing another boy sitting at Billy's place. I can't help but worry about him.'

Her mother lit up a cigarette. 'I know I come over hard

as nails, but I'd rather have Billy here any day than a stranger sitting at his place at the table and sleeping in his bed, despite all the headaches he causes me.'

'I know, Mam. Billy likes to think he is grown up, but he's only a lad still, he's only fifteen. How could anyone have believed he was eighteen?'

'Because he wanted them to, Rosa.'

After a pause, Eira's face softened. Her voice hoarse, she said, 'At least I have my daughter back. It's good to have you home, Rosa.'

Jane and Huw Williams welcomed Rosa's suggestion to invite George to the exhibition and reception in three days' time.

'Of course we don't mind, why should we?' Mrs Williams said.

'I didn't want people to put two and two together and come up with five, or fifty-five.'

'Everyone in Merthyr knows about the Bevin boys, and, from what you say, he is having a tough time. I like to think there might be a family somewhere who has taken our Dylan under their wing.'

The night before the show, Rosa fretted about what she would wear. Her best two frocks were in London still, and she explained this to her mother by saying she had lent them to Molly.

Her mother's eyes narrowed. 'That seems a bit rash, seeing as you spent a fortune on them. And you looked a picture in the blue polka-dot dress. I'll see what I have that will suit you.'

Eira rummaged through her wardrobe and held out a

black dress with a sweetheart neckline that she teamed with a string of pearls, and a green frock with yellow flowers and a full skirt, worn with a yellow cardigan. Her mother was two inches taller with a rounded figure and complained they were too tight. Rosa tried them both on. She was unsure about the black dress as she felt it was too formal, but she instantly fell in love with the green and yellow one. She swirled in front of the mirror and turned her head in all directions, admiring her reflection.

'That's the one for you. It has your name written on it,' her mother approved. 'You can keep the black dress too as it's just been sitting at the back of my wardrobe. It might come in useful one day.'

'Thank you, Mam. I wish Dylan could see me in this, it's just perfect. I feel like Cinderella, all dressed up and ready to go to the ball.'

Rosa and George met Dylan's parents on the steps of the Town Hall, a red-brick, towering building in the High Street, at five o'clock. Rosa had walked past the building many times, but never been inside before, and she glanced up at the clock tower as it struck the hour.

Two days before, a contrite Hettie had popped into the shop to confirm the time and Mrs Williams pressed her about future work.

'There's no reason why Mr Fry shouldn't want to continue using you to make posters for the exhibition; we could work something out with deliveries,' she pronounced.

'That's very good to hear,' Mr Williams said, relieved to be parting on good terms.

Rosa introduced her nervous companion to Dylan's

parents. Mrs Williams took his hands in hers and spoke warmly. 'You're doing a tough job, George. Everyone here knows that. You will look back on this one day and feel proud of what you've done.'

'It wasn't my first choice, I must admit, Mrs Williams.'

Mr Williams led the way into the vast municipal building. Long tables stretched across the back of the entrance hall, and waiters and waitresses filled small glasses with wine. Tea was also available, and hot water bubbled away in an urn on a separate table with biscuits.

Rosa hung her coat up and smoothed the folds of her dress. 'Why, you are looking lovely in that dress. I don't think I've seen it before,' Mrs Williams said.

Rosa pushed some loose strands of hair behind her ear. 'It's Mam's. It doesn't fit her and she gave it to me.'

A waitress approached carrying a tray of drinks. Rosa chose a small glass of sherry.

'I'm usually the one serving drinks. I'm not used to being waited on,' Rosa commented with a faint smile.

'Well, all the more reason to enjoy every moment of it, my dear,' Mrs Williams replied.

The area was filling up with more arrivals and they stepped into the main exhibition room on the left side of the entrance. It was an elegant room, with walls painted a very pale green and decorative cornicing on its high ceiling.

Rosa spotted Hettie in the centre of the room chatting to a group, including some who were dressed in their military uniform. One of her hands was placed casually on Hubert's arm and the other was tipping wine down her throat. She was dressed in a stylish dark blue satin dress with pink bows down the front, and pearls hung from her neck.

Paintings, some vast, filled the walls. Many showed graphic, bloody battles, gunfire and explosions, but it was the tortured faces and desperate expressions of the soldiers that held Rosa's attention. Some of them looked very young, the same age as Billy. She turned to comment on this to Mrs Williams and saw that her eyes were glazed over and she was unsteady on her feet.

'Are you feeling alright, Jane?' Rosa asked softly.

'I felt giddy for a moment. I think it's the shock of Dylan's news and seeing the suffering on these paintings affecting my nerves. I would like to sit down. I wasn't sure if it was a good idea for me to come, but Huw was keen, and I didn't want to let him down.'

Rosa held on to Mrs Williams's arm and led her to the corner of the room, where she slumped in a chair. They had passed Hettie and Hubert deep in discussion, and Rosa caught Hubert's eye. He excused himself, going over to join them and leaving Hettie chatting with the group.

'I saw you have a turn, Mrs Williams. Is there anything I can get you? Some water, perhaps?' the captain asked, his eyes filled with concern.

Mr Williams approached with George and asked anxiously, 'What happened, my dear? Your face is very pale.'

'I was overcome by the horror of these paintings, to see this is what we put our boys through, though I imagine the reality is far worse. I'll be alright in a moment,' she said with a faint voice.

Turning to the captain, Mr Williams said, 'Your paintings are very powerful, young man, to make my wife react this way.'

'I'm so very sorry. That was never my intention, especially

after the news you have had. I've heard they have made stoic people faint.'

Mrs Williams pressed her hand against her chest and inhaled deeply. 'Could I have that glass of water please, captain? I don't mean to make a fuss. It's important that you and your fellow artists show it as it is.'

George stepped forward. 'I'll fetch some for you, Mrs Williams.'

'They'll have some in the entrance hall,' Rosa whispered as he turned to fetch it.

The captain's eyebrows furrowed. 'I don't believe I know that boy.'

'It's unlikely, unless you go down the pits. He's a very unhappy Bevin boy, though he's only been here a week.'

'I can imagine it's dreadful for him,' the captain concurred.

Mr Williams and Rosa made a fuss of Jane while the captain rested his hand on his chin and appeared deep in thought.

When George appeared with the water, Hubert introduced himself as one of the artists and probed, 'Tell me, George, what is it really like being a conscript forced to work underground in darkness all day?'

'I remind myself that I'm doing national service, but I would far rather be seeing the action you've painted here, whatever the risks, than face every day working in a tomb with barely space to stand and water dripping down, hacking away in filthy conditions for a lump of coal. Your paintings are wonderful,' he blurted, his voice inflamed with passion.

Hubert declared, 'You've given me an idea, George. I should like to see it myself. I should like to paint our brave Bevin boys who are working for the war in these hellish conditions.'

'Feel free to take my place. It's not for the faint-hearted.'

'I've seen plenty of action, I can assure you. Just look at the paintings around you.'

Jane rose, placing her weight on her husband's arm. 'I think you should do it, captain. Let everyone see what it's really like for our young lads down there.'

'I most certainly will, when my duties permit. You will be immortalised, my dear boy. If you excuse me, I can see Hettie calling me over. We'll be making speeches soon – I hope you can stay for them.'

Jane insisted she had seen enough of the paintings while her husband and George continued to browse, Mr Williams stopping to chat with business acquaintances.

All at once the room hushed and all eyes turned to Mr Fry as he began to speak, thanking people for their support, and saying that the exhibition had attracted interest nationwide. He singled out Mr and Mrs Williams and Rosa for praise, and made clear his intention to continue using their services to advertise his future shows at venues throughout the country.

Hubert spoke next, paying tribute to the artists for their works that had touched people's hearts and aroused mixed emotions, ranging from fear and compassion to incomprehension and outrage.

His eyes fixed on George. 'It is my intention to return when I can and go down into the pits to paint our bravest men, our unsung heroes, our conscript Bevin boys.'

'How will you do that, then, seeing as they're in darkness?' one man called out.

'That's a good question. The answer is because what I see down below in the darkness will remain fixed in my head like a beacon. Like your forebears, these brave men deserve recognition for their war work.'

'Hear, hear!' cheered one of the attendees. Soon the room was filled with cheering voices.

Rosa grinned. 'Well, George, you've created a bit of a stir tonight.'

'I had no intention to. It's not about me,' he replied uneasily.

'I'm sure Hubert and Mr Fry know how to go about things. Besides, you're not being singled out. You're the inspiration behind the project, and I think it's an excellent idea.'

Mr and Mrs Williams beamed as they were congratulated by Hettie's parents. 'I always knew your work was the best,' muttered Mr Pritchard, puffing on his pipe. 'I shall continue to sing your praises. It's thanks to working for you that our Hettie met Hubert. Hasn't she done well for herself?'

Before they could reply, Mr Pritchard walked away and hailed someone else for a one-sided conversation.

Rosa had gone ahead to the entrance to collect her coat when she heard her name being called out. She caught her breath as she recognised the woman walking towards her. 'Good evening, Lady Gwendoline,' Rosa stuttered, avoiding eye contact, suddenly overcome with a deep sense of unease.

Lady Gwendoline pressed her hand on Rosa's arm. 'I'm sorry to hear about Dylan. Can we have a word somewhere quiet?'

Rosa spun around and saw Dylan's parents and George in conversation with Hubert and Mr Fry.

'It's important. There's a room on the other side of the hallway we can perhaps slip into for a moment.'

Rosa felt a lump form in her throat as she followed her into an empty office. Lady Gwendoline's expression was irked. 'I'm glad I've bumped into you. I was at the palace earlier in the week and enquired about you and was told you had left. I later found out an investigation involving you was being carried out by the palace police. What's this all about? I placed my trust in you. Have you let me down?'

Rosa choked on her words. 'Never. I swear to you I haven't done anything wrong.'

Her body shook with uncontrollable sobs as she poured out what had happened between taking large gulps of air.

'I'm innocent and I don't know how to clear my name. What's going to become of me?' she wailed.

'I suspect that depends very much on the police investigation. Let's hope they find no evidence against you. I'll see what I can find out, but I won't be able to influence the outcome.'

A woman's shaky voice at the door asked, 'Police evidence? Investigation? What's this got to do with you, Rosa?'

Rosa turned to see Mr and Mrs Williams at the door with George behind them. Their expressions were confused.

Lady Gwendoline advised, 'I think you have some explaining to do to these good people, Rosa.'

16

The evening that had started so well had now come crumbling down around her, leaving her feeling wretched.

As Lady Gwendoline walked out of the room, Dylan's parents came towards Rosa. Mr Williams turned to George and said, 'Do you think you could leave us for a minute, lad?'

'I'll wait outside,' he nodded.

Mr Williams closed the door behind him. 'Do you have something to tell us, Rosa?'

Rosa stared at the two kind faces before her, their gentle, enquiring eyes waiting for her to give an explanation for what they had overheard.

'I didn't mean to lie about the reason for coming back. You see, allegations have been made against me that are false.'

'What kind of allegations? And what did she mean about a police investigation?'

Rosa's mouth was clenched. She didn't know how to speak the words she knew would shock and disappoint them.

'I'm accused of stealing silver from the royal household, but I swear on my life I didn't. I've been set up.'

Mrs Williams gasped and held her hand up to her face. 'That is truly shocking. I can't believe such a thing of you, Rosa. When did this happen?'

'I can't say as I didn't take anything, but I was sent home a week ago.'

She lowered her gaze to her feet, ashamed of the unfounded allegation against her.

'Have you told your mother about this?'

'No, I couldn't, I daren't,' she breathed.

Mr Williams scratched his head. 'If you are innocent, Rosa, and I'm not saying for a minute that you're not, you have to believe that the police will get to the bottom of it. Have you given a statement yet?'

'Not yet. I'm waiting to hear when I'm needed, so I can give my side of the story.'

Mrs Williams's shoulders sunk and her eyes showed despair. 'You must tell your mam straight away. She won't take kindly about George knowing first.'

'I know I must. It's a relief to get it off my chest. Do you still want me to work in the shop? I'll understand if you don't.'

Mr Williams glanced at his wife's anxious expression. She raised her shoulders and didn't speak. After a pause, he replied, 'Let us think about this over the weekend. We want to do right by you, Rosa, but we can't take on any more anxiety, not with the worry of Dylan. We'll let you know one way or the other.'

The reply felt like a punch in the stomach. 'I understand,' she choked, dreading how her mother would respond if she lost her job with Dylan's parents too. She squeaked, 'I wish I'd never gone to London. None of this would have happened then.'

Mr Williams sympathised. 'I'm sorry, Rosa, we have to be cautious. If word should get out about you being involved in a police investigation at the palace, our customers may take their business elsewhere.'

That thought had never occurred to Rosa. She bade her farewells to Dylan's parents on the steps, feeling an emptiness inside her, and fear of facing her mother's wrath. George walked a few feet behind, sensing her troubled mind.

Her mother was still out when they returned home. She wasn't surprised as it was still early, not quite nine o'clock, and she wasn't expecting her for another couple of hours.

Rosa removed her coat and threw it over the back of a chair, slumping into it, her head in her hands. George disappeared into his room, leaving her to her thoughts.

She idly picked up a discarded copy of *Woman* magazine and saw underneath a pile of paperwork and an envelope. Her heart skipped a beat when she spotted her name on the front – and the palace postmark dated yesterday. It must have just come today, she surmised. With trembling hands she slid a knife under the back of the envelope and removed its contents. Her face paled as she read:

Dear Miss Edwards,

You are required to meet with Chief Inspector Graham Donaldson and me at Buckingham Palace at 10am on Monday, 1 May 1944 to give a statement regarding the disappearance of valuable items belonging to the royal family from Buckingham Palace.
Enclosed is a rail voucher.

Kind regards,
Superintendent Leonard Hodges
Buckingham Palace Household Police

'But that's the day after tomorrow!' she exclaimed.

She was reading it through again when her mother returned home, kicking off her shoes and walking to the stove to light the kettle.

'Poor Charlie came over poorly, so we left early,' her mother said breezily, placing two cups and saucers on the table.

'Mam——' Rosa began.

Eira glanced at her daughter's shaking hands fiddling with the letter. 'It's not Dylan, is it?'

'No, Mam,' she replied softly. 'There's something I need to tell you.'

Rosa shifted uncomfortably on her seat, her eyes moistening, pausing to catch her breath as she revealed everything.

'I swear I didn't take anything. There's another maid at the palace who doesn't like me. I think she's behind it. What am I going to do, Mam?'

Eira fumed. 'What are you going to do? You are going to tell them to shove off with their wicked lies. Who do they think we are? We may be poor, but we have never nicked a thing in our lives.'

'I know, Mam. But some silver ended up in my room. I don't know how to prove I didn't take it.'

'Monday, is it? Well, I'll be coming with you, my girl. I'll tell them us Edwards could be trusted with the Crown Jewels, never mind a few small silver trinkets, whatever they might be.'

'I thought you'd be angry with me, Mam.'

'Of course I'm flaming angry. I'm furious! But I also know you are truthful. Who else knows about this?'

Rosa explained how she was forced to confess to Dylan's parents after Lady Gwendoline cornered her.

'And George, does he know, seeing as he was there?'

Rosa shook her head. 'Mr Williams asked him to leave the room, though I suspect he got wind something is amiss. It was a horrid end to what had been a lovely evening.'

'I'm coming with you, Rosa. I fancy a trip to London. We'll pack a bag tomorrow and stay overnight in lodgings in Buckingham Palace Road,' Eira declared. 'We'll get this mess sorted together.'

Rosa was pleasantly surprised by her mother's reaction, but a doubt suddenly occurred to her. 'I appreciate your support, Mam, but I don't think they'll let you in the palace. Your name isn't mentioned on the letter and you won't be let in at the gate with me. They have very strict security. Everyone who enters the palace has to be vetted first.'

Eira raised her hands in the air. 'I hadn't thought of that.'

After a pause, Eira suggested, 'How about asking Mr Williams to vouch for you in a letter? You could see him tomorrow. Or Lady Gwendoline might speak on your behalf?'

Rosa shook her head. 'No, I won't do that. I don't want to involve anyone else. I'm innocent and shall go there and tell the truth. I have to prove my innocence myself, and make the police and palace believe me.'

'You've some of your mam's fire in your belly after all. That's my girl. Where will you stay tomorrow night?'

Rosa thought for a moment. 'I have a friend at the

palace who is more like a sister. She told me her home is my home whenever I need it. I shall go there.'

'As long as you are not walking the streets on your own at night.'

Eira opened her handbag and fished out her purse. She produced three crisp one-pound notes and slapped them in the palm of Rosa's hand. 'Here, call it a loan.'

Rosa and her mother embraced. 'You're the brains of this family, Rosa. I have every faith in you.'

17

Next morning, clutching an overnight bag and wearing the smart black dress her mother had given her teamed with sensible black shoes, Rosa felt ready to face the world.

'Dressing your best is empowering,' her mother told her, adjusting how the dress rested on her shoulders. 'It will make you feel in control. Have you got everything?'

'There's one more thing I must take with me.' Rosa rushed to her bedroom and returned with a small box. She opened it and removed the brooch Dylan had given her for her birthday. 'It's for luck. I shall feel Dylan's spirit close to me. And I think it brightens the dress up.'

'That finishes it nicely. You could mingle with the best of society now. Remember, hold your head up high and let everyone see that you have nothing to hide.'

'I'll try, Mam. I wish I was as confident as you.'

'Good luck, Rosa. I'll be thinking of you.'

As Rosa sat in the rail carriage rumbling its way to London, she pondered on her mother's words. She couldn't help but notice how well-dressed fellow passengers glanced at her and smiled. A gentleman sitting next to her, around the same age as her father and wearing a dark suit and bowler hat, was keen to speak to her and hear about life in Merthyr, and they engaged in small-talk, though she was cautious not to give away anything about her troubles.

She had set off after lunch and arrived early evening,

in good time to travel on to Stepney in search of Molly's house. She wondered if it was close to where Alice's aunt lived. Although Rosa remembered Molly telling her she would be welcome any time if she was in trouble, she didn't know Molly's address. She was taking a risk by arriving out of the blue, but felt she had no choice and prayed Molly would be in.

She recalled that it was next to the Three Blind Beggars pub, but had no idea how to get there.

The gentleman who had sat next to her on the train offered to carry her bag when they disembarked at Paddington Station. Rosa gratefully accepted, feeling every bit the lady.

He handed over her bag at the entrance and wished her a good evening. 'Thank you for your company on the train, and for carrying my bag,' she said, glancing around her.

'You're very welcome. I enjoyed your company and hearing about the art exhibition you attended. I do find the Welsh accent very musical and enjoy hearing it spoken. I see you looking around. Are you waiting for someone?' he enquired.

'Oh no, it's nothing like that. I'm going to see a friend in Stepney, but I'm not sure I can remember how to get there.'

'And why would a young lady like you have reason to go to Stepney? It's taken a terrible hammering and is very run down.'

Suddenly Rosa felt lost and vulnerable. 'It's a long story.'

'I may be able to help you. We haven't introduced ourselves properly, have we? My name is Archibald Howell. I'm a solicitor, the founding partner of Howell, Ratcliffe and Fanshawe. And I'm at your service.'

Rosa's jaw dropped as she read the business card he pressed into her hand. 'I'm Rosa Edwards. I'm very pleased to meet you,' she responded in her best voice.

'I have a car waiting for me around the corner. My driver can take you to Stepney if you wish. I assure you my intentions are entirely honourable. I'm meeting friends for drinks a short walk away. The exercise will do me good.'

'But we've only just met. I couldn't possibly accept and put you to so much trouble.'

'I understand your caution, Miss Edwards. Perhaps you need proof of who I am.'

A policeman walked in their direction and greeted the solicitor. 'Good day, Mr Howell, sir. I trust all is well with you.'

'I'm very well, thank you, Constable Gilbert. I wonder if I could ask a favour – could you vouch for my good name to this young lady, Miss Edwards, here who I shared a carriage with on the train?'

The constable looked surprised. 'How do you mean, sir?'

'Could you confirm who I am, my name and business, and if I am a person of good character?'

Rosa flinched, feeling uncomfortable. She raised a hand. 'There's really—'

The constable leaned back, holding his hands across the front of his chest, and in a clear voice pronounced: 'There is no more reputable man I have the pleasure of knowing than Archibald Howell, the finest solicitor in our city. Will that do, sir?'

'Thank you, that will do nicely.' Mr Howell winked, and the constable sauntered off.

'You are quite right to be cautious of strangers, Miss

Edwards. I wouldn't want my daughter visiting unsavoury parts of London on her own this time of day. It's a long journey and you don't want to hang about. I'm a happily married man with two daughters, which should put your mind further at rest. The night is drawing in, it will soon be blackout. My offer to you is made with the best of intentions for your safety.'

'Thank you, Mr Howell. It's just that I'm not used to such generosity, and from a stranger. I will accept your kind offer.'

'Very good. Jarvis is parked around the corner. I'll take you to him.'

He approached a Rover car parked nearby and spoke to a man standing on the kerb by the vehicle. He introduced Rosa to Jarvis and raised his hand to wish her a good evening and safe onward journey.

As she slid onto the back seat, sinking into the comfy leather upholstery, Jarvis took his place in the front behind the wheel and turned to her.

'Where to then, Miss Edwards?'

'It's a house in Stepney next to the Three Blind Beggars pub.'

'It so happens I know it, even though it's not on my usual route,' he replied.

Jarvis was in his fifties, with tobacco-stained teeth and pockmark scarring on his cheeks. The police constable she had seen a moment ago knocked on his window and urged Jarvis to move on. He switched the engine on and set off.

'Do you mind if I ask you a question, Jarvis?'

'What would that be, miss?'

'Does Mr Howell often help strangers in this way? I've

only just met him and could barely believe his kindness towards me.'

Jarvis replied, 'Since his son, Sidney, died – he was torpedoed in the navy and drowned – he has changed his outlook on life. He regrets spending his life building his career and not having more time with his family. Now they come first – and any young people he meets along the way that need a helping hand. He's a proper gent, is Mr Howell.'

'I see. That's very sad, and very noble. My brother is in the navy. He ran off – he's only fifteen, and Mam and me are worried sick about him.'

'He sounds a very strong-willed young lad.'

After a pause, she added, 'My Dylan is missing too. He set off on his first mission with the RAF, but nobody knows what's happened to him.'

'I'm sorry to hear that. It's terrible for you and the poor boy's family. I hope things turn out alright.'

The car glided smoothly past the smart houses in Sussex Gardens and along Marylebone Road. It twisted and turned through Camden Town and her eyes widened at some of the city's finest wonders as they passed: the imposing British Museum, St Paul's Cathedral and the Tower of London, through Wapping and then sweeping down Commercial Road. Jarvis pointed to the piles of rubble and bombed buildings they passed, the aftermath of an air raid which claimed the lives of innocent civilians. He pointed to one building and said, 'A woman in that house was found sheltering in her cellar hours after her roof collapsed.'

'She was lucky,' commented Rosa, staring at the fragmented remains of what had once been a home. One wall had been left standing with a mirror hung lopsided above a mantelpiece, the other three walls a pile of rubble on the ground along with shards of glass, twisted metal, smashed furniture and pieces of ripped fabric from the clothing its residents once wore.

They drove on a bit and Jarvis pointed ahead. 'This is where the King and Queen came after it had taken a terrible hit. It was in the early days of the Blitz in 1940, and the air raid was still on. A school stood there sheltering five hundred homeless people awaiting evacuation, and more than seventy were killed.'

Rosa's ears pricked up. 'What did the King and Queen do here?'

'They walked amongst the rubble and talked to people. Everyone came out that day and forgot their troubles. The Queen put her arm around people covered in blood and dirt and consoled them, just like she was one of us.'

'She really is just like that,' Rosa replied.

'You say that as if you know her,' Jarvis commented, glancing at her through his rear-view mirror.

'Oh no. She sounds that way from what I've read, and from what you've just said. I mean, she could have left London and taken the princesses with her, fled to Canada, away from the war, but she refused. Anyone can see her heart is in London with its people.'

'Got it in one. My uncle comes from these parts and saw the King and Queen that day. His neighbour was really shaken, she was on her hands and knees clawing away at the rubble on the bombsite, then peering down a hole. The Queen asked her why she was doing this and she told her her dog refused to come out, and she wouldn't budge an inch until she had. Do you know what the Queen did?'

Rosa was all ears. 'No. What did she do?'

'She said, "Perhaps I can try. I am rather good with dogs."'

'That's true, she is very fond of her corgis. Did she get the dog out?'

Jarvis cocked an eyebrow. 'Yes, she did. She spoke to people like they were her own kind, saying she knew how they felt as the palace had been bombed too. The crowd erupted and chanted "*God Save the King, God Save the Queen*" at the top of their voices.'

'I can just picture it. Are we nearly there yet?'

'Not far, another fifteen minutes or so. The Three Blind Beggars, you say?'

'That's right.'

The rest of the journey continued with Jarvis giving Rosa a rundown on the Whitechapel neighbourhood, infamous for the murders of Jack the Ripper, and Rosa shivered.

Jarvis braked as he came to a bend and turned into it, slowing down further as he approached a building at the far end of the road. Rosa peered through the window of the car and saw *The Three Blind Beggars* in clear letters on the front and a swaying sign showing three men, bent over and leaning on sticks, with vacant expressions in their eyes. A small house with a black door adjoined it. She saw some figures inside and got out of the car with her overnight bag.

'Thank you for the lift, Jarvis. I didn't realise it was so far.'

'I've enjoyed your company, Miss Edwards, and especially hearing your lovely voice. I could listen to your Welsh accent all day.'

'It's just normal for me,' Rosa smiled.

'Do you want me to wait, just in case you decide you're not going to stay and need a lift back?'

Rosa thought for a moment. 'It might be a good idea if you could, so I can be sure my friend Molly is in. I wouldn't like to be stranded here.'

Rosa knocked twice and stood back. The door was opened straight away by a fair-haired girl with a cheeky face, her hair tied in pigtails. 'Hello. Who are you?' she asked forthrightly, giving Rosa the once-over with her large, curious eyes.

'Is your last name Deakin? My name is Rosa. I'm a friend of Molly Deakin and she told me she lived next to the Three Blind Beggars. Is she in, please?'

The child was pushed aside gently and Molly stood in front of her, her eyes filled with wonderment. 'Rosa! What are you doing here?'

'Thank God you're in, Molly, it's such a relief. I wasn't sure you would be and I didn't know where else to go. I've so much to tell you, if I can come inside,' she replied, glancing around at Jarvis, who was standing by the car with his ear cocked in their direction.

'Who is he?' asked Molly, her eyes narrowing, following Rosa's gaze.

'It's a long story. That's all I seem to be saying these days. He's a driver who kindly gave me a lift here from Paddington Station. He wants to know if I'm staying, or need a lift back.'

'You're staying, of course. Don't you remember me telling me that my house is your house, as long as you don't mind a bit of noise?'

'Oh, thank you, Molly, thank you so much. I'll just let Jarvis know.'

'I'll tell Ma that you're here. She's in the kitchen and will be pleased to meet you.'

Rosa went over to the driver. 'It's fine, Jarvis. I'm staying here. Thank you again for everything.'

'As long as you're sure then, I'll be on my way. Have a good evening, Miss Edwards.'

When Rosa stepped over the threshold of Molly's house she sensed straight away it was a home filled with love. She stood in the sitting room, where an odd assortment of dining chairs were placed around an oval table in one corner, and a sofa stuffed with horsehair was placed under the window. The carpet was threadbare in places and the walls were covered in photographs of Molly with her mother and five siblings, showing a happy, smiling family.

The young girl who opened the door ran up to Rosa and wrapped her arms around her. 'My name is Helena and I am nine years old,' she grinned. 'Do you like playing games?'

An older girl answered for her. 'She likes playing Snakes and Ladders. If you land on a snake she makes pretend you're a German and dive bombs your counter.'

'That sounds fun. You must be . . . ?'

'I'm Rosemary, and that's Benjamin over there with his head buried in a book,' she answered.

'You speak funny,' teased Helena, a mischievous look in her eyes.

Molly came back into the room with an older woman holding a large brown teapot.

'Enough of that cheek, Helena,' Molly said. 'We want our guest to feel welcome. Rosa, this is my ma.'

'I'm pleased to meet you, Rosa,' Molly's mother said.

'I'm Annie Deakin. Molly has told me a lot about you and you're welcome to stay the night.'

'Whoopee!' shrieked Helena. 'I like Rosa.'

'Can you give us a minute or two, children?' Mrs Deakin said. 'We'd like to have a private chat.'

Rosemary led her mischievous sister and studious brother up the stairs. 'It's like Bedlam here sometimes,' Molly's mother went on. 'I imagine you'd like a drink, and we have some cold meat if you'd like a sandwich.'

'That's so very kind of you, Mrs Deakin. I don't mean to put you to any trouble,' said Rosa.

Mrs Deakin stepped into the kitchen and returned a moment later with a cup and saucer and a fresh brew. 'Any friend of Molly's is welcome here. You can call me Annie, by the way.'

'Thank you, Annie. This tea is delicious. I'm parched.'

'I'll put something together for you to eat while you and Molly catch up. Molly's other sister, Phyllis, is sleeping where she works, and her brother Thomas won't be back for a while, so you won't be disturbed,' Annie stated.

'Thomas helps out in the pub next door,' Molly added, 'and uses the back door when 'e returns. Mum swore never to set foot inside after Dad ran off with the landlord's wife. But I told her it wasn't his fault, he was as shocked as us. The money comes in 'andy and she's come round to the idea now.'

Annie went back into the kitchen, and Molly took hold of her friend's hands and asked, 'Tell me, Rosa, what brings you here? Are you in trouble? Tell me everything.'

'Oh, Molly, I don't know where to start. I've been accused of stealing silver from the palace . . . and Dylan . . . he's been officially reported missing.'

Rosa collapsed into Molly's arms and her chest shook uncontrollably, the tears she had held back flowing freely. When she had no tears left and dried her eyes, Molly spoke in a soft voice.

'You poor thing, it sounds like you've had a very rough time of it.'

'Do people at the palace know why I left suddenly?' asked Rosa. 'I've been asked to make a statement to the palace police about the missing silver. I'm going there tomorrow, that's why I'm here. I swear it was nothing to do with me. Cross my heart, hope to die.'

Molly's face puckered. 'I believe you. The police spoke to me about you. They've spoken to other staff who know you, even Jerry, who's furious about it. They say they won't give up until they discover the truth. They intend to make an example of whoever's responsible.'

'Well, it's not me, but I don't know how to prove it.'

'There's something going on. I get the feeling they're doing spot checks. I saw one of the other maids being asked to tip her handbag out as she left, but she was clean. The mistrust in the staff quarters has created tension.'

'I suppose the spot checks are to be expected, in the circumstances. Are you still in Windsor, or back here in London?'

'I'm here again now, as of tomorrow. The other two sisters made a quick recovery and Mrs Hargreaves wanted them back. Or rather, I 'ad the feeling she wanted me gone as soon as possible.'

'What other suspects could there be? I can't think of anyone who would steal from the royal family.'

Molly shrugged her shoulders. 'Nobody knows. Everyone

has vouched for your character. We have no choice but to let the investigation run its course. Jerry refuses to have a word said against you. Whoever the thief is, he or she is bound to make a slip-up.'

Mrs Deakin knocked lightly on the door and entered carrying a tray of cold pork sandwiches and a rock cake. 'We're lucky. The landlord next door has a deal going with a butcher and buys cheap offcuts from him. Says he owes him a favour or two and they rub each other's backs without asking any questions – but don't tell anyone about their black-market racket,' she whispered.

A thought occurred to Rosa. 'Annie, I have a friend from Merthyr staying with her aunt at an address in South Grove. I wondered if it was near here, and if you might know her – a Welsh lady by the name of Ruby Evans?'

Molly's mother shook her head. 'Ah, this is the friend Molly was telling me about that you're trying to find. I don't know her myself, but if there's any gossip to be had in that road, I know someone who might. I'll let Molly know if I hear anything.'

'Thank you, Annie. I can't help but worry about her. It's frustrating to know she could be close by, and that I can't see her.'

'It sounds like you have lots on your plate at the moment. I'll go and see to the children upstairs, and I might turn in early myself. Molly will make you a bed on the sofa, Rosa, if you don't mind that.'

'Thank you, that will do perfectly, I don't want to trouble you. I'm only little and will fit on there nicely.'

'It's very cosy, and we wouldn't have it any other way,' Molly smiled. 'Especially after walking along those

draughty corridors in the castle and sleeping in a basement, or dungeon, whatever it was.'

'Do you remember when I curtseyed and my legs got
cramp?' laughed Rosa, and the two girls fell into fits of
giggles.

'It's so good to see you again, Molly. Whatever happens, I've made a best friend in you, and will be thankful
of that for the rest of my life.'

'I feel the same way, Rosa. You'll get through this.'

With the blackout curtains drawn tightly, Rosa began
to yawn. She was shown where to wash in the outhouse,
then slipped out of her smart black dress, laying it carefully over the side of the chair, while Molly brought in
some spare bedding.

'If it's alright with you, Molly, I was going to ask if I
could travel in with you tomorrow morning, and I'll sit in
a café in Buckingham Palace Road until it's time for my
appointment.'

'Of course you can. I'll say I just bumped into you. I
don't see there's no 'arm in that. Try not to fret about it
too much, Rosa. I'm sure everything will work out.'

Rosa settled herself on the sofa and lay her head on the
pillow. She took her friend's hand and squeezed it. 'Thank
you for being such a good friend, Molly. I don't know how
I can ever repay you.'

18

Rosa and Molly parted company outside Sweet Betty's café, a stone's throw from the palace. 'Will you get word to me somehow and let me know how it goes?' Molly asked as she parted from her friend.

'I promise, and thank you again, Molly.'

Rosa stirred her tea mindlessly, unable to eat the toast she had ordered. Finally it was time to leave. She felt her insides turn to jelly as she approached the palace gates. She sailed past the guards, who ticked her name off their list, and noticed with great relief that Jerry was not on duty; she would have felt too embarrassed to see him. A guard escorted her through a side entrance and down a flight of stone steps to a door with a sign that read *Police*.

The door was slightly ajar. She peeped inside and saw two men in police uniform. One was sitting behind a desk, holding his head in his hands and reading from a folder. His colleague was seated in a corner.

She drew back when the guard knocked on the door. The man behind the desk looked up and invited her to enter. She stepped inside clutching her overnight bag, feeling shaky.

She straightened herself and shook hands as the two men rose and introduced themselves as the two officers whose names she recalled from the letter. She looked about her and saw that one wall was lined with shelves heaving with filing boxes. A large framed picture of the King hung on the wall behind the desk.

The older of the two men, Superintendent Hodges, had long grey whispery sideburns and bushy eyebrows. He offered Rosa a seat, and she removed her coat, her fingers straying to her brooch as she sat down, willing it to bring her good luck.

The younger officer, Chief Inspector Donaldson, hung up her coat and moved his chair closer to hers. He clutched a large notepad and pen. Rosa noticed a sheet of paper on the desk with the words *Police Statement* written on the front. The superintendent leaned over his desk and stared at her intently.

'Thank you for coming today, Miss Edwards. The King and Queen have asked me to bring my investigation to a swift conclusion as staff find it very unsettling.'

Rosa was unable to hold back. 'I didn't do it. I didn't take a thing, I swear it.'

'Now, just listen to me for a moment, Miss Edwards, then you can speak. As you know, an accusation of theft has been made against you and I would like you to provide a statement giving your version. My chief inspector here is making notes of our meeting. Can you start by telling us about yourself, where you worked before you came here and how you came to secure the position here, and then we will address the questions surrounding the thefts.'

With a wobbly voice, Rosa described her employment with Dylan's family and the Valleys Hotel, stating how she was following in her friend Alice's footsteps after she had moved to London. 'I saw a sign advertising my position in a window in Merthyr. If Lady Gwendoline hadn't encouraged me the way she did, I doubt I would have had the confidence to apply for it.'

The superintendent's eyebrows rose at this. He then reeled off a number of items that were missing and asked if she knew of their whereabouts: a silver sugar bowl and milk jug, a large amount of silver cutlery, and some porcelain pieces of small animals, including one of the Queen's beloved corgi that had been gifted to her by the King and she was desperate to have returned.

Rosa answered truthfully, saying she had always been accompanied by other staff in the palace rooms, and stealing anything, even if she had had the opportunity to do so, was the furthest thing from her mind. She mentioned Agnes's dislike of her too, when asked if anyone might have tried to frame her.

When she finished and signed her statement, she declared, 'It's the truth, that's all I can say. I will swear it on oath. Do you know how long the investigation will take?'

The superintendent sat back in his chair and stroked his chin. 'We hope to clear this matter up as soon as possible. You should hear from us within a fortnight.'

'I'm so upset about this. I can't wait to have my name cleared and return, put this horrid business behind me.'

'This may come as a surprise to you, Miss Edwards. I am going to be very frank, if I can count on your confidentiality.'

'Of course, Superintendent Hodges. Do you believe me?'

'All I can say for now is that I have had forty years' experience as a copper and can sniff out a liar. I've nabbed more lords and ladies, as well as ruffians and spivs, than I've had hot dinners.' His eyes were fixed on Rosa's face.

He paused, leaning forward. 'Another matter has since come to light that could have some connection.'

'What do you mean?'

'Let's just say our investigations are continuing. We needed to see you today and have your statement to judge your character and evidence. That is all for now. You will be hearing from us again in due course.'

The superintendent rose and nodded to his colleague, who helped Rosa on with her coat.

'But I'm not sure what you're saying,' she pressed as she walked towards the door. 'Can I tell my mam that you believe me?'

'I'm not at liberty to say any more. There is one more thing I should mention. I believe you are still in touch with staff here. You must keep everything to yourself that was said between these four walls. It's in your best interest.'

'Of course, I understand,' Rosa muttered.

'May I ask your plans for the rest of the day?' the superintendent enquired, his tone softening.

'I shall go to see a friend, Alice, and then return to Merthyr.'

'I hope you have a pleasant day and safe journey back,' he smiled.

The chief inspector handed Rosa her coat and bag, opened the door and accompanied her out into the corridor and up the steps into the courtyard. She had an inkling it had gone well, but couldn't make sense of what the other matter was they were looking into. She held her face up to the sky. Never had the fresh air felt so good.

*

Rosa remembered the Underground route she needed to take to reach the home of Alice's aunt Ruby in Stepney. She'd hastily scribbled a note in case there was no reply, stating that she was going back to Merthyr for a while and keen to see her before she left.

As she approached the house she noticed all the front curtains were closed. A neighbour, a young mother in her early twenties holding a baby in her arms, called out from her front door step: 'There's nobody in. They've gone away for a while.'

'Really? Do you know when they'll be back?' Rosa asked.

'I've no idea,' came the reply.

Rosa had no choice but to push her note through the letterbox. Something isn't right, a voice in her head told her. It's as if she's vanished into thin air, or doesn't want to be found.

It was early evening when Rosa arrived back in Merthyr. She let herself in and found her mother and George were out. The teapot was still warm and she poured herself a brew, her eyes straying to the latest edition of the *Merthyr Express* on the table. She idly flicked through its pages.

There was a photograph on the front page of the Home Guard having a dinner, and an article about local councillors pressing for the demolition of dilapidated homes in Penydarren and Dowlais – including the home where she had been born. Not a moment too soon, she reckoned.

She turned the page and gasped as she recognised two faces: George, their Bevin boy, looking very bashful, alongside a beaming Captain Hubert Fry announcing his new art project at the exhibition. The report, headlined *Artists Show True Horrors of War*, included an extremely complimentary review of the exhibition, stating it had been seen by five thousand people, some of whom travelled miles to see it.

She raised her head when she heard voices outside in the hallway, followed by a knock on the door.

She opened it to see their landladies standing outside. 'Betty? Vera? What is it?' The two sisters were holding their hands up to their throats.

'I'm very sorry, my dear,' Vera choked. 'You should perhaps brace yourself for bad news.'

'You're making me scared. What are you talking about?'

'We were walking past the Williamses' shop and saw a telegram being delivered. Huw opened it and collapsed over the counter, then put the *Closed* sign up on the door.'

Rosa's legs buckled. 'When was this?' she cried. 'You don't think it means Dylan is dead?'

'It was only an hour or so ago. From Huw's reaction, that may be the case. We know how hard this will be to hear, my dear. We're so very sorry.'

'His poor parents. I must go to them now. What can I say?'

'My darling girl, the right words will come to you, and sometimes words are not necessary at all. Grieve with them, be there for them and cherish your happy memories,' advised Vera.

'Will you tell Mam where I've gone if she comes back before me?' Rosa called as she flew out the door, down the stairs and out into the street.

She quickened her pace, tears streaming down her

cheeks, and ran blindly down the steep, narrow streets, brushing against anyone who was in her way.

Breathless, she arrived at the shop, pressed her body against the wall and rested her hand against her chest, inhaling a lungful of air. She ventured round to the back of the building and pressed on the doorbell. Mr Williams appeared at the bottom of the stairs and unlocked the door.

A glance at his puffy eyes and sad expression confirmed her worst fears.

'Is it true? Is Dylan——?'

His sad watery eyes told her the answer.

'No! Not Dylan,' she wailed.

'Come upstairs, Rosa,' he croaked. 'Jane is in a bad way.'

Her heart thumping, Rosa numbly followed Huw upstairs and into the living room. She recalled the last time she had been there with Dylan before he left for war. She had been invited to have Sunday tea with the family and felt shy and nervous.

Jane was seated on the sofa clutching Dylan's photograph, dabbing her eyes, her face contorted with grief. Rosa rushed to her, threw her arms around her neck, and they cried uncontrollably.

When they had no tears left, Rosa asked gently, 'Do you know how it happened?'

Before they could answer, she spotted the telegram on the table and picked it up.

WE REGRET TO INFORM YOU OF THE DEATH OF FLIGHT NAVIGATOR DYLAN WILLIAMS FOLLOWING A HIGH-RISK SECRET OPERATION. EXACT DATE TO BE CONFIRMED. LETTER TO FOLLOW.

Rosa stared at it blankly. 'What does it mean? What secret operation was Dylan on?'

'I've no idea. But I know one thing, our son died a hero,' Mr Williams uttered softly.

'What good is a dead hero? He was so young,' cried Jane. 'I want my boy back.'

She grabbed Rosa's arm. 'We have you still, Rosa. You won't desert us now, will you?'

Huw took his wife in his arms and pressed her shaking body against his. He soothed, 'Rosa has her own life to live, my love. Let's not speak of these things now.' Turning to Rosa, he asked, 'How did your meeting go with the police? Did they believe you?'

'I think so,' she replied weakly. 'But I don't care any more. I'll not leave you as long as you want me.'

'You don't know how much that means to us,' Jane's voice wobbled.

The following day a sign was placed on the window stating: *CLOSED UNTIL FURTHER NOTICE DUE TO FAMILY BEREAVEMENT.*

19

A letter followed two weeks later telling them that Dylan had been laid to rest with full honours in a French village cemetery under the boughs of a holly tree, but its exact location could not yet be disclosed to his family. His bereft parents wept at being denied the chance to have their beloved son home in the Welsh valley that he so loved.

For the first few days after receiving the letter, Jane and Huw locked themselves away with their grief, and Rosa felt the loss deeply; it was as if her heart had been ripped out. They cried together and clung to each other as they relived their happy memories, weeping for the loss of their hopes and dreams, the future they looked forward to sharing, and that was now denied them.

Rosa put all thoughts of the palace investigation to the back of her mind, but felt a deep yearning inside as she realised how much she missed Molly and the chance to cry on her shoulder.

The day that the letter arrived, Rosa suggested, 'Why don't we plant a tree at Cyfarthfa Castle, with a plaque that has his name on it. It's where I feel close to Dylan. He used to liked standing at the top of the hill and looking across the Valleys. It's a beautiful and peaceful place.'

Jane and Huw glanced at each other. Huw said, 'I really like the idea of that, Rosa. Perhaps a rowan tree — it's associated with courage, protection and good fortune. We can see to it and contact the authorities.'

The castle was owned by the local council, and the authorities there readily agreed, sending their condolences to Mr and Mrs Williams for the loss of their brave son. A date was set for the next Sunday afternoon. Once word of it spread, many people in Merthyr announced they were keen to be there, holding Dylan close to their hearts too.

'I don't know how I'll get through it, with all those people watching,' Jane wailed.

Huw soothed, 'This is the only chance we'll have for people to be united and pay their respects. Dylan deserves this.'

Through scalding tears, Rosa had meanwhile shared her sad news in a letter to Molly, who immediately wrote back offering her deepest sympathy, and to come to Merthyr to see her.

I appreciate your kind offer, Rosa wrote back, *but I need to spend as much time as I can with Dylan's parents. Our hearts are broken and we take comfort from being together and talking about him.*

On a warm sunny Sunday at the beginning of June, Rosa slipped on the black dress and pinned Dylan's brooch to it, smiling as she remembered the joy she felt when he'd surprised her with the gift. She accompanied Dylan's parents to Cyfarthfa Castle on foot, walking alongside Huw, who pushed the rowan tree in a wheelbarrow. Huw and Jane wore black armbands over the sleeve of their jacket and Rosa did the same, borrowing a dark jacket from her mother.

As they reached the allocated spot her eyes widened. 'There must be at least one hundred people here,' Rosa whispered, her voice cracking.

Jane's eyes were wet and her bottom lip wobbled. The choir from their chapel were there, standing in line. Hettie was nearby with her parents, alongside Huw's business associates and Mr Fry. Some of the younger people present included Dylan's classmates and teacher, as well as his fellow air cadets and instructors dressed smartly in their uniforms. Eira, Grandma Meryl and George stood towards the front, and her eyes caught her father's bent figure at the back of the crowd, his head bowed in respect. There was even a reporter from the *Merthyr Express* who Rosa recognised from the exhibition reception, his notepad and pen in his hand.

The Williamses refused to have a minister in attendance, questioning why God could not have saved their only child.

Huw cleared his throat and the hushed crowd raised their gaze.

'Jane and I would like to thank you all for coming today,' he began. 'Many of you, like us, have lost someone you love in this bloody war. I don't know how we're going to get through our lives without Dylan. You couldn't have asked for a more caring and capable boy, who didn't have a bad bone in his body and was willing to lend a hand to anyone.'

Huw paused and sniffled, and muffled voices could be heard muttering, 'That's very true,' and, 'He was one of the best.'

Jane's legs swayed and she clutched Rosa's arm as Huw continued.

'Aye, Dylan was one of the best. I only have to look around here to see that he meant something to so many people with his thoughtful ways. I'm not a man of many words, but if Dylan is looking down on us, he will see you all and know the mark he has left on our lives.

'He died a hero, fighting for our country's freedom, determined to destroy the Nazis and their tyranny. We must hope his sacrifice will have been worth it in the end.

'I shall now plant this tree in his memory. We hope one day to be able to return his remains here, but for now, this is Dylan's tree. It's a beautiful spot for us to visit and think of him. He will remain in our hearts for ever.'

Rosa and Jane clutched each other, dabbing their eyes, as Huw dug the spade into the soil. The choir burst into 'How Green Was My Valley', an evocative song that tugged at the heartstrings. The mourners hummed along while Huw positioned the tree and pressed the soil around it, then dug in the brass plaque in front.

When he'd finished Huw straightened his back and raised his chin, staring up towards the sky. Impassioned, he again praised the bravery of his son, telling the crowd how, although most aircrew were over nineteen, Dylan's brilliant navigation skills and confidence as an air cadet had surpassed the expectations of his superiors.

Finally he cleared his throat and read the words on the plaque in a loud, clear voice: '"In memory of Dylan Williams, a boy of the Valleys, aged 18, who gave his life that we may live in peace."'

Amen, chorused the mourners. They remained silent, their heads bowed.

Rosa and Jane stood next to Huw as mourners approached to acknowledge their loss and pay tribute to Dylan's outstanding qualities. Eira and Grandma Meryl supported Rosa and Jane by ensuring they had a moment's peace when their emotions became heightened.

The journalist approached Jane, his notebook and pen poised. 'Mrs Williams, would you be able to say a few words? It's important to write about our local war heroes. People want to know about them.'

Eira stepped in front of him, her nostrils flaring. 'How dare you intrude on this family's grief. Can't you see how upset they are? You are not welcome here. Will you please leave immediately.'

Rosa spotted her father approaching George and watched as they shook hands and walked off chatting, her father patting their lodger on the back. She was deeply touched that George had wanted to pay his respects to Dylan; he had told her his two brothers were pilots, and that his family dreaded the worst happening to them. Their landladies, Betty and Vera Hughes, were there too wearing old-fashioned black skirts, jackets and hats, and Rosa wondered if these were the mourning clothes they wore when they lost their loved ones during the Great War.

Huw put his arm around his wife's waist and she rested her head on his shoulder. Most people had gone, with Hettie and Mr Fry amongst those still remaining. Hettie came up to Rosa and said, 'I'm so sorry to hear about Dylan. I still picture him behind the counter, seeing to all the orders.'

'I'm glad you could make it today, Hettie. That means a lot. How is Hubert?'

'He's overseas at the moment, and news from him is scarce. I guess you know how that feels.' When the words passed her lips she covered her mouth with her hand. 'I'm sorry. I didn't mean to be insensitive. Me and my big mouth. This bloody war jangles my nerves. I really am sorry, Rosa. Dylan thought the world of you. It put my nose out of joint that he preferred you. I'd like to apologise.'

Rosa was taken aback by Hettie's goodwill gesture. She said softly, 'I hope you hear from Hubert soon, Hettie. He's a good man and dotes on you. I appreciate what you said about Dylan. I was as surprised as anyone that he fell for me. If only we could have had longer.'

Hettie shuffled from one foot to the other. 'There is something I wanted to ask, but do tell me if it's not appropriate right now.'

'What is it?'

'Is the shop still taking orders during the mourning period?'

Rosa bristled. 'There really isn't a canary's chance,' she said.

Mr Fry appeared, having overheard Hettie. 'I'm sorry. Please accept my apologies. Hettie was asking on my behalf as we would like to continue working with you.'

'This isn't the time or place. But I thank you both for coming today. It would have meant a lot to Dylan. Now, if you'll excuse me.'

Rosa turned her back on them and walked away, her lips set tightly. Her mother noticed the interaction and asked, 'Is everything alright, love? It looked like they upset you.'

'They did. Can you believe they asked if we're taking orders again.'

'Well, that might not be a bad idea. Now we've had the

memorial service, what else will you all have to occupy yourselves? Life must go on, Rosa, it's what Dylan would have wanted.'

Rosa's eyes narrowed. 'It's too soon, Mam, my head and heart aren't ready to think of work right now.'

Eira counselled, 'The thing is, that's all you do have right now and you're going to need to earn again, seeing as there's still no news from the palace, and it's been more than two weeks since you gave your statement. Why don't you at least think about it?'

After a pause, Rosa said, 'Very well, I should have heard by now. I'll think about it, but it depends on how Dylan's parents feel. I'm going back to their place now. Would you like to join us? And Grandma?'

'Thank you for asking, love. I don't think they will want my company right now, but they need you.'

'And I need them too, Mam. Being with them, being in Dylan's home, makes me feel close to him.'

Eira embraced her daughter. 'You're a good girl, Rosa. I promise you will get through this pain.'

Rosa joined Dylan's parents, taking Jane's arm in hers.

'I never expected so many people,' Huw commented.

'And they all spoke so kindly about our Dylan,' his wife replied.

'He was loved by many, as well,' Rosa added, squeezing Jane's arm and exchanging a warm glance.

Huw asked, 'Was that your father I saw there, Rosa?'

'Yes, that was Da. I'm only sorry I didn't get the chance to speak to him. He seemed to be chatting for a long time with George.'

'I imagine they'd have a lot to talk about,' Jane remarked.

'Perhaps he can give him some advice about working in the mines.'

Huw winked at Rosa. 'Aye, and no doubt he will have invited him to the Miner's Arms to share some ale.'

When they reached home and settled themselves, Huw surprised Rosa by raising the subject she had dreaded mentioning.

'Now we have laid Dylan to rest the best way we can, Jane and I have been thinking . . .' He paused, and Jane nodded, urging him to continue. 'We've been thinking, we can't keep our door closed for ever. We saw you talking to Mr Fry, and in the last few days I've been approached by a couple of businesses enquiring about placing orders.'

Rosa looked surprised. 'I told Mr Fry there wasn't a canary's chance, not yet. I hope I didn't say the wrong thing.'

'We'll just take things one day at a time. People have been most understanding,' replied Jane, patting her husband's arm gently.

'Have you thought what you would like to do next, Rosa? We don't want to hold you back if you wanted to return to London and be with your new friends,' said Huw.

'I'm quite content to stay on here for now, if that's alright with you. When are you thinking of opening again?'

'How does tomorrow sound?'

Rosa hesitated for a second. 'I wasn't sure earlier, but now I think it sounds just right,' she replied with conviction.

The following morning Rosa arrived early. The deep sadness in her gut began to lift a little as she approached the shop. The shutters had been lifted and the bereavement notice had been replaced with a sign stating *OPEN FOR BUSINESS*.

Jane was dusting shelves while Huw's head was bent over a pile of papers. 'I've left everything until I felt ready to face it,' he said, separating them into different piles. 'There's nothing here we can't manage. I'll give Mr Fry a call and arrange a meeting. I wouldn't like to let him down or lose his trade as he's been loyal to us for many years.'

Within a couple of hours the paperwork had been filed and a list made of potential clients to contact. 'Mr Fry has called and asked if I can see him now,' said Huw, breaking into a smile.

After Huw left, the bell on the front door began to ring and the place sprang back to life. 'I'd like to advertise a fundraising bingo night for the soup kitchen at our social club,' one woman requested, ordering twenty posters. Then a well-dressed gentleman ordered leaflets for a promotion for servicemen at his restaurant.

Rosa set about the artwork, using cheerful characters that fitted the outline of the briefs, and when she finished she showed them to Jane. 'You have such a gift, Rosa. I don't know how we would manage without you.'

Huw returned later in the afternoon with a relaxed smile across his face.

'It looks like everything went well,' Rosa commented.

'It certainly did. The exhibition is to be shown in Cardiff later this year, and then London. Mr Fry would like to order posters from us, and asks that you do the artwork again.'

'Why, that's wonderful news. I did wonder if that's what

they wanted to speak to you about,' Rosa replied. 'I'll discuss the design with Mr Fry. He may like to use a different painting for the next promotion.'

Huw rubbed the back of his neck and frowned.

Jane asked, 'Is there something else you need to tell us?'

'There is. It was Hettie's idea.'

Jane's eyebrows furrowed. 'What is it? Are you going to tell me?'

'Hettie wants to dedicate the Cardiff exhibition to Dylan. She says Hubert will paint a portrait of him wearing his air force uniform from his photograph. She thinks it will add the human touch to the exhibition, and wondered if we would agree to it.'

Jane remained silent, her bottom lip quivering.

Huw took a deep breath and continued, 'Mr Fry made the point that it's thanks to the sacrifice made by Dylan, and thousands of other sons, brothers and husbands, that the Nazis haven't invaded our country, and never will.'

Jane sniffled. 'We don't even know the details of his death or where his resting place is. It's too much. We don't know when, or if, we'll be told. No, I don't want this.' She raised her chin, fighting back tears. 'This will only bring everything back. Tell them *No*.'

Huw consoled his wife, drawing her towards him. 'Then we won't agree to it, my love. I'll let Mr Fry know. It was only a suggestion.'

Rosa nodded. 'I think Jane is right. It's too soon.'

'I think we've had enough for one day,' Huw said. 'I know it's early, but I think we should close now.'

'We understand if you want to leave early and spend time with your family, Rosa. They've not seen much of you these last few weeks,' Jane proposed, a weariness in her tone.

'Well, if you're sure there's nothing else I can do,' Rosa replied slowly.

'Nothing that can't wait till tomorrow. You've already done so much for us,' Huw replied.

Rosa picked up her bag and turned at the door as she left, seeing the pained expressions of Dylan's loss etched across their tired faces. Every muscle in her body ached and she felt emotionally drained, saddened that she would never feel his kisses again.

When she placed the key in the door at home, to her surprise her mother flung it open before she could turn the latch.

'I thought I heard you coming up the stairs,' she said. 'You have two visitors.'

20

'Molly! Jerry! What are you doing here?'

The shock and surprise of seeing two of her truest and most loyal friends brought a lump to her throat. Seeing them both sitting there, smiling and rising to greet her, made her gasp for breath, and her hand reached up to her throat.

'Oh, Molly. I'm so happy to see you. What brings you to Merthyr? And you too, Jerry?'

Jerry rose. 'I had some leave and Molly asked me to accompany her here. I'm so sorry to hear about your loss. I really am. Dylan sounds like a champion chap and everyone at the palace sends you their condolences and best wishes.'

'They do?' asked Rosa, her eyes incredulous.

Molly flung herself at Rosa. 'Yes, Rosa. You've been cleared. It's over. You can come back.'

Rosa stared at them with a dazed expression. 'What do you mean, *I can come back*? What's happened?'

'You won't believe it. The thief was Agnes all along,' Molly babbled.

'Agnes? But how? So nobody is pointing the finger at me any more?'

Eira interrupted, 'I hope that wicked girl gets what's coming to her!'

'I don't understand,' Rosa stuttered. 'Is this the reason you're here now?'

Eira got up. 'I'm sure they'll explain,' she said to Rosa. 'Now, if you'll excuse me, I'll pop round the corner to Mrs Larkin's and ask if she can put them up for the night. She takes in lodgers and I'll see if I can get a special rate.'

'That's very kind, Mrs Edwards, and thank you for making us so welcome,' Jerry replied graciously.

After she left, Molly started to tell Rosa everything that had happened at breakneck speed. Jerry raised a hand. 'Slow down, Molly. You're speaking so fast that it's hard to follow what you're saying.'

Molly pretended to be in a huff and crossed her arms across her chest. 'Very well then, you tell her, Jerry, if she can't understand me.'

'Shall we *all* sit down?' he suggested warmly, holding out a chair for Rosa. Molly and Jerry seated themselves either side of her.

Rosa stared at them, a wide smile stretching across her face. 'I just can't believe the two of you are here.'

'I'm just sorry we weren't able to be here yesterday for Dylan's memorial,' Molly said in a soft voice.

'It was only yesterday that the palace police had the final proof they needed,' Jerry said. 'I have a letter for you exonerating you of all the allegations and offering you their apologies. The palace was going to post it, but we wanted to bring it to you ourselves as soon as possible.'

He produced an envelope from his jacket and handed it to her. 'Molly wanted you to hear the news in person. She twisted my arm to come along with her.'

A sob rose through Rosa's chest. 'I've had to suffer an outrageous slur against my name, on top of losing Dylan.

I've been to hell and back. Why would I want to return to the palace?'

'You didn't deserve any of that, Rosa,' Molly said. 'Hear Jerry out, though, he has a better way with words than me.'

Rosa nodded. 'Very well then. How did they know it was Agnes?'

Jerry moved his seat closer to Rosa. 'To start with, Agnes isn't her real name. It's fake. Her real name is Glynis Piper.'

'What! Why would she have a false name?' Rosa queried.

'Because she's a con-woman and a thief.'

'Never! Surely the palace checked her references.'

'If you stop interrupting, Jerry will tell you,' Molly reprimanded gently.

'The reason is because the references were fake too. The palace was presented with two letters attesting to Agnes's good character, but they were written by her accomplices,' Jerry explained. Rosa opened her mouth to speak, but Jerry continued. 'The police took statements from everyone in the palace who had access to the stolen items, which is why the investigation took so long. Not one person had a bad word to say about you, or could conceive of you stealing from the King and Queen.

'Agnes continued to put up a front, and all was quiet for a while after you left. Then a maid called Jenny, who shared a room with Agnes, lost five one-pound notes over a month. At first she thought she had misplaced the money, or even spent it, as she doesn't have a good head for figures, but then she caught Agnes red-handed.

'This only came to light recently, and if we'd known

earlier you would never have been under suspicion. Agnes threatened that if Jenny spoke to anyone about it, she would get her brother to beat her black and blue. The girl was so terrified that she handed in her notice there and then.'

Rosa's hand flew to her mouth, a shocked expression on her face. 'That's wicked. The poor girl – no wonder she left. How was she caught?'

Molly replied, 'I saw Jenny crying when she packed her bags and persuaded her to tell me what had happened. She begged me not to tell anyone and was petrified of Agnes's threats. I couldn't keep it to myself. I told Jerry, and he told the police.'

Jerry took up the story. 'After Jenny left, a new girl called Polly was put in the same room as Agnes. Superintendent Hodges set a trap.'

'What kind of trap?'

'When the new maid was out, and knowing that Agnes was due to return to her room at the end of her shift, they planted two crisp ten-shilling notes in clear view under an ornament on the sideboard, marking them with invisible ink.

'As expected, the notes disappeared, and later that evening a spot check was carried out on all staff. The stolen notes were found in Agnes's possession and she was arrested. Jenny has agreed to help the police and is back at the palace, while Agnes – or Glynis, whatever her name is – is banged up in the police cells.'

'I can barely believe this. What drove her to do it?' asked Rosa.

Molly answered, 'It turned out she was in debt – she

had a gambling habit. She sold everything she nicked. Except the figurine of the corgi, which was found thrown out with some rubbish, with its head smashed off.'

Jerry added, 'The Queen was furious when she was told. She insists Glynis Piper is charged and made an example of. I heard too that the Queen was most upset to hear you had been blamed. The officer who was supposed to have checked her references has been demoted. It's been a horrible business, and I'm glad it's over.'

Rosa gulped, taking in everything she had been told. 'I never did anything against her. Why did she pick on me to frame?'

Molly answered, her voice filled with warmth. 'Because you were an easy target, seeing as you were new and an innocent in the ways of the royal household. I suspect there was a hint of jealousy behind it too, as you settled in very easily and got on with everyone.'

Rosa stood and paced the room, rubbing the back of her neck. 'I appreciate you coming to tell me this and bringing me the letter, but I can't go back to the palace. I can't leave Dylan's parents. They need me to help with the business, now Dylan is no longer with us.'

Molly responded, 'I understand this has come as a big shock and you need time to take it all in. Seeing as we're not going back until tomorrow afternoon, is there any chance we could meet Dylan's parents tomorrow, to pay them our respects?'

Rosa clasped her hands in front of her chest. 'They would appreciate that. I've told them all about you and my work at the palace. Afterwards I'll show you the tree we planted in Dylan's memory at our favourite spot.'

'We'd like that very much, wouldn't we?' said Molly, turning to Jerry, who nodded.

'It's a shame you never got to meet Dylan – you would have all got on like a house on fire,' Rosa warbled, her eyes misting over. Molly placed a comforting arm around Rosa's shoulder, consoling her friend.

Eira returned and informed Molly and Huw that two small rooms were available with Mrs Larkin, and she would cook them egg and ham with boiled potatoes for tea, if they wished.

They readily accepted, picking up their overnight cases left by the side of the door.

Molly hugged her friend. 'Before we go, Ma asked around in South Grove about your friend Alice, but nobody could say anything, though neighbours have noticed the curtains seem to be permanently drawn.'

'That's very strange. She seems to be lying low. What on earth could be the reason?'

Molly shrugged her shoulders. 'Whatever the reason, the truth will come out sooner or later, they can't stay behind closed doors for ever.'

Rosa's face showed strain. Molly went towards the door.

'You've had an exhausting day, Rosa. We'll leave you now and call round for you in the morning. Is around eight-thirty OK?'

'Yes, that would be perfect.'

21

Rosa tossed and turned that night, her mind spinning after Dylan's memorial, the unexpected arrival of her visitors from London, and their shocking disclosure about Agnes. She rose bleary-eyed the following morning as her mother put the kettle on to boil, tipping out the old tea leaves from the night before. 'They've been used twice. Let's make a fresh pot.'

As they sat at the table, Eira remarked, 'You've got two good friends there. They must care about you a lot to come all this way to break the news to you, when the letter would have sufficed.'

'Molly's like a sister to me, and her family are the kindest people you can meet. I don't know much about Jerry, but we get on well and rub along together.'

Rosa pushed away the toasted crumpet her mother set in front of her. 'I couldn't eat a thing.'

'I'm not going to see it go to waste,' Eira replied, pulling the plate towards her and savouring each mouthful.

Rosa grabbed her bag when the doorbell rang. 'That will be Molly and Jerry.' It rang a second time while she found the letter and placed it in the bag to show Jane and Huw. 'I'll see you later, Mam.'

'I thought you were never going to answer,' Molly quipped outside. Jerry was waiting by the front gate and raised his hand.

Rosa took Molly's arm in hers. 'Sorry. I'm feeling jittery and so confused right now. Let's go.'

Rosa pointed out familiar landmarks they passed on the way: the department store where she saw the advertisement, and the town hall where the art exhibition was held. They arrived at the printer's shop just as Huw was unlocking the door and picking up his post, which he placed on top of the counter.

'I'll see to that later. Who do we have here then, Rosa?' he smiled, inviting them in with a sweep of his arm.

'This is Molly Deakin, my best friend from the palace. And this is Jerry Snaith – he's a guard at the palace. They came here all the way from London to bring me some good news. I've been cleared of all the allegations against me. It's in a letter here,' Rosa blurted, handing it to him.

Mr Williams took the letter out of the envelope and read its contents. When he had finished, his eyes shone.

'Well, isn't that just the best news. Jane will be delighted to hear it. It says here you can go back to the palace, Rosa. What do you say to that?'

'I've told you, I'm going to stay here with you both and help with the business. It's what Dylan would have wanted.'

Jane came into the shop from the back room. 'I thought I heard voices. Good morning, Rosa. And these are your friends?'

Rosa introduced her and Huw passed his wife the letter. After she had absorbed its contents, she tilted her head towards her husband. 'Will you excuse us for a minute while we discuss something important? Rosa, where are your manners. Why don't you put the kettle on and show your friends the poster you designed?'

Rosa did as instructed, leaving Molly and Jerry gawping in admiration at her work while she poured water into the kettle and placed five cups and saucers on a tray. While waiting for the water to boil, she looked out the window and saw Dylan's parents in the back yard talking animatedly. Jane's hand rested on her chin as she listened intently, while her husband spoke rapidly, raising his arms and shrugging his shoulders.

She drew back when they turned around to come back inside. Rosa poured out the tea and enough chairs were found for them all to sit on.

'Is everything alright?' Rosa asked. Huw and Jane sat close together, holding hands.

Jane pressed her hand gently across her husband's arm. 'You tell her, Huw.'

'Tell me what? Why do you look so serious?'

Huw handed Rosa her letter back. '*This* changes everything, Rosa.'

Rosa jerked her head back. 'Changes what? What do you mean?'

'When I saw Mr Fry, he said more to me than I've let on. He asked if I would give him first refusal if and when I wanted to sell the business. The thought has crossed our minds, now we've lost Dylan.'

Rosa shook her head, not believing what she was being told. 'But I thought you wanted to keep it going. You have so many loyal customers.'

'We are only carrying on for your sake and the connection you feel here with Dylan. This might be the right time for you to return to London and start afresh. You have to keep living your life. If there is anything this war has taught us, it is that we only have one life, and we should grab what chances we can.'

Rosa's throat clenched.

Jane said, 'I'm sorry, my dear. We don't mean to upset you. Huw and I are tired and ready to give up the business. If we sell to Mr Fry, Hettie will take over the everyday management. It seems to make sense.'

Rosa frowned. 'But are you sure? The business has been with the family for so long. It's come as a shock to hear you even think of such a thing.'

'Of course it has. We think this is the right time for us to move on, and for you too.'

'I see,' mumbled Rosa, feeling an emptiness inside and a deep sadness.

Huw pressed his hand on Rosa's arm. 'I hope you see this would be best for us all. We can't bring Dylan back and we feel a change of scene would be best. We've seen how other families have wallowed in their grief and given up on life. That's not what we want for you, or for us.'

'But what will you do? Won't you be lonely in a new place?' Rosa queried.

Huw grinned. 'I fancy myself as a bit of an artist, not painting war pictures like Hubert, but nature and the beauty of our valleys and coastline around the Mumbles.'

Jane piped up, 'We thought we could take in lodgers for a bit of company and some extra money. We'll stay in touch and visit you, and you must come and stay.'

'It sounds like you've thought it all out. I wouldn't want you to stay here on my account, and maybe it is for the best. I just wasn't expecting it.'

'We were in no rush, but now you have the chance to

return to London, this seems the right time to do it,' Huw replied, turning to his wife, who nodded her agreement.

Molly placed a reassuring arm around her friend's shoulder. 'So what do you say then, Rosa? Are you coming back to the palace?'

'It seems like the decision has been made for me. But I won't leave here straight away. I still need some time here to say my goodbyes. I want to spend time with Da too, see if we can make up before I leave. We parted under a cloud when I saw him last Christmas. I'll write to the palace and let them know I'll return.'

Jerry beamed. 'If you were to visit our capital city, Mr and Mrs Williams, I would be delighted to recommend a show or some excellent restaurants that are reasonably priced.'

Once their next steps had been agreed, the mood in the room lightened, and Molly and Jerry told Dylan's parents about Agnes and her deception.

'None of us believed it was Rosa,' Molly stated. 'Oh, by the way, did Rosa tell you about one of the palace cooks who comes from Merthyr, by the name of Mary Jones? She used to work for one of the ladies from here.'

'Oh yes, Lady Gwendoline!' Rosa said. 'It slipped my mind. Mrs Jones has been very kind to me. I must let Lady Gwendoline know the result of the investigation.'

Jerry leaned forward. 'The chances are she already knows. From what I hear she was involved in stepping it up when it seemed to have stalled.'

'I will write to her with my thanks,' Rosa smiled.

Jerry looked at his watch. 'We'll need to catch our train in a couple of hours. Before we go I would very much like to see Dylan's memorial tree, if you are still able to show us, Rosa?'

'Of course you must take them,' Huw said. 'Let them see the views of our beautiful valley.'

Molly beamed. 'I can see why Rosa is so fond of you both. I'm so very sorry for your loss. Dylan must have been a real credit to you both, and I know how much he meant to Rosa. I'll look after her, don't worry.'

She embraced Dylan's parents in turn and there wasn't a dry eye between them as they set off, with Rosa promising to call in after Molly and Jerry had caught their train.

She turned as she stepped out of the door and saw Huw wipe a tear away. Saying goodbye was going to be harder than she realised – for them all.

Molly waved vigorously from the window of the carriage as the train pulled out of Merthyr. Jerry had surprised her by taking her hand on the platform and awkwardly kissed her lightly on the cheek. He pulled away sharpish when he saw the surprised expression on her face.

'I'm sorry, I didn't mean to make you feel uncomfortable.'

'Of course, Jerry. Thank you again for coming. Will you give my love to everyone at the palace?'

She watched the train disappear over the horizon feeling a tinge of sadness at their departure, and found herself smiling as her hand strayed to her cheek where Jerry had kissed it. Did she imagine his eyes lingering on her? She dismissed the thought that the kiss was anything other than friendly, and realised she was beginning to look forward to returning to the palace.

She was deep in thought as she made her way back to the shop, where she planned to finish work on Mr Fry's new poster design. When she reached the premises she stared at the front door. Why was the *Closed* sign up?

'It's only me,' she called cheerily as she entered, letting herself in through the back door. 'Is everything alright?'

Huw appeared holding a letter in his hand, his face etched with sadness.

'What's happened?' she asked.

'After you all left I picked up the mail from this morning and this letter was amongst it. It's from a fellow pilot of Dylan's.'

'What does it say?'

'Come on through and you can read it.'

'Where's Jane?'

'She gone upstairs to rest. It's all been too much for her.'

As Rosa opened the envelope a photograph slipped from the folds of the letter: it was the photograph of herself that she had given to Dylan. A lump formed in her throat.

Huw placed a comforting arm on her shoulder and pushed a chair close to her. 'It's the photo I gave Dylan before he left Merthyr,' she sobbed.

Huw bowed his head and wiped his eyes with his sleeve. Rosa glanced to the end of the page and saw it was written by a Raymond Shawcross, a name she had never heard before. He wrote: *We were on the same highly secretive mission and agreed beforehand that if anything happened to either of us, whoever survived would return any personal items to the bereaved family. It is my sad duty to do so on behalf of Dylan.*

Raymond offered his most sincere condolences, and apologised that he could only disclose limited information. He continued:

*I am able to share with you the bravery surrounding Dylan's
passing. He was unlucky, being in a plane on his first mission
that took a hit and burst into flames. He parachuted and landed
in a field, where he was found the next day by a farmer, barely
alive. The farmer and his son returned with their cart and hid
him in their home, where they treated his injuries. Dylan drifted
in and out of consciousness and mumbled a girl's name, Rosa, who
I know is the girl in the photograph that was found in his inside
pocket. Dylan showed it to me and spoke very fondly of her.*

Rosa placed the letter in her lap. 'My poor Dylan,' she wept. 'He must have been terrified. He was so brave.'

Huw put his arm around Rosa. 'Yes, he was brave, so many of them are. I hope in time we will learn the true nature of this secret mission. He must have known it was dangerous.'

Rosa picked up the letter and read on. '"Dylan lost a lot of blood and it was impossible to get medical aid to him without the farmer arousing suspicion. German troops occupied the village just a short distance away and had executed local people for doing this. He put himself in extreme danger by taking Dylan in."'

Rosa looked up. 'How can we ever thank him?'

'Maybe one day we will be able to, when this war is over,' Huw said thoughtfully.

Rosa continued reading, staring in disbelief. 'He says one day the farmer hid Dylan under a false floor in the basement when a sudden check was made by the Germans. They got him down just in time.'

Huw clenched his fists. 'Those bastards. It fills me with fury. I hope Hitler and his bloody Nazis burn in hell.'

'Oh they will, there's no doubt about that,' Rosa spat.

Just that week the war had taken a new turn, with Britain and her allies storming the beaches in northern France. There was a massive air attack too; newspapers reported that the sky was filled with aeroplanes that were breaking through German defences. Could Dylan have somehow had a part in this?

The letter finished with Raymond saying that, despite the farmer's best efforts, Dylan was unable to pull through. One morning when they checked on him, he had stopped breathing. The farmer arranged for the burial in the churchyard, with the priest complicit in convincing the Nazis that the coffin contained the remains of a vagrant. The Williamses should take comfort for now that he had a Christian burial.

Rosa's words faltered as she read the final sentences. '"One day you will learn the truth of Dylan's bravery. It was a great privilege to know him and fly alongside him. May God rest his soul."'

Rosa buried her face in her hands and wept into her soggy handkerchief. When she had no tears left she bit her lip and turned to Huw. His face was grief-stricken and the dark rings under his eyes showed his pain.

Her stomach lurched, but she straightened her back and tidied her hair. Turning to Huw she beckoned to the workbench and said, 'Come on, there's work to be done. I want to have Mr Fry's posters ready for when he next calls in.'

Huw steadied himself. 'Has anyone told you, you are a remarkable young lady, Rosa Edwards? No wonder our Dylan fell for you.'

The following day Rosa wrote to Superintendent Hodges thanking him for his letter and saying she would be able to resume duties at the palace the following week, Monday 19 June. She asked him to confirm if this was acceptable, and, if so, to include a rail warrant. She also wrote to Miss Rogers saying she was looking forward to returning, and, having pondered on Molly's update about her friend from home, she wrote to Alice at the Stepney address to let her know she was there for her, whatever trouble she might be in.

As she dropped the envelopes into the post box she heard a woman call out her name. She turned to see Lady Gwendoline dressed in an elegant pale blue suit. 'Ah, Miss Edwards . . . Rosa. I was hoping to see you. Do you have a moment?'

'Er, yes, of course, Lady Gwendoline.'

'We're just a few minutes from Goodwin's. Shall we go there? I'm sure we will find a quiet room. I understand quite a bit has happened since I last saw you.'

Within a short time she swept into the store behind Lady Gwendoline, who greeted staff and customers on both sides. She paused at a glass counter displaying nylon stockings. 'Rosa, would you like a pair or two? It's my treat.'

Before Rosa could answer an assistant was summoned over and asked to wrap two pairs of much-coveted Kayser

Bondor nylons. 'Please add them to my account,' she instructed the shop girl, and gave them to Rosa.

Lady Gwendoline led Rosa up the stairs into an unoccupied office and invited her to take a seat. 'The stockings nowhere near make up for the terrible injustice you have suffered. I feel partly responsible for the trouble you found yourself in as you went to the palace following my encouragement.'

'It wasn't your fault,' Rosa replied.

'Your discretion and fortitude have not gone unnoticed in the royal household, particularly as you had to bear this unpleasantness on top of the loss of the boy you had affections for. I'm so sorry to hear about Dylan. It must be very hard on you and his family.'

'We heard today from a pilot who knew Dylan. Nothing could be done to save him. He was so young, so brave,' Rosa said, and dabbed an eye.

'I'm sure he was. Losing someone you love is very painful, but you are young and pretty and one day—'

Rosa's voice was adamant. 'I couldn't even think of such of thing. It wouldn't be right.'

'None of us can say what the future holds for us. I wanted to let you know how well you are thought of in the palace, after what's happened, so you can hold your head up when you return. Mrs Jones tells me you are always cheerful and willing to lend a hand where it's wanted. I hear you have a good way with the Queen's corgi too, and that you also made an excellent impression on the young princesses.'

'I did? I was only being myself.'

'Don't ever change, Rosa.'

A moment later there was a gentle knock and an older lady appeared holding some folders. 'Excuse me for interrupting, but I have the letters you requested ready for you to sign.'

Lady Gwendoline rose. 'I must attend to these. It was lovely to see you, Rosa. I am very pleased you will be returning to the palace and I'll be sure to look out for you when I next visit there.'

Rosa took her cue. 'Thank you for the stockings. And for putting me at ease about going back to the palace.'

Lady Gwendoline extended her hand and clasped Rosa's in hers. 'You'll be just fine and I'm sure we'll stay in touch, my dear.'

A few days later, a reply from the palace landed on the doormat, including a railway warrant and her staff pass. To Rosa's delight, a postcard arrived from Billy the same day showing a picture of a boat with some brief, reassuring words: *Don't worry about me, I had to get away. I'm alright. Billy.*

She spent the day with Huw and Jane helping them sort out orders that needed finalising. On her way there she dropped a note for her father at his lodgings asking if he could meet her at the printing shop at five-thirty that day, hoping they could make up after refusing to give him money at Christmas.

As she was about to leave the print shop, she spotted him pacing backwards and forwards outside the door. She bade farewell to Dylan's parents and stepped outside, pleased to see her father had made an effort with his appearance and was clean-shaven.

He beamed. 'I don't brush up too bad, do I? Old Widow Isaacson had a clean-out after her Boris died and gave me first pickings.'

'You look really smart, Da. What's brought this about?'

'The truth is, I've met up a couple of times with that lad George. We hooked up after Dylan's memorial, and he gave me a talking to.'

'I see. I had no idea. He's a dark horse.'

'I realised I'm a silly old fool and . . .' He paused, coughing up dark phlegm and spitting it out.

'Da, your chest, have you had it seen to?'

'Aye, there's naught anyone can do. I was told to cut down on the booze straight away, and that's why I'm cleaning myself up. I didn't want you to be ashamed to be seen out with your old man.'

'What do you and George talk about?'

'He told me straight that I should be there for you, even though things didn't work out with Mam, that too many lives were being ruined by the war, and we should be there for the family we have.'

Rosa stared with her jaw open. 'That's very philosophical of George. I thought we could walk to Cyfarthfa Castle. Is that alright?'

He took her elbow and they walked together along the path. When they reached the castle, Rosa led him to the bench she had sat on with Dylan during their last meeting.

Rosa's lip wobbled. 'I owe you an apology, Da.'

'Whatever for, lass?'

'I'm sorry you never got to spend time with Dylan. It's just that—'

He coughed, his chest lurching forward. He produced a handkerchief and coughed again, bringing up fluid stained with dark markings.

'Your chest sounds worse, Da.'

'Don't you worry about me, Rosa. I'll be alright. It warms my heart to see how well you've done. You've made your old man proud, working at the palace. Do you get to see the King and Queen, or the princesses?'

'Shush, Da, you know I can't talk about that kind of thing, you never know who might be listening.'

Rosa pressed her hand on her father's arm, then rested her head on his shoulder. She closed her eyes and for a split second imagined she was sitting alongside Dylan and looking forward to a bright future together.

She spent her remaining time in Merthyr giving her mother's rooms a good tidy. Mr Fry praised her latest work, implying there might be a job for her if she wanted to consider it. Rosa was flattered, but politely declined, believing her future now lay in London.

'Promise you'll come and see the exhibition in London. I'll send you some tickets,' Hettie said, smiling, surprising Rosa by the warmth of her farewell hug.

When it came to say goodbye to the Williamses, Jane produced a small red box.

'We'd like you to take this.'

'What is it?' Rosa asked, taking hold of it.

'We know you and Dylan had only been together for a short while, but he went to war feeling loved by you and, who knows, the chances are he would have proposed if he had returned home.'

Rosa lifted the gold ring from the pink satin lining and counted ten diamonds shimming around the band.

'Why, it's beautiful. It must be worth a small fortune. But I don't understand, why do you want me to have it?'

'We told Dylan that when he found the girl he wanted to spend the rest of his life with, I would give her this ring after they wed. You are the closest that came to.'

Rosa struggled to find the right words. 'Wed? Well, it was early days—'

'It's an eternity ring,' Jane continued. 'It used to belong to my mother, she gave it to me, and I have nobody to pass it on to. I would like you to have it.'

Rosa held it up to the light. 'I've never seen anything so beautiful. If only Dylan could have given it to me.'

She slid it on her finger and it fitted perfectly. She held up her hand and admired it. Tears sprung from her eyes. 'I promise I will treasure it.'

'There is something else,' Jane said, her voice soft, glancing in Huw's direction.

He took the cue. 'We know you will respect Dylan's memory. But he wouldn't want you to spend the rest of your life wallowing in misery. We want you to allow yourself to be happy. One day, you will find someone else to love.'

Rosa inhaled a sharp breath. 'None of us can say what the future holds.'

'That's true, but do you think Jerry may be just a little fond of you?'

Rosa's eye's widened. 'Jerry? You surely don't think—?'

'He seems very fond of you, to have come all this way,' Huw went on. 'As I said, we wanted to let you know you shouldn't hold back if you have a second chance of happiness – not on account of us.'

'Jerry is just a friend, a good friend. I'm not interested in another fella.'

Jane pressed her hand on Rosa's arm. 'Huw's right, my dear. Now, promise you will stay in touch and let us know how everything is going. We shall worry about you.'

Rosa hugged Jane and Huw, all three choking back tears and wiping their eyes. 'I promise I will,' Rosa stammered.

On her way home, Rosa took the path that led up to Cyfarthfa Castle for a final visit before her departure to London, traipsing along the steep, narrow streets that twisted and turned past the rows of terraced houses. When she arrived at the top she strolled through the parkland, stopping when she reached Dylan's memorial tree.

She fingered her ring and whispered, 'I may be leaving Merthyr, but I shall always remember you, Dylan, wherever I am.'

23

On the morning of Rosa's departure, Eira handed her daughter her small case. 'It's a very long time since I've been to London. I might surprise you with a visit, once you're settled back in.'

Rosa hugged her mother. 'That would be lovely, Mam.'

'You take care of yourself. Promise?'

'I promise, Mam. I'm glad I can return and hold my head up high. And I must try and find out what's happened to Alice. I feel it in my gut she's in trouble.'

'She was always headstrong, didn't have a sensible head on her shoulders like you.'

'She's my friend, Mam. I want to help if she's in trouble.'

'You are soft-hearted, Rosa Edwards. Be off with you now, before you miss your train.'

To her surprise her father was at the station. 'George told me you were leaving this morning. I wanted to see you off.'

A couple of nights before, Rosa had spoken to George about the change in her father, thanking him for his kindness towards him. She was astounded when George told her, 'He did it for you, Rosa.'

'Da, take care of yourself. I'll write to you,' gulped Rosa.

'It's you who must take care in London, lass.'

A guard blew his whistle and called, 'All aboard!'

Thomas watched Rosa board her carriage. She opened

the window and a tear trickled down her cheek as she saw him wave his handkerchief till the train was out of sight.

She shared the journey with servicemen travelling to join new postings. The talk was about the latest string of fierce attacks on London from a new weapon in the sky that needed no pilot – the flying bombs, or doodlebugs, as they were known, that were targeted on the city and would then plummet to earth and explode.

It was a cloudy, overcast day and on the chilly side, and Rosa was glad her mother had suggested she wore a rain-coat over a light blue sweater with a grey flannel skirt. She continued her journey from Paddington Station by bus, changing at Hyde Park Corner for a second bus that stopped in Buckingham Palace Road. She didn't at first pick up on the animated chatter around her, peppered with the words 'bomb' and 'palace'.

A woman speaking in a louder voice made her ears prick up and she bolted upright and tapped on the woman's shoulder in front of her. 'What's happened? What is everyone talking about?'

The woman spun around. 'Haven't you heard, love? The Guards' Chapel took a direct hit yesterday during the morning service. Dozens of people have been killed.'

'Dozens? Are you sure?'

Her first thought was Jerry. Would he have been there? Was he killed? She pressed her face against the window for any sight of the bombed area. The bus drew to a halt a couple of streets away and she saw crowds of people in the distance amongst a large pile of rubble.

She leaped off the bus and flew along the road, her heart pumping faster than ever. The chapel was part of

Wellington Barracks, home of the royal guardsmen. Panicked, all she could think was whether Jerry had been inside at the time.

As she got closer to the stricken site, evidence of the huge damage became apparent. From her position behind a barrier she saw rescue workers, ambulance, police and Home Guard everywhere. Many of the onlookers were in floods of tears and gathered as close as they could in search of missing family.

The front of the chapel where the alter was positioned remained standing, with fragments of its adjoining walls, leaving a hollow shell where the direct hit had landed, destroying the roof. Several journalists were busy scribbling in their notebooks while photographers snapped away.

'Can you please all move on,' one of the officers hollered. 'This is a rescue operation still, and those we recover won't appreciate sightseers.' Another voice bellowed, 'Didn't you hear? Clear orf, else you'll be arrested for obstruction!'

'Those bastard Nazis,' shouted one of the angry bystanders. 'Killing innocent people in the house of God. I hope they burn in hell!'

Rosa looked away as a lifeless body covered with a blanket was carried from the rubble – but not before she had seen a man's arm dangling from the stretcher, wearing the same khaki sleeve of Jerry's uniform. She stepped over a child's shoe and teddy bear, and prayed they had survived.

Rosa had never witnessed such carnage and devastation before, the frightful sights and frantic sounds that she would never be able to forget.

She turned and fled, feeling she wanted to throw up. After a moment she steadied herself and caught her breath. She stumbled to the palace just a few minutes' walk away, her eyes searching frantically for Jerry at the staff entrance gate.

'Hello – Miss Edwards, isn't it?' one of the guards asked, his eyes dull.

'It is.' Her words faltered. 'I've just been to the chapel. I can't believe the destruction, with so many dead and injured. Do you know if Jerry Snaith was there at the time?'

'I'm afraid not. The casualty list is being drawn up. More than one hundred died, that's all I know. Did you know him?'

Rosa stifled a sob and nodded.

'I'm sorry, love, I can't tell you any more. I have no idea myself.'

Rosa's shoulders shook and she walked unsteadily across the courtyard to the staff entrance. A guard checked her paperwork and she made her way down the steps and through the labyrinth of endless tunnels. Staff were scurrying about, their expressions pained, many leaving the palace carrying trays of sandwiches, perhaps to offer at the scene of destruction.

She felt relieved to reach her room, and slumped on the bed. She couldn't put Jerry out of her mind, particularly the fear that he could be dead, and the realisation of just how deeply she cared about him.

Her maid's outfit was laid out neatly on the bed. She slipped out of her clothes and hung them up, then quickly ran a comb through her hair, washed her tear-stained face and slipped into her work clothes.

In the kitchen, Mrs Jones glanced up, wiping her brow with the side of her arm. 'It's good to have you back, Rosa, and I'm glad that the nasty business about Agnes has been sorted once and for all. We're in shock here – what a day to return. You've no doubt heard what happened yesterday, with the chapel bombing. Many of our own guards and their families were there and have been killed or injured. How much more bombing can we take?'

'I saw it on my way here,' Rosa replied, shaken and sensing the heavy atmosphere in the room. 'I'll never forget the sight. What can I do, Mrs Jones? I'll do anything to help.'

'The rescue teams have been working all round the clock. I think they need more refreshments – it's the least we can do. Can you carry a couple of flasks of tea over with these paper cups. I've added milk and there are some sugar cubes too.'

Molly burst into the kitchen carrying an empty tray, having just returned from the bombsite. She caught Rosa's anxious expression. 'Judging by your face, I can see you're knocked for six. I'll give you a hand if that's alright, Mrs Jones?'

'Very well. Here's another flask for you, Molly, and some more Marmite sandwiches. The first batch went down a treat.'

Molly paused. 'I've just heard one of those killed is the sister of Mr Penn,' she said, referring to the Queen's private secretary.

'Poor man,' Cook said. 'He went over to assist with the search and found his sister's body. It's just too bloody awful.'

Molly and Rosa set off with their trays. 'I've never seen anything so dreadful in my life,' Rosa said, 'and they're still bringing bodies out. I saw a dead guard being carried out. I'm worried if Jerry—' Rosa's bottom lip wobbled.

'I haven't seen him since we came back,' Molly said. 'We can ask around, but there's so much confusion at the moment. We must try not to think the worst.'

'That's easier said than done,' Rosa replied, her eyes downcast as she walked steadily with her laden tray down the passageway and out into the fresh air.

They reached the security barrier and were told they couldn't go any further. 'Thank you, ladies. Place it down there, will you. We'll leave them there for you to collect,' an officer instructed.

Rosa hovered as Molly tugged at her arm, but she brushed her off. Trembling, she plucked up courage to ask the guard, 'Do you know if a Jerry Snaith was here at the time? He's a guard at the palace and we're his friends. We're anxious for news of him.'

The officer scratched the back of his neck. 'The name doesn't ring a bell. I can't tell you anything for sure. Sorry, love. I must press on.'

Rosa and Molly returned to the palace, where Cook was co-ordinating more refreshment trips to the bomb-site. They continued backwards and forwards with trays for hours, until finally the rescue efforts were halted for the night.

'Just imagine if it had been the palace that was hit, and the King and Queen were killed. It doesn't bear thinking about,' Rosa said as they sat with cups of tea at the kitchen table.

Mrs Jones remarked, 'It's thanks to God's mercy that they have survived. The palace was hit numerous times during the Blitz, but they still refused to leave the country. The worst time was in September 1940 when we were hit twice in one week. One in the quadrangle broke a water main and caused water to spout ten feet high, but thankfully nobody was killed. The King made sure everyone was down in the shelter, but the Queen wouldn't go until she had her corgi in her arms. God bless them. I worship the ground they walk on.'

'It must have been terrifying,' Rosa replied, wide-eyed.

'I can't say it's something you get used to. As the King said, we are not going to let German barbarity beat us. Treacherous acts such as this merely strengthen our resolve.'

Rosa shuddered. A thought occurred. 'Do you think the Nazis meant to blow up the palace instead of the Guards' Chapel?'

'Possibly. That's why the princesses are kept outside London, but do what they can to support the war effort. They do their bit to "Dig for Victory" at Windsor by growing produce, and I hear the young Elizabeth has green fingers. They've raised money by putting on pantomimes every Christmas, and I daresay they've knitted socks for the soldiers too.'

Just then, Miss Rogers came into the kitchen. 'The Queen would like to pass on her thanks to you all for everything you did today. As you can imagine, she was devastated to learn that Olive Penn, the sister of her private secretary, Mr Penn, was amongst those killed. She has written to Arthur offering her sincere condolences – she really feels for his suffering, and for everybody's.'

'Thank you for letting us know, Miss Rogers. It's good to have Rosa back too. She's been a real trooper, going backwards and forwards with refreshments for the rescue team,' said Mrs Jones.

'Yes, it's good to see you again, Miss Edwards. There is something else; the King and Queen will host a gathering for the rescue teams in the next week to thank them. The search is still going on, meanwhile, and we must hope that more survivors can be found.'

The end of the week came with no news of Jerry. Rosa had asked in the Guards' office, and was told it was too early to say for sure which men were killed there.

Molly suggested, 'Why don't you come over tomorrow for the weekend? You'd be welcome, as long as you don't mind sleeping on the sofa again.'

Rosa shook her head, her eyes downcast. 'That's very kind, but I'm feeling done in and want some time alone.'

Her friend consoled her. 'I understand. You've been through a lot these last few weeks.'

'Truth be told, I'm also worried about Alice and plan to return to her aunt's house to see if she has returned. I have an inkling that something is terribly wrong. I don't understand why I haven't heard from her.'

'Well, don't go getting yourself into any sort of trouble. You know where I am if you need me.'

Rosa sighed. 'I do, but I'll be fine. I also have letters to write home to Mam and Dylan's parents. I know they'll be worried about me. Please give your mam and family my love. You are blessed to have them, Molly. I'll see you on Sunday evening.'

The following morning Rosa set out for South Grove in Stepney. The weather was foul and she dressed in her dark blue raincoat and carried an umbrella. She again scribbled a note for Alice informing her she was back at the palace, in case there was no reply.

Rosa's pulse quickened as she stepped out of the Underground at Stepney Green, her umbrella held high as the rain lashed down. When she reached the house, she froze. She noticed a large black car parked outside. Two men were standing on the pavement in front of the gate, one wearing a trilby hat and mackintosh and holding a large camera with a flash-gun, which he pointed in her direction. Rosa gasped and shielded her face. The other man stepped forward, his collar turned up, as rain trickled down the back of his coat.

'Excuse me, miss. Are you anything to do with the family here?'

Rosa opened her mouth to reply, but her instincts warned her against it. She didn't like the forceful manner of these two men, whose eyes had lit up at the sight of her, their faces almost pressing against hers so she could feel their breath. She stepped back and held her arm over her face, suddenly realising they must be reporters. But why are they here? she pondered, feeling increasingly anxious.

She pushed past them and knocked on the front door. She heard voices inside and called out, 'Alice, it's me, Rosa. Will you open up please?'

She pressed her ear against the door. A man's voice was speaking in a firm tone and she could hear crying over it. Suddenly the front door burst open. A man in his thirties stepped out, placing a small notepad and pencil inside his jacket pocket, his raincoat gripped under his elbow.

'Who are you? What business do you have here?' he asked tersely, looking over her shoulder.

'I've come to see my friend, Alice. My name is Rosa Edwards. Is everything alright? Can I see her?'

'I'm afraid not, so 'op it.'

He turned his back on her and called inside, 'Jack Finchley and his sidekick are still there, Guv.'

'We're coming out now,' a man's voice called back.

'No. Please don't do this,' a woman's voice cried.

'Alice!' cried Rosa.

She pushed her way inside the house as an older man with the bushiest eyebrows she had ever seen placed handcuffs on her bewildered friend.

'Rosa!' she gasped, shaking from head to toe.

Rosa gripped her arm. 'What's happening, Alice? Why are you being arrested?'

Alice's eyes were puffy and her bottom lip quivered. She panted for breath, her chest heaving. 'I can't—I didn't—'

Rosa's eyes almost popped out of her head when the figure of an older woman appeared who she recognised from Merthyr. 'That's your mother! Why is she being handcuffed?'

The older man pushed Rosa aside. 'It's time to go. Keep your heads down, seeing as the Press are outside.'

'Where are you taking her?' blurted Rosa. 'Can I see her later?'

'She'll be at the local nick. You can see her after we've taken our statements. Now leave us to get on with our job, else you'll be arrested for obstructing a police officer in the course of his duty.'

He grabbed Alice under her elbow and the younger officer took her mother's arm while shielding their faces from the flashing camera bulbs the best they could, leading them into the black car. The camera flashed again, catching Rosa's agitated expression.

Aunt Ruby appeared at the front door. 'Get off my property,' she ordered the photographer when he stepped onto her garden path.'

He stepped back and snapped Alice's distraught aunt waving her hands in the air, then retreating into her house and slamming the front door.

The car sped off as the photographer grinned at Rosa and said, 'Make sure you buy the *Express* on Monday. Your face will be on the cover alongside your friend's. Did you know she's a baby-killer?'

24

The terrified expression plastered on Alice's face was fixed in Rosa's head. She stumbled to a nearby teashop and found a table in a corner. She fingered the menu, unable to take in what was on offer.

'What can I get you, luv? I haven't got all day.' It was the fourth time the waitress had asked.

'Err, just tea and a teacake, please.'

'Are you alright, luv? You look like you've 'ad a right shock.'

'I have, but I'll be alright.' Rosa's voice quivered.

She couldn't believe the horrendous accusation levelled against Alice. Alice a baby-killer? It was impossible to believe she could face such a wicked accusation. How and when did she have her baby? Why was her mother arrested too?

When her order was brought to her, the waitress quipped, 'What's all that fuss about round the corner? People are saying a young girl was arrested for murder! You never can tell who's living next to you these days, can you?'

Rosa ignored the question, but the waitress persisted. 'I think I know the girl they're talking about. She used to come in 'ere for a cuppa and seemed nervous, like. The girl was only about your age and you could see she was up the duff. She came in with an older lady I took to be her mum. I 'ope she 'as a good brief to sort out the mess she's in.'

The waitress's words sharpened Rosa's mind. She dug deep into her bag. Her fingers probed desperately, discarding her purse and handkerchief, her comb and lipstick, and some old bus tickets. *Where is it?* she thought frantically. *I'm sure I put it in here.* Flustered, her fingers eventually found what she was looking for, and she read the words on the card she had dug out: *Archibald Howell, Solicitor, Howell, Ratcliffe and Fanshawe, Family and Criminal Law.*

An address in Park Lane and phone number were printed below.

I'll call him, that's what I'll do, she thought to herself. I bet Alice doesn't have a solicitor. I'll see if he can help her.

She inhaled a breath and rose, flung what she owed onto the table, and rushed outside without touching what she had ordered.

She stumbled down the road gathering her thoughts, and after a few minutes she stopped a passer-by and asked where the nearest phone box was. She was directed to the next road where she found the call box, inserted two pennies and dialled for the operator.

'Piccadilly 3861 please, operator.'

She hopped from foot to foot, praying for Mr Howell to answer the call, that he would be in his office on a Saturday. She felt a huge sense of relief when she heard a man's voice say, 'Good morning, may I help you?'

'I need to speak to Mr Archibald Howell. It's urgent. I met him recently and he—'

'This is Mr Howell speaking. I recognise your accent — you're the girl from Wales I met on the train, I believe?'

'Yes, that's me. Am I glad to speak to you! I didn't know who else to turn to,' Rosa gabbled.

'Slow down and tell me, how can I help? You were most fortunate to catch me in today as I don't usually work weekends. I had some papers to sign and was about to leave for a social engagement.'

Rosa's hand flew to her throat as she tried to slow her rapid breathing. Between gasps of air, she blurted out how Alice and her mother had been arrested and led away in handcuffs in front of the Press. 'The photographer said she was a baby-killer. I can't believe it. Alice wasn't with child. She's not married and not seeing anyone. There must be some mistake.'

Mr Howell's tone was sombre. 'This sounds very serious indeed and we need to act quickly. Their lives could depend on it. I need to make a call and cancel my prior arrangements.'

'So you'll see Alice? I tell you, she's no killer. Will you help her?'

'I sense that this case will cause huge outrage throughout the country. I specialise in taking on cases of the most heinous nature. You say your friend isn't a killer: my job is to make a judge and jury see it that way too, which depends very much on her defence.'

'So, you'll help?'

'I will if she would like, but she must agree to me representing her. Her mother will need representation too. I shall have to check they've not already briefed a solicitor. I know the police station in Bethnal Green where she's been taken and am on their rota as duty solicitor. I will ask Jarvis to take me there without delay.'

A thought flashed into Rosa's mind, but she felt guilty for even thinking it. Sensing there was more, Mr Howell probed gently, 'Is there anything else I need to be aware of?'

'It's just, bearing in mind my position at the palace, I wondered if it would go against me if my friendship with them became known. A part of me thinks I shouldn't get involved, but I can't abandon her.'

'I can see this is a delicate situation for you and I assure you I shall be as discreet as possible.'

'Thank you, Mr Howell. I don't know who else I could have turned to.'

Rosa's legs gave way, overcome with emotion as the enormity of the consequences of the charge levelled against her friend sank in. If convicted of murder, Alice and her mother would hang. But none of it made sense. What baby? And Alice wouldn't hurt a fly.

'Can you go to the station, Miss Edwards? I'm sure your friend would like to see a kindly face.'

'I will if I can, but is it allowed? The police officer said I wouldn't be able to see her until she had given her statement.'

'I shall call the station now and ask them to delay taking any statements until I have had a chance to see your friend and her mother. If you are able to wait until the statements are taken, you should be able to see one or both of them afterwards.'

'I've got all day. I'll find my way there. Will you tell Alice I'm here for her, whatever trouble she's in.'

'You're a very good friend, Miss Edwards, especially in these circumstances. I shall cancel my engagement and leave without delay.'

After she hung up, Rosa stumbled out of the phone box, oblivious of the two women waiting outside to make their call. Scowling, they pushed their way into the booth. 'I'm sorry, but my friend's life depends on it,' she said, feeling giddy at the enormity of her words.

She had no idea how to get to the police station and looked around for a friendly face to ask. A butcher's boy on a bicycle had paused on the kerb to light a cigarette and Rosa headed towards him. 'You're in trouble, are you, miss?' he winked, eyeing her up and down.

'Oh no, nothing of the kind, but my friend is. There's been some kind of misunderstanding, and I want to see her.'

He advised the bus she needed and pointed across the road to the stop. Rosa thanked him and waited, each second feeling like an eternity. When it arrived she hopped on and found a seat, whispering the police station as her destination to the conductress, who eyed her with a suspicious sideways glance.

She shuddered as she eyed the bombed-out buildings she passed and thought of the ordinary families who had perished. It was a scene she was becoming increasingly familiar with and it was clear to see that London was a target for Hitler, while homes in Merthyr remained standing, but the poverty and suffering they endured was still felt.

It was half an hour before a voice boomed, 'Next stop Bethnal Green police station,' making Rosa jump from her seat.

The station had a large black lantern hanging above its front door and its name clearly carved in the stone facade. She recognised the reporter and photographer from outside Alice's house lolling about outside, but their backs straightened and their faces brightened when they saw her approach.

''Ello again, luv,' said the snapper, an eager tone in his voice, his fingers fidgeting on the shutter. 'Are you popping in to see your friend?'

His colleague sauntered towards her. 'I expect you could do with a few extra bob or two. If you give us the exclusive on your friend, you could earn yourself a pretty penny.'

Rosa's jaw dropped. A fury rose within her. 'I have no intention of speaking to you. I am sure this is all a misunderstanding, so you'd better watch what you write.'

She pushed past them and into the station. The entrance lobby had a number of posters on the wall advertising for Special Constables, and notices advising people to contact police or an air-raid warden if they were bombed out and had nowhere to go. She opened the door to the reception. A sergeant, his arms sprawled across a large wooden counter, was turning the pages of a ledger in front of him. Without looking up, he asked, 'Can I help you?'

'My name is Rosa Edwards. I've come about my friend, Alice Evans, and her mother, Beryl. I believe they are here?'

The officer looked up. He was middle-aged and balding, with small, currant-like eyes, red freckles and a bushy moustache to match. 'I'm afraid that isn't possible. What is your connection with them?' he asked, leaning forward.

'I'm Alice's best friend, from Merthyr. I was at the house in Stepney when they were arrested. I'm worried about them.'

'You'll have to ask the officer who's leading the case. He's taking statements from them at the moment.'

'But he can't, not yet, not until their solicitor arrives. He was going to call you,' she blurted, her face reddening.

'You seem to know a lot, Miss Edwards. As a matter of fact, he has. If you take a seat over there, we'll let you know if you can see them. I warn you, it might be a long wait.'

'I don't care how long it takes, I'm staying until I see Alice,' she declared.

Rosa perched herself on a wooden bench at the end of the reception, watching people coming and going to report a theft or assault, and being led away to make statements. After half an hour with no news, she paced the reception, trying her best to keep out of the sergeant's gaze. Her mind turned to a comment the waitress had made about Alice being 'up the duff'. Could that be true?

Two hours later she ventured outside in search of a café, but, spotting the reporter and his colleague and fearing being pounced on, she scuttled back inside the station.

Her stomach was rumbling and the sergeant called her over. 'I expect you could do with a cuppa?'

Rosa replied appreciatively, 'Oh, yes please, if it's no trouble. Is there any news?'

'I'll see what I can do. And no, there's nothing more I can say. These things take time.'

He beckoned a young police constable who appeared from the room behind him, and pointed in Rosa's direction. Fifteen minutes later the officer returned with the tea and a spam sandwich. 'With our compliments. The sergeant is worried you'll pass out from hunger.'

Rosa's cheeks flushed. 'Thank you. I must admit I am famished.'

When she had devoured every last morsel, she returned the tray to the sergeant. 'I can see that went down a treat,' he said, curling his moustache in his fingers.

'It did, it was very kind of you. I couldn't face going outside with that reporter still standing there,' she replied.

'That will be Jack Finchley. He's the crime editor on the *Express*.'

Rosa's eyebrows furrowed. 'Crime editor? How did he know the police were arresting Alice?'

The sergeant shrugged his shoulder. 'No doubt he has his sources.'

Rosa pondered for a moment. 'It can only be someone from here. Who else would know?'

'It's not for me to say,' he muttered, as a door behind reception sprung open and Mr Howell walked through with the officer who had arrested Alice.

Someone who wants a few bob on the quiet, Rosa thought to herself.

After a further half hour wait, the sergeant called Rosa over. 'I'm afraid you've had a long wait for nothing. You can't see your friend today, but her brief wants you to join him.' He pointed to Mr Howell in the room behind, then lifted the flap on the counter and she went through to join him.

Rosa opened her mouth to speak, but Mr Howell told her to follow him and they walked briskly along a corridor towards the back of the building.

'But I want to see Alice,' she wailed.

Mr Howell replied calmly, 'Follow me this way so we

miss the Press at the front. Jarvis is parked at the back. Alice and her mother are in serious trouble. I thought you should know, though right now she is in a state of shock and can't face seeing you.'

'Tell me, what have they done?'

'They are charged with murdering Alice's newborn baby, a boy just one week old.'

Rosa recoiled, her eyes widening. 'No! Never, I don't believe it. I had no idea she was even expecting.'

'I'm afraid it's true. Come, my dear. I will tell you everything. I'm sure I can vouch for your confidentiality.'

Rosa's stomach churned as she followed Mr Howell to his car outside the back of the police station. Jarvis tilted his head in her direction and opened the passenger door. 'Good day to you, Miss Edwards.'

She was too numb to reply and climbed into the back seat. Mr Howell sat alongside her.

'Perhaps we can drop off Miss Edwards in Buckingham Palace Road, Jarvis.'

On the journey, Mr Howell recounted what Alice had written in her police statement. 'Alice realised she was in the family way at the end of last year. She'd had a fling with an American serviceman on leave in Merthyr. It turned out he was married and promised to divorce his wife and marry her when she told him she was expecting. Instead of keeping his word, this man, a Dennis Mitchell, moved out of his rooms and couldn't be traced.'

Rosa's bottom lip shook. 'He was married? I had no idea. He must have led her on and she would have been in a desperate state. I think I saw him with another girl after she left for London. It would break her heart to know.'

'Maybe she did know, for it is my belief that she felt deep shame after being abandoned by this man. Her mother put two and two together when Alice began vomiting in the morning. They were terrified her father would find out. He has a weak heart and they were afraid the shock of it would finish him off.

'It was agreed that she would find a job in London – anything – which is how she came to work for Lord Jeremy and his wife. She could see they were unconventional, that was part of the appeal for her, as she hoped they would accept her situation. She planned to tell them the truth and explain she was going to have the baby adopted. But, I'm afraid, it didn't work out that way.

'One day Alice was asked to shift some heavy boxes of books in Lord Jeremy's office and she tripped and fell. She was in agony and cried out that she was worried about her unborn baby. Lady Iris said she had to leave immediately, which is when she moved in with her aunt Ruby in Stepney.'

The solicitor paused for breath. 'I realise this is a lot for you to take in.'

Rosa stuttered, 'Poor Alice. Now I understand why she left Merthyr so suddenly.'

Mr Howell continued, 'Alice and her mother heard about a couple who wanted to adopt through the nursing home. They even met the couple, and it was agreed to hand the baby over to them as soon as it was born. However, when the day came, the couple changed their mind, saying they wanted a baby girl, not a boy.

'Alice was desperate, not knowing which way to turn. The matron put her in touch with a couple of adoption agencies, which she called on their behalf. After being discharged from hospital, Alice and her mother wrapped the baby in a blanket and went to the agencies, but neither wanted to take the boy, saying they only had interest from families for children from the age of three.

'Alice and her mother were really desperate now. They had no idea where to go or what to do. They had promised Aunt Ruby not to take the baby there and arouse gossip from her neighbours.'

Rosa gulped. 'So, what did they do?'

'This is when it gets really difficult to recount the events. They are truly shocking, and you need to brace yourself.'

'What do you mean?' Rosa said, her voice wobbling.

'Police spoke to witnesses who saw Alice and her mother in the Rose and Crown public house in Islington at around seven o'clock. They appeared nervous and couldn't quieten the baby, which was crying its head off. The women ordered a couple of sherries each, downed them in one gulp and then left.'

'Where did they go next?'

'They went into the ladies' public conveniences across the road, and—' The solicitor paused and took a deep breath. 'This is very hard for me to say, it's so shocking.'

Rosa raised her chin. 'I'm not afraid to hear it. Please tell me.'

'I feel I must because if you don't hear it from me, you will read about it in the papers when the case goes to court,' he replied softly.

'You're making me scared now.'

Mr Howell's voice cracked. 'According to her statement, Alice pushed the baby's head down the toilet and her mother flushed it. The poor little thing didn't stand a chance. A post-mortem is being carried out as I speak to you.'

Rosa pressed her hand against her mouth and cried, 'No! That is the most wicked and cruel thing I have ever heard. I can't believe it of Alice.'

'It's one of the worst crimes I've ever encountered. Alice and her mother claim the baby was still alive when they left it there on the floor and planned to return the next day. He was discovered by a cleaner the following morning, dead.'

Tears streamed down Rosa's cheeks. 'I don't believe a word of it! Alice would never kill a fly, let alone a baby.'

'It was clearly a desperate act. Her mother thought it was best for Alice and her husband.'

'They both could hang for murder, couldn't they,' Rosa whimpered.

'I'll do everything I can,' Mr Howell promised, pressing his hand on her arm.

25

That Sunday evening back at the palace, Rosa confided to Molly about the terrible crime her friend was accused of, and cried on her friend's shoulder. 'I can't believe it,' Molly gasped. 'And to think she was staying not far from us. No wonder they hid behind their curtains. What's going to happen to them?'

'I don't know, it's too horrible for words. I'm scared for Alice and her mam, and I'm scared if the King and Queen discover I know her and think I'm no longer suitable to be a palace maid.'

Molly assured her, 'It wouldn't come to that. Miss Rogers would vouch for you, and that posh lady you know from Merthyr. Mind you, what that girl did was wicked. You're a good friend, Rosa. A lot of people would have washed their hands of them in the same circumstances, including me.'

'I couldn't do that, though it tears me apart to think about what she might have done. This isn't the Alice I know. I find it hard to believe. I can't bear to tell Mam, but she'll find out soon enough. It's only a matter of time before the whole of Merthyr hears about it.'

Something else preyed on her mind; there was still no news of Jerry. It had been over two weeks since she last saw him and she clung to the hope that he had been posted somewhere and that his whereabouts had to remain secret.

Alice's life-or-death predicament now filled her head.

She had barely slept a wink since Mr Howell's graphic account of the death of the infant. It hadn't occurred to her at the time to ask if the baby had a name. Surely the boy had a name, even if it lived only week?

Meanwhile, that Monday the King and Queen had invited officers and men from the American Forces to a reception, and the palace kitchen had all hands on deck. Miss Rogers popped her head in to see that all the refreshments had been prepared to her exacting standard, ready for the arrival of their guests.

Earlier in the war, the Queen and Mrs Roosevelt had formed a close bond, and the wife of the American President had travelled to the United Kingdom to visit their troops. Now well over two hundred people were due to arrive at the palace in the afternoon, and Rosa forced a smile as she carried trays to the Grand Hall. Cook informed Rosa that this was the royals' favoured location for entertaining on a large scale, partly because it was easy to get down to the air-raid shelters in the bowels of the palace if there should be a sudden warning, as had happened on at least two occasions.

Two buffet tables, each forty feet in length, were set up in the Grand Hall, left and right of the ornate staircase. Mr Corbitt had worked his magic, securing extra sugar and margarine under permits from the Westminster Food Office, but alas, no butter could be given. He had further excelled himself, much to the delight of the Queen, by sourcing a brand of American coffee popular with the forces. She gave orders too that the Americans should be supplied with their favourite toasted-tobacco cigarettes, which Mr Corbitt obtained through the United States Embassy.

Dozens of loaves of bread were sliced, had margarine slapped on them, and were then covered with a paste prepared with grouse shot at Balmoral. Tomatoes, cucumbers, lettuce and cress were also provided for the royal guests as unrationed commodities, grown on the royal estates in Sandringham and Windsor. An assortment of small cakes had been made too, ginger and lemon drizzle, as well as Victoria sponge.

Molly nudged Rosa's arm gleefully. 'All the maids are keen to see the Yanks. I wonder if they'll give us some chewing gum. Or maybe some stockings?'

'Not now, Molly, I'm not in the mood,' she replied dully, the fate of Alice pressing heavily on her mind.

Miss Rogers checked everything was laid out correctly and instructed Rosa to make coffee. Rosa stifled a yawn.

'Is anything the matter, Rosa? You have big grey shadows under your eyes and you appear somewhat distracted and slower than your usual self.'

Before Rosa could conjure up a reply, Miss Rogers was called away to check on something else, urging her to smile and sharpen up as she left.

Rosa positioned herself behind one of the long tables, fixing a forced smile on her face. She poured countless cups of coffee, serving dozens of handsome uniformed American servicemen, as well as a number of servicewomen, as they mingled with royalty, including King Peter of Yugoslavia, a slim figure dressed in uniform. The King was dressed in khaki, rows of medals pinned above his left breast pocket, and walked down one side of the hall speaking to guests, while the Queen, in a pink floral silk dress and a long string of pearls, did the same along the other side, leaning forward as guests replied, taking great interest in what they said, and charming everyone.

More than once Rosa apologised for spilling coffee into the saucer as she poured. 'No harm done,' a square-jawed serviceman assured her.

This hadn't gone unnoticed by Miss Rogers, who caught Rosa's eye and frowned. Rosa straightened her back and forced herself to be alert. When she looked up again she saw Miss Rogers in the corner holding a newspaper, with the Queen's private secretary pointing to the front page and glancing in her direction with a disapproving expression.

Rosa's hands shook as the housekeeper approached. 'May I have a word with you, Miss Edwards. Please come into my office.'

'It looks like someone's in for it,' drawled one of the American guests, biting into a slice of ginger cake.

Rosa's pulse soared as she followed Miss Rogers down the steps and along the corridor until they reached her office. She gripped a copy of the *Express*, and Rosa knew that it must be about Alice.

Miss Rogers slammed the paper on her desk and demanded, 'What is the meaning of this?'

Rosa picked it up and stared at a photograph of herself standing next to Alice as she and her mother were hauled by police in handcuffs into a car. The headline screamed *Baby-Killer and Mother Charged with Murder.*

'I can explain,' Rosa stuttered in a soft voice, as her legs gave way.

'I can see you are very shaken. Take a seat, and tell me all about it.'

The housekeeper passed Rosa a handkerchief as tears came to her eyes. When she had composed herself, Rosa poured out everything and watched Miss Rogers's face pale as she described the baby boy's death in the toilet.

Afterwards, she appeared visibly shocked. 'That's the most terrible thing I've heard. You should have informed me of your association with this family straight away. It is clearly going to be a sensational court case and attract the attention of the Press.'

Rosa stumbled on her words. 'I had no idea about it when I went to see Alice at her aunt's house, or that I would have my photograph taken. He was a horrible man. I swear this isn't the Alice I know. Her father is strict and has a poor heart and—'

The housekeeper's nose flared. 'That is no excuse. Tell me, Miss Edwards, did you speak to the reporter? Does he know you work at the palace?'

'Oh no, Miss Rogers. I never said a thing, except to say I wasn't going to speak to him.'

'We cannot have the palace brought into this. In the meantime, continue to keep your lips sealed and let justice run its course,' the housekeeper instructed.

'Yes, Miss Rogers.'

'You may return to your duties and help with the clearing up. Dry your eyes first and do stop your hands from shaking.'

'Yes, Miss Rogers. Thank you.'

Trembling, Rosa did as she was asked, trying her best to carry on as normal and force a smile, even though she felt ripped to pieces inside.

The reception was drawing to an end when Molly

rushed over to her. 'What was that about? I saw Miss Rogers with a face like thunder.'

'I can't say anything. I have to keep my lips sealed.'

Rosa kept her head down for the next few days, doing her best to keep in Miss Rogers's good books. On the Friday, the housekeeper called her into her office again and said, 'I thought you should see this.' She handed Rosa the latest edition of the *Express*. 'It says here they've been committed to stand trial next Monday at the Old Bailey.'

Rosa's bottom lip wobbled. 'So soon! I'd like to try again to see Alice this weekend, if you have no objection. She must be terrified.'

After a pause, Miss Rogers said, 'I have no objection, as long as you keep your employment here to yourself. And be sure to keep your distance from the Press.'

Elated, Rosa replied, 'I promise. Thank you, Miss Rogers.'

Molly handed Rosa a blue and yellow headscarf on the Friday evening. 'Here, you can borrow this if you like to disguise yourself, just in case that scumbag reporter is still hanging around the police station. Pull it down over your face and nobody will know it's you.'

'Thanks, but no thanks. That will only make me look more suspicious. I'll nip in the back way if he's hanging around the front.'

The two girls embraced as Molly left to spend the weekend with her family. Rosa stopped by the post office in the palace and picked up two letters addressed to her. She recognised her mother's handwriting and opened it.

Dear Rosa,

Everyone in Merthyr has seen your photograph on the front of the paper. Are you mad, getting caught up in this trouble? I don't know what to say to people about it when they ask. I always knew that girl was trouble. She's brought shame on Merthyr. Write to me straight away and tell me you're having nothing to do with her, else I'll be coming over on the next train.

Your anxious Mam.

The next letter was from Jane Williams.

My dear Rosa,

We've seen your photograph in the paper – everyone has! We can't believe what we read about Alice and Beryl Evans and the terrible death of her baby boy. Knowing your fondness for Alice, we expect you will be doing your best for her. This must be a terribly anxious time for you and if there is anything we can do, you only have to ask. You are much cherished in our hearts and minds.

Hettie was asking after you and sends you her best wishes. What a funny girl she is!

With our fondest love,
Jane and Huw

Rosa scribbled a hasty reply to both, explaining the circumstances of her photograph and ignorance of the charge, how she had, quite by chance, encountered a solicitor who was representing Alice and her mother, and her shock at the murder – and the terrible consequences of a guilty verdict.

She posted them the following morning as she set off once again for Bethnal Green police station where Alice was still detained while police continued their questioning.

As she arrived and came out of the Underground, a paperboy bellowed, *'Baby-killer and mother face trial on Monday! Read all about it!'*

Rosa kept her head down as she proceeded to the station, a short walk away. A queue had formed outside a butcher and snaked a good hundred yards down the road after word of a delivery of bacon, while the shelves at a nearby fruit and veg shop had been cleared, the extra veg in demand to bulk out meat pies. To her relief, there was no sign of the reporter or photographer hanging around the station entrance. She paused for a moment, then braced herself and stepped inside. A different sergeant was on duty behind the counter.

'Yes, miss. What can I do for you?' he enquired, tapping his pencil on the surface.

'May I see Miss Alice Evans, please?'

His grey eyes scrutinised her closely. 'And what would a nice girl like you want to do with a girl like Alice Evans?'

'She's my friend,' Rosa replied, raising her chin.

'I see. I'll have to check with my superior. Wait here a minute and I'll ask.'

Rosa watched the sergeant disappear behind the door. She shuffled from foot to foot, feeling her insides turn to jelly.

He returned with another officer. 'We've checked with

Miss Evans and she will see you. You have fifteen minutes. Constable Baldock will accompany you.'

The sergeant lifted the flap on the counter and she followed the constable along a corridor to a door labelled *Interview Room 1*. The constable said, 'If you take a seat here, I'll bring the prisoner up from her cell.'

Rosa felt a shiver run along her spine at the words 'prisoner' and 'cell' in connection with her friend. She seated herself on one of two chairs in front of a desk. It was a cold and hostile room, the grey door made from reinforced metal with a small window at the top covered by a metal flap.

A few minutes later the door was flung open and Alice appeared. Rosa ran towards her, but was ordered to stand back. Alice turned to the constable and held up her cuffed wrists. 'Are these really necessary? I'm hardly likely to make a quick escape.'

'Rules are rules, miss.' Then, addressing Rosa, he said gravely, 'I'll be standing outside. You have fifteen minutes.'

When they were left alone, Rosa wrapped her arms around Alice in a bear hug. She felt Alice's chest heaving and her heartbeat pounding as if it were going to explode. She took her friend's hands in hers, feeling the cold of the metal chains, and stared into her pale face and her drawn, haunted expression. This wasn't the happy-go-lucky girl she knew in Merthyr, the pretty girl who turned heads wherever she went. The Alice she saw now had grey rings circling her puffy eyes and a defeated expression. She sniffled into a handkerchief she fished out of the pocket of her drab grey skirt. Her hair hung limply around her shoulders. She wore a plain blouse and thick grey stockings with flat black shoes.

She blurted, 'Oh, Alice. What have you done? Is it true you killed your baby boy?'

Her friend's eyes creased and she buried her face in her handkerchief, nodding slightly.

'How could you? But why?' Rosa wailed.

Alice shook her head and looked up, tears streaming down her cheeks. 'If only I could turn back the clock . . .' Her voice trailed off. A moment later, she warbled, 'Thank you for sending the solicitor to me. The police asked me if I had one, but I don't know about these things.'

'Is Mr Howell helping you?'

'He is, but I doubt he can save my neck.'

Rosa squeezed her friend's hands. They felt icy-cold in her grip. 'He'll do his best, Alice. What drove you to it?'

Alice stifled a sob. 'I don't know what came over me. The Yank wanted nothing to do with me once I told him I was in the family way. He said I was just a bit of fun, and then it turned out he had a wife back home who he had no intention of leaving. I was ashamed of being up the duff and didn't want to drag you, or anyone else, into my mess. But I couldn't hide it from Mam and she flipped.'

'What you did was wicked. It's splashed all over the papers.'

'So I hear. The jailer showed me the headlines and told me I'm the most hated woman in the country. Poor Mam, I can't even speak to her or see her. I worry about how she's doing.'

'Maybe Mr Howell can ask for you, or pass on a message?' Rosa suggested.

'He's coming in this afternoon. I can ask again then. I don't know what I would do without him.'

After a pause, Rosa asked tentatively, 'Have you heard anything from your father since this happened?'

Alice shook her head. 'Mr Howell has tried, but he says he's washed his hands of us, me and Mam. He blames me for dragging Mam into it and ruining their lives and good name.'

A knock on the door and the appearance of Constable Baldock brought their meeting to an abrupt end.

Alice clutched her friend's hand tightly. 'Thank you for coming, Rosa. Will you be able to come to the Old Bailey on Monday? My case is scheduled for the afternoon.'

Rosa's forehead creased. 'I'm afraid I can't, I'll be at work. I'll be thinking of you both. Stay strong, Alice.'

They rose and she hugged Alice tightly. Words now failed her, feeling her friend's body stiffen. She pulled away and watched Alice being led back to her cell, her shoulders slumped, with the demeanour of a condemned man. Alice glanced over her shoulder at the door and said, 'I loved him, you know, my baby Johnny. Do you believe me?'

Rosa's hands flew to her face and she let out an anguished cry. Hearing the baby's name felt like a stab in her heart and she pictured a chubby baby with dimpled cheeks.

'I believe you, Alice,' whispered Rosa, as her friend vanished from sight.

The tenth of July started off like any other day for Rosa in the palace. She made her way to the staffroom and sat idly stirring her spoon around her porridge.

'I don't need to ask what you're thinking about,' Molly commented, plonking herself next to her.

'I can't think of anything else,' Rosa retorted, her expression downcast.

'She was desperate, and her mind wasn't right,' Molly replied.

'I know that, but even so—'

Molly continued, 'We shouldn't have too busy a day. The King is visiting a munitions factory in the north and the Queen is calling in on an emergency centre for bombed families. I expect we'll be cleaning the silver again.'

Molly's words barely sunk in. Rosa felt wretched at the thought of her friend hanging for her crime, but tried to hide her true feelings, afraid of incurring the wrath of Miss Rogers.

The morning passed much as Molly had anticipated. They applied plenty of elbow grease to shine the silver serving plates and cutlery, the candelabra that sat on the table, as well as the tea and coffee sets, rubbing away until they could see their reflection. It was the kind of mindless task that Rosa wanted that day.

When it had all been done, Miss Rogers inspected the work and gave a nod of approval.

Rosa and Molly were about to set off for lunch when the housekeeper called Rosa over. 'You have a visitor, in my office. I will give you a moment together.'

'A visitor? I'm not expecting anyone,' Rosa queried, her eyebrows knitting together.

'Well, go along then. It's rude to keep her waiting.'

Rosa's fingers twisted in her hands as she made her way to the housekeeper's office. The door was slightly ajar. She knocked softly and pushed it open and was unable to disguise her surprise when she saw a familiar figure standing in the room.

'Lady Gwendoline!'

'Yes, it's me, Rosa. Come inside, will you?'

Rosa stepped into the office and closed the door behind her. 'Miss Rogers said you wanted to see me. I'm not in trouble again, am I?'

Lady Gwendoline flicked her hand in the air. 'No, Rosa. I hear you have settled in well again. I suspect we both have the same troubling matter on our minds – the trial today of Alice Evans and her mother.'

Rosa nodded. 'I can't think of anything else. What's going to happen to her and her mam? Will they hang?'

'I can't say, but there is every chance they could. It's a terrible case, one of the worst of its kind. I can't let it rest, as I know Alice from the Valleys Hotel. I've always believed her parents to be good people and the whole of Merthyr is shaken to its core.'

Rosa whimpered, 'What can we do? What can anyone do to save them from the rope?'

'Let's take it one step at a time. I plan to be at the hearing this afternoon and Miss Rogers has kindly given you permission to accompany me, if you wish.'

'She did?' Rosa replied, gobsmacked.

'Indeed she did. Cook has said you can be spared as your tasks for the day are all completed. I plan to take a cab, and I think your friend would like to see you there.'

'Well, in that case, yes. I'll come.'

'We just have time to finish these sandwiches Miss Rogers has thoughtfully provided, before you change quickly. There are too many for me, and as you haven't got time for lunch, you're welcome to share them.'

Rosa's eyes widened. 'Really?'

'She's not really a dragon, you know.' Lady Gwendoline's eyes crinkled as she bit into an egg and cress sandwich.

26

Rosa and Lady Gwendoline shielded their faces from the flash-guns as they entered the Old Bailey just before two o'clock. The criminal courthouse, the most famous in the land, hadn't escaped the ravages of war. Three years before, a corner of it had been obliterated in one of the worst raids of the Blitz that had also caused severe damage to Westminster Abbey, the destruction of the Commons Chamber in the Houses of Parliament and significant damage to the British Museum.

On the dome of this famous landmark stood Lady Justice, defiantly unscathed, holding a sword in her right hand and the scales of justice in her left, symbolising the power to punish and the fair administration of justice.

Despite the damage, the legal wheels continued to turn in the main court building. Rosa stared all around as she scurried alongside Lady Gwendoline over the marble floor and in her anxious state she barely glanced at the walls depicting allegorical paintings representing Labour, Art, Wisdom, and Truth.

They found the day's cases pinned on a wall and read *Rex v Alice Anne Evans and Beryl Henrietta Evans*. 'Rex is Latin for King,' Lady Gwendoline explained. 'The trial commences in Court One at two o'clock. That's good, we're just in time.'

She approached a court usher draped in a black flowing

gown, who directed them to the cramped public gallery on the first floor. Spectators huddled close, and the two of them squeezed themselves onto the wooden bench on the front row, with a bird's-eye view of the oak-panelled courtroom.

A number of men, including Mr Howell, were seated below, heads bowed, reading papers tied in ribbon. Their heads were locked together over a particular point on one of the pages, with Mr Howell speaking animatedly. They then spoke to men wearing white wigs, who Lady Gwendoline said were barristers who would present the case on behalf of both the Crown and the defence.

Rosa spotted the reporter from the *Express* crouched over his notebook, already furiously scribbling away, alongside others who had pens and notebooks placed on a bench within easy reach. Rosa cringed as she observed their eager expressions, waiting to devour their prey.

A few minutes later the chattering in the courtroom fell silent and all eyes fell on the dock. A prison officer appeared from steps that led to the cells below, followed by Alice, her mother and another prison officer. Mr Howell approached the dock and had a quick word with them both before returning to his seat and nodding to the barrister in front of him.

Alice looked up to the public gallery, scanning those in attendance. Her eyes settled on Rosa for a couple of seconds. The fearful expression on her friend's face tore at her heart. As Rosa raised her hand slightly, Alice looked down, having been nudged by one of the prison officers to look ahead.

The jostling on the benches and the jeering sounds

from those close by was unlike anything Rosa had experienced before; it felt as if the crowd was baying for blood.

Suddenly a voice called out sharply, 'Please stand. Rise in court. Silence please.'

The judge entered and paused in front of a long bench facing the dock. He stared intently at the two defendants, before seating himself in a high-backed ornately carved chair. The atmosphere was electric and Rosa felt partly petrified and partly in awe.

Everyone sat, while Alice and her mother remained standing, and the charges were read out by the clerk to both – the wilful murder of a one-week-old baby boy.

'How do you plead to the charge?'

'Not guilty, your honour,' replied Alice and her mother in turn, their voices barely audible.

'How could they be so wicked?' one woman hissed to her companion next to Rosa.

'I hope they burn in hell,' her friend spat.

'They deserve to hang. Pass me the rope and I'll do the job for them,' said another, punching his fist in the air.

Rosa shuddered, her blood chilling, at the hatred hurled at Alice.

The jury was sworn in and the prosecutor, Sir Henry Childerley, KC, outlined the case. He was robust in presenting evidence against the two women, emphasising that they had admitted to committing a terrible act against a helpless infant, and, crucially, that they had intended for the infant to die. He declared it was a premeditated act of the most heinous and despicable nature that he had ever encountered. The top part of the baby's clothing was still wet when the infant was discovered, having been held head down in the toilet and water flushed. His throat had also been throttled. The defenceless child was then left on the toilet floor to die in those surroundings, if the angels had not already released it from its agonies.

Alice wept and buried her head in her hands, while her mother dabbed her eyes, fighting back tears. Two women seated behind Rosa began crying on hearing the evidence. A lump formed in Rosa's throat and Lady Gwendoline passed her own handkerchief with her initials embroidered in the corner.

After a pause, Sir Henry glared at the defendants and thundered, 'Have you ever heard of a more sickening crime against a baby just a week old?'

Rosa clenched her fists in her lap as Alice was called to give evidence. She walked unsteadily to the dock. 'I swear I didn't know what I was doing. I just knew that we couldn't take the baby home for the shock would have killed my father. I was so upset. My mind was in a whirl,' she uttered to a hushed courtroom.

'Can you raise your voice please, Miss Evans?' the judge asked.

Alice was visibly upset, her hands tightly gripping the sides of the witness box. Spectators in the public gallery tilted their heads sideways, craning their necks, desperate not to miss a word.

'We thought he was still alive when we left him. We saw him kick his little legs. We were going to go back for him the next day and try another adoption agency. I wasn't in the right frame of mind. I was in a terribly anxious state.'

The next moment Alice collapsed, still gripping the

sides of the witness box. The clerk rushed over to her with a glass of water.

'Take a deep breath, Miss Evans,' her defence barrister, Robert Crawley, KC, advised in a sympathetic tone.

After pausing for a few minutes, Alice continued her evidence, her eyes welling up. 'If it hadn't been for my father and his weak heart, I would have kept my baby, regardless of the shame of having an illegitimate child. I hoped he could be found a good home, but nobody wanted to take him. What was I supposed to do? I was worried out of my mind. I just wish I could have taken him home.'

Alice's harrowing evidence brought tears to Rosa's eyes as she imagined the fear and desperation that had gripped her at that moment, having just given birth, and nowhere to take her child.

The evidence Alice's mother gave was the same. She had a tendency to look down when she spoke, and the judge reminded her several times to look up and address her answers to the jury.

'What was your part in this wicked crime?' asked Sir Henry, drawing out each word, his eyes focused on her.

Beryl dabbed her eyes, choking on her words. 'I— I—'

'Let me tell the jury what you did, Mrs Evans, and will you be so kind as to confirm if what I say is correct.' He paused, rubbing the back of his neck. 'While your daughter held this defenceless baby's head down the toilet, you flushed it, the shock of which caused him to have a heart attack. This was your grandson, just one week old, born into a family who wanted rid of him, by the foulest means.'

'You wicked, evil woman!' screamed a woman from the public gallery.

'Hang them! Hang them!' chanted another, standing and raising her fists.

Beryl whimpered, 'I don't know why I did such a thing. We didn't know what we were doing.'

Sir Henry read from her police statement as Beryl bowed her head: '"I pulled the chain while Alice held the baby's head in the water in the lavatory. Alice tried to squeeze its throat. We put it on the floor and had to leave it. We knew he was still alive for he was wide awake and kicking."'

Shocked gasps echoed around the packed courtroom.

Alice's Aunt Ruby was next to the witness box. She vouched for their genuine intention to have the baby adopted. The shock of these terrible events caused Alice's father to have a seizure and, as a result, he had been left weakened and too ashamed to leave his house.

When all the evidence had been called, and the summing-up by the judge completed, the jury left the courtroom to consider its verdict. It was five-thirty and the judge urged them not to rush their decision, to take as much time as they needed.

Rosa's heart was pounding so hard she thought it was going to explode. Her cheeks flushed purple and she and Lady Gwendoline exchanged a worried glance.

'She should've kept her knickers up instead of dropping them for any Tom, Dick or Harry,' the spiteful woman next to her commented.

'Ignore them, Rosa,' Lady Gwendoline muttered. 'Shall we go for some tea?'

They found a tearoom around the corner where a

number of court officials had also headed, including Mr Howell. He approached Rosa and she introduced him to her companion.

Lady Gwendoline asked, 'Tell me truthfully, Mr Howell. How do you think the case is going? Clearly they have admitted causing the death of the infant. What does the outcome of the case hinge on?'

He pulled out a chair at their table. 'May I join you? I can then elaborate on some of the finer legal points the jury has been asked to consider.'

'Please do,' Lady Gwendoline responded, sitting down alongside Rosa.

Mr Howell proceeded to explain the key points. 'It very much depends if the jury believe the balance of their minds were disturbed in carrying out this act. None of the witnesses commented on Alice being distressed shortly beforehand, particularly customers in the public house across from the lavatory where they spent time just before it happened. My hope is that the jury will see it was a desperate act and they will be convicted of infanticide.'

'I don't understand,' Rosa said. 'What's the difference between infanticide and murder?'

'It's not very well understood. The jury needs to accept that Alice was in a vulnerable mental state after having her baby and desperate to protect her father from a heart attack when she committed the terrible act, and therefore not of sound mind. If they believe that, it is deemed by law to be an act of infanticide, and could save her neck.'

'I see. If she had been the old Alice I knew and could

have taken her baby home to care for him instead of being scared out of her wits, then she would never have killed him and there would be no murder, or infanticide, charge.'

Mr Howell concurred. 'You put it very well.'

Lady Gwendoline pondered for a moment, cupping her chin in her hand. 'The girl was in a terrible state worrying about the impact that being an unmarried mother would have on her father. She was absolutely besides herself. I would class that as being in a fragile mental state. Anyone can see that, surely.'

'We have to hope the jury sees it that way,' the solicitor replied, frowning.

'Let's hope. The judge, in his summing up, stated that to be worried *out of your mind* was not the same as having the balance of your mind disturbed following the recent birth of a child, on the grounds that Alice hadn't fully recovered from giving birth. I can certainly see the difference.'

'Exactly,' Mr Howell confirmed. 'We've put forward the best case we could. Their fate lies in the hands of the jury.'

'I wonder how long we'll have to wait,' Rosa said. 'Alice and her mum must be terrified.'

It was just after seven o'clock when the jury returned, having agreed to reach their decision there and then. Their expressions were grave and they stared in the direction of the dock as the two defendants were brought up from the cells. The judge entered the courtroom and everyone rose.

After he sat down, the judge asked the foreman of the jury, 'Have you reached a decision on which you are all agreed?'

'Yes, your honour.'

'Do you find Alice Anne Evans guilty or not guilty of the wilful murder of the week-old infant?'

'Guilty, your honour.'

Alice cried out, 'No! I didn't mean it.'

A prison guard placed his arm on her shoulder and pushed her back into her seat.

The judge continued, 'And do you find Beryl Henrietta Evans guilty or not guilty of the wilful murder of the week-old infant?'

'Guilty, your honour.'

Beryl sobbed into her handkerchief.

'Will the defendants please rise,' the judge instructed.

The two women rose and held on to each other, sobbing.

He cleared his throat. 'After hearing all the evidence and giving it their fullest consideration a jury has found you both guilty of the wilful murder of a young baby in a case that has shocked the nation.

'There is only one sentence I can pass – and that is the death sentence.'

The judge placed a black cap atop his wig.

'The sentence of this court is that you will be taken from here to the place from whence you came and there be kept in close confinement until the day that you be taken to the place of execution and there hanged by the neck until you are dead. And may God have mercy upon your soul.'

A loud cheer erupted in the public gallery and Alice and her mother collapsed. They were aided to a standing position as the judge continued, 'The jury have asked that you be shown mercy. I shall pass on their recommendation to the Home Office for due consideration.'

He nodded at the prison guards who gripped the women.

Mr Crawley rose instantly. 'May I have a quick moment with my clients, your honour?'

The judge gave his assent and the court filled with chatter while he spoke with them both.

He then addressed the judge. 'Your honour, I would like to give notice that we shall appeal immediately.'

'Very well, Mr Crawley, so be it,' the judge replied. As he rose the court clerk declared, 'This court is dismissed.'

People had already made their way out, with reporters rushing to file their story.

Rosa leaned over the public gallery as Beryl disappeared down the steps to the cells. Alice was about to make her descent, clearly distressed, unable to stand unaided. Rosa cried out, leaning over the gallery above, her eyes stinging with tears. 'Alice!'

Alice spun around and looked up, her fearful eyes locking with Rosa's. She swayed and the guard pushed her along, almost making her fall.

Rosa grabbed Lady Gwendoline's arm. 'Did you see her eyes, pleading with me? We must do something to save them both.'

'Come, Rosa. I agree. We have work to do if we are to save them from the rope.'

27

There was only one topic of conversation in the staff quarters at the palace – and indeed, throughout the country – should Alice and her mother hang?

Miss Rogers took Rosa to one side the day after the hearing. 'I appreciate this is very upsetting for you, Miss Edwards. I believe there is to be an appeal, and in the meantime there is nothing you can do. We are short-staffed today and the Princesses Elizabeth and Margaret will be having lunch here after they pay a visit to their dentist. I need to be able to rely on you to be at your best.'

Rosa straightened her back, realising she had to step up and not let standards slip. 'Of course, Miss Rogers.'

'Excellent. After lunch the King has a meeting here with Mr Churchill.'

Rosa's mouth dried at the thought of being in the same room as the Prime Minister. She'd seen his photograph in the newspapers, but later today she would see him in the flesh and the thought of being so close to this great man, who the country relied on to win the war, made her stomach wobble.

As if reading her mind, Miss Rogers's lips curved up. 'You've nothing to be nervous about, Miss Edwards. Mr Churchill is very affable and will have very important matters to discuss with the King.'

As she scurried back to the kitchen, Rosa brightened

at the thought of seeing the two princesses again. It had been several weeks since Princess Elizabeth's birthday and her cheeks flushed as she recalled the indignity of being summoned by Mrs Hargreaves and forced to leave under a shadow amid the false accusations of theft.

By twelve-thirty the trolleys were laden with steaming bowls of consommé, plaice and an accompanying white sauce, seasonal vegetables, and dainty apple tarts. The table in the dining room had been laid for four, and the glasses sparkled from the beacon of sunlight that shone on it. Jugs of water were laid out and in the centre was a pretty floral arrangement of roses and greenery from the palace gardens.

Rosa and Molly put the food on hotplates on the sideboard, and a moment later the royal group appeared. The King had a serious expression and was dressed in military uniform, while the Queen listened attentively to her husband, placing her arm on his shoulder and appearing to reassure him. When she was within hearing distance, Rosa overheard her say, 'The nation has complete faith in you – Mr Churchill says so.'

Rosa almost tripped over one of the Queen's corgis and spluttered with relief, 'That was close.'

The hound scooted under the table to sit by the Queen's ankles, and she turned to Rosa and said, 'You manoeuvred that very well. Dookie seems very fond of you.'

Rosa's cheeks flushed. 'I wouldn't want to hurt him. He's just being playful.'

The Queen beckoned Rosa closer. She was immaculately made-up and dazzled in a lilac dress with lace edging the neck and cuffs.

'It's very good to see you again, Miss Edwards. I heard about that frightful business with the other maid.'

'It's very good to be back, your Majesty,' Rosa demurred, astonished that the Queen remembered her name.

The two princesses bounded in chatting animatedly together, and took their places at the table, nodding a greeting to Rosa.

'It's been a while since we've seen you,' Elizabeth said, smiling warmly. Margaret greeted her with a cheeky, 'Hello again. How are your legs today?'

A tall, greying butler, Albert, who had been with the royal family for twenty years, was in attendance, keeping a close watch on Rosa and Molly to ensure everything was in order; he was to serve at the table and they were to watch for his cues. He caught Rosa's eye and indicated for her to take her place.

As the meal progressed, she couldn't help noticing how the family interacted with each other like any other family – with affection and courtesy, listening attentively as they spoke.

While clearing dishes towards the end of the meal, Rosa's ears pricked up hearing the Queen mention Alice's court case. 'My dear friend Lady Gwendoline has taken a keen interest in this as she knows of the family. Apparently they come from the same town as her in Wales. It's the most terrible crime I've heard. How could a mother be so wicked?'

'No, it's not like that!' Rosa yelped before she could stop herself, covering her hands with her mouth as she realised her faux pas.

She turned to see Albert's pursed lips mouth the words, 'Over here, now!'

Rosa bobbed an awkward curtsey and retreated. 'What do you think you are doing, Miss Edwards. Please be sure to keep your mouth shut from now on.'

'I apologise. It won't happen again,' Rosa assured him.

After the meal was finished and Rosa prepared to serve coffee, Princess Elizabeth approached her. 'You cried out a moment ago, when Mama mentioned the court case. I wondered why.'

Rosa bit her lip and kept her mouth shut, glancing around for Albert, who was out of sight. Molly stepped forward. 'Rosa's too upset to say, and maybe I shouldn't tell you. But seeing as you ask, and we can't tell a lie, the truth is, Alice Evans is her best friend and comes from Merthyr, like her. Rosa was at the trial with Lady Gwendoline.'

Rosa shot Molly an anxious glance, opening her mouth to speak. 'It's true, Alice is my friend, ma'am. We're hoping the appeal will go in her favour.'

'I see. No wonder you are upset. These cases are never just black and white. If Lady Gwendoline has taken an interest, I'm sure she will do what she can and ensure all legal avenues are explored.'

'She's been very kind. Alice and her mam need all the help they can get,' Rosa murmured.

Princess Elizabeth returned to her seat and conversed with her mother. The Queen stared at Rosa as the princess continued speaking. She listened attentively and nodded, before turning around and speaking to her husband. Fifteen minutes later the party left the room and Rosa and Molly cleared the table.

'I hope I didn't speak out of turn,' said Molly. 'You never know, they might be able to help. Did you see Her

Majesty taking it all in when the princess told her you knew them? I couldn't stand by and say nothing.'

'Don't be daft. What can they do? Nobody can do anything now.'

Later that afternoon Rosa and Molly wheeled a trolley laden with Earl Grey tea, toasted crumpets and teacakes with margarine and raspberry jam, and fruitcake, which Cook said the Prime Minister was partial to. They were asked to provide enough for six, as other high figures of state would be joining the meeting.

As usual, a guard was on duty outside the room, but today the butler took the trolley from them when they knocked on the door. 'They are in the middle of a very confidential discussion and you are not permitted to stay.'

Rosa craned her neck and saw a short, balding man puffing on a fat cigar seated next to the King, who inhaled deeply on his cigarette. Molly grabbed her by the arm and pulled her away as the door closed in their faces. 'You heard what the butler said. Come on, before we're both given our cards.'

'I couldn't help myself. I've never seen Mr Churchill close up before.'

Later that evening, over supper in the staffroom, Miss Rogers approached Rosa. 'I thought you would like to know – the appeal date has been set for next Thursday.'

'So soon?' Rosa gasped.

'Lady Gwendoline asked me to let you know. She is in touch with Mr Howell and Mr Crawley and wants to assure you that everyone is doing what they can.'

'I wish there was something I could do too.'

Miss Rogers shook her head. 'I know this must be very

hard for you, but I understand Mr Crawley is an excellent barrister and will do his best for them both. We have an investiture that afternoon with around three hundred guests. We will need every spare hand we have that day.'

'An investiture?'

'The King and Queen are dedicated to honouring servicemen and women for their bravery. You will be required to serve them refreshments in the Great Hall and must put this business behind you.'

Unbeknownst to Rosa, Lady Gwendoline had sprung into immediate action to save the necks of Alice and her mother. When she returned to Merthyr she found, much to her surprise, that despite the despicable crime, people were vocal in the defence of the doomed mother and daughter.

The *Merthyr Express*'s front page headline announced a petition: 'Save our Merthyr Mother and Daughter'. Within the first two days more than five hundred people signed the petition, and the groundswell of support took everyone by surprise.

Rosa asked Cook, 'Why do you think so many people are behind our Alice?'

Cook answered emphatically. 'She did wrong, there's no doubting that, but folk believe Alice wanted to keep her baby and found herself in a desperate situation. The poor thing fretted about her father's health and what taking the babe home would do to his heart, and on top of that she'd been used for sexual gratification by a Yank, only to be discarded by him like an old pair of dirty socks. The scoundrel!'

'Yes, that's exactly it. Poor, poor Alice. I will do my best for her.'

Eira wrote to Rosa, enclosing a copy of the *Merthyr Express* article: *Even the Chapel has started a petition amongst the congregation and is sharing it with the churches. We are flabbergasted by how many have signed. George has even taken it to the coalface with him and is getting men to sign it.*

A thought occurred to Rosa. *Why didn't I think of that? I shall start a petition here, in the palace.*

She knocked on Miss Rogers's door and, when she entered, was surprised to see Lady Gwendoline in the room.

'I do apologise. I didn't mean to interrupt.'

'What can I do for you, Rosa?' the housekeeper asked.

'I wanted to ask if I could start a petition here with palace staff, asking for mercy for Alice and her mam so they don't hang.'

Miss Rogers frowned. 'I shall have to ask the Queen's permission. I will do so this afternoon.'

Rosa glanced in Lady Gwendoline's direction, hoping she would back her suggestion, as momentum was gathering now with the two petitions in Merthyr.

'Rosa, that's an excellent idea,' Lady Gwendoline said. 'The Home Office has to consider the jury's recommendation for mercy, and public opinion, which is very evident from our petitions. People believe in Alice's defence, that she was in a desperate state and could see no way out after her hopes for the baby to be adopted came to nothing. These facts will hopefully sway the Home Secretary on his final decision. The voice of the public cannot be ignored. I also have a petition circulating amongst my influential friends in London. The appeal hearing is only two days away. I shall be there.'

'How do you think it will go?' stuttered Rosa.

'I wish I could say. It comes down to matters of law and we have to leave that to Mr Howell and Mr Crawley in the hope they can persuade the appeal judge in their favour.'

Rosa left the room, deep in thought. There would barely be time to gather a huge number of signatures for the palace petition, but she was determined to get as many as she could.

Later that evening Miss Rogers confirmed that the Queen had no objection, and provided several sheets of paper for the petition. With fire coursing through her veins, Rosa went into action and used the same wording as the *Merthyr Express*'s appeal.

She left the petition on a side table in the staffroom. The following morning Mr Corbitt pushed it in front of tradesmen with a pen and they added their scrawl. Within a couple of days two hundred names had been added.

When the day of the appeal arrived, Rosa was a bag of nerves. Dark circles around her eyes showed she had barely slept. The thought of eating breakfast made her stomach heave, and she forced herself to sip a mug of cold tea before setting about her duties. A radio was switched on and the appeal hearing was the lead news story of the day.

Meanwhile, the kitchen was a bustling hive of activity as refreshments for the investiture guests were laid out. Staff had arrived early to set out trestle tables, crockery and the urn for tea and coffee in the Great Hall. Cakes and biscuits had been baked the day before and were placed alongside sandwiches, making a very fine spread.

At ten o'clock, Rosa and Molly were in position to serve refreshments as the Great Hall started to fill. A queue had formed at one end of ordinary-looking men and women the same age or older than her parents, dressed smartly in their Sunday best and carrying their gas masks: no chance was being taken after the recent onslaught close by at the Guards' Chapel.

They had a dignity about them, and some of the ladies who chatted amongst themselves dabbed their eyes. They were lined up in front of the King, who was dressed in his full military uniform, a sword hanging from his hip, and was listening attentively to a distinguished-looking gentleman in a ceremonial outfit, a red sash diagonally across his tailcoat, who flicked through pages of notes.

Albert stood next to Rosa. He whispered behind his hand, 'The King considers this one of his most important duties. The people gathered here are the bereaved family of servicemen and women who gave their lives for their country and must be treated with the greatest respect.'

'You mean, the men who died are being honoured now?' Rosa queried.

'Exactly. They are being honoured posthumously. Their sacrifice is being rewarded and their honour means their legacy will live on. If they have family, their children will know that their father died a hero.'

Rosa reflected on the sadness of it for families. 'Who is that gentleman talking to the King?' she asked.

'That's the Lord Chamberlain, the Earl of Clarendon. He reads out the citations describing acts of bravery. He was bereaved himself in tragic circumstances nine years ago when his eldest son was killed in a shooting accident in South Africa.'

Before Rosa could press him for details, the Lord Chamberlain and the King took their positions in front of them. The Earl cleared his throat and read the first name on his list: '"Flight Lieutenant David Gregory: awarded the Distinguished Flying Cross. His plane was shot down by enemy aircraft over Normandy and he was killed instantly. He assisted in the destruction of six enemy aircraft at night, displaying a high standard of skill and resolution, and was a most keen and devoted member of his aircraft crew."'

Rosa watched in awe, craning her neck to see over the large numbers in attendance. She listened as one heroic tale after another was recounted of personnel from the three services, the Medical Corps and even chaplains.

She was deep in concentration and didn't notice two figures walking towards her until they were close by. Rosa rubbed her eyes, staring in disbelief. 'Jane! Huw! What are you doing here?'

Huw produced a letter from his inside pocket. 'It's Dylan. He's been honoured for his bravery.' He dried his eyes with his jacket sleeve and a lump formed in Rosa's throat. She spun around to look for Albert, expecting a reprimand for neglecting her duties, when Miss Rogers suddenly appeared.

'It's good to see you've met up.'

'You knew about this?' Rosa asked.

'Well, yes. Lady Gwendoline mentioned it and took me into her confidence when she was here. Don't worry about Albert, he'll understand once I explain the circumstances.'

Rosa hugged Jane and Huw. Dylan's mother explained, 'We wanted it to be a surprise. We know what you're doing to support Alice and Beryl. Do you know there are two thousand names on the petition now?'

'That's incredible. I hope and pray it makes a difference. The appeal hearing is this afternoon. I couldn't bear it if . . .'

Huw took Rosa's hand in his. 'We've signed the petition. Everyone is doing their best for them, Rosa. Now, we would like you to join us when we meet the King to accept Dylan's medal.'

'Me? But is it allowed? I'm not even dressed properly,' she said, pointing to her black dress and white apron.

'That's not important. We'll ask if you can come with us. Dylan would have liked that.'

'I am nervous,' Jane admitted. 'I expect you've met the King a few times now, Rosa?'

'Oh yes, just a few times,' Rosa quipped, a mischievous twinkle in her eye. 'We're on first-name terms.' Noticing Jane's alarmed expression, Rosa added, 'I'm just teasing. My knees still shake when I see him, but he is very kind.'

The proceedings were suddenly interrupted as a piercing shriek from the sky drowned out conversation.

A voice boomed, 'Can everyone please make their way to the air-raid shelter in an orderly manner. Our staff will direct you to the basement.'

Rosa panicked as everyone around her ran. 'We're not going to die, are we?'

Jane looked petrified and gripped Huw's arm. Molly beckoned to them urgently. 'Come quickly, follow me.'

'Will there be room for everyone?' Huw asked, glancing at the mass exodus.

'Oh yes, have no fear there,' Molly replied.

The sound of the flying bombs screeching overhead and explosions nearby could be heard clearly. People pushed forward and scrambled down the staircase, shoulder to shoulder, their eyes fearful as the eerie sound echoed around them, until they reached the bowels of the palace.

The walls of the shelter had been reinforced and chairs and benches were scattered around. The shelter spread the length of three or four rooms and, to Rosa's relief, the lights were on. 'I thought we were going to be stuck here in pitch darkness. I wonder how long we'll have to stay here?' she asked.

Voices around her echoed her thoughts. 'I can't believe this is happening. Wait till I tell my folk how I was stuck in an air-raid shelter with the King.' Another voice hissed, 'Those bastard Nazis. I hope our boys are giving them what they deserve. Who do they think they are, bombing our King and Queen as we honour our heroes!'

Miss Rogers found Rosa. 'I'm glad to see you made your way here. This is probably the safest shelter in London, built especially for emergencies such as this.'

'I had no idea it was so big,' gasped Rosa, staring around in awe.

'The King has his own office here with a telephone line direct to the War Office and Number Ten, as well as Windsor Castle. It has air ventilation and all the comforts he needs. He has dinner here sometimes when he works late.'

'Really! That is very reassuring,' Rosa said.

The chatter around her quietened when the Lord Chamberlain stood on a bench and raised his arm. 'Can I have silence please. Quiet, everyone!'

The room was hushed, aside from the loud screech of the flying bombs, as the Earl continued, 'The King is going to address you. Before he does, I would like you all to promise that you will not tell a soul about this shelter. It wouldn't do for this kind of sensitive information to find its way into the wrong hands. Do you all promise?'

'Aye, aye,' chorused the gathering, or variations of confirmation.

He stepped down and the King took his place on the bench. His words faltered as he stuttered, 'You . . . have . . . all . . . come . . . here for a special . . . purpose. I do not . . . intend that you should . . . have a wasted journey. We will not be defeated in our aim . . . to honour the brave men and women who gave their lives fighting to defeat Hitler . . . and Nazism. I intend . . . for the investitures to continue.'

'Hear, hear!' chorused the gathering. 'Three cheers for the King. *Hip, hip, hooray! Hip, hip, hooray! Hip, hip, hooray!*'

The Lord Chamberlain proceeded to call out names. Families came forward to collect distinguished awards in honour of their loved one who had died so valiantly. Suddenly Jane and Huw's names were called and they beckoned to Rosa to join them. She shuffled along with them, but remained standing behind as they took their place in front of the King.

Jane curtseyed and lowered her eyes while Huw bowed. Rosa bobbed a knee, deeper than usual, praying that she wouldn't get stuck again.

The Lord Chamberlain boomed: '"Flight Lieutenant Dylan Frederick Williams: the Distinguished Flying Medal for displaying bravery during his first active sortie. After the aircraft was hit by anti-aircraft fire over Normandy, the pilot struggled to fit his parachute. Flight Lieutenant Williams regained control of the plane under the pilot's instructions and continued enemy attack, until they were both able to bail out, ultimately saving the life of the pilot. Flight Lieutenant Williams died of his wounds. He displayed courage, fortitude and devotion to duty of the highest order."'

'You must be . . . very proud of your . . . son. He paid the ultimate sacrifice . . . with his life, and I promise you . . . it will not be in vain. I give you my word . . . we will win this war.'

'Thank you, Your Majesty. We shall treasure those words and the honour bestowed on our son.'

The King tilted his head, glancing over Huw's shoulder. 'Is our young Welsh maid . . . with you, by any chance?'

'She is, Your Majesty. Rosa and our Dylan, they were very close.'

'I see,' he replied, his eyes fixed on Rosa's face. 'Will you step forward please, young lady?'

Rosa's cheeks flushed and she raised her face to meet the King's kind eyes.

'I had no . . . idea of your very sad . . . loss,' he stuttered. 'The Queen and I would . . . like to extend . . . our heartfelt . . . condolences. It would give us . . . great pleasure if you . . . could also join us when we host . . . a tea in the palace . . . at a later date . . . with other bereaved families.'

'We would all be honoured, Your Majesty,' Huw and Jane replied, their faces glowing with delight.

The investitures continued, the families exchanging heroic stories and showing off the posthumous medals to those around them, a camaraderie forming from being forced together so closely. There was hardly a dry eye in the room as the final citation was solemnly read out.

'I shall never forget this day as long as I live,' Huw said, his eyes moist, after the all-clear had been given at the end of the afternoon and they emerged from the underground shelter, blinking as their eyes became accustomed to the light.

As they stood in the palace courtyard ready to leave, Rosa turned to Jane. 'I wonder how the appeal went this afternoon. Would you mind if I try and find out?'

'Of course not. We would like to know too. By the way, we thought we might see Jerry here?' Jane asked softly.

Rosa's eyes showed concern. 'It's not always easy to stay in touch and I haven't seen him since he returned from Merthyr, though I checked and his name isn't amongst those killed in the Guards' Chapel. Nobody I ask knows his whereabouts. I can only hope he's on one of his secret missions somewhere.'

'Let's hope so. He seems a good sort. By the way, we have found a little place on the coast in Swansea and will be moving there once all the paperwork is completed. You are welcome to come and stay any time.'

Rosa wiped a tear from her cheek. 'I'd like that very much. You're like family to me.'

She embraced Dylan's parents, clinging tightly, a lump in her throat. After she pulled away she watched their forlorn figures, arm in arm, disappear out of the palace gate, wondering when she would see them again.

Her ears pricked at the bellowing of a newspaper boy outside the palace: '*Mother and daughter lose appeal! Special late edition. Read all about it!*'

'They're done for,' sobbed Rosa, slumped over the table in the palace staffroom.

Miss Rogers appeared with a sombre expression. 'I see you've heard the news. Lady Gwendoline is here to see you.'

Lady Gwendoline was pacing Miss Rogers's office when Rosa appeared.

'I was hoping they stood a chance,' Rosa said, her voice wavering. 'Why did it go against them?'

Lady Gwendoline shook her head. 'The appeal was brought on the grounds that the verdict was unreasonable, given Alice's vulnerable state of mind following the birth of her child. The judges rejected this argument, saying they heard nothing new in support of the appeal.'

'Is there nothing we can do now? Will they both hang?'

'We must hope that all is not lost. They said the jury's urgent recommendation to show them mercy would be considered in the proper quarters. We must also hope they take heed of the nation's petitions supporting them. There are over five thousand signatures all combined, and we must get as many more as we can. The Home Secretary can surely see that Alice is a young girl who was acting out of desperation. This will remain on her conscience for the rest of her life.'

'It must be torture for poor Alice and her mam, sitting

in their cells wondering if they will live or die. If the people who signed it can see that poor Alice and her mam were out of their minds, why can't the judges? Are they blind?' said Rosa.

'In a way, yes, as they are tied by their interpretation of the law. I suppose they can't see beyond the terrible crime they committed.'

'There's no escaping that. If a petition is our last resort, I'll keep pushing it. I'll do anything to save my friend and her mam. But how long do we have?'

'Only a week. Their execution is set for six o'clock on the morning of Friday 28 July. If the plea for mercy is heeded, they will serve a very lengthy prison sentence, maybe life, but they won't hang.'

Rosa swallowed hard. 'At least I could still see Alice. Do you know who has the final word?'

'This may surprise you. It will be His Majesty and the Privy Council.'

Rosa's hand flew to her mouth. 'I didn't know. Surely he'll agree to it?'

'He goes on the recommendation from the Home Secretary. Mr Howell is urging that we gather as many signatures as we can and send them to him within the next three days.'

Three days later, at 5.30 p.m., Rosa set off to deliver her petition to Mr Howell's office in Pall Mall. She found him seated behind a vast desk covered in a thick pile of paperwork.

'I came as soon as I could get away from work,' Rosa blurted, staring at the huge mountain of papers. 'Are they all signatures for Alice and Beryl?'

'They are. I am quite overwhelmed by it. Churches of all denominations have signed it, and the mayor in Merthyr. Lady Gwendoline has some very high-profile signatures on her petition, and the local people really got behind their newspaper's appeal.'

Rosa placed a large brown envelope on his desk. 'Here's some more for you, at least five hundred people, including palace staff and their associates. How many names do you have now?'

The solicitor rose from behind his desk and came over to Rosa, taking both her hands in his and shaking them vigorously.

'Including the latest push, we have at least eight thousand names, an extraordinary amount. I must get these to the Home Secretary immediately. They are considering the case tomorrow.'

'I must see Alice,' Rosa wailed. 'Am I allowed? She must be scared witless.'

'Leave it with me. I'll ask my secretary to telephone Holloway and see if you can visit. When are you thinking of going?'

'This evening, if it can be arranged.' Rosa fidgeted with her hands.

Mr Howell stepped out of the room and Rosa's eyes fell on the petition. To think that thousands of people cared about the fate of Alice and her mother was both humbling and heartening. *Why should they care about Alice and Beryl?* But they clearly did; Alice's desperation had resonated with them.

Mr Howell returned. 'Very well, you can see her for half an hour. Officially, visiting time has finished, but they are allowed to use discretion when capital punishment has been passed and is close to . . .'

Rosa pressed her hands against her ears. 'Don't say the words. I don't want to hear those words.'

Jarvis knocked on the door and entered. Mr Howell said, 'The prison is a good distance. Jarvis will take you now, if you wish. Do let Alice know we are doing all we can. I shall visit her tomorrow. Right now, I am going to deliver the petition. I have a contact there who is working late and expecting me.'

'You've thought of everything, Mr Howell. It was a most fortunate blessing for us our paths crossing that time on the train.'

'I have thought the same,' he replied.

On the drive to the prison Rosa asked Jarvis, 'Have you been to the prison before? I wonder what it's like. I've never been to one.'

'I've been a few times; it's part of my job, driving Mr Howell there to see prisoners. He's never 'ad a case like this, though, where the death sentence 'as been passed.'

Rosa stared blankly out of the window as they passed wreckages of bombed buildings on their way out of central London, through Camden, and onto a straight stretch of road that took them to Holloway.

Jarvis pointed out a Victorian public house they passed, the Nag's Head, which, he claimed with relish, served the best jellied eels in the city. It was a short distance from the prison, which was easy to spot; a vast building with distinctive turrets and towers. In its time it had housed suffragettes during their brave campaign for women to have the vote, and other high-profile inmates including the fascist Oswald Mosley and his wife, Diana Mitford.

Jarvis drew up outside the entrance and a shiver ran down Rosa's spine as she stared up at the facade.

'It's grim, isn't it! I'll wait for you here. Go straight ahead and knock on the door and give your name,' Jarvis instructed, stretching behind the wheel and opening up a newspaper.

Rosa walked unsteadily to the huge Victorian door. She'd been running through what to say when she saw her friend and hoped the right words would come to her. Her knock was answered promptly by a severe-looking woman whose cold, penetrating eyes made Rosa freeze. Rosa gave her name. 'We've been expecting you. Open your bag.'

'What for?'

'Well I'm not after your lippy, you daft sod. We search all visitors.'

Rosa complied and the guard then ordered, 'Raise your hands.'

Satisfied that Rosa was not concealing any contraband or illegal items, she nodded. 'Follow me.'

Rosa's heart pounded and she quickened her short steps to keep up with the guard's strides as they marched through a quadrangle. Rosa realised she was passing cells, each with four iron bars across a shutter for guards to peer inside. Her guard had a large bunch of keys secured around her waist that jangled as she strode ahead.

At the end of the path they turned right and marched along another corridor. The guard paused at the end and reached for one of her keys to unlock a door to some steps going down. When they reached the bottom the piercing sounds of women screaming and banging on the metal doors was deafening.

'These mad women never learn,' snarled the guard.

'Sod you, you screw!' yelled one inmate in such a loud voice that Rosa leaped forward. To her horror, the guard removed a baton from her pocket and banged it against one of the doors. 'Shut yer face up, yer slag.' Rosa flinched, stepping backwards. The noise quietened for a while, but soon started again. They came to the end of the corridor, where two female guards were positioned, and Rosa's guard banged on one of the doors with her baton.

'Visitor for yer.'

'For me?' a soft voice replied that Rosa instantly recognised.

The jailer searched on the bundle of keys, raised one, then slipped it into the lock.

Rosa's heart skipped a beat when the door opened. 'Alice!'

Alice rose from her iron-framed bed and stared in disbelief. 'Rosa? What are you doing here?'

The guard stepped forward and spoke in a hard tone that made her shiver. 'You can have half an hour in the visiting room. Me and Mrs Yeo here will be outside.'

Rosa's heart sank as she observed Alice's gaunt face and sunken dark-ringed eyes. There was a fragility about her that brought a lump to Rosa's throat. They followed the guard into a nearby room with a table and two chairs. Mrs Yeo closed the metal door behind them with a bang. 'We'll be outside, looking in,' Rosa's guard warned, opening the cover across the small window at the top of the door.

'Oh, Alice!' Rosa sobbed.

'I'm done for,' cried Alice, holding tight to her friend as they embraced, her body shaking.

Rosa stroked her face. 'Alice, I've come to tell you we're all doing what we can for you and Beryl.'

Trembling, Alice forced the words through her thick throat. 'I'm scared, Rosa ...' Her chest shook as she sobbed uncontrollably. Rosa passed her a handkerchief, stroking her hair as she composed herself. 'They tell me I'm going to hang on Friday, in three days' time. And poor Mam too. She should never have been caught up in my mess. They've even been in to measure and weigh me for ... for the drop.'

'Don't speak like that, Alice. You mustn't give up hope,' said Rosa, her voice wavering. 'Mr Howell is doing everything he can. People are pulling together to save your life. We have four petitions signed by at least eight thousand people. Mr Howell says he's never known anything like it.'

'Really? Words can't express how grateful I am, but I don't see how anything can save us now, as our appeal failed. I know what I did was wicked. I'm not even allowed to see Mam and I worry about Da. Who is going to look after him after ... ?'

'Your da will be alright. Mam will keep an eye on him.'

The din from the cells could be heard in their room. *'Baby-killer! You deserve to hang.'*

Rosa flinched. 'How can you put up with this? It would drive me mad.'

'I don't have a choice. I can't sleep a wink at night. It goes on all the time and all the guards do is bang on the door themselves and yell, only ten times louder.'

Rosa shuddered. 'Poor you. I wish there was something I could do for you.'

'You've done so much already, Rosa. Seeing as I'm condemned to die, I don't know what more anyone can do.'

'There's still a chance, Alice. Mr Howell is taking the petitions to the Home Secretary. He can't ignore the thousands of signatures. We are fighting your case, even Lady Gwendoline, until . . .'

'You mean to say "until the end", when I'm hanging by my neck,' Alice sniffled, dabbing her eyes with her sleeve. 'It would be a release for me, after what it's like here.'

'Oh Alice, please don't say that,' begged Rosa, handing her a handkerchief.

'I feel I'm already in hell. Word soon got around what I did and I've been banged up in solitary for my safety. As you can imagine, baby-killers are the most hated prisoners. I can't even go in the exercise yard in case I get attacked.'

Rosa listened with tears in her eyes as Alice poured out her misgivings and regrets. 'I was a fool and am paying the price for it. Nobody ever asks if I had a name for my son, my little Johnny. He had the bluest eyes, Rosa. How I regret what I did. I wish I had ignored my fears and taken the consequences. I'd give anything to turn the clock back and hold him in my arms again.'

Before they knew it, the minutes had flown by and Mrs Brown marched in. Alice rose and flung her arms around Rosa's neck. She gulped back sobs and choked on her words. 'If I never see you again, thank you for all you've done. You've been the best friend, more than I deserve.'

Tears streamed down Rosa's burning cheeks and her arms clung tightly to her friend. 'I love you, Alice. I shall always love you, whatever happens.'

'You've had yer time,' Mrs Brown commanded, pulling them apart. She took Alice brusquely by the arm and Rosa followed, watching as her friend was forced into her cell. She cowered in a corner, covering her ears with her hands to block out the deafening jeers and cries.

Rosa was led outside, where she raised her face upwards towards the sky and inhaled the fresh air. Jarvis took one look at her tear-stained face and handed her a silver hip-flask. 'I can see you're shaken. Have a few sips of this.'

Rosa's hand shook as she undid the cap and sniffed its contents. 'Brandy? I've never tasted that before.' She threw her head back and poured the warm liquid down her throat, feeling her insides burning.

'You've done all you can, miss,' Jarvis consoled her as he drove deftly through the city's streets. He maintained a silence for the rest of the journey, observing Rosa's stricken face. It was early evening, and from her seat Rosa observed people going about their daily lives. She contemplated that they may each have faced a personal tragedy caused by the war, as she had herself with Dylan's death, and the uncertainty of Jerry and Billy's fate. But losing a childhood friend to the hangman's noose was more painful than words could describe.

'A life for a life.' In her mind it was a barbaric way to punish a young girl who regretted her actions – actions that were due to her being out of her mind with worry and seeing no other way out.

*

Within half an hour of being back at the palace, Miss Rogers approached her. 'I need you to pack your bag, Rosa. You and Miss Deakin are off to Balmoral tomorrow.'

'Balmoral? That's in Scotland, isn't it?'

'It is. The Queen and princesses plan to visit there next week and I need you both to check everything is in order for their arrival.'

'Oh, but . . .' Rosa began to say, a catch in her throat, her face panicked.

'I know what's on your mind, Miss Edwards. Lady Gwendoline has kept me informed. But really, there is nothing more you can do. It might help you to be away while . . .'

Rosa's face creased. 'We only have a couple of days to save them.'

'I know,' replied Miss Rogers, her voice softening as she placed her hand on Rosa's shoulder.

Molly appeared alongside her. 'Come on, Rosa. I'll 'elp you pack.'

'How long will we be away?' she asked.

'For a couple of months, unless there are unforeseen circumstances.'

Rosa's chin trembled.

'Lady Gwendoline or myself will call Balmoral with any news.'

As Rosa lay in bed that night, she saw Alice's haunted face in her head and heard the tortuous screams of the inmates. She pressed her face into her pillow and cried herself to sleep.

'But it's so far away,' Rosa wailed the following morning when the distance she was to travel struck home.

'We should look on it as an adventure,' encouraged Molly, trying to keep her friend's spirits up.

It was almost 6 a.m., and they were already at King's Cross station, waiting to board the Flying Scotsman on platform one, due to depart at 6.15 a.m. A cheerful guard had informed them it was the fastest engine in the land, with speeds of up to 100mph, and they would arrive in Edinburgh in a blink. The train had originally been painted apple green, but was now wartime black, in common with all railway stock. From Edinburgh they would switch to a local train taking them to the town of Pitlochry, where they would be met by a driver from Balmoral for the last couple of hours of the journey. Snacks had been prepared for them and were tucked in their bags, and Miss Rogers had arranged for them to have a meal on board.

'I'm glad of that, seeing as it's going to take all day,' Rosa moaned as she made herself comfortable, surprised to see that all other seats were taken.

'I've heard it's beautiful there,' Molly chirped in an attempt to distract Rosa from her anxious thoughts. 'Mr Corbitt has been and says it's the Queen's favourite royal home and very close to her heart, especially the fish and game right on her doorstep. She comes from a

Scottish family and the princesses were there when war was declared.'

Rosa rubbed the back of her neck, her eyebrows furrowed. 'I'm sorry, Molly, but I can't think of anything else except Alice and her mam. I'm so impatient for news.'

Molly opened her bag and produced a ball of pale blue wool and a knitting pattern cut from a magazine. As she delved deeper into it, she ventured, 'I've brought something to take your mind off it. How's yer knitting?'

'Knitting? Me? Nah. I've never been able to get the hang of it. I must take after Mam – she can't knit either, so I've never really had the chance to learn before.'

'Come on, I'll show you. It will take yer mind off things. Two pairs of hands are better than one, we can knit a sleeve each.'

'Knit a sleeve? I wouldn't know where to start. I shall be useless and drop stitches,' Rosa protested.

'You'll have to concentrate then, that's the whole point. I'm making a cardi for Ma. I want it to be a surprise for her birthday.'

Rosa took the wool that Molly handed to her, along with a pair of knitting needles. 'I do like the colour. Where did you get your wool from? I hear it's nigh on impossible to find these days.'

'I've unravelled a couple of jumpers that Ma made for the little'uns years ago and found three skeins of wool that were left over. It was stumbling across them in the back of the wardrobe that gave me the idea.'

'You're so clever, Molly, how you can make ends meet,' Rosa said. 'Very well, I'll have a go, if you show me what to do.'

After a few wobbly starts, Rosa's eyes focused on the job in hand and she followed the instructions to a tee. After a couple of hours Molly looked up from her yarn. 'You're doing a great job, Rosa. We'll have it finished by the time we arrive in Edinburgh.'

Rosa grinned as the train continued at great speed on its northward journey. Besides a couple of short breaks to stretch their legs, and an early lunch in the dining car where they gobbled tomato soup and bread rolls, braised steak with mash and cabbage, and jam roly-poly with custard, they remained in their seats.

Somewhere past Berwick, Rosa became restless, casting her knitting aside as her mind turned from Alice to Jerry, who she still had no news about. A warm feeling filled her chest as she pictured his kind face and recalled the soft kiss he'd planted on her cheek. It aroused a similar feeling to her memories of Dylan, but she immediately brushed such thoughts aside.

Rosa snapped back to the present as the train slowed, then screeched to a halt and she was relieved to see they had arrived at their destination.

'I'm sorry, I've not quite finished it yet. I hope it isn't too much of a disaster,' sighed Rosa, handing back her knitting.

'For a first effort it's brilliant,' praised Molly.

As Rosa stepped onto the platform with her bag, she looked around. 'Where do we go now?' she pondered. 'We have half an hour before our connection, according to Miss Rogers's schedule here.'

'I'll ask someone,' Molly replied, looking for a guard.

Rosa spotted one in the distance and went over to him.

He gave directions in his thick Scottish accent. 'Can you repeat that, please? I don't understand what you're saying,' Rosa said as politely as she could.

'Aye, and I suppose your dialect is easy to understand,' he grinned before repeating his directions.

The train rocked from side to side as it gathered speed out of Edinburgh. Its seats were harder and the slower pace and louder engine made it far less comfortable than the Flying Scotsman.

But what the second train lacked in comfort it made up for in the spectacular scenery it passed. Rugged heathland and hills were splashed in a purple haze of heather and glorious sunburst yellow of gorse like a blanket on both sides.

'Oh, it's so beautiful. I didn't realise how much I missed the hills and countryside, even though it's very different here to Wales,' Rosa murmured.

Molly was equally awestruck. 'Blimey. It's really something. Look at them hills – they go right up to the sky. I've never seen anything like it before, being a London girl.'

It was late afternoon when the engine crawled into the small station at Pitlochry. 'It's so quaint here,' Rosa commented, noting the buildings made in local stone.

They made their way to the front entrance as Miss Rogers had instructed. Just as she had said, a stout, bearded man wearing a tartan kilt was waiting for them, lolling against a black Rover car. 'Welcome to the Highlands, lassies. I'm Fraser McBean and I'll be driving you on,' he said in his thick accent.

Rosa and Molly introduced themselves, shaking his hand while their eyes fell on his kilt.

'This is our family tartan and I can tell you it's darn comfortable to wear. It's our national dress and we're proud of it.'

'I didn't mean to stare,' Rosa gulped, sliding into the back seat while Molly stretched out in the front.

As he pulled away, Fraser said, 'You've had a long day travelling. Mrs McDonald will have a meal for you when you arrive. We have a couple of other guests too from London, so you'll have some city company.'

'It's been a long day,' Molly agreed, wondering who the guests might be.

'What's it like living here, Mr McBean?' Rosa asked.

'It's very special, that's what it's like. I can tell you're not a city girl, are you, Miss Edwards? We had Mrs Jones, the cook from Buckingham Palace, come one year. She's a good sort, that's for sure, and, judging from your accent, you're from the same part of the world as her.'

'You've met Mrs Jones?' Rosa exclaimed.

'Oh yes, and a good dancer she is too. But that story is for another time. You'll love it here, lassies. There is nowhere else in the world I would rather be. You'll see what I mean once you've settled in and walked in the hills.'

Rosa smiled. 'I love it already. The best thing is I don't see any bombed-out buildings. It's so tranquil, compared to London.'

'You wouldn't get me setting foot there. The Queen knows that. She's from these parts too, you know. Tell me about yourselves, and before you know it, we'll be at Balmoral.'

The warm welcome and friendly banter from Fraser McBean immediately put Rosa and Molly at ease. He listened with great interest as Rosa told him about life in Merthyr, the loss of Dylan, and the dramatic events at his investiture, and he chuckled when Molly described her siblings and the fun they had together. His face clouded at first when Rosa told him about her father, and lit up when she described the change in him since meeting George. He nodded without comment at Billy's escapades, and smiled when she spoke with fondness about her mother.

'We're no longer strangers now, are we, seeing as I know all about yer kin?' he chuckled.

After they had driven for almost two hours, the roads became narrower, with room for only one vehicle to pass.

'Look, there's a deer. And another!' Rosa yelped excitedly.

Molly jumped off her seat. 'I can see the castle.'

'Yes, that's Balmoral,' Fraser said.

'It's like a fairy-tale palace,' Rosa gawped.

'I can't believe I'm here. I feel I'm in heaven.'

'I told you it was special,' Fraser grinned, drawing to a halt at the back of the castle.

Rosa and Molly got out and stretched their arms above their heads after the long drive. They spun around on their heels, taking in the spectacular sight of the magnificent castle, its looming towers and turrets in grey stone soaring high above them, set amongst luscious lawns and surrounded by trees.

Fraser removed their bags from the boot of the car. 'You must be in need of a wee drink. Come along and meet Mrs McDonald, she'll look after you.'

They followed him through the back door. Stag heads stared down on them from the walls and their heels made a soft sound as they walked along the stone floor and down a staircase into a warm kitchen.

A cheery woman wiped the flour from her hands onto her apron and approached them. 'My, you are two bonny lassies. I'm Hilary McDonald, the cook here, and I expect you're famished after your journey. I'll be laying out a meal in the staffroom in half an hour, but I've just made a brew and I'll pour you a cuppa while you catch your breath.'

They plonked themselves on a bench along the sturdy kitchen table where Mrs McDonald had started making pastry. Glassy eyes on the heads of more beasts shot on the estate stared down on them with sad expressions, giving Rosa the shivers. But the kitchen was filled with the sweet aroma of shortbread which tickled her taste-buds, and her face brightened when Cook placed some on a plate in front of her.

'Nobody can resist my shortbread, especially the Queen. Go on, help yourself – but no more, mind you. I don't want you ruining your appetite.'

Cook was right. The soft buttery biscuit melted in Rosa's mouth and she summoned her best willpower to resist a second helping. Molly licked her fingers and declared they were the best she had tasted – even better than Mrs Jones's.

Rosa's face suddenly clouded and she bit her bottom lip. Molly pressed a hand on her arm. 'I can guess what's on your mind. Remember what Miss Rogers said – either she or Lady Gwendoline will call you here when there is news.'

Rosa whispered behind her hand, 'I should mention this to Mrs McDonald, and let her know how urgent the call will be.'

After doing so, Cook assured Rosa she would inform the housekeeper, Mrs Gillespie. 'It's not usual for staff to have calls in the office, but if you say it's arranged by the palace, that shouldn't be a problem.'

'It's really, really important,' Rosa implored. 'I won't be able to sleep unless I hear.'

They were shown to their room by Fraser. 'The palace maids have been very comfortable here,' he said, opening a door the second floor.

To their great delight, they had two beds in a light airy room with views across the grounds. They had matching mint-green candlewick bedspreads, and wallpaper and matching curtains decorated in ferns. It wasn't a huge room, but small and cosy, and a welcome change from being cooped up in the bowels of the palace. A bathroom was next door which they were to share with staff in other rooms along the corridor.

After a quick wash and change into fresh clothing, Rosa felt revived.

'You look really pretty in that dress. Lemon suits you,' Molly admired. 'Are you ready?'

'I am. I wonder what we'll have to eat.'

'Whatever it is, it's bound to be delicious, I can smell it from here. If you remember, they grow lots of produce here and send it to the palace.'

They found their way back to the kitchen. Cook was placing vegetable tureens on a trolley. 'Can I help?' offered Rosa.

'Everything's done now. We have fresh whiting for dinner this evening, caught just this morning. I hope you like fish.'

Rosa's eyes creased. 'I can't say I've ever eaten whiting before. What's it like?'

'It's soft and white and flaky, the Queen is very partial to it. We have lots of fish here, all caught locally on the day it ends up on your plate.'

'I'm sure we'll love it,' Molly piped up.

'Go and take a seat in the first room on the left, that's where the staff eat, and I'll be with you in a minute.'

As they made their way there, Rosa moaned, 'I'm so famished. Can you hear my tummy rumbling?'

As she stepped into the room a man's voice said, 'I thought I recognised that lovely Welsh accent.'

'Jerry? It can't be you!' Rosa cried, her jaw dropping.

'It bloody well is,' Molly yelped, before he could reply.

'I'm as shocked as you. What are you both doing here?' he asked, his eyes wide in disbelief.

Rosa's eyes remained fixed on Jerry's face. 'We've been sent by the palace to prepare for a visit by the Queen and princesses next week. We've been worried sick about you, Jerry Snaith. Why didn't you let us know you were safe?'

'I would have done if I'd known it mattered to you,' he replied softly, his eyes staring into Rosa's face for an answer.

'Oh Jerry, of course it matters. I thought after the Guards' Chapel bombing that you—'

'I wasn't there, but would have been if I hadn't been posted here. I lost many good friends that day.'

'I'm sorry to hear that. I was there, looking for you. What brings you here?'

'It so happens I'm here for the same reason as you, though I'm checking security is tight before the royal party arrives. My presence here is naturally secret – none of the other guards knew.'

A coughing sound caught their attention. 'Good evening, ladies. I've heard all about you from Jerry. My name's Martin Cunliffe, Marty to my friends, and we're working on the same task.'

Molly held out her hand and gave her biggest smile to the handsome dark-haired man with soft brown eyes and a warm smile. 'Very pleased to meet you, Martin. Any friend of Jerry's is a friend of mine.'

Rosa introduced herself as Mrs McDonald entered pushing the trolley laden with their dinner.

'I see you've introduced yourselves. Shall we take a seat?' she said, pointing to their places. 'Do help yourselves,' she added with gusto. 'There's plenty for everyone. Fraser is finishing something off and will join you as soon as he can, and the same goes for me.'

'What about the other staff?' queried Rosa. 'Will they be joining us?'

'Not this evening. Our staff numbers are low when the royal family are not in residence. If they are local, they tend to return home at the end of the day, unless there are duties here they are required for. As for Mrs Gillespie, she prefers to eat in her room.'

Jerry pulled out a seat for Rosa next to him, while Martin did the same for Molly, who shyly giggled behind her hand at his gentlemanly gesture.

They helped themselves to the white fish and parsley sauce that Mrs McDonald had cooked to perfection, and piled their plates high with fresh vegetables.

Jerry listened attentively as Rosa poured out how

desperate she was for news about the fate of Alice and her mother, whose lives were hanging by a thread.

Jerry frowned. 'I had no idea about any of this. The story hasn't reached the newspapers here. Time is against them, but a miracle could happen. If the palace said they would call you with news, I'm sure they'll keep their word.'

After they'd finished eating, Rosa paced the room, wringing her hands. 'I can't bear the waiting. It's gone seven o'clock.'

Just then a woman in a plaid suit entered the room. 'Miss Edwards?' she asked, staring at both Rosa and Molly.

'That's me,' blurted Rosa.

'There's a call for you in my office.'

She rushed over. 'I've been waiting for this call. Please, please, let it be good news.'

She followed Mrs Gillespie up winding stairs and along a corridor, to a room with her name on the door. 'The phone is on the desk. I'll be back in a few minutes. I hope you speak politely. I know what you London girls are like.'

Rosa tried to make sense of what she had been told. *Speak politely*? Well, didn't she always speak well? And besides, she was from Wales.

She eagerly gripped the telephone receiver. 'Miss Rogers?'

A polished, clipped voice replied, 'Good evening, Miss Edwards. This is Princess Elizabeth.'

'Princess Elizabeth? Really? I don't understand. Is it really you, Your Highness?'

'I assure you it is, though I can imagine you were not expecting to speak to me.'

'Well, no, ma'am. Miss Rogers said she would phone me, or Lady Gwendoline. I don't understand.'

'First, let me tell you the good news and then I will explain.'

'Good news!' gasped Rosa.

'It is agreed that the death sentence is reprieved for both Alice and her mother.'

Rosa's hand clasped her chest. 'So they're not going to hang? What will happen to them, ma'am?'

'They have been given life sentences, which means they are going to spend a very long time in prison instead.'

'Oh, I see. That's wonderful news. It means I'll be able to visit Alice.'

'I expect so, Miss Edwards. I thought you should know.'

'It's very kind of you to inform me, but – I don't mean to appear rude, but—'

'You want to know why I called. Let me explain. On my eighteenth birthday I became a Privy Counsellor and able to act on behalf of my father, the King, if he is out of the country, which he is at the moment.

'One of the duties includes approving recommendations from the Home Office, such as this. The recommendation was made after consideration was given to the huge groundswell of support from thousands of people in the country; even a bishop signed the petition asking for mercy to be shown to Alice and her mother. The counsellors were also persuaded by the fact that it wasn't a premeditated murder, but a terrible, tragic act committed in a moment of desperation.

'Hearing about the case from you, and your personal

interest, aroused my interest too. Now I have signed the reprieve papers, I hope your mind is put to rest on what has been a most distressing case.'

'It has, and thank you, miss – I mean ma'am. I mean, Your Highness,' said Rosa, suddenly tongue-tied.

'Ma'am is fine, Miss Edwards. I was informed you started a petition at the palace. That is most commendable.'

Rosa felt her heart thumping inside, as if it would explode.

'Well, good evening, Miss Edwards. I hope you sleep soundly now you know.'

Rosa fled out of the room – and straight into Jerry, who was standing outside the door with Molly and Martin.

'I thought you might need a shoulder to cry on, in case the decision went against them.'

'You're never going to believe this,' Rosa gushed, smiling from ear to ear.

Jerry took her hands in his. 'Judging from the expression on your face, it looks like it's good news?'

She ran into his arms and he swung her around. 'It is! The death sentence has been reprieved and been replaced with life in prison.'

'Hooray!' exclaimed Molly.

'It's thanks to you and everyone who signed the petition!' said Jerry, as he released Rosa and punched the air.

'That's not all. You'll never guess who called me to break the news.' Rosa grinned.

'Miss Rogers? Lady Gwendoline? Mr Howell?' suggested Molly.

'None other than Princess Elizabeth herself. She signed

the reprieve on behalf of the King. I couldn't believe it
when I heard her voice.'

'That's remarkable,' Molly exclaimed. 'It reminds me
of when we served tea one afternoon and the Queen
was reading the newspaper report about the case. You
looked upset and the princess wanted to know why, and
I told her.'

Rosa thought for a moment. 'That's right, so you did,
and she remembered. How very kind of her to call me
herself. It's still going to be tough for Alice though,' she
added, recalling the shrieks from fellow cellmates.

Jerry led Rosa a few steps away. 'I just want to say how
I admire your courage and determination to stand by your
friend, in spite of the terrible crime she committed. Many
girls would have washed their hands of a friend who did
such a terrible thing. You make an impression on all the
people you meet, like Miss Rogers and Lady Gwendoline,
Huw and Jane, and even Princess Elizabeth, who all put
themselves out for you.'

'Stop it, Jerry. You're making my cheeks turn red with
your compliments. I can feel them burning.'

'I've never told you before, Rosa, but I find your rosy
cheeks very appealing.'

'You do?'

'I know you are grieving for Dylan, and I don't want to
push you, but one day, I wondered—'

Rosa's hands flew to her face before Jerry could finish
his sentence. Her heart was pounding. 'Are you saying,
you and me—?'

He took her small hands in his. 'Yes, that's exactly what
I'm saying.'

Rosa hesitated, seeing Dylan in her mind's eye. 'I don't know what it is we have, Jerry, but I know I can't bear the thought of anything happening to you, like Dylan.'

'Well that's a great start. I'll settle for that,' Jerry beamed.

'You will. But on one condition?' she replied, her expression earnest.

'What would that be?' he replied, stroking her flushed cheek and raising her chin.

'That you don't go off and disappear again without telling me, and make me worry like mad.'

'I think I can manage that,' he laughed, scooping her in his arms and bringing his lips down on hers for a long, slow kiss.

'You don't know how long I've wanted to do that,' he whispered, as he placed her feet back on the ground.

A shocked voice bellowed, 'Miss Edwards! I can't believe what I am seeing with my own eyes. You've only been here five minutes and are already getting up to no good. It's always the same with you London girls.'

'But I'm from Wales, Mrs Gillespie. And right now I'm the happiest girl from the Valleys and the Highlands and London all put together.'

Afterword

People often ask me, 'Where do you get your inspiration from?' It's a question often put to authors.

I remember being at an event when Jeffrey Archer was asked this, and my answer is the same as the one he gave – people tell me their stories.

I was inspired to write Rosa's story after it was told to me by her daughter, Jan. Rosa really was a pit-miner's daughter from Merthyr Tydfil in Wales who went to Buckingham Palace to work as a royal coffee-maid in 1944 after seeing the position advertised in a shop window.

She really did meet a royal guard at the palace called Gerald Snaith, and they fell in love.

But the book is fiction and their romance inevitably faces challenges against the background of World War II. Although many of the historical events on these pages really happened, characters were created to bring these stories to life.

I asked Jan how Rosa would feel knowing I had written about her life, and she replied, 'Mum would be surprised, humbled, excited, proud and really pleased. She was a conscientious worker and so caring and kind. I learned so much from her.'

I've tried to stay true to Rosa's spirit – in real life, the royal family warmed to her infectiously happy nature.

Rosa really did have rosy cheeks, a heart of gold and touched people's lives, and through these pages she has touched mine.

I hope I have done her story justice.

Acknowledgements

It's been a joy and a privilege to write about Rosa's life, and I have her daughter Jan to thank for sharing it with me.

Jan's email out of the blue telling me how her mother left Merthyr Tydfil as a poor pit-miner's daughter to start a new life as a royal coffee-maid in Buckingham Palace stayed in my inbox for a couple of years before I began thinking about it, due to other writing commitments.

It was a 'pinch my arm' moment as I began writing this book and I thank Jan for entrusting it to me.

Factual accuracy is hugely important to me and I turned to Merthyr historian Huw Williams to fact-check the Welsh storylines. I am immensely grateful to him for his meticulous attention to detail in poring over every word of my first draft. My visit to Cyfarthfa Castle, spending a day with Huw and learning about the town's history, gave me a sense of place, and ability to visualise it when writing about the town. I am greatly indebted to Huw for his time and expertise.

Neil Storey is a fount of all knowledge when it comes to World War II, and I can trust him implicitly to check the facts from this time with a fine-tooth comb. Thank you, Neil, for being there for me and giving me peace of mind.

I have to thank Julie Crocker, a senior archivist at the Royal Archives, for promptly and ably replying to my emails when checking historic royal details with her, providing a valuable service to me.

I am immensely grateful to South Wales Miners' Library for sharing valuable audio files with me, which I was riveted by, recounting miners' stories from days of old.

The book could not have happened without the representation of my former agent, Elizabeth Counsell at Northbank Talent Management, who secured the book deal with Penguin. I am now ably managed by Marissa Constantinou at Northbank.

Madeleine Woodfield has been my constant enthusiastic and supportive editor at Penguin and it has been a pleasure for me to see that she understands my characters and cares for them as much as I do.

I would like to thank the background Penguin team who I don't get to meet, from the talented cover designer to the marketeers, and my excellent copy editor, Eugenie Todd, for making it a final, polished product.

I thank my family for sharing my writing journey and understanding why I need to lock myself away in my office.

Most of all I thank my readers who I hope will take Rosa to their hearts, as I have. I hope you have enjoyed her story.

Find out what Rosa and her friends
get up to next in *The Royal Maid Finds Love*!

Available to order now.

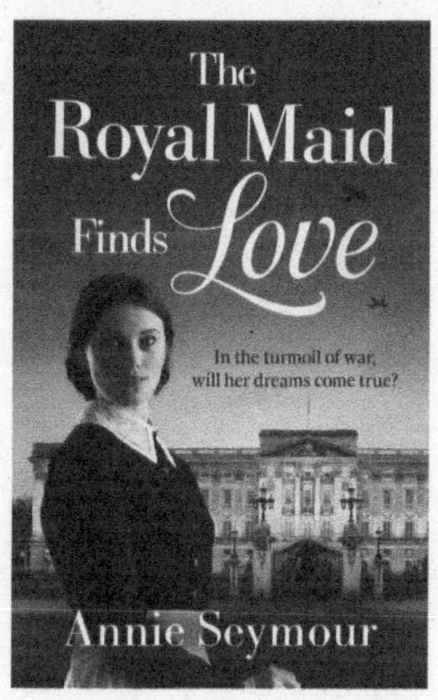

As World War II nears its end, Rosa Edwards, royal
maid at Buckingham Palace, risks losing it all
when her good nature is taken advantage of.
Will the royal guard she loves stand by her, or
should the pit miner's daughter return home in
shame to Merthyr Tydfil in Wales?

NURTURING WRITERS SINCE 1935 

He just wanted a decent book to read ...

Not too much to ask, is it? It was in 1935 when Allen Lane, Managing Director of Bodley Head Publishers, stood on a platform at Exeter railway station looking for something good to read on his journey back to London. His choice was limited to popular magazines and poor-quality paperbacks – the same choice faced every day by the vast majority of readers, few of whom could afford hardbacks. Lane's disappointment and subsequent anger at the range of books generally available led him to found a company – and change the world.

'We believed in the existence in this country of a vast reading public for intelligent books at a low price, and staked everything on it'
Sir Allen Lane, 1902–1970, founder of Penguin Books

The quality paperback had arrived – and not just in bookshops. Lane was adamant that his Penguins should appear in chain stores and tobacconists, and should cost no more than a packet of cigarettes.

Reading habits (and cigarette prices) have changed since 1935, but Penguin still believes in publishing the best books for everybody to enjoy. We still believe that good design costs no more than bad design, and we still believe that quality books published passionately and responsibly make the world a better place.

So wherever you see the little bird – whether it's on a piece of prize-winning literary fiction or a celebrity autobiography, political tour de force or historical masterpiece, a serial-killer thriller, reference book, world classic or a piece of pure escapism – you can bet that it represents the very best that the genre has to offer.

Whatever you like to read – trust Penguin.

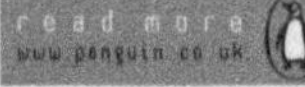